THE APEX

DM SEARLE

The Apex by DM Searle published by Nightscape Press Limited.

ISBN number: 978-1-7384438-1-9

Copyright © 2024 by DM Searle

ABOUT THE AUTHOR

DM Searle is the author of crime thriller *Back*. *The Apex* is his latest gripping tale of mystery and suspense. He lives in the heart of vibrant Camden Town in north London, where he enjoys writing speculative thrillers and other stories.

Feel free to connect with him on social media or drop him a line at dm@dmsearle.com

'… nature, red in tooth and claw …'
Alfred Lord Tennyson

"There is no god besides me. I put to death and I bring to life."
Deuteronomy 32:39

ONE

1

Kristen Hardy stared into the eyes of the Mother of God. *Please*, she prayed silently, *keep my baby safe*. She waited for a sign that she had been heard but the painted mural remained silent on the stone pillar. If the Virgin Mary *was* hearing petitions, they were more likely those being uttered by Father Connolly, who was leading Mass from the front. Our Sacred Heart was one of the bigger Catholic churches in Cambridge and the priest's words echoed off every wall, a familiar, almost Gregorian sound that ordinarily would have instilled in Kristen a sense of calm. But not today. Try as she might, she could not let go of the knot in her stomach. She bit her lip and reluctantly turned away from the mural, trying to focus on the service. Beside her, her best friend was texting. Of course she was. Kristen was usually indifferent to Bree's blasé attitude towards her own religion, and to the Mass in particular. But this morning it felt wrong. Bree froze as she caught Kristen looking at her. She shrugged, flashed a cheeky smile, and slipped her phone back into her handbag. Kristen tried her best to smile back, but the look of concern that crept over Bree's face told her she hadn't succeeded. Kristen turned away, afraid she might cry. The last thing she needed was a scene in church. Bree gently touched her elbow. 'Hey, you okay, hon?'

Kristen reached across and squeezed Bree's hand, still avoiding her gaze. Darius, on Bree's other side, stared at his wife. 'Can you be quiet, sweetheart?' he whispered.

'*You* be quiet,' Bree shot back. 'Krissy's upset about something.'

'I'm okay,' Kristen said quietly.

'See?' Darius tutted. He placed a finger on his lips.

'Don't you dare shush me,' Bree said.

'*Shsssh!*'

The second shush came from the pew behind them. Chastened, Darius gave seventy-year-old Mrs Gibbins an apologetic wave and turned back around to glare at his wife. Kristen, meanwhile, gripped Bree's hand firmly and made an effort to join in with the words of the Gloria, which Father Connolly was encouraging everyone to sing. The cadences of the hymn, which she had heard countless times over the years, created a harmony that filled the air. Slowly, it calmed her. Kristen glanced back up at the mural and pictured the Holy Mother looking down on her with grace and love. Surely, her prayer would be heard in her hour of need. Besides, how difficult would it be for God to grant her request? He *was* God, after all. Hadn't he made the stars?

2

It had all begun with the stars. Kristen had been eleven years old, gazing up at the night sky on a summer camping trip in Cornwall with Bree. The weather was so warm that Bree's parents had allowed the girls to sleep out in the open campsite field, covered only in their sleeping bags. Kristen had found this an exciting prospect, but nothing had quite prepared her for her first glimpse of the Milky Way. Growing up in Cambridge, Kristen had enjoyed only a muted view of the stars, dulled by the glow of street lamps. But in the remoteness of the countryside, she saw with her own eyes what it was to have the heavens truly shine above you. The sprawling, magical constellation literally made her catch her breath. It was like a window into something Grander and Beyond. The longer she stared, the more it seemed to make the normal things in her life, like homework or netball and her favourite TV shows, seem small and inconsequential. She was so enthralled, in fact, that she barely paid attention to Bree's pronunciations on who was the coolest Spice Girl. As a giddy sensation percolated in her gut, Kristen realised what she was feeling was *wonder*.

'C'mon, Krissy,' Bree said. 'Posh, right? No competition.'

Her voice was unmistakably laced with disappointment that Kristen hadn't been paying attention.

'Sorry,' Kristen said, finally pulled out of her reverie. 'But it's just so amazing, don't you think?'

'What is?'

'The stars!'

'Pop stars?'

'No, *stars* stars,' Kristen said, pointing up. 'Just look at them. Aren't they just beautiful? Like someone designed them just for us.'

'What makes you think someone designed them?' Bree asked.

Kristen shook her head like it was the most ridiculous thing she'd ever heard. 'How could anyone *not* think that?' she said.

3

Kristen came to realise that there was beauty everywhere if you only knew where to look. Some examples were obvious, like a stunning sunset or a colourful rainbow. But there were other things too, that to her mind were just as awe-inspiring as anything in nature, spiral galaxies included. Like music or friendship. Or love. In fact, the more she pondered it, the more convinced she became that there had to be something very special about life if it contained all these beautiful, wondrous things. And if that was true, then maybe there was something special about human beings too. Maybe they were no random accident, the product of mere *biological soup* as her science teacher insisted. Instead, what if Someone Upstairs had created all these beautiful, wondrous things purely so people could enjoy them? And what if, Kristen then wondered, He had done so because He loved them?

Over the course of the next year, Kristen began to see people differently. It dawned on her that every person, no matter who they were, had intrinsic value. This idea so permeated her thinking that she surprised herself one day after school when a charity ad came on the TV. It was an appeal to help the victims of a terrible earthquake in India and, by the time it had ended, she was crying uncontrollably.

'Kristen! What on earth's the matter?'

Her older sister, Jacqui, gave her a stern, quizzical look from their open-plan kitchen. Kristen could barely answer. 'It's just so sad,' she said at last. 'All those people suffering with no one to help them.'

Her sister shrugged and carried on helping their father prepare dinner.

The following week, Kristen asked Bree whether she could accompany her family to Mass. She knew the Honeywells were Catholic but knew very little about church. But she had the impression that the people who went there believed in Someone Upstairs and in helping those in need. So she was excited when Bree's parents agreed to take her. Kristen's father, however, was less than thrilled.

'Just don't let them brainwash you,' he warned. 'They're good at that.'

Kristen promised him she wouldn't. She knew her dad meant well. When the girls were younger, their mum had died of cancer. Twelve-year-old Jacqui had developed a tough exterior that lasted to this day, but six-year-old Kristen retreated into herself for the better part of three years. Her father had been overprotective of her ever since. But he did not forbid her from going.

Kristen's first Mass made a big impression on her. She sat quietly between Bree and her parents while a burly priest addressed the congregation. He spoke eloquently about the Sermon on the Mount, parts of which Kristen remembered from school. She was particularly struck by the message of social justice in Jesus's teachings. *Blessed are the poor in spirit. Blessed are those who mourn.* She had no idea what any of the rituals meant but she liked the sense of atmosphere and the singing. She remembered looking around the congregation and seeing men and women, old and young, and many different races, all united in purpose. It felt like a family. Kristen was so instantly at home that she asked to return with the Honeywells the following Sunday. A fortnight later, she had volunteered to help with the soup kitchen for the homeless. Bree's mum was astonished that Kristen had thrown herself into the church so fervently. But her behaviour only puzzled her best friend. One afternoon, Bree confronted her about it when they were hanging out in her bedroom.

'Why do you flippin' want to go to church, Krissy?' she asked. 'Mum and Dad make me. But no one's making you.'

Maybe God is, Kristen thought. But she didn't say it. Bree was her closest friend and she didn't want to upset her any more than she already had. But she had also crossed a line that there was no going back from. And so regardless of Bree's bewilderment, Kristen kept willingly coming back to Mass every Sunday. Week after week. And then, year after year.

4

As twenty-six-year-old Kristen queued for the Eucharist, she reminded herself that God always heard the prayers of his children. Father Connolly gently placed a wafer on her tongue and she recalled her first communion at this very altar when she had turned thirteen. She closed her eyes, took a sip of the communion wine and savoured the familiar feeling of belonging not only to a community, but to something greater than herself. Retaking her seat, she bowed as she waited for the Mass to end. When it did, the congregation shuffled through the double doors at the back of the church. Kristen followed Bree and her husband, aware that Bree kept looking at her quizzically. But now wasn't the time. At the doorway, Father Connolly shook hands with each member of the congregation as they exited. Bree ignored the ritual and instead gave the priest a sloppy kiss on his forehead.

'Thanks for the talk, Father,' she said.

'It's called a *homily*, Bree,' Darius corrected.

'Whatever,' Bree said. 'He did good. I stayed awake the whole time.'

She patted Father Connolly on the chest. 'Your singing, on the other hand … well, that's a work in progress, Father.'

The priest chuckled, his bushy grey beard bobbing merrily up and down. 'I'll try harder next week, Bree,' he said. 'I promise.'

If Darius had been lighter skinned like his wife, Kristen was sure he would have blushed a deep red. 'I'm *so* sorry about her, Father.'

'No need to apologise, Darius. We are all as the Lord made us. And your wife is always such a delight.'

'You tell him, Father!' Bree said as she trotted merrily down the church's steps.

Darius mouthed a *thank you* to the priest and hurried after her. Kristen was next. She offered her hand, but instead of taking it, Father Connolly gently touched her shoulder.

'Is everything all right, Kristen?' he asked. 'During communion, you seemed … troubled.'

Kristen opened her mouth to speak, then shut it again. Her cheeks were wet and she realised tears were running down them. Connolly, looking over Kristen's shoulder at the line behind her, leaned forward to gently whisper into her ear. 'Why don't you wait for me in the presbytery?' he suggested. 'We can talk in private.'

Kristen joined her friends in the church's car park. She buttoned her coat against the autumn weather as Darius unlocked their Toyota.

'You want a ride?' Bree asked.

'No thanks, Bee,' Kristen said. 'I need to speak to Father Connolly.'

'Okay, hon,' Bree said. 'You call me later if you need to, okay? I'm always here for you, girlie. Know that.'

'I know. You guys still up for coming over for dinner sometime?'

'A night off from cooking?' Bree said. 'You try and stop me.'

Kristen smiled at her. Darius climbed into the driver's seat and leaned over to open the door for his wife. 'Let's definitely try to get a date fixed,' he said. 'We'll bring a bottle of wine.'

'Two,' said Bree, grinning.

She blew Kristen a kiss as she entered the passenger side. 'Love you, girlie,' she called through the window.

Kristen watched the car's rear red lights diminish as it disappeared down the road, heading out of Cambridge town centre. She reminded herself that friends were a blessing, especially loyal friends. And whatever her faults, they didn't come any more loyal than Bree. In the car's wake, crisp brown leaves swirled above the asphalt, whipped up by a wind that had sprung up from nowhere. It made Kristen shiver.

5

'So, Kristen,' Father Connolly said warmly, 'what's troubling you?'

They were in the presbytery adjacent to the church, sitting in the study. The priest was behind his desk, a high stained-glass window above his head. Cloud-filtered light illuminated a colourful figure of Christ with a child on his lap, surrounded by His disciples. Kristen sat in the chair opposite, trying to ignore her nerves. It wasn't easy, but Father Connolly seemed to sense this. He leaned casually back into his chair as if to remind Kristen they were old friends now, and she needn't put on graces. Finally, she found the courage to speak. 'Marcus and I ... well, the thing is, we've been trying, you see.'

Connolly's bushy eyebrows rose. 'Trying?'

'To have a baby,' she said.

'Oh. Yes. I see.'

'It ... we've ... I mean ... I had a couple of miscarriages. Before.'

She stopped there, doing her best not to descend into tears. Memories flooded back. The first time she had been at home. As a nurse, she should have spotted the signs, but somehow she told herself it might just be stomach cramps, perhaps something she ate. She had spent an hour sitting on the toilet, her eyes closed, trying to block out what had really happened. By the time Marcus came home, she had managed to get it together, tidy herself up and even put on a lick of make-up. She didn't say anything to him, telling herself if she chose her moment she could control her emotions. It didn't work. When she opened up a couple of days later, she'd ended up sobbing into her husband's arms, which was all that had prevented her from shattering into pieces. When it happened again just a few months later, she had told Marcus straight away. Kristen shook her head, trying to shake the memories off. When she looked up, she was surprised to see Connolly dabbing the corners of his eyes with the sleeves of his black cassock.

'Forgive me, please,' he said. 'I know it's not my grief.'

She was dumbstruck. 'It's ... all right, Father.'

It was all she could think to say. Why had she never talked to Father Connolly about this before? Was it because she blamed herself for what had happened? It was as though she had let go of her dark secret and she felt lighter for it. There was no reason not to tell him the rest. 'The thing is, I'm pregnant again,' she said.

Father Connolly smiled with surprise. 'What? That's wonderful news, Kristen. Congratulations.'

'It's only been a few weeks.'

She glanced down at her belly.

He nodded. 'And you're worried.'

She sighed. 'Oh, Father, I just don't know if I can go through it again.' She stared at the priest imploringly. 'I've prayed, Father. Prayed so hard that God won't take this one. Not this time. I couldn't bear it.'

'Have you spoken to your GP?' he asked softly.

She fidgeted in her seat. 'Yes. He told me I'm perfectly healthy. But it doesn't mean it won't happen again.'

Her palm circled her belly again, as though drawing an invisible shield around the small life that was growing inside. 'I've been praying to Mary and asking her to intercede for me,' she said.

She pulled out her rosary as if offering him proof, but Connolly waved it away.

'Kristen,' he said. 'This isn't about your efforts. What happened to you happens to a lot of women. It's very sad, and very common.'

She studied the beads, remembering how many times she had worked them. 'What about confession?' she asked. 'I come once a week, but perhaps if I made it more often. Perhaps some sin—'

'Oh, my dear,' Connolly said. 'Please. No. God is kind and all-loving. Whatever sins you have committed, and we all sin, He would not punish you by taking away your baby.'

'Then why did He take the others?' she asked.

Father Connolly's eyes brimmed with compassion and Kristen could see he was trying to form the right words. After a while, he pointed up at the stained-glass window. 'Do you know where this scene is from?' he asked her.

She nodded. 'Matthew.'

'That's right. Chapter nineteen. The people brought little children to Jesus for Him to lay hands on them and pray for them.'

Kristen stared at the child sitting on Christ's knee in the window.

'Our Saviour loved children,' Connolly said. 'I wish I could tell you why He calls some home early, but there are some mysteries we will never know.'

She sniffed. While Kristen believed that the babies she had lost were in heaven now, it still didn't help much with the sadness. And it certainly didn't do much to quell her fears now. 'Oh, Father,' she said. 'How am I going to get through the next few weeks?'

Connolly nodded. 'Do you remember the story about the footprints in the sand?'

Kristen did, but didn't say so. She didn't want to stop the comfort the priest was hoping to offer.

'A man arrives in heaven. He looks back on his life and sees two sets of footprints in the sand,' Connolly said. 'They represent the times in his life when Christ walked beside him, from his birth until the day he died. The man notices that at times there is only one set of footprints and asks God why He abandoned him. And God replies, "No, no, those are *my* footprints. This was me, carrying you."'

Connolly reached across the desk, offering his hands. Kristen took them. His strong but gentle fingers squeezed hers.

'His footprints are there, Kristen. You just have to look for them.'

He let go and smiled kindly at her. 'You must trust Him to carry you through this, Kristen. I will pray for you.'

'Thank you, Father,' she said.

She touched her stomach again, visualising the life that was still forming. There were still eight weeks to go before she would be out of the danger zone. Father Connolly was right. She had to find a way to trust that God would somehow carry her.

6

As she walked home from Our Sacred Heart, Kristen was buffeted by a powerful wind. She knew Father Connolly's counsel was wise. Surely God would spare her the pain of losing yet another child? Despite the best efforts of the elements, her feet eventually found their way to the small terraced house on Northfields Avenue that had been her marital home these last two years. She let herself through the front door quietly because Marcus often liked to sleep in on a Sunday. Treading softly through the living room, she was surprised to see her husband standing out in the garden, the mop of his hair flapping in the wind. She put her bag down and slid the patio door open. Marcus turned, his eyes scrutinising her as if she were a stranger. Anyone else might have been puzzled by his confusion but Kristen knew she had merely disturbed him while he'd been lost in thought. 'Darling.'

'Kris!' he said. 'When did you get back?'

She kissed him on both cheeks. 'About thirty seconds ago,' she said. 'I thought you might have been sleeping.'

'I was thinking about the future,' he said. 'I had a call from the production company.'

'The ones who said they liked your book?'

Marcus had written a popular science book that had shot up the *Times* bestseller list. Kristen had always told him it was only a matter of time before it led to greater things.

'They want to pitch it to the BBC,' Marcus said, grinning like a schoolboy. 'They asked if I was interested in presenting it too.'

Kristen felt a flood of happiness for him. 'Oh, darling, that's wonderful news. Now let's get you in before you get blown away.'

Marcus's straggly ash-brown hair was blowing across his face, but he didn't seem to notice. Kristen led him back inside, closing the glass door behind them to keep the tempest out. 'I'll put the kettle on,' she said cheerily. 'Jubilee blend?'

'Please,' Marcus said, still beaming.

He always looked so much younger when he smiled. As she set the water to boil, she turned to look at his happy expression again. This was such a great turn of events.

'So how was … you know?' Marcus asked.

It was Kristen's turn to smile. 'Oh, church? You can say the word, you know.'

She heard him tut quietly.

'I'm showing an interest, Kris. Isn't that what you say you want me to do?'

'I think it's great that you pretend to,' she said.

Marcus sighed. 'It doesn't mean I don't care about *you*.'

'I know,' she said. 'And I hope *you* know that you're welcome to go with me, anytime.'

'I did go,' he said. 'You made me say some vows in there, remember? I wore a suit and everything.'

'Yes, and you haven't been back since.'

Marcus laughed and turned his attention to the spread of magazines on the coffee table. He picked up *Country Life* and pretended to flick through it. 'Kris, if God actually *did* exist,

I'm pretty sure the last thing He would abide is an atheist in His house.'

'Well, the invitation's always there,' Kristen said, as she took two china mugs from the cupboard shelf. She opened the teapot lid and placed the strainer on it.

'So … tell me more about this offer,' she said.

'It's early days,' Marcus said. 'Nothing is signed. But if it all goes ahead, I might have to travel. A lot.'

Kristen stiffened. 'How much travelling are we talking about?' she asked.

She had not told Marcus about the pregnancy yet. Although he didn't often express his vulnerability, she knew that he had grieved the last two miscarriages deeply, just as she had. Now she wondered how he would feel this time if everything went to plan. Given what they had lost, wouldn't he rather stay close to home, to be with a healthy child if they were blessed with one?

'I don't know the details yet,' Marcus said. 'Though I do know they want to base it on the research in my book. So that's a lot of countries.'

Another thing that was now up in the air, Kristen thought. She would have to ask God to give her a lot more patience in the coming days. 'What about your research at the university though?' she asked. 'Will you have to give it up?'

'We'll see,' he said. 'But it's a possibility, yes.'

She nodded. 'I'm so proud of you, darling,' she said.

'Thank you, Kris.'

Kristen opened the tin lid of the tea caddy and scooped the leaves into the strainer. It was all finally happening. Marcus was getting the recognition he'd worked for and surely deserved. The question was, could she make him even happier in a few months' time? *Footprints in the sand*, she reminded herself. It was important to remember that God was always there. The kitchen window rattled as rain hammered against the glass, making Kristen jump. This was especially true, she thought, when it felt like events were out of control.

7

Since becoming a person of faith, Kristen had believed that events were never out of control. Rather, she trusted that God guided her life every step of the way, according to a divine plan. Often, she would look back on things that had happened to her and spot patterns or coincidences that she had missed at the time. She also believed that this included meeting her husband at work. Inspired by stories of Christ's compassion in ministering to the sick, Kristen decided to follow His example by becoming a nurse. She completed her nursing degree at twenty-two and was offered a job at St Anthony's hospital in Cambridge, where she had worked ever since. Kristen remembered the day she met Marcus like it was yesterday. She was on a break and, having been on her feet all day, needed somewhere to rest. The hospital's cafe was on the tenth floor. It was busy at the best of times, and today only one of the green Formica tables had a spare seat. Sitting opposite it was a young man with floppy brownish hair, dressed in a corduroy jacket and trousers.

'Excuse me,' she had said. 'Is this seat taken?'

Floppy-Hair looked up at her with brilliant hazel eyes.

'Uh, no,' he said. 'Please. Help yourself.'

He appeared to be in his late twenties or early thirties. From his plummy-ish accent, Kristen guessed he wasn't from a poor family. She sat down, placing her styrofoam cup of coffee on the table and smiled. The man said nothing, staring at the black liquid in his own cup.

'You're brave, drinking the coffee here,' she said.

'This?' he said, tapping his cup, finally working out what she had meant. 'Oh, this is tea.'

'Oh,' Kristen said. 'You drink it black? Without milk?'

'I find tea to be somewhat like life,' he said. 'Dark, mysterious and complex.'

Kristen frowned. 'What?'

She thought it was a strange thing to say.

'It's just a little joke,' he said, looking sheepish. 'I simply prefer the taste, that's all. Though I will say they could do with some better blends.'

She nodded. 'NHS needs more funding.'

It was her turn to try a joke, but hers apparently horrified him.

'Oh God, I hope you didn't think I was complaining,' he said. 'You do such wonderful work here. I didn't mean to sound like some sort of snob.'

'It's okay,' she said, surprised at his sudden earnestness. 'I wasn't being serious.'

She winked at him and took a sip.

'I'm serious, though,' he said. 'I'm so grateful for what you all do. You're taking such good care of my friend.'

Kristen caught a shimmer in his pupils and realised he was feeling emotional and had been trying to suppress it.

'Is ... your friend all right?' she probed gently.

'He's stable now, thankfully.'

'I'm pleased to hear that,' Kristen said.

'Can you believe he managed to poison himself with deadly nightshade? I mean, how unlucky is that?'

Kristen's ears pricked up. 'Wait, you're Harry's friend?'

'Harry Dean, yes. You know him?'

'They brought him in a few hours ago,' Kristen said.

'They haven't let me see him yet, but the doctors assured me he's going to pull through.'

'He'll be fine,' Kristen said. 'He's on my ward. They administered charcoal as an emergency intervention. It seems to have done the job. He's stable and sleeping now. I just left him for my break.'

'You're his nurse?' the man asked.

He visibly relaxed when Kristen nodded and his shoulders slumped as he leaned back in his chair. 'Thank you so much for taking care of him,' he said. He smiled and extended a long arm across the table. 'The name's Marcus.'

'Kristen,' she said.

She let him take her hand and give it a gentle squeeze. She didn't mind the contact. In fact, she found that she quite liked it.

8

Harry Dean's story was remarkable. Kristen vividly remembered when the paramedics first wheeled him into Accident and Emergency. Harry had been critical, his face a dark purple and his breathing severely restricted. The first time she saw him, Kristen thought the ambulance crew must have had their work cut out for them. Harry had to weigh one hundred and sixty kilos, perhaps more. His size belied his relatively young age. She was shocked to learn he was only twenty-four. Once the emergency team had stabilised him, he was transferred to Kristen's ward, where she took care of him for the remainder of her shift. He was constantly monitored with an ECG, his breathing supported by oxygen and his body pumped full of saline and fluids to wash any residual traces of the poison he'd ingested. Kristen cared for him over the next few days. She was there the moment he first woke up, terrified and disorientated. Her hands gently cupped Harry's as he instinctively reached for the mask strapped to his face.

'It's okay, dear,' she said. 'You're in hospital. That's just oxygen to help you breathe, okay? You're all right.'

Her voice had the desired effect, the alarm going out of

Harry's eyes as he looked at her with gratitude. But that didn't stop him panicking frequently after that, sometimes two or three times an hour, squeezing Kristen's hand like a little boy, asking her if he was going to die. Whenever he pressed the call button, Kristen ran to him, stroked his head, reassured him that all the poison had been flushed from his system. Eventually, he would calm down and thank her over and over. By the time Kristen had her third shift with him, it was clear she was his favourite nurse.

'I suppose you think I'm an idiot,' he said.

'I don't like to think bad things about people,' she said.

She understood why he would say so, however. Harry had been hiking through a nature reserve just outside Cambridge with Marcus, the man she'd met at the cafe. The two of them had stopped for a picnic and Harry had got sticky fingers eating a jam doughnut. He wiped his hands on the nearest bunch of green plants. It was incredibly unlucky.

Deadly nightshade, as it was commonly called, could still be found in woodlands all across the UK, but it was rare. Rarer still that Harry had unknowingly used its leaves as nature's napkin and then touched more food with those same fingers. As a result, he had ingested the plant's toxins. Less than an hour later, after Harry had suffered severe convulsions and hallucinations, Marcus made a frantic call to 999. It was a miracle he had received treatment in time.

'Funny name, *Belladonna*, isn't it?' Harry said one morning.

Kristen was taking his blood pressure, winding a cuff tight around one chubby arm. 'I'm sorry?'

'It's another name for the nightshade.'

'Oh,' Kristen said.

'It means beautiful woman,' he said with a sigh. 'I mean, who wouldn't want to touch one of those?' Harry looked down as the cuff tightened. 'At least I'm somebody's main squeeze,' he said.

Kristen rolled her eyes.

'I know,' he said, with a smile. 'I don't deserve to be here, making terrible jokes.'

The machine released the pressure and he met her eyes. 'Seriously,' he said. 'Thank you for everything.'

Later that day, Marcus paid his friend a visit. When Kristen returned from her break, she found Harry asleep and Marcus by his bed. Now that she saw him standing up for the first time, it was impossible not to notice his height. Easily six foot three, practically a giant compared to her five-foot-five frame. He carried a bumper book of crosswords in one hand.

'You bought him puzzles?'

Marcus turned to Kristen and nodded. 'He … uh, well, he'd want to keep his brain challenged.' He trailed off shyly and stared at the linoleum floor.

She smiled and took the book off him, which earned her a grateful look. 'That's very thoughtful,' she said.

She placed the book down on a PVC side unit by the window, where Harry's personal things were stored.

'They were deliberately designed to be that big, you know,' Marcus blurted.

'What were?'

'The windows,' he said. 'Back in the nineteenth century, hospitals began putting in large windows. It was believed that light possessed a calm, healing quality, like nature or gardens. It was part of what they called the *moral treatment* … the theory that patients deserved more dignity.'

'Oh? I didn't know that.'

'Of course, studies have shown that a caring and supportive social network can help with recovery too,' Marcus said. 'It's something our ancestors understood well. When one of the members of the tribe was ill, the whole tribe suffered.'

It was fascinating to listen to him. He spoke with such confidence, as though giving a lecture, while simultaneously casting nervous glances at the bed, IV lines and machinery. Instinctively, Kristen placed her hand on his forearm.

'He'll be all right, you know,' she said.

Marcus stopped talking and swallowed. He stared at his friend. The ECG rhythm blipped steadily on the black monitor mounted to a trolley. Then, as if some part of him felt he was being watched, Harry Dean slowly opened his eyes. He blinked in confusion.

'Aury?' he murmured weakly.

Later, Kristen learned that *Aury* was Harry's silly nickname for Marcus, short for *Marcus Aurelius*. Marcus glanced back at Kristen as if seeking permission to have a conversation with his friend. Kristen nodded encouragingly.

'Harry, how are you feeling, old boy?' Marcus said. 'You didn't half have us worried.'

Harry reached out a large hand and beckoned Marcus nearer the bed. When he obliged, the hand closed fast around Marcus's wrist. 'Aury, I owe you my life,' he said. 'Whatever you need, now or in the future. Say it and it's yours.'

Marcus stiffened. 'Come on, Harry, don't be so dramatic. You'd have done the same for me.'

'But if you hadn't called the ambulance ...' Harry said.

He closed his eyes and sighed, then apparently overcome with exhaustion, slipped back into sleep again. Marcus gave Kristen another appreciative look. 'Thank you so much again for taking care of him.'

'He's a good friend,' she said. 'You care about him a lot. I can see that.'

'Yes, yes, exactly.'

He smiled at her. It was a cute smile. Again, she felt sorry for him. He might tower over her, but she knew he would be comforted by a hug. It was all she could do not to offer one.

9

In truth, she was not hugely surprised when Marcus called her on the ward a week later. His voice had a slight quaver as he asked her whether she had any plans during the week.

'I, er, thought maybe, I, um, could buy you a drink,' he said. 'For looking after Harry.'

It wasn't the first time Kristen had been asked out by a patient or one of their visitors. She turned them down usually, but something about Marcus intrigued her and she agreed. When the day of the date arrived, she felt she could have predicted the pub he'd chosen; it was characterised by obscure real ales and the faint odour of old men's sweat. Marcus sat on a stool with an empty one next to him, presumably for her.

'Thanks for, er, coming,' he said, standing up and brushing down his corduroy trousers. 'What can I get you?'

Kristen asked for a dry white wine. They sat in silence, a palpable awkwardness growing between them. Kristen realised it would be up to her to break the ice. 'So,' she said. 'How is Harry doing?'

'He's glad to be home. And he couldn't be more grateful for how incredibly well you looked after him.'

'Oh, bless him,' Kristen said. 'You two been friends a long time, then?'

Marcus relaxed. Her giving him permission to talk about himself loosened his tongue; he talked for England after that. He started with his relationship with Harry. Kristen discovered the men were postgraduates at Cambridge University. Marcus had studied anthropology while Harry's field was neuroscience. They had met when attending a lecture on social psychology, given by a visiting guest speaker. After it was over, a handful of students had retired to the pub to debate what they had heard, Marcus and Harry among them. It didn't take the pair long to discover where their fields of interests overlapped. After a few pints of ale, they found they had personal hobbies in common too, including a keen interest in local history. Kristen listened with genuine interest, charmed by the story of their geeky bond. She interrupted Marcus at one point to ask why he had wanted to study anthropology. This turned into another long monologue in a tone that she would later come to think of as Marcus's Lecture Mode.

'Anthropology is not simply a dry academic subject,' he assured her. 'It touches everything in our daily lives. Take this pub, which is based on early Roman taverns. We often look to the past to shape the world around us.'

Marcus talked confidently and intelligently, yet he clearly didn't know how to fully relax in the company of a woman. It was such a strange combination and she couldn't quite work out what it was that kept her there, listening so intently. But she did.

She agreed to a second date. This time, Marcus took her to a Tuscan-inspired restaurant, where he managed to ask some questions about her. Had she always lived in Cambridge? Where were her family from? Did she have brothers and sisters? Though he reeled these off in a deliberate, practised order, Kristen didn't feel like she was being interviewed. She sensed Marcus was aware that their last meeting had been pretty one-sided and was trying to do his best not to talk about himself this time. She liked him all the more for it.

'So why did you choose to become a nurse?' he eventually asked.

By now, they were on their second bottle of wine. Kristen hesitated. She'd been asked the question many times, even by her father, who once had hopes that she might go on to work in a much higher-paid profession. Forming her answer as articulately as she could, she tried to explain to Marcus how she believed in the existence of a God who loved people, and how she felt called to take care of the sick. Marcus listened attentively while she explained that her time studying nursing at university and her practical placements on hospital wards had felt to her like a divine calling. Finally, she finished. Marcus paused, took a big gulp of Chianti and fixed her with an intense stare.

'I'm an atheist,' he said. 'You should know that about me.'

Kristen put her glass down next to her plate of gnocchi. 'So, is this a deal breaker for you?' she asked.

She decided she might as well be direct. Marcus looked at her for what seemed like the longest time, then spoke with a passion she had not yet heard in him, even when in Lecture Mode.

'You know the worst kind of people in my opinion?' he said. 'People who don't think about any of … this.'

He waved a hand around him, and Kristen understood he wasn't referring to the restaurant.

'I mean, the basic questions one should ask,' he continued. 'How did we get here? Was there some divine origin, as you believe? Or was it simply chaos, a random act of a quantum singularity followed by billions of years of slow evolution?'

He swirled his wine as if there was further wisdom inside

the crimson liquid, then looked into her eyes once more. 'I might disagree with you, Kristen. Profoundly, even. But I admire that you care enough about the question itself that you have pursued your own path. I respect you immensely for being so principled.'

Though she had only just met Marcus, and was confident in her beliefs and had no desire to be validated by anyone, Kristen was blushing. It was all too much. She had to lighten the tone. She reached for the menu and scanned the dessert list. 'Look at this,' she said. 'They've got panettone cake … how can you *not* believe in heaven?'

10

Kristen became lost in the whirlwind romance that was their courtship, engagement, wedding and honeymoon. In just a matter of months, they were husband and wife. The next couple of years were perfect, despite Marcus not being a Catholic. But that was something she figured she could learn to live with. The only major challenge came when they decided to try for a baby. The first miscarriage tested Kristen's faith deeply, as had the second. And now here she was again, daring to hope that this time all would be well. The weeks that followed her confiding in Father Connolly passed by in slow motion. Each morning, when she visited the bathroom, dark thoughts chased after her like shadows. But when, each morning, everything seemed all right, she felt a weight lift off her heart and said a prayer of thanks. She continued to work her shifts at St Anthony's hospital as normal. Focusing on her patients, many of whom were suffering even greater hardships, was a helpful reminder that she wasn't the only person in the world who had trials. On Sundays, she went to Mass with Bree and Darius, where she made a point of staring up at the mural of Mary as if to remind the Holy Mother that she was still here, pleading for the life growing inside her.

. . .

The time ticked by. Her belly slowly swelled. Eventually, the so-called safety zone arrived. And much to Kristen's relief, she discovered that she had crossed it. She finally told Marcus. It almost broke her to see him burst into tears, his usual stiff-upper-lip-ness crumbling like dust as he asked her how far along she was. She told him she hadn't wanted him to worry, that she only wanted to share the happy news when she was certain it *was* going to be happy. They held each other for so long it made Kristen wonder if they would ever let go. The thing they had been trying for, that had brought them so much pain, finally seemed possible. She wished then, as she had so many times before, that Marcus shared her faith. That they could drive to Our Sacred Heart to light a candle together, say a prayer of thanks. But she knew Marcus felt gratitude in his own way. Even if, for him, it was just a random card the universe had dealt them.

11

Life had progressed quickly with Marcus's book being adapted into a TV show. His increasingly packed schedule meant the dinner party Kristen had promised Bree and Darius kept getting delayed. After weeks of last-minute cancellations and postponements, however, they finally succeeded in having the couple over. Giddy with excitement, Kristen answered the doorbell promptly at seven one Friday evening. Darius kissed her on the cheek as Bree handed her a bottle of champagne. 'I have news,' she whispered cryptically in Kristen's ear.

'Me too!' Kristen said. She led them both into the living area.

'Where's Marcus?' Bree asked.

From behind them, in the corridor, the door to the spare room opened.

'Did someone mention my name?' he said.

'There you are!' Bree chirped, kissing him on the cheek.

Kristen watched in sympathy as her husband, who often struggled with people invading his personal space, pulled back as if he'd been slapped.

Darius offered his hand. 'Thank you for having us over.'

Marcus nodded, looking relieved to have been given a more muted greeting. 'You are most welcome.'

They began with the hors d'oeuvres, which Kristen had meticulously prepared that morning. She poured them glasses of champagne. Darius stood by the corner bookcase in the living room, examining the books on display.

'Bree tells me you've written a book,' he said.

'It's going to be on telly!' Bree told him.

'Congratulations,' Darius said. 'Is it this one? You mind?'

Marcus shook his head as Darius removed the book with Marcus's name on the spine. The title was *The Rites Stuff*. He stared at the cover, which featured a series of illustrated black skulls and bones.

He frowned. 'Evolutionary theory?' he ventured.

'Anthropology,' Marcus said. 'Though I am also an evolutionist, which I'm sure you know. I don't know whether that means you'll be less likely to want to read it.'

'*Marcus*,' Kristen warned.

She really hoped this dinner wouldn't sour before it had even begun. She knew her husband's penchant for starting debates. But Darius did not seem offended.

'It's okay, Kristen.' Darius looked at Marcus. 'The Catholic Church has long embraced the theory of evolution. In fact, Pope John Paul the Second declared it to be the mechanism by which God chose to bring about the world.'

'God Himself rubber-stamping evolution, eh?' Marcus said with a sardonic half smile. 'That's quite an idea.'

Kristen hastily sandwiched herself between the men in case she needed to head Marcus off at the pass. His shyness somehow didn't seem to cover switching into Lecture Mode, especially when it came to arguing about religion.

'So what made you want to write the book, Marcus?' Darius said. 'If you don't mind me asking?'

'Not at all,' Marcus said, taking a champagne flute from Kristen. 'I find human behaviour fascinating. Especially ancient human cultures. And I wanted to arouse the same passion in the average man or woman on the street, as it were. Plus, I felt it would put my combined knowledge of human biology, evolutionary psychology, and linguistics to good use.'

'Always said he was too smart for you, Krissy,' Bree said. She was settling in on the sofa, stretching out across it and dangling a leg over one of the arms.

Kristen handed both their champagne glasses to Darius. 'Ha *ha*,' she said. 'I'm going to check on the roast. Everyone okay for now?'

The group confirmed that they were. Kristen swallowed and went into the kitchen. With a bit of luck, Marcus would continue to behave himself, and no one would storm out halfway through the dinner she had spent all day preparing. Especially when she had such exciting news to share.

'You write every day?' Darius was asking as Kristen returned to the room.

Marcus confirmed that he did. Kristen picked up an empty bowl – Bree had already devoured the nuts – and pointed to the spare bedroom door.

'Marcus locks himself away every spare hour he gets,' she said. 'I'm not allowed to disturb him when he's working. He gets very cross.'

Marcus smiled. 'A bit of an exaggeration, darling,' he said. 'But, yes, I do need my private time. Kristen knows that about me.'

'I don't know how you write about all that boring history crap,' Bree said.

Kristen saw Marcus wince and then pretend he hadn't.

'Different people find different things interesting, sweetheart,' Darius said. 'Even you like things others would say were boring.'

'Like what?'

'I don't know. Candy Crush?'

'Hey, I'll have you know I'm the queen of the Crush. I *crush* the Crush.'

The conversation lulled, but Kristen didn't mind. It was rare that the four of them got together, and she was just glad they weren't embroiled in a heated discussion about religion. The oven timer rang, saving any more awkward pauses. She invited everyone to sit down at the table while she excused herself. She returned with the leg of lamb and was gratified to hear the appreciative *oohs* and *ahhs*.

'Marcus, would you mind?' she asked.

'Of course,' her husband said, standing up from the table.

He picked up a chef's carving knife and, with a meat fork in the other hand, cut through the rosemary-embedded skin and into the flesh. 'You know, Bree, one of the reasons I enjoy all that *boring crap*, as you so endearingly put it, is that I believe our past can tell us a lot about how we are today. Take this meal, for example. Human beings have found great significance in coming together over the slaughter of animals since the start of recorded history.'

'That's a cruel way of putting it,' Kristen chided him.

'It's just nature, darling. Kill or be killed and all that. We're just fighting for our place in the food chain.'

'Mmm,' Bree said, smelling the aroma of the lamb Kristen had cooked. 'Sorry to say this, but I'm glad we get to eat this poor little bugger.'

Marcus smiled and cut two more slices off the leg. 'What's more, doesn't your church have the breaking of bread?' he continued. 'Society is rooted in rituals around death, food and life. It's fascinating when you think about it.'

Bree stared at him dumbly, looking unsure how to respond. Kristen moved quickly to refill everyone's champagne glass and noticed Bree hadn't touched hers. She went to top it up anyway, but Bree quickly cupped her hand over the glass.

'Don't tell me you drove, Bee?' Kristen said.

'Don't be silly,' Bree said. 'Darius doesn't trust me enough to insure me on his precious little car.'

'That's what I thought. So why—?'

Kristen frowned before the epiphany came. 'Oh my gosh!' she said. 'You're not …?'

'Can confirm.'

Kristen let out an excited squeal.

'Ten weeks,' Bree said. 'I know some people say we should wait before telling anyone.'

'Yes, some people did say that,' Darius said with a resigned sigh.

Bree punched him on the shoulder. 'She's my bestie, Dee,' she said. 'How can I keep a thing like this a secret from her?'

'Oh, Bee, I'm so happy for you,' Kristen said.

The women hugged and Bree started to tear up.

'Isn't it wonderful news?' Kristen said, turning to Marcus.

'Yes, marvellous,' Marcus agreed.

He put down the carving tools and took the bottle off Kristen. 'I think this calls for a celebration,' he said. 'Darius?'

Darius nodded, grinning. Marcus filled up two flutes and clinked glasses with him. 'To fatherhood,' he said.

'I wanted to tell you before, Kris,' Bree said. 'But Darius kept saying … oh, it doesn't matter. Hey, Marcus, that's not very gentlemanly of you. Why don't you pour your lovely wife a drink too?'

Marcus gave Kristen a guilty look.

'Wait, what? What's going on here?'

Kristen shrugged. 'I guess today might be, well … a double celebration.'

'What do you mean?' Bree asked. 'Why wouldn't you be drinking?'

'For goodness sake, Bree,' Darius said.

Bree turned back to him. 'What? What am I—'

And, like Kristen, the veil fell from her eyes. 'Oh. My. God.'

'Sweetheart! The Lord's name,' Darius said.

'I'm sorry,' Bree said. 'I meant Oh My Days. Obvs. Krissy, I just can't believe …'

'I know,' said Kristen. 'Me neither.'

More squealing ensued. Marcus finished carving the roast and invited everyone else to pass their plates. Darius readily handed his, but the women were no longer engaged with dinner.

'Come with me! You need to tell me everything! Right now!'

Bree had already pushed her chair up and grabbed Kristen's wrist. 'We'll be back,' she said. 'Save some for us, okay?' Before the men could object, she pulled Kristen across the oval white rug and towards the patio door. She found the latch easily enough and the pair stepped out into the terraced garden.

'Oh my God,' Bree said again, closing the glass door behind them.

She pulled a packet of cigarettes out of her clutch purse.

'Bree, what are you—?'

'Yada yada. I've quit. For obvious reasons. But sometimes I just need the prop, okay?' She slipped an unlit cigarette between her lips. 'Oh my God, Krissy.'

'I know.'

'So how far are you gone?'

Despite the freezing weather outside and not wearing a coat, Kristen lifted up her sweater a little, revealing the bump that now swelled beneath her T-shirt.

'Officially twelve weeks,' she said. 'I'm sorry I didn't tell you. I wasn't sure it was going to be … all right.'

Her friend nodded. Kristen had already cried on Bree's

shoulder more than once. 'And your doctor says you're okay?' she asked.

'I had my scan,' Kristen said. 'It all looks good.'

Bree leaned forward and the women drew warmth from each other. 'Oh, Krissy, that's *so* wonderful.'

Kristen hugged her back tighter. 'I was so worried, especially after …'

'Of course, of course. But it's okay. You're okay now.'

'Father Connolly said I needed to have faith. And he was right. I prayed, Bree. And God heard me. He heard, Bree. Now we're both going to be mums.'

'I know,' Bree said. 'I'm so happy I could shit.'

Kristen laughed. 'Okay, maybe try and be a bit less happy. Come on, let's go inside before we freeze to death.'

The funny thing was, Kristen wasn't feeling cold. She felt as though she was wrapped in a warm shawl. Like she was being covered in God's love and grace. It was a beautiful, wondrous feeling.

TWO

1

Kristen watched her daughter skip through the brambles ahead, oblivious to the possibility they could both get very lost, very quickly. The bright July sky was obscured by a verdant canopy of trees – a mix of oak, beech and ash. She had never been in this part of the New Forest before and was naturally hesitant. But Abigail was undeterred.

'Why can't we go back to the path, Abi?' she asked.

'I told you, Mother,' Abigail said. 'I saw a deer.'

Kristen was feeling breathless as she struggled to keep up. 'So what?' she said. 'We see them all the time.'

'This one's unique, Mother. If I'm right. Come *on*.'

Abi's enthused skipping continued as she veered around tree trunks like they were obstacles on a course, chasing down the phantom shadow that just moments earlier she swore was an animal. 'We're getting close, I can sense it,' she said.

'Abi, I'm tired. Do we have to?'

'God, Mother, why are you always so exasperating?'

'Hey,' Kristen said. 'Watch your tone there, missy.'

Abi's bony shoulders tensed. She hated being called missy. But she deserved the rebuke. What eleven-year-old spoke to their mother like that? For that matter, what eleven-year-old used words like *exasperating*?

'Well? Do you have something to say to me?' Kristen asked.

'*Sorry*, Mother,' Abi said.

Her voice was laced with just the right amount of sarcasm to give her plausible deniability. Kristen sighed. She worried about Abi's attitude sometimes. It was probably nothing more than growing pains, but lately, the two of them were rubbing up against each other more often. It bothered her a lot.

'Look, Abs,' Kristen said. 'I appreciate I'm not your father. But I did get up this morning, and very early on a Saturday too.'

Abi stopped. She turned around and regarded Kristen thoughtfully. 'You're right,' she said, this time with obvious sincerity. 'I apologise.'

'It's okay,' Kristen said.

Perhaps as an olive branch, her daughter reached a hand out and Kristen took it. 'This way. It's not far.'

Kristen allowed herself to be led through a gap that opened onto a small copse. Here, knee-high grass was punctuated with tufts of daffodils and clusters of white-petalled flowers that Kristen couldn't name but had no doubt her daughter could. Abi put a finger to her lips and crouched down on her haunches. Kristen copied her, though, at thirty-seven, she was finding the pose more taxing than she would have done a decade ago. Then mother and daughter slowly crept closer to the centre of the clearing ... until Abi froze and pointed. Kristen saw the creature for the first time. Small, reddish-brown and sporting a white patch on its chest, the deer had apparently stopped to chew something it had found along the ground. They watched it in awe. The deer's head snapped back, giving Kristen a brief glimpse of two cute ears flicking back and forth. Dark brown eyes stared at them before the deer sensed danger. The creature scampered off into the undergrowth. As quickly as that, the show was over.

'No antlers,' Kristen said. 'So, a female?'

'Oh, very good, Mother.'

'See? Who needs your father, after all?'

Abi smiled and laid a soft hand on Kristen's arm. 'Oh, Mother,' she said. 'You *are* adorable.'

2

They re-entered the woodlands and headed back towards the path they'd abandoned.

'That was a roe deer, the smallest of the species native to the forest,' Abi explained. 'There are only around four hundred or so. Father says they were hunted to extinction here and had to be reintroduced by the Victorians.'

'Oh?' Kristen replied.

She could well imagine Marcus pontificating about the history of the deer, amongst many other forest-related topics, on one of the regular nature trails he and Abi made on Saturday mornings.

'Do you know who first named this place the New Forest?' Abi said, not quite teasing, but almost.

'Actually, I do, Miss Clever Cloggs.'

'Who then?' Abi asked as if she didn't quite believe her.

'William the Conqueror,' Kristen said.

'Correctamundo, *Mater*.'

'Please,' Kristen said, 'don't ever call me that, okay?'

She wasn't overly keen on *Mother* and *Father* if she was being honest. Marcus had used these titles in front of Abi ironically at home, ever since she was a little girl. For some reason Abi apparently thought it was hilarious to copy him. But the Latin versions were beyond grating.

'Fair enough. I apologise,' Abi said. 'But you *are* right. William named it *Nova Forester*. Of course, forest meant something very different back in 1079.'

'It did?'

Kristen knew Abi was just parroting more of what Marcus had told her, but she wanted to appear engaged. It was a special honour being invited to stand in for Marcus, and she didn't want to seem uninterested.

'It means *hunting grounds*,' Abi said. 'A place where the king and his officers would chase after beasts for food and sport. It's lucky we have roe deer, or any other deer, left at all.'

'But they won in the end, didn't they?' Kristen suggested. 'Because it's illegal to hunt in these woods now, so they're free to roam wherever they like. They can finally live without fearing death.'

Abi mulled this over and gave Kristen an approving nod. 'That's true,' she said.

They eventually rejoined the path, much to Kristen's relief, and made their way back to the car park. Kristen handed Abigail the water bottle from her small backpack and Abi took a grateful sip.

'Mother, why don't you ever go out walking with Father?' Abi asked, giving the bottle back. 'I'm sure he'd love you to.'

Kristen shook her head. 'Your father knows how I feel. I told him long ago it wasn't my thing.'

It wasn't for want of trying. Kristen had accompanied Marcus on many walks back when they had lived in Cambridge. She loved spending the time together, but she just couldn't abide Lecture Mode, which Marcus inevitably slipped into whenever they passed anywhere of any historical significance. 'Darling,' she'd said to him. 'You know I love you very much. But I'm your wife, not one of your students.'

'Things have changed, Abs,' Kristen said. 'It's more important the two of you go out together.'

'Why's that, Mother?'

'Well, this is where your father grew up,' she said.

When Abi was two years old, Marcus's parents had decided to emigrate to Spain. Marcus had offered to buy their family home from them, helping them out financially and giving his own burgeoning family a chance to upgrade. Kristen, who had always fantasised about moving to the country, had considered it a win-win. 'Your father was raised in Granny and Granddad's house,' she said. 'I think it's more special for him to share his walks with you now, because he's also sharing childhood memories. It means a lot to him to pass them on to his daughter.'

Abi smiled at this. 'Still, I'm sure he'd appreciate it if you went out with him once in a while.'

'Maybe,' Kristen said. 'But the truth is, I'd prefer to spend time with your father doing things that are fun for *both* of us.'

Abi picked up a long stick and absently swished it around in the air like a sword.

'But what about you, Abs?' she asked. 'How come you never get bored with these walks? Don't you ever just wish you could switch it up for a change? Do something else together?'

'Like what?' Abi asked.

'I don't know, something fun.' *Oh crap*, Kristen thought. *I sound just like Bree.*

Abi twirled her stick around like a cheerleader's baton, her tongue sticking out as she interrogated the question in her mind. 'Anyone's father can do fun,' she said. 'But not everyone can take you back into the past. Make you feel like you're actually there. Father's rather unique, really.'

Yes, he is, Kristen thought. It was one of the reasons she had ended up falling so hard for him. Lucky for Abi, she supposed.

3

It was lucky for all of them, Kristen thought on the drive back to Ashworth, the small village they called home. As she navigated the narrow country lanes, she reflected on how fortunate she was to have enjoyed a morning out like this. Though a decade had passed, she had not forgotten the anxiety she had when she had first fallen pregnant with Abi. She thanked God every day that He had protected her and the baby, and that today she was blessed with such an intelligent, talented and beautiful daughter. A daughter who, to Kristen, was perfect in every way, even if she did dote on her father a little too much. She caught her eyes in the rear-view mirror and saw the flicker of guilt in them. She had no right to be envious of Marcus's relationship with Abi. But she was, at least a little. *But maybe it's not jealousy I'm feeling,* she told herself. *Maybe I'm just sad that Abi and I don't have what she clearly has with Marcus.* And, if that was the case, wasn't it her responsibility to do something about it? Find new ways mother and daughter could bond? She had become so lost in that last thought that she was surprised to discover she was already home.

Kristen steered the Land Rover up the long gravel drive

towards Orchard House. The sight of the five-bedroom property never failed to charm her, not only because of its mock-Tudor aesthetic, but because she loved the idea that it contained happy memories of Marcus's childhood. Kristen parked in front of the portico and shut the engine off. Abi remained in her seat. She was laughing heartily, her phone gripped tightly in both hands. Kristen gently removed one of her white ear pods.

'We're home, Abs. What's so funny?'

'It's just Father!'

'He's on the phone right now?'

'No, Mother it's the show. They have their own YouTube channel, see?'

She held out the screen. The channel's logo and the title of Marcus's show were displayed under a video that featured a dense green jungle. While Kristen had never watched *The Rites Stuff* on anything other than broadcast TV, she had seen most of the episodes.

'That's the one in Borneo, isn't it?' she said.

'Yes. Where Father gets his hat stolen by an orangutan!' Abi squealed in delight.

That particular scene had passed, but Kristen could see Marcus talking to camera. He was holding up a hominid skull circling his index finger above the cranium. She couldn't hear what he was saying because Abi still had her earphones connected, but it must have been something witty because her daughter was still chortling. Kristen smiled. Even seven thousand miles across the other side of the world was not a big enough divide to come between father and daughter. She should be happy about their special bond, not envious.

'Come on, you,' she said. 'Let's get you inside. It's just one more sleep before you get to see him again in the flesh.'

4

The next morning, they set off to Heathrow airport to meet Marcus straight off his flight. He was returning from the latest recon with the TV production crew, a trip that served as the prelude to the actual shoot, which would start in earnest in the autumn. *The Rites Stuff* had just been renewed for its eighth season by the BBC, so Kristen was no stranger to being a production widow. But she continued to miss Marcus terribly during the months he was away. Abi could barely contain her excitement all the drive up. As her father emerged from the Arrivals hall, she practically vaulted over the barrier to launch herself into his arms. Marcus laughed as they collided, the pair almost falling over his wheeled luggage. Embracing his daughter tightly, he smiled at Kristen. 'You miss me too?' he asked.

'We both did,' Kristen said. 'I'm afraid I made a poor forest companion.'

'She really did,' Abi confided audibly in Marcus's ear.

Behind him, several members of the production crew ambled past, nodding politely at Kristen. The man leading their charge was Tim Barnes. Clean-shaven, with slick blond hair, Tim was the only one wearing a suit. Kristen suspected he wore it to let everyone know he was Executive Producer.

He beamed. 'Kristen, how are you?'

'Not as tanned as you,' she said. 'Where's Steve?'

'Oh, he never picks me up any more,' Tim said, waving goodbye to the last of the crew. 'He grew bored of my foreign adventures years ago.'

'You guys get what you needed?'

'Well, we managed to visit all the locations in Marcus's new book,' Tim said. 'You know, your husband's research is so good, you'd never know he'd never actually been to any of them.'

'Well, I'm ticking them off now,' Marcus said, finally putting Abi down.

Kristen swapped places and hugged him.

'Easy now,' Tim said. 'You don't know where he's been.'

'Oh, I'm sure he'll tell me,' Kristen said. 'He doesn't care whether I'm bored of his adventures or not.'

Tim smiled.

'Darling, I'm famished,' Marcus said. 'Any chance we can stop for a bite to eat somewhere?'

Kristen turned back to Tim. 'Why don't you join us for lunch? We can give you a ride home if you want. It's not that far out of our way.'

'You sure?' Tim asked.

'Absolutely,' she said. 'You boys can give us the highlights of your trip.'

They stopped at a pub near Tim's house in Kingston upon Thames that Tim had heard did good food. At a corner table by the open window, Marcus ordered a chicken baguette, which he demolished within seconds of its arrival.

'So what was it like, Father?' Abi asked.

Marcus was still chewing his last mouthful, so Tim

stepped in for him. 'It's a beautiful place,' he told her. 'Do you know much about the Philippines, Abigail?'

'I know it's an archipelago,' Abi said.

'That's right. It consists of over seven-and-a-half-thousand islands. Your father did a lot of research on the Mangyan people who live on Mindoro island, so we spent a few days there trying to talk to some of the tribal chiefs about filming.'

'How long have those people lived there, Father?' Abi asked.

Kristen noticed she'd propped her palms underneath her chin and was gazing up at him adoringly.

'Not as long as some, Abi-girl,' Marcus said, dabbing his mouth with a napkin. 'The original inhabitants of the region are thought to be *Homo Luzonensis*. They lived on the island of Luzon roughly fifty thousand years ago.'

'Wow,' Abi said.

'We know a fair bit about them too,' Tim added, 'thanks to the Callao cave on the north of the Luzon island. It's a popular archaeological site.'

Marcus took a sip of his cider. 'Archaeologists have found all kinds of things inside that can tell us about prehistoric man in the region.'

'What kind of things?'

'Bones and remains, mostly,' Tim said.

'Did you go there?' Abi asked her father.

'Just for a day,' Marcus said.

'We made some enquiries about licences,' Tim said.

'And *you* made a new friend,' Marcus said.

The producer grinned. 'It's true, I might have been singled out by an enterprising local.'

Seeing Abi's raised eyebrow, he elaborated. 'Anywhere that becomes a rich archaeological site often brings a rush of amateurs having a go at digging around themselves. In this case, a local man who lived on the island claimed to have unearthed some items of value. He was keen to sell some of them to me.'

'Were they genuine?' Abi asked.

'That's my princess,' Marcus said. 'Exactly the question you should be asking.'

'Actually, they were all genuine,' Tim told her. 'He had quite the collection too. I ended up buying several fossils from him.'

Kristen placed her hand on his arm. 'I hope you bought a gift for Steve over there too, or you'll be in trouble.'

Tim chuckled. 'Then maybe I *am* in trouble.'

'If I don't hear from you, we'll start looking for another producer,' Marcus teased.

'I'll do it,' Abi said. 'I'd love to come with you next time.'

I bet you would, Kristen thought. *Then you could follow him around all year*. She was immediately appalled at the petty stab of jealousy. Where was this coming from, honestly? She was better than this. 'Come on, guys,' she said. 'Let's hit the road. I'm sure you're all jet-lagged and I, for one, would like to get home.'

5

They dropped Tim off at his home, a detached house on the outskirts of town. Zane, Tim and Steve's chocolate Labrador, came bounding down the driveway the second they pulled in, as if sensing Tim's presence inside the car. Abi cooed as the dog leapt onto his hind legs and licked Tim's face like there was no tomorrow.

'If only Steve missed me this much,' the producer joked.

Marcus helped Tim with his luggage and the Hardy family left man and pet to it.

They were back on the motorway, Abi in the back seat with Marcus so she could cuddle up with him.

'Father, can we get a dog?' she asked.

'No, Abi-girl,' Marcus said. 'You're not old enough yet. I keep telling you.'

'Oh, please? I promise I'll take care of it,' Abi said.

'Let's talk about it on your next birthday, all right?'

She sighed. 'Okay, Father.'

For the next hour, she quizzed Marcus about every aspect of his trip. Clearly excluded from the conversation, Kristen concentrated on the motorway traffic, trying not to feel like a glorified chauffeur.

'Darling,' Marcus said, breaking his latest anecdote, 'are you in a hurry?'

Puzzled, she looked at the needle. She was doing seventy-five.

'Could you slow down a bit?' he asked. 'It's not like we have anywhere to be.'

Kristen stared at him in the rear-view mirror. 'Well, I just thought if we made good time, Abi and I could still make evening Mass,' she said.

She caught Abi staring back at her, then at Marcus. Something unspoken passed between them.

'What?' Kristen said.

Abi looked guilty and gave her father an imploring look.

'Marcus, what is this?' Kristen said.

Marcus sighed. 'Kris, Abi and I have been talking.'

'On WhatsApp,' Abi added.

'I …' Marcus began, but wilted.

His face had developed that awkward expression he acquired when he knew he needed to be socially empathetic but wasn't sure how to say the right words.

Abi took over for him. 'Father says I don't have to go to church any more.'

'What?'

She might as well have told Kristen she was moving out.

'But, darling, we always go to church.'

It was, in fact, their thing. And their only thing. She and Abi went to Mass every Sunday at St James's, the local village church. It was as regular a ritual as the Saturday walks, but it was one activity that Marcus never invited himself along to, something that was solely theirs.

'I know, Mother. And I know you enjoy the two of us going. But Father thinks I shouldn't any more. He says religion is fine when you're a child, but that I'm growing up now.'

'I see.' Kristen gripped the steering wheel harder. 'And do you think your own mum is a child?'

She watched Abi's face expectantly. But her daughter just sighed. 'No, Mother, of course not. I'm sure Father didn't mean you.'

'Actually, Father can be pretty rude,' Kristen said. 'Even about me. Especially when he knows there are some things I feel very strongly about.'

Marcus shuffled awkwardly in the back, fiddling with his seat belt. He refused to meet her eyes in the mirror. 'Let's talk about it when we get home, Kris,' he said. 'Please.'

She was surprised that Marcus so willingly offered to drop the subject. Maybe he was too jet-lagged from the flight to get into it. Or maybe even he could sense that he had upset her. When she checked again ten minutes later he had closed his eyes, Abi's arms and legs curled around him like a snake. She wondered if it was genuine tiredness or just an excuse to avoid the topic. Either way, this was something they would have to thrash out.

6

Both father and daughter were soundly asleep when Kristen eventually arrived back at Orchard House. The sound of the engine dying stirred Marcus. He rubbed his eyes and gently moved Abi aside to help Kristen with the suitcases. Kristen unlocked the front door; Marcus wheeled the luggage inside and carried it up to the master bedroom.

'What shall we do for dinner, darling?' Marcus asked. 'I'm sure you're too tired to cook. We could go to the Lamb's Head?'

She was struck then at how easily he seemed to have forgotten their conversation, and her irritation returned. 'Why did you tell Abi she didn't have to go to church without talking to me?' she said.

'Oh. You want to do that now.'

'Give me one good reason.'

Marcus sighed. 'I can give you plenty,' he said, 'but I'll settle for what I told her. You have the autonomy and the right to believe in fairy tales if you want. But we shouldn't be pushing that stuff on her. I'm sorry.'

'You can be sorry all you like,' Kristen said, trying not to react to the way he said *fairy tales*. 'But Abi is my daughter too. And we agreed we'd raise her Catholic.'

'We agreed,' Marcus said, tersely, 'that *you* could raise her Catholic until she was grown up enough to decide for herself.'

'Eleven years old is *not* grown up, Marcus. I'll respect her decision when she's old enough to make it. But she isn't yet.'

Marcus stared at her in disbelief. 'Isn't that the age you chose to believe? What gives you the right to have a choice at that age but not Abi?'

Kristen felt her hackles rise. 'How dare you?' she said. 'You know how seriously I take my faith.'

'But isn't that the point, darling? It's *your* faith. Not hers. I'm just saying that maybe you need to compromise a little.'

Now Kristen was certain her blood was beginning to boil. '*Me* compromise? I wanted to send her to St Kathryn's. But no, you said. You insisted she go to a state school, regardless of how well she would have flourished there.'

'She *flourishes* better in a secular setting, Kris.'

'Oh, and you know that because ...?'

'Well, I don't exactly see the national curriculum teaching kids that some first-century Jewish zombie can turn into bread and wine.'

She felt heat flush through her cheeks. 'You can be a real bastard sometimes, do you know that?'

Before Marcus could reply, Abi appeared in the doorway, looking foggy.

'Hey, Abs,' Kristen said in a calmer voice.

'I woke up and thought I was still in a dream,' she said. 'You two were gone.'

'Sorry, princess,' Marcus said. 'We didn't want to wake you.'

Abi frowned at her parents. 'Okay, well, I'll be in my room, okay? Call me when it's time for dinner.'

She vanished, and Kristen turned back to Marcus.

His expression was contrite. 'I'm sorry, darling,' he said. 'It's just something I feel quite passionate about.'

Kristen unzipped the suitcase on the mattress and began pulling her husband's clothes from inside it. 'Sometimes I don't get why you married me,' she said.

'Because I fell in love with you,' Marcus said.

'You wanted to marry someone who believes in fairy tales?'

Marcus sighed and sat down on the bed. 'No two people are alike, Kris,' he said. 'It doesn't mean we don't love each other. It's not as if you didn't know I was an atheist when we met.'

'And it's not as if you didn't know how important my faith is to me.'

'Of course,' Marcus said. 'I try my best to understand that, even when I don't agree with it.'

'But you still think I'm stupid?'

'I think on this, you're wrong, yes. But so bloody what? Are couples supposed to believe all the same things? Vote the same way? Have the same politics and opinions on every issue? How boring would that be? I love you, Kris. I have done from the moment I first saw you.'

She sighed, stacking a pile of socks. 'I love you too,' she said. 'I guess when it comes to Abi, it's tricky. We both love her and want what's best for her.'

'You're right, of course,' Marcus said. 'I suppose we just have to find a way to have these difficult conversations.'

'Yes, and without being mean to each other,' Kristen said. She stroked his cheek. 'I never mock your beliefs, you know.'

'Yes,' he said. 'I know. That's because you are gentle and kind and considerate. And I'm an arsehole.'

'Well, on that much we do agree.'

He smiled weakly, moved around the bed and wrapped his arms around her. She felt him close, his heart beating next to hers. She loved him with all hers. Despite their difference, she always had.

7

Now that he was home, Marcus returned to his usual routine of retreating upstairs to his study to work on his next book. Unlike the cramped room in their old Cambridge home, Orchard House's study was spacious and furnished with all the creature comforts he needed. He mainly emerged for meals and in the evenings, so he could sit with Kristen and watch television. On Saturdays, he reprised his role as the expert local historian and took Abi out into the forest, showing her more of the places he had enjoyed exploring as a young boy.

But Marcus was not young anymore, something Kristen was acutely aware of with his fortieth birthday approaching fast. It fell on the last weekend in August which, although over six weeks away, didn't give her much time to prep. She was planning to host a party in their garden, though not a surprise party, which she knew Marcus would hate. Somewhat unexpectedly, Marcus was enthusiastic about the idea. Normally one to downplay birthdays, he seemed uncharacteristically keen to embrace this one. Kristen suspected he was satisfied with what he had achieved at this milestone in his life. It was deserved too. He'd written six popular science bestsellers and hosted eight seasons of one of the UK's most-watched TV shows. He was also happily married and blessed with a bright, intellectually curious daughter who wanted to emulate him. What more could a man ask for? The only thing Kristen knew he missed was his postgrad research. When she first met Marcus, he practically lived at Cambridge University. But there was no room in his life for that now. With the TV show and his publisher's ten-book contract, Marcus barely had an hour to spare in his day. Sometimes she felt lucky he managed to fit her and Abi in at all. Kristen insisted he did no work on his birthday, however. She was determined to make it a day he'd remember forever.

The planning began at the kitchen table on Saturday afternoon. Kristen had barely started making notes when Abi wandered in and asked what she was doing. When Kristen told her, she became excited and asked if she could help.

'I don't think so, Abs. It's all in hand, I think.'

'There must be something I can do,' Abi insisted.

Kristen chewed lightly at the end of her pen, considering. 'Tell you what,' she said. 'Why don't you write your father a speech?'

'What about?'

'How much he means to you. All the things you love about him. You can read it out loud at the party.'

Abi swallowed. 'Mother, I don't know. That's speaking in public. You know how shy I can be.'

I'm not sure I do, Kristen thought, but knew her daughter was being sincere and loved her too much to say anything.

'You don't have to, sweetie,' she said. 'I just think it would mean a lot to him. You are his little princess, you know.'

Abi's cheeks flushed, but Kristen could tell the idea

appealed. She fetched a notebook and pen from her bedroom and returned to her spot at the table. 'Okay, Mother,' she said, removing the lid from her pen. 'What shall I include?'

'Whatever you want, sweetie. Maybe start with your early memories of him.'

Abi frowned as though this was too obvious a suggestion. Before she could respond, Marcus emerged unexpectedly from the study upstairs.

'Hello to my two favourite ladies. Don't mind me, just filling up on coffee.'

He looked at Abi, who smoothed out the page in her notebook.

'What's all this?' he said.

'You'll see,' Abi said, her tongue poking out as she scribbled down some thoughts.

'Oh, a secret, is it?'

He walked over to Kristen and kissed her forehead. 'And what are you up to?'

'Nothing much, darling,' Kristen said.

She moved over to the sink to run the hot tap as if to start some washing up.

'I see,' he said. 'Anyone fancy a walk? The woods are looking very inviting today.'

Abi shook her head. 'Things to do, Father.'

Marcus chuckled. 'Very well,' he said. 'I can see you two are occupied with something.'

He made himself a cappuccino using the machine on the counter and trotted out of the kitchen.

When he was gone, Abi spoke again. 'Mother, I've been having a think about church.'

Kristen was instantly transported back to the car journey from the airport and how upset she had been. 'Oh?' It was all she could manage.

'Yes,' Abi said. 'I think I might have been premature.'

'Premature?' Kristen repeated, feeling confused.

'I've been trying to decide what I believe, you see. I know you and Father have such different ideas and he was just keen for me to think for myself.'

Yes, Kristen thought. *If by 'think for yourself' you mean agree with him.* But she said nothing as her daughter continued.

'I can see Father's point of view, and it sort of made sense for a while, but then I realised that Father doesn't have all the answers.'

Kristen could barely believe her daughter could utter such a statement. 'He doesn't?' she asked gently.

Abi laughed. 'No, he doesn't. He's so super clever, but in some ways he's not as smart as you.'

Now Kristen was intrigued. 'How so?'

'Well, for one thing, it's smart to look after your community, isn't it? Your life is always connected to the lives of your neighbours, the people around you. It's fundamental to society. Father should understand this better than anyone, but for some reason he doesn't.' Abi pointed to Kristen. 'But you do, Mother. You've been a part of St James's church since you and Father moved here. Who raises money for the local charities? Who visits the sick and elderly in the village who have no one else? Who does old Mrs Hanner's shopping every week?'

Kristen felt her cheeks flush, but her daughter wasn't finished.

'It's true, I have yet to process the claims the Christian church makes and come to my conclusions. But I do know that's not all that's important. Supporting the poor. Feeding the hungry. Following the example of Jesus.'

She slid off the table and, with no sense of embarrassment, hugged Kristen as hard as she could. 'That's what you teach me,' she said. 'I know I don't show it often, but I'm grateful for that, Mother. And I'm also not ready to let that go yet.'

Kristen nodded and pulled Abi in close to her. Her daughter, eleven years old but going on forty herself, trotted back to the table. Kristen, meanwhile, turned around, facing the window and the sink. She was crying tears of pride that she was too embarrassed for Abi to see.

8

Though there was plenty to organise, it all came together seamlessly on the day. The catering company Kristen had hired erected an imposing marquee in the sizeable back garden. In the end, eighty-one people confirmed, with some family staying overnight. Marcus's parents, Henry and Rosalind, had flown in specially from Spain. Kristen's father and her sister Jacqui had also arrived earlier that afternoon and were already availing themselves of the champagne. Kristen stayed by Marcus's side from the moment the first guests arrived. She had made a real effort to dress up for the occasion, deliberately buying an overpriced designer dress and getting her hair done in the only salon in the village. She knew she'd probably overdone it. In contrast, Marcus had put on an old linen suit, which was complemented by his straggly crow's nest of hair and a scuffed pair of loafers that had seen better days. But what he lacked in fashion he made up for in charm. And today, he was in his element. He moved slowly from guest to guest, kissing cheeks, shaking hands, never forgetting a name, even the plus-ones. Most people were huddled inside the marquee, seeking shelter from the sun. At one end, where the white canvas had been rolled up to allow a welcome breeze through, Tim Barnes was sharing a joke with his husband Steve.

'Marcus!' Tim said when he saw them approach. 'You don't look a day over sixty.'

'He's a funny man, isn't he?' Steve said. 'You can see why I married him.'

'Darling, I thought you told me you'd taken Tim off the list,' Marcus said.

Kristen shrugged. 'He must have slipped through security.'

Tim handed Marcus a wrapped box. 'Slipped this through them too,' he said. 'Happy birthday, old man.'

Marcus handed his champagne over to Kristen and took the gift. He removed the wrapping and opened the box. Inside was a black shawl-like cloth, which he unrolled carefully in his palm.

'What is it, Father?'

Kristen turned to discover Abi had appeared behind them. She too had made an effort, even putting on a dress and allowing Kristen to tie her hair in a ribbon.

'It's a knife,' Marcus told her. 'Not just any knife either.'

'It's from Luzon island,' Tim said. 'From my amateur archaeologist.'

Abi reached out to touch it, but Kristen stopped her in time.

'You can look, but don't touch, Abs, okay?' she said.

Abi nodded. 'It looks old,' she said.

'Yes, it's made from flint,' Marcus explained. 'But it's incredibly well preserved because it's been buried inside a dry cave. It's extremely rare to find one intact.'

He ran his fingers along the edge of the tool. 'And it's still sharp.'

'Did it belong to the *Homo Luzonensis*?' Abi asked.

'Goodness,' Tim said, 'your daughter has a good memory, Marcus.'

Marcus smiled with pride. Kristen could hardly blame him. Their daughter retained knowledge like she was a walking encyclopaedia.

'Was it used for hunting?' Abi said.

'Yes, it was,' Marcus said. 'Most likely to keep the bearer warm.'

Abi shot him a puzzled look.

'The remains of deer carcasses have been found in the Callao cave,' Marcus explained. 'Which means *Homo Luzonensis* wore animal skins. So someone probably used this for skinning animals.'

'Cool,' Abi said.

'Very cool,' Marcus agreed.

He turned back to Tim. 'But I'm afraid I can't accept it,' he said.

'Why not?'

'Because I know its true value.'

Kristen understood what her husband meant, but it seemed Tim did not. The producer shook his head and looked at Steve. 'See? I told you he'd be like this. Marcus, without you we wouldn't even *have* a show. Don't worry about what it cost. It's your birthday.'

'I'm not talking about cost,' Marcus said. 'I'm talking about its cultural and historic value. This piece belongs in a museum.'

Tim blushed and Kristen felt a flush of pity. She knew he hadn't meant any harm.

'Marcus, you know how I feel about all that British Empire acquisition stuff,' Tim said. 'I would never deprive any culture of anything of value. There are literally hundreds of fossils in the Philippines. If I thought one would make a difference, I'd never have bought it.'

'I know,' Marcus said. 'And I appreciate it's not like these are the gates of Babylon you've brought back. But still, out of principle, I'm afraid I can't accept. I do hope you don't think me judgemental. I know you meant well.'

Tim looked increasingly embarrassed. 'I'm so sorry, Marcus,' Steve said. 'I did tell him to get an expensive whisky. Next year, maybe.'

Kristen touched Tim's elbow as her husband slowly wound the black cloth around the dagger. 'It really was a nice gesture,' she said. 'I'm sure Marcus is grateful for the thought, aren't you?'

Tim sighed and took the fossil back. 'It's okay, I should have checked with you first,' he said. 'I am sorry, Marcus. At least let me get you something. How about I take you out for dinner?'

'You can treat me when we're back in Manila,' Marcus promised. 'I'll pick the most expensive restaurant, don't worry.'

Polite smiles were exchanged. Though Marcus had only been trying to move the conversation on, the mention of Manila reminded Kristen it would only be a few weeks before she would become a production widow again. *Best not to think about it*, she thought. *Today is supposed to be a happy day.* Just then, she spotted Bree and Darius making their way across the lawn.

'Will you please excuse us?' she said.

Grabbing Marcus by the arm, she inclined her head sideways, indicating to Abi that she should follow too. As for Marcus, he looked grateful to be pried away.

9

Bree and Darius waved as the trio exited the marquee. A smaller figure trailed behind them. She was about Abi's age, only slightly skinnier, with buoyant frizzy hair and light brown skin.

'Hey, girlie,' Bree squealed, breaking into a slight run.

She hugged Kristen tightly. Kristen hugged her back before breaking free to kneel down. 'Hello, Poppy,' she said warmly. 'Nice to see you! Do you have a cuddle for your Aunty Krissy?'

The girl ducked shyly behind Bree as though she wasn't eleven at all, but three.

'Happy birthday, Marcus,' Darius said.

'Thank you both for coming,' Marcus said, beckoning to one of the passing catering staff.

A tray appeared before their newest arrivals.

'Ooh, bubbly,' Bree said, grabbing two flutes and necking the first instantly.

Darius gave her his customary eye roll but gratefully took a drink for himself. The waiter returned to the marquee where more thirsty guests were waiting.

'Good turnout, Marcus,' Darius said. 'This all looks very lovely.'

'Good tunes too,' Bree said.

She pointed at an outdoor wireless speaker, through which a medley of eighties hits were being streamed from inside the house.

'I'm afraid this was all Kristen's doing,' Marcus said. 'Take a bow, darling.'

Kristen didn't, instead wanting to soothe the social anxiety of the girl cowering behind Bree. 'My goodness, Poppy,' she said. 'You have shot up, haven't you? You'll be taller than me soon.'

The girl looked doubtfully at Kristen.

'Go on, honey,' Bree said. 'Say hello! It's only Aunty Krissy.'

'H-hello,' Poppy said meekly.

'Gosh, how long's it been since we last saw her?' Kristen asked.

'Oh, probably a year,' Darius said. 'When did you two have the spa weekend?'

The women agreed that it had been a year ago, at least, maybe more. Kristen smiled at Poppy. 'You remember Abigail, don't you? Abi, come over here.'

Abi stepped forward.

'This party really isn't going to be much fun for girls your age,' Kristen said. 'Abi, why don't you take Poppy into the house? Maybe the two of you can watch a movie or something.'

Abi sighed. 'But, Mother, I was hoping to mingle. This is like being relegated to the children's table.'

'Princess, don't be rude,' Marcus said.

'But Father, I want to stay with you. I want to talk with the adults.'

Marcus shook his head. 'When we have guests, it's our job to make sure they're entertained. Go now.'

Abi stared at her father, her eyes pleading for a reprieve. But Marcus stood firm. Her expression became visibly pained. 'Fine,' she said. 'If that's what you really want, Father.' She stared at Poppy. 'Follow me then.'

With an obvious huff, Abi spun around and stomped towards the rear of the garden. Poppy swallowed and looked up to her mother.

'It's okay, sweets,' Bree said. 'Go play. I'll come find you later.'

Slowly, hesitantly, Poppy plodded cautiously in the same direction as Abi.

'She's turning into a little woman,' Kristen remarked.

'I don't know about that,' Bree said. 'She's scared of her own shadow, that one.'

'I think she's just lovely.'

'Yeah, well at least you don't have to worry about yours coming out of her shell. I see she's still going with the whole *Mother Father* skit?'

Kristen laughed. 'I can't shake her out of it, Bee. I keep telling her she sounds precocious, but I think she thinks it's charming or something.'

'Well, at least it's on-brand, honey. Look at this wonder pad. If this isn't a place where a child can be precocious, I don't know where is.'

Kristen blushed. Bree had stayed over at the house many times since she and Marcus had moved here, but she never failed to feel embarrassed when her friend teased her about their comfortable lifestyle. 'It's all the TV money,' she said, not for the first time. 'Without it, Marcus would never have been able to buy his parents out.'

She glanced at Marcus, but his gaze seemed distant again. He was shuffling his feet, looking beyond them and around at the other guests. 'You okay, darling?' she asked.

'My apologies,' he said to the group. 'I'm just looking out

for Harry. He was supposed to arrive this morning, but his flight's been delayed.'

'Harry Dean,' Kristen explained to Darius. 'He's an old uni friend of Marcus's. They studied at Cambridge together.'

'A very long time ago now,' said Marcus. 'I'm very much looking forward to seeing him again.'

Kristen rubbed his shoulder.

'Aw, Marcus's bestie is coming over for his birthday,' Bree said. 'That's sweet.'

To Kristen's surprise, Marcus's cheeks reddened.

'Listen, girlie, I'm roasting,' Bree said. 'Any chance we can get out of the sun?'

As they all moved towards an area of shade, Kristen just about caught Abigail out of the corner of her eye. From her body language, it was clear she was still in a mood. She knew Abi would have much preferred to stay with the adults. But Kristen thought it was good for her to engage with kids her own age sometimes. More than that, it was healthy. For once, Abi would just have to accept that she was still a kid and not a grown-up. She'd get over it soon enough.

10

Poppy trailed after Abigail with some reluctance. It was obvious the other girl didn't want to play with her. But Poppy's mum had told her to go with her, so she had. Abigail led her around the back of the house, past lots of balloons tied to trees and garden furniture, all with the name 'Marcus' and the number forty. They passed a big white tent where many grown-ups were standing around inside, just talking. Poppy thought Aunty Krissy was probably right. This party wasn't going to be much fun for an eleven-year-old. But that still didn't mean she wanted to be stuck with Abigail. The two girls had often been thrust into each other's company over the years because their mums were best friends. But although Poppy was around the same age as Abigail, they couldn't have been more different. Abigail liked the sound of her own voice far too much. In fact, she liked talking as much as any adult Poppy had ever met. She suspected Abigail would much rather be inside that tent, jabbering away about the news or whatever boring stuff the adults were discussing.

Abigail took her through the open patio doors and into the kitchen. Poppy had been here many times before but never failed to be impressed at its size. In the middle of the kitchen was something her mother had told her was an *island*, though it looked to her like a giant white table. It also looked big enough for them to play fort inside. Although Abigail probably didn't play fort; she most likely considered it a silly kids' game.

'Where are we going?' Poppy asked.

'To the theatre of the imagination,' the other girl said.

Confused, Poppy followed her through the hallway and up the stairs until they turned into a room midway down the passage. She remembered this place. It was the only room in the house that was full of books.

'If they're going to insist on confining us, we might as well read,' Abigail said, sweeping her hand at the shelves that lined every wall. She tapped her forehead. 'They can't imprison us in here now, can they?'

Poppy stared slack-jawed at the sheer volume of both hardbacks and paperbacks on display. 'Are these books all just for adults?' she asked.

Abigail shook her head. 'Father says no books should be off-limits to anyone. But this shelf here is full of children's classics.'

Poppy drew closer and ran her eyes across some of the titles. It was a mix of older and newer books. *Harry Potter. The Adventures of Huckleberry Finn. The Tale of Peter Rabbit. Where The Wild Things Are.* Some she'd heard of and some she hadn't.

'You like to read, right?' Abigail said.

Poppy nodded nervously. She *did* like to read, but she doubted she had read anywhere near as many books as Abigail. That girl was what her mother called *silly smart*.

'Grab whatever takes your fancy,' Abigail said.

'What's a good one?' Poppy asked.

'Well that's a subjective question,' Abigail said. 'It really all depends on your taste.'

'My mum doesn't like to read much,' Poppy said. 'Except magazines sometimes.'

'Mother says reading is reading,' Abigail said. 'And that every person should read for pleasure, whatever they like. Sometimes Father and I can spend a whole Sunday afternoon curled up on the sofas reading books.'

Poppy didn't know what to say to that. She'd never spent any time reading with her dad or her mum. 'That sounds nice,' she finally managed, after worrying she'd been quiet for too long. 'You do a lot of things with your dad?'

Abigail stared out of the window and down at the party. 'Usually,' she said. She glanced back at Poppy. 'You know what? Let's leave these adults to their child-free event if that's their wish.'

'What?'

'Let's take our books to the woods! I can show you a secret place no one knows about.'

'I don't know,' Poppy said with a nervous swallow. 'I'll have to ask my mum.'

Abigail rolled her eyes. 'Your mother doesn't care what you do,' she said. 'Isn't that obvious? The adults just want you and me out of their way. So let's leave them to it.'

Poppy swallowed. 'I d-don't know,' she said. 'Aren't the woods … dangerous?'

Abigail laughed. 'Only in stories. I know these woods like the back of my hand. They're nothing to be frightened of.'

The other girl frowned. 'But what if we get lost?'

'We won't. Now come on, choose a book and we'll grab a snack from the kitchen. And then we'll have a party all of our own.'

Poppy stared at the other girl, feeling very unsure. But she also didn't want to appear silly. Despite their similar ages, Abigail was basically a grown-up in a younger girl's body. If she said the woods were safe, then Poppy was inclined to believe her. So, somewhat hesitantly, she agreed.

11

The adults sat around the oval wrought-iron garden table, under the shade of a large umbrella. Bree complimented Kristen on her heating stove, which stood sentry-like in the middle of the lawn. 'It makes pizzas, right? I was telling Darius we need to get one of those.'

'Do it,' Kristen encouraged her.

Marcus's phone buzzed on the table and he glanced down at the screen. 'He's here,' he said. 'I told him just to make his way around the back.'

A few moments later, Marcus waved. Kristen turned around to see Harry ambling along the lawn, ruddy-faced and out of breath. 'Sorry, all,' he said as he eventually reached the quartet. 'The taxi driver got a little lost.'

Both of them stood up. Kristen grabbed Harry by both shoulders and kissed him on one cheek. 'Lovely to see you, darling.' She turned to Marcus. 'Darling, help Harry with his case.'

Marcus moved in to take Harry's suitcase from him.

'Thank you, Aury,' Harry said.

'Harry, dear, I've made up a bed for you,' said Kristen. 'Marcus will show you. Then come and join us out here.'

'Well, we've got our orders,' Marcus said, laughing. He led Harry into the house, slapping him on the back as the two of them chatted excitedly, talking over each other.

'So that's Markie's bestie?' Bree said. 'He seems nice.'

'He's very sweet,' Kristen said. 'I'm just so happy he could take time off for this. It'll mean so much to Marcus.'

The men rejoined them some twenty minutes later, both with a beer from the kitchen. Once all were seated, Kristen introduced everyone formally. Harry smiled shyly at the group. Beads of sweat had formed on his brow, but she couldn't tell if he was nervous or just hot.

'So what's it like, living in Geneva?' Darius asked. 'Do you miss the UK?'

'Sometimes,' Harry said. 'But I've been there so many years now, I think of it as home.'

'Never been to Geneva,' Bree said. 'It sounds friggin' cold.'

'Hey, wasn't there that terrorist attack at the airport recently?' Darius said. 'I saw something on the news.'

'Yes, fortunately they arrested the man,' Harry said.

'Religiously motivated, wasn't it?' Marcus said.

Kristen's heart sank. It might be his birthday, but she didn't want him upsetting her friends. 'Darling, let's not go there,' she suggested.

'Oh, don't be ridiculous, Kris. We're all grown-ups, aren't we? And just for the record, I have nothing in particular against Muslims. I am, in fact, strongly against all religions.' He turned to Bree and Darius and smiled. 'As my wife will tell you, I'm convinced they're all as dangerous as each other.'

Kristen saw Darius tense, about to take the bait. *Don't do it, don't do it, don't do it,* she prayed silently in her head. But it seemed it was too late for that.

'Is that so, Marcus?' Darius said, raising an eyebrow. 'And why exactly would you say that?'

12

Mum and Dad aren't going to be happy about this, Poppy thought. She trailed after Abigail to the back of the garden and an iron gate built into the hedgerow. None of the guests paid them any attention as the older girl slid the bolt across. On the other side, a well-trodden path snaked its way across a field. Abigail skipped along it, holding the straps of her pink rucksack. She had changed out of her party dress, swapping it for a more pragmatic T-shirt, jeans, and trainers that were more suited to their impromptu odyssey. Poppy followed skittishly behind, her heart sinking a little as the music from the garden faded. Her dad would be especially cross with her. He didn't like Poppy going anywhere without permission. Mum was a bit more relaxed, which sometimes annoyed Dad. But there was no doubt they would both be angry that she had not told them she was leaving the party. Abigail had insisted though, saying it served them right. Why *had* Poppy gone along with her? She was eleven now and could make her own decisions. But she knew the answer. She wanted to prove she wasn't scared. She'd felt embarrassed when Abigail laughed at her earlier about thinking the woods might be dangerous. It had been a dumb thing to say. Now Poppy secretly wished that there would be something dangerous waiting for them in there. Something big and scary, like a bear. She knew that bears didn't live in English woods but part of her would love it if one did come crashing through the forest at them. Then Abigail would quickly change from being *Miss Know It All* to being *Sorry, Poppy, You Were Right*.

'What are you smiling about?' Abigail asked, breaking Poppy from her reverie.

'Nothing,' Poppy said, looking away.

She was hardly going to tell Abigail what she had been thinking.

'You're a bit of an introvert, has anyone ever told you that?'

'No!'

'Do you even know what an introvert is?'

'Yes, of course I do,' Poppy said, though in truth she didn't.

They arrived at the edge of the forest, where Abigail picked up another path. Poppy was surprised at how much darker it became once the trees blocked out the light. The girls followed this new trail until Abigail veered left and into the undergrowth. Here, the air smelled muskier and Poppy could hear the sound of lapping water. They trod slowly down the side of an embankment. It wasn't steep, but the ground was covered in many loose stones that threatened to trip them up. At the bottom, they came across a stream. Bolstered by the confidence of local knowledge, Abigail skipped across two stepping stones and onto the opposite bank. Poppy moved more cautiously, concerned her trainers might slip against the wet stones. She joined Abigail on the other side. Her eyes were beginning to adjust to the twilight effect of the shade now and she saw the woodlands in more detail. She heard noises, scurrying that sounded like squirrels, or rats. Abigail resumed a walking pace again.

'Did you know that millennia ago, neolithic tribes used to hunt in these woods?' she said.

Poppy shook her head. She didn't know what *neolithic* meant or half the fancy words Abigail liked to use.

'These woods are rich with evidence of them,' Abigail said.

'Who?'

'The Neolithic, silly. They left behind hunting tools and other objects. Father says they were the first humans to develop permanent dwellings and make cultural leaps, like making pottery and paintings.'

'Oh?' It was all Poppy could think of to say.

'They were first to have pets too. Do *you* have pets?'

Poppy confirmed she did not.

Abigail sighed. 'I really want a dog,' she said. 'Father doesn't think I'm ready. But I am.'

Poppy struggled to keep pace with the other girl, in all senses of the word. She was out of breath. With the same confidence she showed leaping across the stones, Abigail practically slalomed around trees, weaving her way towards her intended destination, wherever that might be. After a while, Poppy lost track of which way they were facing. And her legs started to ache. Eventually, however, Abigail reached a grassy bank and waved Poppy over. 'We're here,' she said.

Poppy joined her at the crest of the bank, which bordered another river, or possibly a different part of the same river as before. Hovering above it was an old tyre hanging from a rope tied to a weeping willow branch that extended halfway across the water.

'See?' Abigail said. 'Told you this would be fun.'

Poppy chewed her lip nervously.

13

'I'm sorry, but it's true,' Marcus said, staring across the table at Darius. 'How many wars have been started throughout history because somebody forced their beliefs on others?'

'Hey, come on, darling,' Kristen said diplomatically. 'Let's drop it.'

'I've never forced my beliefs on others,' Darius shot back.

Marcus waved at him dismissively. 'Fine, I acknowledge that in your case that may well be true.'

'That's very gracious of you,' Darius said tartly.

'But the chances are if you believe in something dogmatically, you're going to be predisposed to thinking in black-and-white terms. Which, in turn, makes it easier to become an extremist.'

'Darling, you also think in black-and-white terms,' Kristen reminded him. 'And you're being very rude to Darius.'

Marcus groaned. 'See, that's the problem right there,' he said. 'As soon as you criticise religion, somebody tells you to be quiet in case somebody else takes offence.'

'Well, maybe if you didn't call people extremists,' Kristen said.

'She's right, Marcus,' Darius said. 'Just because one idiot

did something stupid doesn't mean you get to tar all religious folk with the same brush.'

'Yes, but sometimes the shoe fits,' Marcus said. His voice was calm and low but there was a tightness to it.

'What do you mean by that?' Darius said.

'Well, it's not like the Catholic church hasn't had their share of extremists.'

'Really? Like who?'

'Those behind the Crusades. Or the Inquisition. I could go on.'

'Please don't, darling,' Kristen said.

'Look,' Darius said, 'we can all agree that sometimes religious people do bad things.'

Marcus took a swig of his beer. 'The truth is that it's simply impossible to radicalise someone who's an atheist. We're the only ones who can think for ourselves.'

'I think that's a very patronising thing to say,' said Darius softly.

'It's not my problem if other people choose to believe nonsense,' Marcus said.

'I'm sorry, but that comes across as really arrogant.'

'That's Marcus for you,' said Kristen. 'He's the be-all and end-all of all knowledge. And he doesn't like it when people disagree with him.'

'Actually, I welcome it,' Marcus said. 'I embrace being challenged on my own propositions. It's just that no one here has been able to challenge me with a decent rebuttal.'

'Well, I can rebut you,' Harry said.

The group fell silent. Kristen had almost forgotten that Harry was present. Marcus stared dumbly at his friend.

'You?'

'Only the part where you talked about people choosing what they believe,' Harry said. 'Nobody does that, not even you, Aury.'

Marcus's eyebrows shot up. Kristen wouldn't have been

surprised if her husband keeled over. '*Et tu*, Harry? You've been an atheist for as long as I've known you. Surely you haven't changed sides?'

Harry chuckled. 'No,' he admitted. 'But you can't blame anyone for their beliefs. They're hardwired into our brains.'

'What are you talking about?' Darius asked.

Harry had the full attention of the group. Even Bree had stopped looking at her phone. Kristen could see that part of him regretted speaking up, uncomfortable at having the audience. He cleared his throat nervously.

'Everything around us is data,' he said. 'Our brain is the world's most complex neural network, a computer that's constantly receiving input and automatically reacting to it, whether it's to the environment, or our friends and family. Which means our beliefs are essentially outside our control.'

'You're arguing something rather esoteric, then,' Marcus said. 'A sort of biological essentialism?'

'Essentially, yes,' Harry said with a grin.

When he saw no one had reacted to his joke, he dropped it.

'Go on, Harry,' Kristen said, touching his arm. 'Don't let Marcus put you off. Please.'

Harry nodded at Kristen before continuing. 'When we are exposed to any external stimulus, our brains produce neuro-chemical reactions – what we think of as our thoughts and experiences. Our consciousness fools us into believing it's *you* generating these, but it isn't. It's only your brain.'

'You're saying our brains act against our own will?' Darius asked. 'Isn't that impossible?'

'Not at all,' Harry said. 'And I can prove this very easily with a famous experiment. Whatever you do, do *not*, I repeat, do *not* think of a pink elephant … now, what did you just do?'

The group were silent. Kristen suspected that all of them had just pictured the same thing.

'We are just puppets to our biology,' Harry said. 'Our neurons hold all the strings.'

'But if that were true, it would have a lot of implications for free will, wouldn't it?' Marcus said. 'Why do we even bother punishing criminals, for example? If they're not culpable for the choices they make? Wherein lies our own agency, ontologically speaking?'

'*And* I'm out,' Bree said, returning to her phone.

'The philosophical implications of this are outside my purview,' Harry said. 'All I know is that neurobiologically speaking, people don't actively choose their beliefs. Even in the domain we call spirituality.'

Darius shook his head, his frown deepening. 'Is there really evidence for this? Scientifically, I mean?'

'For the part about spirituality?'

'Sure, why not?'

Harry nodded. 'Numerous MRI studies have been conducted on the brains of religious people that clearly show blood flow lighting up parts of the frontal lobes during prayer and meditation.'

'So?' Darius said. 'What does that prove?'

'That different parts of the *physical* brain are active whenever a person is in a religious mental state. Similar studies have shown that when people were exposed to words and imagery that have religious or spiritual meaning, there is marked activity in the prefrontal cortex. In other words, beliefs themselves are intrinsically related to brain activity. You can't have one without the other. Biological changes are directly connected to belief.'

'Hmm ... but why couldn't it be the other way around?' Darius asked. 'How do we know the belief doesn't happen first and the brain changes as a result? How can we tell which is cause and which is effect?'

Kristen saw Harry's face light up.

'That,' he said, 'is *exactly* the question. And it is the very question my own experiments were set up to answer.'

'Experiments?'

Harry looked at Kristen guiltily. 'I wonder whether perhaps this isn't the time,' he said. 'I'm conscious this is supposed to be a party.'

'Preach,' Bree said.

'Actually, Harry, I'd like to hear more,' Marcus said. 'You've always been a little coy about your research. Now you've got me curious. I'm sure no one minds you telling us about it. Unless anyone objects?'

He searched the faces of the group. Kristen nodded, Darius following suit. Bree stopped what she was doing and looked up. 'Sure, go on, professor, tell us all about it. As long as we're not being marked.'

Harry smiled nervously. 'Very well,' he said.

14

'I don't know how much Marcus told you about me,' Harry continued. 'For the last five years, I've been working for a non-profit organisation – the Bennett Foundation. Have any of you heard of it?'

Bree shrugged. 'The only foundation I know is the stuff I try not to let Darius see me slap on my face every morning,' she said.

Harry gave her a warm smile as if he was genuinely tickled by the bad joke. Kristen suspected he probably was. 'This is the other kind,' he said. 'The Bennetts were a wealthy Victorian family. Industrialists and entrepreneurs. And like a lot of those sort of folk back in the day, they aspired to be philanthropists. So, in 1862, they made it their mission to help the insane.'

'So it *does* have something to do with religion,' Marcus said.

'Darling,' Kristen said. 'Please, just let Harry talk.'

Harry nodded his thanks at her. 'It all started when Albert Bennett's nephew George was rumoured to have gone mad in his early thirties. Today, we would say he had a nervous breakdown. But they didn't know the concept back then. Out of compassion for his nephew, Albert set up a charitable foundation, whose purpose was to investigate the various diseases of the mind. Today, it's evolved into medical research into the brain itself and in trying to understand more about neurobiology. Ultimately, we are seeking medical learnings that will benefit the whole of humanity.'

'That's great, Harry,' Kristen said. 'It's so good that you're helping people.'

'So what about these experiments?' Darius asked.

Harry turned towards him. 'For the last three years, we've been exploring neuro-*theology*. It's a very specialist but established branch of neuroscience. Our work was inspired by all the big names in the field, people like Ramachandran, Beauregard, De Manti ...'

'Oooh, yes, all the big names,' Bree mumbled without looking up.

Harry ignored her. 'We first started with a study group of around two hundred people. It was a diverse group that included Christians, Muslims, Jews, Hindus, and Wiccans. But what they had in common was they all claimed to have had spiritual experiences.'

Kristen's ears pricked up. 'What kind of experiences?'

'It varied,' Harry said. 'Some of them claimed to have communed with God. Others to have had various epiphanies, revelations, achieving Nirvana and so on.'

'Hearing voices?' said Marcus. 'Like good old Joan of Arc?'

Kristen glared at him, but Marcus just shrugged. 'You know the old joke,' he said. 'When a man speaks to God, it's called prayer. But when God speaks to a man it's called schizophrenia.'

'Joan of Arc might well have been schizophrenic,' Harry said. 'Without a time machine, we'll never know. But human history is full of well-documented religious experiences, from Tasmanian devils to Sufism to American Pentecostalism.

Many intelligent people from many religions claim to have had ecstatic experiences of varying sorts.'

'Crazies, in other words,' Marcus said.

'Well, now you're echoing the same Victorian attitudes the Bennetts had to face,' Harry said. 'But the point is, these were otherwise normal, functioning members of society. And they were able to consent to us experimenting on them.'

'You still haven't said how,' Darius said.

'We stimulated parts of their brains,' Harry said. 'Like the right hemisphere, for example, which is mostly responsible for creativity and storytelling.'

'Hey, yeah,' Bree said, looking up again. 'Someone said I was right-brained because I was arty at school.'

'You're probably referring to the left-brain versus right-brain fallacy,' Harry said. 'It's a popular myth, but the truth is, we all use both our lobes. But it *is* the right brain that forms narratives. It likes to make sense of visual data and emotional processing, whereas the left brain is the centre for language and abstract reason.'

Marcus finished his beer and placed his bottle on the table. His eyes were fixed on his friend with fascination. 'So, the right brain is the more religious one?' he asked.

'In a manner of speaking,' Harry said. 'But the brain is far more complex than that. So we stimulated other parts too, using magnetic current.'

'Transcranial stimulation?' Marcus asked. 'I've heard of that.'

'Yes, we call it TCS for short,' Harry said. 'But our method is coupled with carefully selected audiovisual input. Tell me, have any of you heard of a God helmet?'

'God *what*?' Kristen said.

'It's a hardware device,' Harry said. 'The original TCS machine. A neuroscientist named Michael Persinger conducted a series of experiments back in the eighties. He was one of the first to attempt to artificially induce spiritual experiences by deliberately manipulating the brain's electro-magnetic activity.'

Kristen frowned. She wasn't sure how comfortable she felt about this idea.

'Did it work?' Marcus asked.

'That all depends who you ask. But we took our inspiration from those early experiments. We've even designed our own version of the God helmets, very much next generation. But, unlike Persinger, we tested subjects who were *already* having spiritual and religious experiences. Our aim was to see if TCS could reduce them.'

'And did it?' Kristen said. Now she was curious, still considering the possibility that something as fundamental as spirituality could be so easily manipulated.

'It did much more than that,' Harry told her. 'When our initial trial was over, the majority of the subjects professed little to no ability to connect with the supernatural at all. But it wasn't just their experiences that changed. It was their fundamental beliefs too.'

Harry looked at Kristen's face and then at the group, who were waiting for him to sum things up. 'To paraphrase R.E.M.,' he said, 'they lost their religion.'

15

Kristen wanted to make sure she understood what Harry was claiming. 'So they became non-believers?' she asked.

Harry nodded. 'Some even officially renounced religion altogether. It took many weeks, but with the right focus on the right areas of the brain, it proved to be as simple as turning off a switch.'

'Impressive,' Marcus said. 'And do you think you'll get corroboration?'

'I do, in time. We've been running more trials since, trying to iron out any kinks. We hope to publish by the end of the year.'

'Did you know this was going to happen?' Darius asked.

'We knew it was a possibility, yes,' Harry said. 'It's part of what we were testing.'

'I don't understand,' Kristen said. 'I thought you said the Bennett Foundation was about medicine and helping people. Why would you want to destroy people's faith?'

The idea seemed incredible to her.

'We didn't want to do that, exactly. We were simply trying to see if it was possible to curtail spiritual experiences in the human brain.'

'But why?' Kristen asked.

Harry put down his beer glass. 'There are a number of dissociative disorders that involve patients who have what you might class as supernatural experiences. Schizophrenia, bipolar disorder, psychosis, post-traumatic disorders. We hypothesise that if we can reduce these experiences, perhaps we can positively affect the underlying disease.'

'But you didn't test patients actually diagnosed with those conditions?' Darius asked.

'No,' Harry said. 'First we needed to test the hypothesis. And the best way to do that was to recruit people of different faiths. This gave us a much wider spectrum to test. Not to mention these were ordinary, functioning members of society who are otherwise fully *compos mentis* and thus able to give informed consent.'

'But why would they give their consent to something like this?' Kristen said.

'They all had their reasons,' Harry said. 'Some were curious about the authenticity of their own experiences. Others were simply keen to know how much biology played a role in them.'

'And, of course, they were all financially compensated for their participation,' Marcus said.

'They were. But you do them a disservice, Aury. The main reason they gave us was actually one of altruism. Being spiritually minded folk, their hope was our research could one day help relieve the suffering of others.'

'And you believe it will?' Kristen asked.

'I hope so. We now have several new trials running, building on the first stage of this research. Once we have passed peer review, the hope is to move on to narrow trials targeting specific dissociative disorders. This research has the potential to seriously advance our understanding of these and hopefully pioneer new pathways of treatment. It's very exciting work.'

Kristen shook her head. She was trying to process Harry's words. She sympathised with his goal. God knows, she had cared for people who suffered from hallucinations and the like, believing all sorts of things that weren't there and who needed help. But she felt a deep objection to Harry's account of the test subjects who no longer believed in their religions. The implications of this were profoundly disturbing to her. Was faith really just a by-product of the brain? Something that could easily be erased with a few well-placed electrical currents?

'I just … I struggle to accept what you're claiming, Harry, darling,' she said. 'My faith teaches that we are more than just brain cells.'

'She's right,' Darius chipped in. 'Some of us happen to believe in a spiritual realm. You can't study everything under a microscope because not everything is made of matter.'

'Yes, like the soul,' Kristen said.

'Exactly,' Darius said.

'I'm sorry, but there is a God out there, who really exists. He's not just in my mind.' Kristen had a flashback to the Mass she had gone to in Cambridge when she had first fallen pregnant with Abi. She remembered how intensely she had prayed to the Holy Mother to spare her any more pain. And then she thought of Abi. The love and purpose of her life. 'He's real,' she insisted. 'He answers prayers.'

It all sounded flimsy, she knew. But something was welling up inside her. Her eyes were getting wet. She was getting emotional.

'Darling—' Marcus began.

'Sometimes even the cleverest people can be wrong about things, you know,' she said.

She hated how incoherent she sounded. They were all staring at her, wondering what had brought about this outburst. All apart from Bree, whose eyes were filled with empathy and understanding. Marcus looked embarrassed.

Harry's cheeks turned a shade of rouge. He cleared his throat.

'I'm so sorry, Kristen,' he said. 'I … um, I didn't mean to denigrate your faith, or anyone else's. I feel I have over-stepped the boundaries of where I should have kept this conversation. I wasn't thinking. Why don't we drop this topic altogether if everyone is amenable?'

The group mumbled eager agreement. But for Kristen, it was too late. She apologised and excused herself, retreating into the house, where she locked herself in the guest bathroom and tried her best to stop the tears that were falling freely.

16

Poppy stared at the tyre swing.

'It's been here for years,' Abigail said. 'It may not look it, but this part of the river's deep enough to swim in. But if you swing hard enough, you can land on the bank without touching the water.'

Poppy wasn't convinced.

'I'll show you,' Abigail said. 'Watch me. It's fun, I promise.'

The older girl removed her pink rucksack and threw it onto the opposite bank before climbing up the willow's trunk. She shuffled confidently along it, then lowered herself down at the point the rope was bound. As she descended, Poppy noticed that knots had been tied at regular intervals in the rope, providing makeshift handholds. Abigail used these to reach the tyre itself, tucking her feet inside the hoop and gripping the outside with her hands. Then, she leaned back, pushing with her knees until the tyre became a swing. When she let go, she landed gracefully on the grassy knoll on the other side, performed a forward roll and emerged triumphantly like a gymnast, arms up in the air.

'See? You just need enough momentum,' she called back.

Momentum. That was another big word, Poppy thought. She was not at all convinced she could repeat the manoeuvre, but she had come too far to back out now. With jangled nerves, she copied Abigail and traversed the trunk. As she crossed over the point where the rope was tied, she felt the branch bend with her weight.

'It will hold,' Abigail assured her. 'Just be quick about it.'

Slowly, Poppy used the knots to lower herself onto the tyre as Abigail had done. The sight of water below made her draw a sharp breath.

'Momentum!' Abigail reminded her.

Poppy swung back and forth a few times. When she finally had the courage to leap off, she landed short of the crest of the opposite bank. But Abigail caught her arm and pulled her up to safety.

'See? You did it! You're okay,' Abigail said. 'Now come on, we're almost there.'

The girls moved on into another clearing surrounded by bushes. In the centre was a yew tree with a cavernous hollow, deep within its enormous trunk. Poppy gasped. It was like the mouth of a cave, full of excitement and danger. Abigail went first, crouching as she disappeared into the black void that was the entrance. Poppy followed in after her. The air was dank and cool inside, and the sounds of the woodland became muted. There was a soft *whoosh* and the hollow lit up in a flash of unexpected light. Abigail had struck a match. She touched it to a candle on a foil tray that Poppy had only just noticed by their feet. Abigail blew out the match.

'I've been coming here for years,' she said. 'And no one else has ever found it.'

Both girls had to stoop, but the interior was big enough to accommodate them. It was like a secret den, with lots of stuff on the ground. Magazines, a seat cushion. Some books. And a red blanket that had been spread inside as though ready for a picnic.

'Wow.'

'Seriously, you mustn't tell a soul about this,' Abigail said.

'I-I won't.'

'I'm only showing you because you live in Cambridge,' she said. 'I mean, it's not like any of your friends would ever come down here, is it?' She sighed happily and flopped down onto the blanket, then fluffed the cushion and invited Poppy to join her. 'Sit, sit,' she said. 'Now we can relax and read our books. And leave Father and Mother to their silly party.'

17

Although Abigail could 'talk for England' (as her dad often said about her mum), Poppy was surprised that she remained quiet for the next half an hour as both girls got stuck into their books. Poppy had chosen *The Hobbit*, which she was already fairly familiar with because she'd seen the movie. Abigail had picked up *Lord of the Flies*, which, even with what little she knew of the story, sounded way too scary for Poppy. The light was just about good enough to read in and the hollow was a fun and cosy place to be. But the candle didn't last. The wax was already low when they entered and was now coalescing into a lumpy pool. Conceding defeat, Abigail blew out the dying flame and suggested they continue outside. The girls exited the hollow and spread out on the grass in the summer sunshine. Abigail lay on her back and shut her eyes, tilting her head back. 'This is how lizards must feel,' she said dreamily.

Poppy didn't know about lizards but she did know the grass was lovely and soft, like a lush green bed. Abigail rolled onto her side and retrieved her book, offering Poppy a packet of crisps from the rucksack. Poppy ate them readily and soon became absorbed in her own book again. After that, she lost track of time. She never wore a watch and her parents forbade her to own a phone, so she had no idea how long they had been out for. But it felt like it was getting late.

'I suppose we ought to think about going back,' Abigail said as if she had read her mind.

Poppy agreed. Abigail put her book away, slung her rucksack over one shoulder and whistled happily as she headed off in a different direction to the tyre swing.

'Wait, where are you going?' Poppy asked.

'Did you want to swim back?'

Poppy looked across the bank and at the expanse of water. The trunk stopped halfway across the river and the rope was too far away to reach from this side.

'Relax,' Abigail said. 'I know another place we can cross.'

Abigail led the way, trailing along the riverbank and taking them further and deeper into the forest. Fifteen minutes later, she pointed out a spot where the water was shallower, the riverbed visible. The girls removed their shoes and waded across. They replaced their footwear when they reached the other bank.

'Don't forget, not a word about the hollow, okay? It's my secret place.'

Poppy assured her she wouldn't breathe a word to anyone.

They followed an invisible path back through the woods that only Abigail seemed to know about and emerged into an expansive glade. If Abigail had not been her guide, Poppy was pretty sure she'd never find her way out of the forest again.

'Have you ever been to Stonehenge?' Abigail asked as she stomped confidently towards a cluster of bushes at the far end of the glade.

'No,' said Poppy, trailing behind her.

'Father promised he'd take me. It's truly a marvel of the

Neolithic age. Some say it was a burial site. How they got those stones all the way from—'

Poppy could have done without yet another lecture and might even have zoned out if it weren't for the strange spectacle of Abigail's head careering forwards. It took a moment for her eyes to feed her brain the relevant information, but when it had, Poppy understood that Abigail's shoe had snagged on a tree root jutting from the ground, yanking her forward sharply, and slamming her down face first with force. Such a spectacle might have been comical if it weren't for the loud crack her skull made as it landed on a large rock embedded in the ground. Poppy froze, puzzled at first as to why a treacle-like substance oozed from Abigail's left ear. It shook Poppy from her daze, and she flung back her head to shout '*Help!*' at the top of her voice.

18

Kristen composed herself. She knew that she had overreacted and had been far too sensitive about Harry's research. She understood why it had upset her, but that was still no excuse. This was meant to be Marcus's special day, and she had almost spoiled it with her emotional display. Nobody was disproving her faith. Nobody could disprove anyone's faith. This day was not about her and it was time to get the party back on track. Double-checking she had no traces of panda eyes, she returned to the garden, where she was pleased to see that people were spilling out of the marquee and mixing with their group around the table. Soon, Kristen was listening to a conversation about the pollen count, soon followed by the latest celebrity gossip from a reality TV cooking show. Nothing heavy duty or upsetting. *Back to normal,* she thought, feeling grateful. Marcus appeared by her side and put his arm around her. She smiled and squeezed him back.

Eventually, it was time for speeches. Kristen stood on one of the wrought-iron chairs. The *ding-ding-ding* of her spoon against the side of her flute made Marcus wince, as she knew it would. The guests gradually hushed and gathered round.

'Ladies and gentlemen. *Friends.* Thank you so much, all of you, for being here to celebrate my husband's milestone.'

'A milestone around my neck,' Marcus said, which made Harry snort.

It also caused a smattering of laughter amongst some of the guests. Kristen let it fade out before continuing. She had forgotten half the notes she'd made so drew instead on her memories of how she and Marcus had first met, and how grateful she was for the life they had made together. She saw her father nod at her as she talked about the importance of family. 'All of you have been so special to us. Each of you is like family in your own way, and I'm so grateful for you coming down …' There were some affirming murmurs among the crowd. 'Even at the grand old age of forty, there are some traditions that you're never too old for,' Kristen said. 'Although we couldn't fit all the candles on a cake, so sorry about that, Marcus.'

It was Kristen's turn to elicit a few laughs. 'But I do think that we should sing happy birthday,' she said, 'if you're all agreeable.'

Marcus feigned embarrassment as the tune was carried poorly by the guests, albeit with heartfelt gusto. When the chorus was done, he joined Kristen at her side. 'First of all,' he said, raising his voice, 'I want to reiterate what Kristen has said about you all coming down here. I do so appreciate it. Getting to forty … well, to some that is a terrifying prospect. But in my case I'd staved off the dreaded midlife crisis. I feel fortunate in that I have achieved many of the dreams I cherished as a young man. I'm lucky enough to have contributed somewhat to helping more people understand who we are and how we got to where we are as a species.'

He shook his head, smiling. 'God, that sounds pretentious, doesn't it? Please, ignore all that. I, of course, only have one achievement that I am most proud of. Meeting the love of my life. And, of course, my daughter Abigail.'

There was applause from the guests and one '*Hear, hear.*'

'I believe she's even prepared a speech,' Marcus said. 'I hope it isn't too embarrassing.'

Kristen joined Marcus in scouring the gathered crowd. But Abigail was nowhere in sight. Nor was Poppy. She glanced at Bree, who shrugged her shoulders casually. *They're probably doing something more fun*, that shrug suggested. Kristen turned back to Marcus, who was frowning.

'Well, it seems she's nowhere to be found,' he said. 'Perhaps she's indoors, talking to her peers on TikTok or whatever kids do with their time now.'

He smiled, looking thoughtful, then continued. 'Actually, my daughter isn't like most other children. I know a lot of parents say that, but she's particularly different. Mature beyond her years. Observant, intelligent. And incredibly well adjusted. Now I know what you're thinking. That sounds like me, right?'

He paused again for laughter. 'But the truth is, while I might be able to claim credit when it comes to her interest in anthropology, her sweet and generally kind nature is entirely down to my wife. Kristen, I thank you for giving me such a wonderful life and a family any man would be rightly proud of.'

Several guests applauded. Kristen was only half listening. She was wondering where Abi had got to.

'Seriously, Kristen has been my rock. Thanks to her, I'm counting my blessings rather than desperately seeking a Maserati to mollify my midlife crisis.'

'Ferraris are better,' Tim Barnes heckled.

Marcus reacted with a smile. 'How would you know, Tim? You're a disgustingly long way from having to contemplate automotive therapy.' He paused. 'Although I suppose filming with me all these years might have given you an insight into old fossils.'

He raised his beer glass. 'To good health and long life.'

There followed a rousing echo of the toast as the crowd raised their glasses in unison. Marcus kissed Kristen on the cheek, but her attention was elsewhere. She gave him a perfunctory kiss back and excused herself. There was a niggling in her stomach that she didn't like. And it was slowly getting worse.

19

The air cooled as the afternoon transitioned into early evening. Poppy had not left Abigail's side, except for one time when she desperately needed a wee. She was scared and tired, her throat sore with all the shouting for help. Her voice had echoed back at her around the trees, but no one had come.

Please let her be okay, she prayed silently.

In between the yelling, she had continually been praying to Jesus to save Abigail. Maybe that was why the girl's chest was still rising and falling. But she remained unconscious. The blood on her head had clotted, and it didn't look like any more was coming out. The rest had already soaked into the ground, staining the leaves a dark brown colour. Poppy had no idea what to do. What if no one ever found them? What if Abigail survived the fall but then they both died from hunger or thirst? How long could you go without water or food? As soon as she had that thought, her tummy rumbled. Abigail's rucksack was still strapped to her back but she had told Poppy earlier they were out of snacks. How could she think of food at a time like this? Honestly! She touched her dry throat. What she wouldn't give for a Coke right now. She considered the other option again, which was running for help. For the last hour, she had been too scared to risk it. She had been worried she might get turned around. And even if she did manage to find her way back to the house, what if she couldn't lead the adults back to this place? It seemed hopeless. She sat on the ground, the leaves crunching underneath as she brought her knees up and buried her head between them. As she rocked back and forth, she became aware that Abi's breathing was sounding more laboured. Maybe she was about to get worse. Poppy shook her head. She had no choice. She couldn't just sit here and do nothing. Risky as it was, she had to at least try and go for help.

20

Kristen checked the far end of the garden and behind the marquee. No sign of the girls. Maybe they were still inside, watching a film like she had suggested. She hadn't even thought to fetch them for the speeches, which was silly of her. She searched the house, starting with Abigail's room. Empty. So were all the guest rooms. Finally, she checked Marcus's study, even though Abi knew full well it was strictly off-limits. She wandered back to the kitchen. Where could they have got to? The niggle of worry intensified. She told herself she was overreacting. The girls couldn't have got far. She returned to the garden and considered rejoining Marcus. He was holding forth before a group of ex-colleagues from Cambridge. But then she checked her watch. It had to be at least five hours since she'd sent the girls off. She glanced nervously at the back garden and the hedgerow that bordered it. She made for the gate and peered through the bars. They weren't in the field. That left the woods. Kristen had never liked Abi going into the forest alone, so she'd agreed with Marcus to get her a mobile phone. If the girls had gone wandering, Abi knew to take her phone with her. Kristen ran back to the house, fetched her mobile and dialled Abi's number. She heard continuous ringing but Abi did not pick up. An automated voice eventually announced the person she'd called could not be reached. She hung up and tried again, only to get the same result.

'Everything okay?' Darius asked.

He appeared at the glass doors leading out onto the patio. Bree was behind him, a concerned look on her face. 'What's going on, Krissy?'

'I can't find the girls,' she said. 'I think they might have wandered into the forest.'

'They're in the woods?' Darius said.

'Are they all right?' Bree asked.

'I hope so but I'm a bit worried. They should have been back by now.'

Kristen moved past the pair and into the garden again, beckoning them to follow her. 'Marcus put one of those tracker apps on all our phones,' she said. 'We should be able to find Abi with it. Let's grab him.'

21

Poppy moved blindly through the woods, only guessing if she was heading in the right direction. She was sure she had been going in circles and, after a while, her calves began to ache from running. At one point she thought she might have heard a phone ringing, but the sound was too far away and she couldn't be sure whether she was imagining it. She shouted out whenever she could, though her voice was becoming weaker each time, just like her legs, which were starting to feel rubbery. Eventually, she stopped, sat down and closed her eyes. This was hopeless. She was lost. Poppy pictured poor Abigail lying there, with no one to help. The shadows of the surrounding trees felt like they were enveloping her. The tears fell before she could do anything to stop them.

22

Marcus remained composed after Kristen pulled him away from his friends and told him the news. 'Don't worry, darling,' he said. 'The app will pinpoint Abi's location.'

He took Kristen's phone and opened a tracking app, which he'd installed a couple of years ago. He cupped his hand over the screen, shielding it from the sun, so Kristen could see what he was doing. Marcus selected Abigail's phone and a blip appeared on a local map.

'She's about a mile south,' he announced. 'Fortunately, we still get a good signal out here.'

'Thank God for technology, eh?' Darius said.

'I'll go,' Marcus said.

'I won't be any good in these heels,' Bree said. 'You go with him, Darius.'

'I'm coming too,' Kristen said.

Marcus gave her a look as if to say that wouldn't be necessary, but Kristen gave him one back. Hers said to never get in the way of a worried mother. He knew better than to object.

23

Marcus led their party, moving swiftly through the trees. The trio crunched their way through twigs and branches, Kristen on the heels of her husband, while Darius brought up the rear. A growing sense of urgency was in the air. Kristen was sure they were all feeling it. They pushed through the foliage and came upon a stream. Marcus paused, rotating the phone, getting his bearings.

'I think she's somewhere over that way,' he declared.

Kristen nodded, trusting his judgement. It wasn't like she had a lot of choice. They waded through the ankle-deep water.

'Wait!' she said.

They were halfway across the stream.

'What is it?'

'I thought I heard someone shouting.'

Darius cocked his head.

'I don't hear anything,' he said.

Her nerves were fraying now. The sooner they found the girls, the better.

'Let's just keep following the signal,' Marcus suggested.

They crossed the stream and their shoes were soaked

through. Marcus announced they were about five hundred metres or so away. It felt like the longest five hundred metres of Kristen's life, not helped by her husband regularly checking the orientation of their position in relation to Abi's. The one thing Kristen didn't want to think about was why her daughter's blip had not moved since they'd set out.

24

Poppy was still crying when, unexpectedly, a miracle happened. Three figures emerged from a small clearing ahead of her. One of them was her dad. A second later, strong arms wrapped around her and scooped her up. Her father hugged her tight and repeatedly kissed her forehead.

'You're okay, Pops. I got you. Daddy's got you!'

'Abigail!' Poppy cried.

'Where is she, sweetheart?'

A woman's voice. Poppy turned and saw Aunty Krissy standing next to her. Her dad placed her back down on the ground. Behind her, she heard Mr Hardy calling out Abigail's name.

'I had to l-leave her,' Poppy said. 'I w-wanted to get help.'

'Poppy, where was Abigail last?' Aunty Krissy said.

'By the rock,' Poppy said. 'She fell!'

Before she knew it, she had cradled her hands in her face and let out a long sob. 'I'm so sorry,' she wailed.

'It's okay, sweetheart,' her father said. 'Is Abigail hurt?'

'Her head, Daddy. She tripped and hit it on a rock. She didn't wake up.'

'Oh, dear God,' Aunty Krissy said.

Then came the sound of frantic scrunching of branches and twigs.

'There's a rock here!' Mr Hardy yelled. 'There's a trail of blood. It looks like she tried to get up. Kris, get over here!'

25

It felt like a dream. Kristen moved towards Marcus, not even feeling the nettles and branches that slapped against her body. She saw the rock Poppy had mentioned. It was smeared with blood, just as Marcus had said. Her husband appeared from behind a bush, holding up a pink rucksack in one hand. He removed Abi's phone from inside it.

'She's not here,' he said, his face pallid. 'It looks like she might have regained consciousness and wandered off. She could be anywhere!'

There was panic in his eyes, and Kristen could tell he was trying to not assume the worst. She looked around the immediate area and saw no clue as to which direction their daughter might have gone. She felt helpless and desperate.

26

Poppy held her father's hand as he pulled her after Aunty Krissy and to the spot where she had left Abigail. Mr Hardy removed a phone from a pink rucksack, and her heart sank. *Abigail was carrying it this whole time!* Why didn't she tell her? She could have used it to call for help. She felt so guilty she barely heard what Aunty Krissy was saying to her.

'P-pardon?'

She knelt down and looked gently into Poppy's eyes. 'I said, do you know anywhere she might have gone, sweetheart?'

Poppy swallowed. She didn't, but she felt awful that she had abandoned Abigail and hadn't known about the phone. And she was anxious to help Aunty Krissy.

'Maybe she went to the secret place,' she blurted.

Aunty Krissy looked confused. 'What secret place, sweetheart?'

'It's inside a tree,' she said. 'Near where the tyre swing is … on the river.'

'Where is that, darling?'

She shut her eyes and shook her head. No, that was silly. Why would Abigail have gone there? 'No, it's too far away.

I'm so sorry – I don't know where she went!' she cried and buried her face in her hands.

Her dad knelt down and wrapped his arms around her.

'It's okay, sweetheart,' Aunty Krissy said.

'Kris, leave her and keep looking!' Mr Hardy shouted. 'Abigail! *Abigail!*'

27

Kristen scoured the perimeter of the glade, joining Marcus in calling out Abi's name. She was grateful it was summer and that the light hadn't faded yet. But that didn't mean her visibility wasn't obscured by the natural foliage. Marcus's voice eventually became a tiny burble in the background. She heard nothing except her own heartbeat as she scrutinised every pile of leaves, every bit of mud, every tree trunk. At last, she saw a glimpse of denim. Then she caught sight of sparkly jeans and a hint of white trainers. Abi was lying face down in the leafy mulch. There was blood on the back of her skull. Kristen yelped in shock and fell to one knee, her training taking over as she felt for a pulse on her daughter's neck. To her relief, she found one. She carefully examined the head wound, touching the blood-soaked strands of Abi's hair. It had congealed, thank God. There appeared to be no more bleeding. She ran her hands across Abi's shoulders, arms and legs. No limbs appeared broken.

'Marcus!'

Her husband had wandered further afield, in the opposite direction to Abi's path, but he came running back in seconds.

'Oh God, no!'

They didn't have time to wait for an ambulance or for paramedics to find their way through the woods. Kristen's nursing instincts took charge and she told Marcus in a calm and measured way that they were going to have to move her. Marcus nodded and bent his knees so he could gently scoop up his daughter. Darius appeared behind them, clutching Poppy to his chest.

'Kristen, what can I do?'

'Help us navigate,' she said. 'We need to get back to the house. And quickly!'

With Poppy in one arm, Darius used his free hand to use his phone as a compass. Marcus fell in behind him. Kristen kept pace with him, one eye on Abi's chest, making sure it continued to rise and fall. She allowed each footfall to remind her that they were one step closer to home, and help. It felt like she was submerged in water, her adrenaline-fuelled heartbeat beating like a kettle drum. Somehow, they emerged from the forest and into the field that backed onto their garden. How long the journey had taken, Kristen couldn't say. She was vaguely aware of a crowd of concerned guests, of wide eyes and shocked whispers. She saw black dots swimming in the periphery of her vision but didn't black out. Holding steady, she followed Marcus into the back garden, pushing past her sister Jacqui towards the open French windows of the living room. She heard Marcus yell at her to get the car keys. Through the corner of her eye, she saw Poppy leap from Darius's hold into Bree's arms, followed by both parents surrounding her, embracing each other as a family. Kristen's heart felt crushed as she wondered if she and Marcus would be able to do the same before the night was over.

'The keys, Kris!' Marcus barked.

'S-sorry, yes,' she said.

She dashed into the kitchen, fetched them off the hook, then opened the front door as Marcus ran through the house. She charged ahead of him, pressing the button to unlock the Land Rover. She had the back door open in seconds, and Marcus laid Abi down. How his arms must have ached, she thought. Only a parent's instinct could have carried her for that long.

'Put her on her side,' she instructed him. 'Keep her airways clear. That's it.'

Darius burst through the front door. 'Hey, need me to drive?'

'What about Poppy?' Kristen said.

'She's okay, Bree said she's fine. Just a couple of scratches. I can take you.'

'No, stay with her,' Kristen said. 'Keep an eye on her. She's probably dehydrated. You'll find some electrolyte powder sachets in the bathroom cabinet. They're for vomiting and diarrhoea but they'll do. If her condition changes, call 999.'

She turned back to Marcus. 'Want me to drive?'

'No, you stay with Abi,' Marcus said. 'In case she wakes up.'

'You sure?'

'I'm okay, Kris.'

He clambered into the driver's seat while Kristen shuffled in, shifting Abi gently along the seat. She closed the door behind her seconds before she felt the gravel kick under the tyres as Marcus slammed his foot down on the accelerator.

28

Kristen gasped, daring to open her eyes. She was in the hospital waiting room, her head against Marcus's shoulder.

'Hey,' he said.

'I fell asleep,' Kristen said. 'How could I have gone to sleep?'

'Your body's exhausted,' he said. 'We've been waiting for hours. It's good that you rested, trust me.'

He pinched the bridge of his nose and sighed. Kristen straightened up, blinking at the same harsh white lights of the King's Hospital Southampton's A&E department that had greeted them hours before. About half the waiting chairs were full. Other people, like her, not wanting to be here on a Saturday night. She leaned her head back on Marcus's shoulder, grateful for his strength and his calmness. He had driven as fast as he dared, pulling up into the A&E bay, asking Kristen if she was okay to park the car while he carried Abi in. When she had come running in herself a few minutes later, she was relieved to find her husband in the triage area and Abi on a hospital trolley bed, already being examined by the emergency staff.

'Concussion to the head,' a nurse explained to the ER doctor.

'Vitals?'

'Steady. Heart rate's eighty. BPM's ninety over seventy. Airways are clear.'

The doctor, a hefty man who looked like he was about to turn into the Hulk and burst through his white coat, nodded at a nearby porter who came over to push the bed towards a set of swinging doors.

'Where are you taking her?' Kristen demanded.

The medics and doctor didn't answer, instead talking to each other in rapid tones as they continued to make their medical assessment. Kristen asked again, raising her voice higher. The doctor glanced at her and nodded. 'You're the mother?'

'Yes! Is she going to be okay? Tell me!'

'Darling.' Marcus put his hand on her shoulder. His tone was meant to be comforting. Kristen knew what he meant. *Leave this be. Abigail was now in good hands.*

'We're just going to do a few scans,' said the doctor.

He called out to a passing ER nurse. 'Hannah, could you please take ... the parents to the waiting area? Thank you.' He turned to Kristen. 'We'll do our best to take good care of her,' he said. 'Please, try not to worry.'

They were deposited in the lounge area, where they waited for an agonising hour until a young Irish nurse returned to inform them Abigail had been taken to an operating theatre.

'We took a CT scan of her head and saw a clot that concerned the doctors,' she said gently.

'Oh no,' Kristen wailed. 'No no no ...'

Marcus squeezed her hand.

'I'm sorry I can't provide more details, but a doctor will come and explain everything to you soon, okay?'

They had fretted for another two hours with no news until

eventually Kristen had succumbed to a mixture of exhaustion and fear and had fallen into a deep sleep.

'No updates?' she asked Marcus.

'Nothing yet,' he said. 'I've asked several times. I suppose no news is good news.'

She fell back against his arm. 'Oh Marcus,' she said. 'What if—'

'We can't afford to give in to speculation, Kris,' he said. 'It will only make us more distressed. We must try and be patient and wait for solid information.'

Kristen shook her head, made herself inhale a slow breath. She let it out and repeated the process. After a few minutes, she felt a little calmer. Marcus was right. Getting all upset wouldn't help either of them. And the last thing she wanted was to add to Marcus's own stress. She knew he was just as worried about Abi. He was also right; they needed solid information. The kind of information she hoped the big burly doctor from earlier, now walking towards them, could give them.

'Mr and Mrs Hardy? I'm Doctor Rosen. Will you come with me, please?'

29

Rosen led them into a dark office around the corner and closed the door. Instantly, Kristen felt trapped, as though the room had become airtight. The doctor flipped a switch and a series of LED bulbs above them gradually illuminated the room. He invited them to sit but Marcus continued to stand. And from the way he held her, he seemed to be encouraging her to do the same.

'Please,' he said. 'Just tell us.'

Rosen nodded and opened a folder that Kristen had only just noticed he'd been carrying. He produced a sheet and held it up to them. 'This is the scan of your daughter's head,' he said.

Kristen stared at the sheet. At first she thought it was an X-ray because it looked like a black-and-white picture of Abigail's skull. Then she remembered X-rays had to be held up against the light. This was more likely a printout.

'The dark area you can see indicates a subarachnoid haemorrhage,' Rosen said, pointing.

There was a blacked-out part of the skull, covering the top and most of the left side.

'A what?' Marcus asked.

'It's an aneurysm?' Kristen said, choking.

'Abigail was transferred to our neurology department where she underwent a procedure called coiling. It's a standard procedure in these circumstances. Essentially a coil is inserted into an artery in the leg, which is then tracked through to the brain. We call it coiling because small coils are inserted into the aneurysm, making sure it's isolated and so doesn't risk rupturing again.'

'I know what coiling is,' Kristen said strenuously. 'Is she going to be okay?'

'The procedure was a success,' Rosen said. 'We were able to stop the bleeding and stabilise your daughter.'

Marcus let out a sigh. Kristen's knees weakened. This time, the strong arms of her husband failed to provide the usual support, so she caved forward, almost falling into Rosen's arms.

'Thank you, Doctor. Thank you so, so much. I …'

She burst into tears and hugged him. Rosen patted her back awkwardly as Marcus finally sat down.

'It's what we're here for,' Rosen said. 'I have to say I didn't perform the procedure. I'm not a neurosurgeon but I was part of the team taking care of her. I'm sorry no one has updated you for a while. We were busy looking after Abigail and you can't rush this sort of thing.'

Marcus said nothing, hunched forward with his face buried in his hands. Kristen continued to hug Rosen as though he was a long-lost relative she hadn't seen for years.

'Thank you thank you thank you,' she whispered.

Her heart was bursting with so many feelings she didn't know how to distil them. Rosen let her express her emotions for a few minutes more, then gently handed her back to Marcus.

'When can we see her?' Marcus asked.

'Soon,' Doctor Rosen said. 'She's in ICU now, so she'll be sedated and intubated. We'll need to monitor her for the next few hours. Once we're satisfied that she's stable we'll transfer her to a general ward and likely revive her. That might be as early as tomorrow but it's more likely to be the day after.'

Kristen reached for Marcus's hand and squeezed. Only then did she notice how badly she'd stained poor Doctor Rosen's white coat with her mascara. She sniffed, able to smile at the embarrassment she felt, but also relishing her deep relief. Rosen closed the folder in his chunky hands and gave them both a solemn look.

'Mr Hardy and Mrs Hardy, I recommend you count your blessings. Your daughter is very lucky. Someone up there must be looking down on her.'

30

There was no point in going home. Marcus made no objection when Kristen told him she was going to seek out the hospital chapel. It was exactly the same as the one at St Anthony's, a multifaith, multipurpose room, much like the ones in airports. A fake stained-glass window adorned the back wall, with green, white, and blue shards forming a flower motif. Innocuous, religion-agnostic. Who could object to a flower? A symbol of hope, whatever your beliefs. However, it was still a step too far for Marcus, who opted for the waiting room and to make calls back to the house and update whoever was still awake at this ungodly hour. It was a shame, because not only was the chapel empty, but the rows of long benches that vaguely emulated pews were a darn sight more comfortable than the waiting room chairs.

It was the perfect space to commune with God, Kristen thought. She believed that God was everywhere, which meant He could hear her prayers in a multifaith chapel just as much as if she was in St James's in Ashworth. She grabbed one of the red cushions that had been placed on the benches and laid it on the floor, went down on her knees and folded her hands together in prayer, just as she had when she was a girl. She whispered words of thanks, allowing herself to feel the powerful gratitude that flowed out from her like a positive glow from her soul. She put it down to God reassuring her that His hand was indeed at work in her life. Muttering one last 'thank you', she rose to her feet and went to find her husband. He was off the phone, standing by the vending machine and drinking coffee, his eyes closed. She wondered if he had lowered himself to secretly thanking God too. Sometimes situations of stress did crazy things to people.

Just before 8 a.m., the Irish nurse found them in the waiting lounge. While Abi hadn't been approved for transfer from the ICU and remained in a temporary coma, they had been granted permission to see her. The nurse led them to the right room, and Kristen rushed to Abigail's bed. 'My sweet girl,' she said, kissing her daughter's forehead.

Abigail didn't move or twitch. There was nothing about her to suggest she was even living save the mechanical ventilator that continued to pump air into her lungs through a mouth tube. A bright cloudless sky, however, brought sunshine through the window, which Kristen took as another sign of hope. A second nurse came in to take Abi's vitals, assuring the two of them it was all right to stay for a while. Marcus sat in a chair beside Abigail's bed, watching as Kristen whispered words of comfort in her ear.

'Darling, it's Mother,' she whispered. 'Don't be afraid now, these people will look after you. I need you to be strong, okay? Be strong and you'll be okay.'

She was rambling, she knew. But it also felt like she was doing *something*. She glanced at Marcus in the morning light. He looked gaunt. Like her, he hadn't eaten anything since yesterday. 'Let's get some breakfast,' she said. 'Abi's not going anywhere.'

Kristen worried she would struggle to eat. But she found herself wolfing down the hot panini sandwich in the cafeteria. The truth was, this was one of the best meals she had ever eaten. Perhaps it was a combination of the hours of tension in her body, the anxiety in her mind and the sick feeling deep in her gut, but every mouthful was a primal pleasure. Marcus wolfed his food down with equal vigour as though he was an animal in the wild. When Kristen finally, regretfully, finished the last bite, she was left sated in a way no meal had ever managed to leave her before.

They returned to Abi's ward, Kristen seizing the opportunity to text Bree an update about Abi's condition, promising to call as soon as she could. She felt guilty, having received a flood of concerned texts and messages from both her family and Marcus's. But there was no way she would have had the emotional bandwidth to keep them all in the loop. Besides, she thought as she *whooshed* the text off, one message to Bree would mean everyone else would be updated in seconds. The thought made her smile, her first in over eighteen hours. She was still smiling as she and Marcus entered the ward and approached Abi's bed, where she saw something not unfamiliar to her from her many years working as a nurse. Her daughter was still there and still attached to the same leads and pipes as before. Only she was shaking, as if someone had sent a thousand volts through her body. Her head jerked back like a marionette's, her arms flapped about on the mattress like beached eels in their last throes. The ECG monitor beeped frantically.

'Help!' Kristen shouted.

A nurse rushed in, took one look at Abi and pressed a button on the wall above her head.

'She's seizing,' she told a second medic, who ran in behind her.

As her daughter continued to thrash around in the bed, Kristen sensed a swarm of people converge around her, along with a small trolley she knew from experience contained crash paddles. Hands gently took her shoulders and steered her and Marcus way from the bed, and time itself slowed to a crawl. She just about managed to turn her head back one last time as she was led around the corner and out of sight. Some part of her brain refused to process what she was seeing, fully expecting the doctors who were now on the scene to stop attending to Abi and fall about laughing with the nurses, all of them pointing to Abi who, jumping out of bed, would also be chortling. *Sorry, Mother,* she would say. *I couldn't resist pranking you. I am genuinely sorry, but don't worry, I really am fine! Did you know Father says the first hospitals were likely built on the Indian subcontinent before 200 BCE?* In her strange new slo-mo world, Kristen was still expecting this to happen, even when they sat her down back in the waiting room next to her husband. Even when another nurse brought her a cup of water, accompanied by the doctor who knelt down in front of her, and even when she heard Marcus wailing at the top of his voice when the doctor announced, in a calm and clinical manner, that their one and only daughter, the love of her life, was dead.

THREE

1

Time passed Kristen by in a fog. There were blotches of lucidity, where she was aware of who she was and where she was, able to grasp the horror of what had happened. The rest was a merciful mix of Diazepam and the after-effects of the heavy sleeping pills the doctor had prescribed. The first few days were the foggiest of all. She had vague snippets of being hugged and held by Jacqui and her father. Both remained at the house for another week, cancelling plans so they could be with her. Kristen was remotely aware of Marcus, during brief snatches at night, when she would wake to the sound of him sobbing quietly into his pillow behind her. She didn't have the strength to comfort him. She was barely able to console herself.

Bree was her rock from the very start. Whenever the wisps of her mind fog cleared, she would be there by her side. Whether it was sitting in the funeral director's home, going through the brochure slowly with her so they could pick out exactly which coffin Abigail would have wanted (*who even asks that about their own child?* Kristen remembered thinking), or at the house, fielding sympathetic neighbours who continued to stop by every day. Bree did all the talking, thanking well-wishers for their thoughts and prayers and receiving their gifts of homemade dishes, flowers and cards. She was a whirlwind of activity in the house, cleaning, tidying, on top of making all the necessary arrangements for the funeral. Cups of tea appeared constantly. There were times when Kristen thought this was how the rest of her life was going to play out – her trapped in some strange time loop, where every time she blinked she was in another room, with another soothing hot drink. Bree was always there, and for that, Kristen was immensely grateful.

The Fog continued. Kristen had no idea how long it had been since that awful morning at the hospital. All she knew was whenever her clarity returned, so did the pain. She had never felt anything like it. Even when she had lost her mum at such an early age, there had been nothing like the hot needles of raw grief that cut and stabbed at every part of her, constantly, until she could stand it no more and longed to return to the Fog. She continued to be dimly aware of Marcus lying beside her at night, his familiar snoring. She didn't dare wake him. Just like she never attempted to speak to him when her mind cleared. Not because she didn't love him. On the contrary. It was the fear that if they talked about it, it would make Abi's death more real somehow. Like Marcus was the only person who could officially confirm that it had really happened, robbing Kristen of the power to tell herself it was still all a dream. But it was more than that. Just as she could barely cope with her pain, she could not bear to look into Marcus's eyes for fear of seeing his. Which was why she continued to reach for more sleeping pills and the blissful relief the Fog offered.

2

One afternoon, she woke from a pill-induced nap and sat bolt upright, her heart beating fast. Bree appeared from the kitchen, carrying a tray with a cafetière and a plate of biscuits. 'You're awake, girlie,' she said, placing the tray down on the low table. 'How are you feeling?'

'When do we bury her?' Kristen asked.

Bree's eyes glimmered with empathy. 'Friday, honey,' she said. 'The day after tomorrow.'

Kristen nodded, closing her eyes. She knew then that, as much as she didn't want to, she had to find a way to step out of the Fog.

3

She forced herself to stop taking the pills. Which in turn made time slow to a painstaking crawl. She spent a day and night curled up on the sofa, arms wrapped tightly around her knees, just staring off into space. An awful memory returned. Doctor Rosen talking to her and Marcus. Explaining the complication of Abigail's transient ischaemic attack, how it was followed by the unexpected brain bleed that had spread rapidly. By the time the medical staff had worked out it was happening, it was already too late. The vivid details returned to her, as did the weight in her chest. But still Kristen refused the succour of the drugs. She was determined to be clear-headed enough to say goodbye to her daughter. In the evening, Bree took her out into the garden and made them hot chocolates with more than a sniff of brandy. They sat in silence in the iron chairs, quietly being in each other's company.

'Where's Marcus?' Kristen asked.

Bree told her he was throwing himself into his work and that he usually spent every day locked away in his study and barely emerging. Kristen nodded. 'I envy him, you know,' she said as she sipped her hot chocolate brandy. 'I wish I had his ability to distract himself.'

Bree shook her head. 'It's just compartmentalising,' she said. 'Men are better at it, especially when it comes to the important shit.'

Her phone beeped, and she fished it out of the fleece jacket she was wearing. The guilty look on her face and the hasty way she returned the phone told Kristen who the sender had been.

'It's okay to reply, you know,' Kristen said. 'I know it's Poppy. You don't have to feel guilty because you still have a daughter.'

Bree returned her look with an expression of pity that almost crushed her.

She looked away, back towards the hedgerow fence. 'Don't ignore her, seriously. Life is precious. Your child is precious.'

Bree burst into tears at that and lunged forward, throwing her arms around Kristen. 'Oh, Krissy, I'm so, so sorry,' she sobbed.

Kristen patted her gently on the arm. 'I mean it, be glad Poppy is alive.' She sniffed. 'Never stop being glad.'

More sobs now, and Kristen felt Bree's weight go dead in her arms. A shadow fell upon the women then, and she glanced up to see her husband standing by the sliding glass door.

'We need ...'

He trailed off, looking awkward. Kristen could tell the last thing he wanted to do was disturb whatever was happening here. In her new sobriety, Kristen was finally able to resume the role of a wife. 'It's all right, darling,' she said. 'There will be plenty more tears ahead. What is it, my love?'

'I'm sorry,' he said. 'It's just, we don't have much in the fridge.'

'I'll go shopping.' Bree sniffed and sat up starkly, gently pushing Kristen away.

'No, that's okay,' Kristen began.

'Let me go, Kris. It's the least I can do for you guys. Besides, I've been eating all your food too.'

Kristen blinked fast, trying to blow further wisps of the Fog away from her mind. 'How long have you been here, Bree? Looking after me?'

'It's been two weeks now, girlie,' Bree said.

Kristen gasped. 'My God, Bree. What about your work? What about your life?'

Bree told her she'd asked for a leave of absence at work while Darius remained in Cambridge, tasked with looking after Poppy. 'It's all good, Krissy. I told you, honey. I'm here for you. For both of you.'

She gave Marcus a sideways glance, but Kristen knew that she was mostly here for her.

'I can't ever thank you enough,' she said.

But Bree shook her head sharply. 'It's nothing,' she assured her.

Kristen knew that wasn't true. She had no idea how she could ever repay her friend.

They moved back inside the house and Kristen took their mugs to the kitchen. On the way, she passed the silver crucifix standing alone on the mantelpiece and paused to stare at it. She had placed it there when they had first moved in. It had always been there, watching over their daily lives, as God Himself was supposed to have been. And yet where was God in all this? Nowhere, as far as Kristen could see. It was Bree, mere flesh and blood, who had shown up in the end. Meanwhile, the One Who Had Made the Stars had been utterly silent. Kristen was feeling a peculiar new twist of grief's dagger. Other people who had experienced a loss as terrible as hers might start to doubt the existence of a loving all-powerful God. Yet Kristen still retained unshakeable faith in the reality of His existence. But that meant that she was now left with the perplexing question of why her God had chosen to do this to her.

4

The day of the funeral came. Without the pills, Kristen slept little the night before. At 4 a.m., she lay in bed, arms tucked behind her head, occasionally rolling to one side to check her phone. It took an eon, but eventually 6 a.m. arrived and she slid desultorily off the mattress and into the bathroom. After she'd peed, she returned to find Marcus still dead to the world. She envied his snoring, which sounded so contented. Let him enjoy a little more time oblivious to the day ahead.

The small village church of St James was full for the first time in many years, but not with locals. Today's congregation were mostly from Kristen's old Cambridge church, many of whom had come because they knew her and had heard the news. Darius and Bree were in the pew behind her, Bree quietly sobbing into her black lace handkerchief. Jacqui and Kristen's father were to her left, as were Henry and Rosalind Hardy, who had flown back from Spain. Marcus sat on her other side, by the aisle. *Well, I've finally got him to come to church*, she thought darkly. The priest, Father Nolan, stood on the raised dais by the altar, nodding at the last of the congregation as they drifted in. Nolan was twenty-six, just one year older than the minimum age required for ordination.

Kristen liked him well enough, but had found that his relative youth robbed him of any charisma or gravitas. Today, he seemed like a lost little boy, nervously shuffling papers at the lectern.

Ave Maria played serenely in the background, its bleak serenade offering zero comfort. Then she heard the doors opening, signalling the moment she had been dreading. The coffin, carried by six volunteers from Our Sacred Heart, entered the church. A hushed silence fell on the congregation. As the pallbearers slowly moved the coffin, Marcus trembled and quiet sobs escaped him. It broke Kristen's heart in two. She cast her mind back to the Fog she had safely hidden in for so long. How selfish she had been. She had allowed herself to avoid reality so completely that she had not been there for her husband. Now she felt profound guilt. Marcus's shaking became more pronounced as he tried to steady himself. Kristen grabbed his hand and squeezed as hard as her own inadequate strength would allow.

The pallbearers placed the coffin on a bier as the music faded. Father Nolan sprinkled the casket with holy water. 'In the waters of baptism Abigail Hardy died with Christ,' he said. 'She rose with him to new life. May she share now with him in eternal glory.'

Nolan took his place back at the lectern and invited the congregation to sit. After a brief reading of scripture, he delivered the one and only eulogy, since neither Kristen nor Marcus could bring themselves to speak. The young priest spoke warmly of Abi, of how she was loved by all and had been taken back up to heaven all too soon. As Kristen listened, she waited for him to say something that would make sense of what had happened. Nolan, however, spoke only in platitudes. He described how Abi was resting in Christ now and waiting for the day when she would be raised up again. But that day seemed a long way off. Behind the lectern was a free-standing statue of Jesus on the cross, three-quarter life-size. Kristen gazed at the crown of thorns on Christ's head. Did God even understand what she was going through today? He might have lost a Son but, as the faith regularly reminded her, He had got him back in three days. Kristen, on the other hand, would spend the rest of her days alone. Before she knew it, everyone was standing for prayers and she was not ready when Father Nolan asked the pallbearers to move the coffin outside. Kristen was worried Marcus would not be able to walk. But Darius, seeing his emotional state, ducked out into the aisle and offered to help. They each took an arm and slowly helped him shuffle towards the open door.

Outside, the rite played out just as Kristen had witnessed in so many other funerals. Only she couldn't find the same comfort she had often felt when it was someone else's grief. None of the talk of life after death resonated with her. All she felt was grief and anger. It was all happening too fast. Young Father Nolan had already finished the committal and Abi's coffin was being lowered into a hole in the ground.

'… for you are dust,' Nolan said. 'And to dust you shall return.'

'No,' Marcus cried. '*Please, no.*'

This time his legs gave out and Darius caught him. Kristen felt her own chest sobbing. *Oh, Abi. Oh, my poor darling girl. I'm so sorry.* The first spade went in. She was supposed to throw a handful of dirt on top of the coffin too, another detail Bree had kindly talked her through. But she didn't want to now. It felt too final. Her eyes stung, and she suspected her mascara had smeared all over her face. She dabbed her face with a handkerchief but it was too late to fix her appearance. Not that she cared. She felt a hand on her shoulder.

'I'm so sorry, Kristen,' her father whispered.

She touched his fingers and shut her eyes and became aware of a series of sniffles, small and contained. When she opened her eyes, a young girl dressed in black was standing beside her. For a horrible moment, Kristen was convinced it was Abi, alive again, watching her own funeral with deep sadness. But the illusion was temporary. How had she not spotted Poppy this whole time?

'It's all right, sweetie,' Bree said, rubbing Poppy's head. 'Abi is in heaven now, with Jesus.'

Kristen turned to her friend, then back to the hole in the ground. She still believed that, deep inside her heart. Yet somehow it brought her no comfort. Instead, all she felt was an increasing internal turbulence. This was all God's fault. He had allowed this to happen. The question that burned inside her was *why?*

5

Later, at the house, her guests ate the canapés the catering company had provided. Marcus had excused himself as soon as they arrived, seeking refuge upstairs in their bedroom. He was clearly emotionally exhausted. Kristen wished Harry Dean had been able to make the funeral, but he was attending a neuroscience-related conference in Bonn, where he was the keynote speaker. Marcus had insisted he didn't need him to come, and had even suggested he preferred they catch up afterwards without the distractions of the day. But Kristen was not convinced. Her husband could have done with his best friend right now. Looking around the sea of faces, it was hard not to see the gathering as a twisted version of Marcus's birthday party in reverse. Kristen had been to her fair share of wakes. They were supposed to be sad, yes, but they were also an opportunity to celebrate the life of the departed. But there was none of that here. What was there to celebrate about the life of a child cut down too early? But that didn't stop the guests from saying flattering things about Abi when they came over to offer their condolences. How sweet natured she was. How smart and witty. Her English teacher, Mrs Kelly, was in tears describing what a wonderfully gifted young lady

Abigail had been. *Had been*, Kristen thought miserably. After a while, she had to get away from the well-wishers. She found Bree out back, smoking by the rowan tree.

'Got another one of those?'

'You've never smoked in your life, Krissy.'

'It's a day of firsts,' Kristen said.

Bree chuckled darkly and opened the lid of her Marlboro Golds. She lit the end for Kristen who, rather predictably, coughed harshly as soon as she took the initial drag. But the second drag went down easier, and the third after that. Within ten minutes, Kristen was smoking like a natural.

'You'll be okay, girlie. I'm going to be here for you in this.'

Kristen blew out a plume of smoke and stared at the red tip. 'I don't think I'll ever be okay,' she said.

'Don't say that.'

'I'm not being maudlin, Bee. Just realistic. I can already tell. The colour's just gone out of the world. I don't think it will ever come back.'

'You've just buried your only child,' Bree said. 'Of course you feel like that.'

'Kristen,' a man's voice said, startling her.

She turned around. 'Father Connolly?'

Connolly wasn't wearing his cassock; instead he was dressed in a standard funereal suit. Kristen guessed he must have been trying to blend in so as not to step on Father Nolan's younger toes. She cast her mind back to Connolly's study in Our Sacred Heart and the stained-glass depiction of Christ with a child on his lap. *Our Saviour loved children*, she remembered him saying. *I wish I could tell you why He calls some home early, but there are some mysteries we will never know.* That was certainly one of them, she thought. The whole thing was a fucking mystery.

'Tough day,' the burly priest said.

'You could say that,' Kristen said, trying her best to keep the bitterness out of her voice.

'I just want you to know we're all praying for you,' he said. 'You still have your Christian family in Cambridge. We're always here for you. *I'm* always here for you.'

They were meant to be words of comfort, coming from the man who had answered all her questions about the faith when she was a girl. But instead of thanking him, Kristen let out a harsh laugh. 'And what comforting words would you offer me, Father? More stories about footprints on the sand?'

Connolly looked stung, but she didn't care.

'I'm sorry,' he said. 'I know you're in pain. I can't imagine what you must feel.'

'No, Father, you can't.'

Kristen pointed her cigarette towards the clear afternoon sky. 'But *He* can, can't he? He can do anything. Including protecting my precious little girl. So where the hell was He?'

Kristen surprised herself, with both her language and the vitriol in it. But heat of the moment or not, she didn't regret it.

The priest nodded solemnly. 'It's normal to wonder where God is in all of this.'

She stubbed her cigarette carefully on a section of bark where it wouldn't mark, and rolled the butt inside a tissue.

'That's exactly the problem,' she said. 'I *know* where He is. Sitting up there in heaven, watching this shit show. Why did He allow her to even be born if He intended to snatch her life away so soon?'

Before Connolly could answer, she stormed away from them both, her mind racing with questions that she knew he would never be able to answer. And an anger she worried she would never be able to quell.

6

That night, after the last of the guests had left, Kristen lay in bed in her pyjamas. Marcus was spooning her, resting one hand over her stomach. Tomorrow, the house would be empty again. In the morning, Kristen's sister would return to Glasgow and her father to Cambridge. Marcus's parents had booked a lunchtime taxi to Gatwick to catch a flight back to Seville. Bree had already left and returned to her family.

'What do you want to do about her room?' Marcus said.

He seemed more like himself again, or at least composed enough to be able to talk. Kristen squeezed his hand. 'I can't think about that right now, darling,' she said.

'I understand.'

They lay quietly together, losing track of the time.

'How are you holding up?' he finally asked.

'Probably the same as you.'

He sighed. 'Yes. I'm sorry I lost it today. It just hit me, you know. The reality.'

'Don't apologise for that, for goodness' sake.'

He pulled in closer and hugged her body tighter. 'I thought it was a beautiful service,' he said.

'Yes.'

'Father Nolan did a good job,' he said.

'Yes,' she agreed.

It was strange to hear him being complimentary about a religious service, even one that had the import of today's.

'I envy you, you know,' he told her.

'What do you mean?'

'Your beliefs. It must be a comfort to think that Abigail is in the afterlife somehow. That her soul will live on.'

Kristen shook her head. 'It doesn't feel like much of a comfort,' she said.

'Still,' he said. 'To be able to believe that she's not really gone. You're fortunate.'

She said nothing. It really didn't feel that way at all. 'Actually, Marcus, it's I who should envy you,' she said. 'You don't have to try and figure out why God wanted to take Abi like this. Why He didn't want her to graduate, get married, have kids. Grow old. You believe in a cold indifferent universe. You don't have to make sense of what happened because random chance makes no sense anyway. I mean, if it's all just meaningless ... well, you can make your peace with that.'

In the darkness of the bedroom, she sensed him processing this, before eventually answering.

'Well, I certainly can't make sense of it.'

Yeah, well that makes two of us, Kristen thought.

7

The days dragged. As empty as Orchard House felt, Kristen elected to spend them indoors, wandering from room to room, her thoughts adrift and listless. She tried her best to focus on taking care of her husband. But Marcus continued to isolate himself in his study, immersing himself in his latest book. He no longer emerged in the evenings to watch television, choosing instead to keep writing. No doubt it stopped him focusing on Abi. Kristen could hardly blame him. She took him his meals, often leaving trays outside the door when he begged her not to be disturbed. At midnight, he would come to bed and slip his arm around her, a reminder that they were still a team, even if they were both only holding on by a thread. When the first Sunday after the funeral arrived, Kristen discovered she did not want to go to Mass at St James's. The same was true on the second Sunday. Halfway through the following week, Father Nolan called around to the house.

'H-hello, Mrs Hardy,' he said when she opened the door.

He sounded nervous and slightly croaky. Kristen stared at him neutrally.

'H-how are you holding up?' the young priest managed.

'Just like you'd imagine,' she said.

But she wasn't sure if Nolan *could* imagine. He likely had no idea how to manage a parishioner who was experiencing this kind of trauma. How could he know what it was to lose a child when he was practically a child himself? She was about to open her mouth to say that she wasn't up to company when a voice from the hallway broke in unexpectedly.

'Father Nolan?'

Marcus closed in behind her, placing a gentle hand on Kristen's shoulder. In the other, he was holding an empty mug, apparently the reason he had wandered downstairs.

'Hello, Mr Hardy,' Nolan said, nodding politely.

'Did you want to come in?' Marcus asked.

Father Nolan looked taken aback, which was exactly how Kristen felt. She could never have imagined Marcus inviting a priest into his home. But then these were far from normal circumstances.

'Th-that would be very kind,' Nolan said.

Kristen wanted to object but Marcus had made it impossible. She reluctantly stepped back to allow Nolan inside.

'Darling,' Marcus said, 'shall we offer the Father a drink?'

For a moment, his voice felt too distant to be real. Then she realised the two men were both looking at her expectantly.

'I ...'

'Do you drink coffee, Father?' Marcus said. 'We have a pretty fancy machine.'

Kristen remained speechless as her husband waved his cup at their impromptu guest.

'That sounds lovely,' Nolan said. 'Thank you.'

They sat awkwardly in the living room. Kristen had transitioned into autopilot and taken on hospitality duties as soon as Marcus had invited the priest to sit down. As she'd busied herself with the coffee machine in the kitchen, she had heard the men exchange small talk about the weather. They had fallen silent when she returned with the tray, however. She handed Nolan a latte and her husband his usual cappuccino, but she herself had nothing. Father Nolan sipped his drink and looked at Kristen.

'We haven't seen you for Mass lately, Mrs Hardy,' he said. 'Everyone's been asking after you.'

Kristen bit her lip. Part of her wanted to launch both barrels, loaded with her burning questions. She imagined the poor priest feeling horrified, unable to offer anything of comfort, anything that made any kind of sense. Of course, it wouldn't be his failing. None of it made sense. Instead, she said, 'I don't think I'm ready. I'm not sure when I will be either.'

Nolan nodded sympathetically. 'Of course,' he said. 'I just wanted to check in on you.'

She didn't know what to say to that. But it was Marcus who spoke next. 'The service, Father. It … it was beautifully done. I wanted to thank you.'

Nolan looked touched. 'Of course,' he said.

'Can I ask you something?' Marcus said. 'That ritual you performed. Sprinkling the water? Why do you do that?'

Nolan looked keenly back to Marcus. 'It's … it's a way of asking for peace and God's protection for … departed souls.'

'*Hmm.*'

Kristen watched Marcus carefully. She wondered whether he would tell Nolan what he thought of that notion and of the kind of people who believed such a thing. But he only nodded. 'I've been saying to Kris how much I envy her,' he said.

'Oh?' Nolan seemed puzzled.

'Having faith, I mean,' he said. 'I feel of late that it would be a great comfort to believe that there was an afterlife.' He smiled bitterly. 'But unfortunately I'm a man of science and reason. No offence, Father.'

'None taken, Mr Hardy,' Nolan said.

'That said, I can see there is utility in religion.'

'Utility?' Nolan asked.

'Emotional and psychological comfort,' Marcus said. 'In believing that this isn't all there is.'

He waved his hand around the room. It reminded Kristen of the night they had shared a dinner all those years ago, when he had told her that he respected her.

'How nice it must be to be able to have that,' he said.

He turned in his chair and looked deeply into Kristen's eyes. She saw love in them the like of which she had never seen. It almost made her want to cry.

'You should go back to church, Kris,' he said. 'I know you have been feeling lost. But your faith has always been your anchor. And if there was ever a time you needed that, it's now.'

Kristen couldn't take in what she was hearing. She had never heard Marcus talk about her beliefs in this way. The idea that he should envy her was patently absurd. Her faith had not helped her in her grief as he imagined. Rather, it had failed her when she had needed it most. She glanced back at Father Nolan. 'I'm sorry,' she said. 'Like I said, I'm just not ready.'

Nolan looked pained. 'I understand, Mrs Hardy,' he said. 'Especially after everything you've been through. But I wanted you to know that we all miss you very much.'

And I miss my daughter very much, Kristen thought. They sat in more uncomfortable silence. It was a relief when the priest finally made his excuses and left.

Grinding days became sluggish weeks. Marcus continued to seek sanctuary in his study, with only the faint sound of tapping keys through the study door signalling to Kristen that he was still alive. That, and the awful low sobs that she was sure he didn't think she could hear. They no longer ate meals together, their only intimacy the late-night arm that snaked around her in bed. Kristen's thoughts continued to go around and around on a circular track. She felt a constant mix of confusion and anger. Why had God allowed this to happen? Although she had meant what she said about not being ready to return to church, she did try one afternoon to find solace in the Bible. She retrieved her copy from the bureau in the bedroom, flicking through its pages until she found the Book of Job. According to the famous story, God had taken all of Job's family, his wife and daughters, apparently to test Job's faith. When Job had demanded why, God simply reminded Job that He was mysterious and there were some things that were just too lofty for a worm like him to understand. A convenient answer. Or perhaps, more accurately, no answer at all. She could not understand why

Job didn't hate God for the rest of his life after that. How could he not?

The dreams started not long after that. Dreams of Abi as a baby. And as a toddler. Memories, mostly. They were a special kind of torture, and resulted sometimes in Kristen waking up suddenly, panting, sweating. Taking a few moments to adjust to the darkness of the room, and the reality of reality. And always, the same question kept returning. Why? *Why, why, why?*

One thing she knew. She was pissed off at God. Not only for what He had done, but because of His deafening silence. She had tried to pray, many times. But He did not answer. Not so much as a *you're-too-lowly-a-worm-to-understand-My-ways*. It seemed God deemed it better that she wrestle with deafening silence, content to let her live out her grief for the rest of her life. To leave her confused and tortured, and without any answers. A special kind of cruelty, reserved just for her.

One night, she woke from yet another vivid dream about Abi, her mind and heart confused, her thoughts twisting around like a cyclone. She checked her phone. It was just after 3 a.m. Gently, she moved Marcus's arm off her and slid off the bed. She slipped into her dressing gown and went downstairs, where she made herself tea. The oppressive silence of the house compelled her to take her drink outside. The night proved surprisingly clement given the hour. Settling on a chair by the long oval table, mug in hand, she listened to the sounds of the forest. Owls hooted, crickets chirped, and she heard the general rustling of other night creatures going about their business. Above her, the sky was clear, lit by a quarter moon. She stared at the table and recalled the heated discussion that had taken place around it on Marcus's birthday. What was it Harry Dean had claimed that had so upset her? Her belief in God, in the specialness of humanity, was all the result of unguided neurons firing away randomly in the background, responding solely to external data. That it was just blind biological processes in her brain that produced her so-called faith. Another memory flashed before her, of Harry Dean explaining what his research had discovered.

To paraphrase R.E.M. ... they lost their religion.

How had he put it?

It took many weeks, but ... it proved to be as simple as turning off a switch.

An idea crystallised in Kristen's mind, and she knew what she had to do.

She wasn't sure how early was too early on a Sunday, but she also didn't care. Nor did she care that she was disturbing Marcus's most hallowed sanctuary. Her husband continued to snore heavily as the study door creaked and Kristen let herself in. She flipped open Marcus's MacBook on the desk, prompting it awake. Her heart sank as she typed the password *Abigirl1*, which she only knew because she remembered him telling her in case she ever needed to get into his machine. And this morning, she most certainly did. She grabbed the mouse and clicked on Marcus's contacts. She didn't have Harry Dean's phone number and didn't want to tell Marcus why she needed it, at least not yet. So this was the only way she knew to contact him directly. She found him easily enough and pressed the phone icon. Warbled ringing through the Wi-Fi was followed by the black screen dissolving into a view of an expansive living room. The decor was Scandinavian – dark wooden floors, pristine white walls lined with bookshelves. A leather sofa stood to the left, and beyond it a window that looked out onto urban apartment blocks across the street. She heard rummaging sounds, then saw a chunky hand gripping the laptop to turn it around.

'Kristen?' Harry said, his expression confused.

'How are you, dear?' she said.

He regarded her with what looked like pity, and for a moment, she resented him for it.

'I'm well, thanks,' he said. 'Is everything all right? Is Aury all right?'

'That's up for debate,' she said.

He nodded solemnly. 'And the funeral? Did it ... I mean, did it go as best it ...?'

She spared him the awkward struggle to find the right words. 'It was a beautiful service,' she said. 'But that's not why I'm calling. Harry. I need your help.'

He nodded. 'Anything.'

Kristen settled into Marcus's chair and let out a long breath. Then she put her proposal to him.

9

'Kristen,' Harry said when she finished. 'I ... I can't.'

'Why not?' she said. 'You told me yourself it was like turning off a switch.'

He squirmed as he appeared to recall the confident claim he'd made in their garden. 'It's not that simple,' he said. 'I'm supposed to run double-blind tests on carefully screened test subjects. I can't just include my friend's wife in a trial for personal reasons.'

'Then find a reason,' Kristen said. 'Use me as a test case. I've been a believer since I was twelve years old. Surely my brain would make for a fascinating study.'

'Kristen—'

'Harry, please. I wouldn't be calling you if I didn't need this.'

He fell quiet, a sheepish expression in his eyes. 'Please, Kristen,' he said at last. 'You know I would do anything for you.'

'Then do it,' she insisted. 'Or have you forgotten how I was there for you when you needed me? All those times you woke up so afraid you were on the verge of dying. Who came straight to your side every single time? Held your hand, huh? Who helped you through it? You owe me, Harry.'

She hated bringing their history up. Her role as a carer had never been performed with the expectation of getting anything back in return. But she was desperate for his help. Much as she hated guilting him, she needed him to agree to this.

Harry winced, shutting his eyes. 'You're right,' he said with a deep sigh. 'I do owe you.'

His face became still, and for a moment, Kristen worried their connection had crashed. But then he nodded.

'Let me think about it,' he said. 'It needs to be done for proper, scientific reasons. It can't just be a favour.'

'I understand, Harry,' she said. 'Thank you.'

She was so relieved, she wanted to cry. She realised how much she had been counting on Harry's help. He promised to get back to her soon. Kristen ended the call, closing the laptop's lid as the wisps of their conversation continued to linger in her mind. A shadow cast itself over the desk, and she turned in the chair to see Marcus, in his dressing gown, staring at her accusingly through the door frame.

'What are you doing, Kris?' he said.

She told him. And waited for his reaction. She hoped it would be one of kindness and empathy.

Instead Marcus just glared at her. 'Have you gone completely mad?' he said.

'Darling, I need this,' she said softly. 'I need Harry to help me if he can.'

Marcus shook his head. 'You want him to tamper with your brain? You don't need his help, Kris. You've got your faith!'

She pushed the chair away and stood up sharply. 'Don't you dare talk to me about faith,' she hissed. 'You were the one who through our entire marriage told me faith was the opposite of reason.'

'Is that what this is about?' Marcus said. 'You're angry at me? Then lash out at me, Kris. I can take it. But you don't need to do this.'

She moved past him into the hallway, her irritation mounting. 'Please don't tell me what I do or don't need to do,' she said. 'You don't understand what it's like for me. I can't sleep. I can't eat. Nothing makes sense and I hate the God I was supposed to love. I ...'

She stopped by the banister, placing one hand on the ball-shaped finial, and spun back around to him. 'I ... I'm stuck. I need some kind of peace. Please.'

Her voice softened as her anger fell away, and heavy sadness took its place. Marcus's breathing calmed down too, the rises and falls of his chest returning to pre-adrenaline levels. He refused to meet her eyes, looking down at the cream carpet instead.

'What if ... what if it changes you?' he asked. 'There could be no going back from this.'

A single tear rolled down her cheek. 'Maybe I don't want to go back, darling.'

'But then I'll have lost a wife and a daughter,' he said miserably.

'I'm sorry, Marcus,' she said. 'There's nothing you can say to change my mind. If Harry agrees, I'm going to go through with this.'

'Kris, I think this is a mistake,' Marcus said.

But she was already moving down the winding stairs, seeking another space in the house to be alone with her thoughts. Thoughts that she hoped might have a chance to finally be silenced. But only if Harry came through for her.

FOUR

1

At the beginning of October, Kristen boarded a plane at Gatwick. As her flight took off, bound for Geneva, she wondered if Marcus's concerns would prove to be justified. Despite his protests over the last few weeks, Kristen had insisted she would see her decision through. Marcus continued to raise objections until Harry Dean eventually sent through a proposal and a schedule. Its arrival finally convinced him that Kristen was serious and not likely to back out, though that didn't stop him from calling Harry personally to discuss his objections. The two men had a long conversation on speakerphone with Kristen in earshot.

'She'll be perfectly safe, Aury,' Harry insisted.

'I don't like it,' Marcus said, looking over at Kristen. 'It sounds invasive.'

What Kristen didn't like was the fact that she was openly being discussed like a possession, as though Marcus was lending Harry his car. But she was glad that Harry managed to persuade him the treatment would not cause permanent harm.

'All right,' Marcus said at last. 'But I still don't approve.'

And that was just fine with Kristen. Her only concern was

whether it would work, followed closely by whether Marcus would cope okay with her being away from home twice a week. This latter worry, however, disappeared when, a week after the call with Harry, Marcus announced that he would be flying to the Philippines to shoot the new series of *The Rites Stuff*. 'The show must go on, as they say,' were his exact words. But Kristen knew what he really meant. Throwing himself into work was his way of coping, just as this odyssey to Geneva was hers. The green patchwork fields of England disappeared beneath the strata of white clouds and Kristen sat back in her seat, closed her eyes and, for the first time since the funeral, thought about what the future might hold.

Her plane touched down at Geneva airport less than two hours later. Kristen had no luggage, and so was out of customs in no time. She grabbed a taxi outside the terminal and passed the directions Harry had emailed to her driver. She had never been to Switzerland before and was struck by how beautiful Lake Geneva looked.

She remembered how curious she'd been as to why a British charity would choose to have a base here. Her own research into the Bennett Foundation provided no answer. Instead it had given her a potted history of the organisation to date. She discovered the Bennetts had generally only funded projects in the United Kingdom. During Victorian times, after poor George Bennett had become manic, these comprised of several mental institutions, spread wide across the country. Sadly for George, and indeed for anyone else suffering mental health afflictions at the time, treatment usually involved being locked up, away from normal society, often in over-crowded and brutal conditions. Attitudes only changed in the twenty-first century, when the foundation invested in more modern mental health hospitals, in the vein of the Maudsley in London. Here, all that old money was finally able to fund pioneering research and treatment for conditions like depression, anxiety, bipolar disorder, and schizophrenia. It had been an interesting education, but it had taken Marcus, always happy to slip into Lecture Mode, to explain to her why Geneva. According to him, the city was already home to innovative projects like the Hadron Collider, and apparently there were a great many scientific minds and talent to recruit from at the prestigious universities. There was also the fact that one local university had also pioneered the special magnetic machines Harry Dean was using on his test subjects.

The institute was built in the early 2010s, before Brexit. However, the Swiss government continued to offer favourable tax arrangements due to the foundation's charitable status. In a strange way, Kristen was glad to have to travel abroad for this. The extra distance somehow felt like she was embarking on a new chapter in her life. She hoped it would be.

The taxi passed north of the lake and continued through the outlying town of Lausanne. They headed further north still, the urban landscape quickly falling away. Soon, Kristen was on a rural highway with Swiss mountains as a backdrop. She caught sight of the facility up ahead, and was struck by how wealthy the foundation must be. The institute was the size of a small airport, surrounded by a car park and ringed by a high security fence. In the centre of the site was a structure that resembled a bio-dome, its glass exterior reflecting the sun, giving it a tinsel-like sheen. As her taxi approached the main gate, Kristen spotted a crowd standing in a field across the road, holding up placards. Two policemen stood sentry-like in front of them, arms crossed, watching them carefully. As her vehicle drew near, she heard raucous, angry shouting. The crowd was a mixture of men and women, young and old. But most noticeable was how the scene resembled some kind of multifaith convention. There was an imam, a rabbi, a Sikh and even a Catholic priest who reminded her a little of Father

Connolly. The taxi slowed, and she was able to read some of the slogans on their signs.

RELIGION IS NOT A DISEASE

BAN DECONVERSION THERAPY

NO FAITH IN SCIENCE

A young woman dressed in a hijab banged loudly on the glass window, which made Kristen jump and the taxi driver curse. One of the cops stepped in, placing his hands firmly on the woman's shoulders and leading her away. The taxi turned into the entrance drive and pulled up to a hut by the gate. A security guard emerged and asked Kristen for her name and form of ID. She handed him her passport as he spoke briefly into a shoulder radio. Moments later, he opened the gate and the taxi moved in quickly, leaving the chants and shouts from the crowd behind. Though she had no reason to believe the protestors had violent intentions against her personally, Kristen felt relieved when the gate closed behind them.

2

The driver dropped her off near the dome's main entrance and Kristen gave him a handful of francs that included a generous tip. She walked past a row of six white vans parked in priority bays and arrived at two glass doors, which slid open to welcome her inside. The vast atrium was distinguished by a central white column, eight storeys high. Each level circled the column, with walkways occasionally extended out towards the glass of the dome. At certain junctures, flights of stairs would connect a walkway to the one above it, creating a labyrinth that reminded Kristen of an Escher painting. Etched on the marble floor beneath her feet were the words *Welcome to The Bennett Foundation*. Underneath that, in a smaller font, was the phrase *Salutem Pro Anima*, which Kristen remembered from the institute's website meant something akin to *health for the mind*. A Scandinavian-looking blonde greeted her warmly at the white doughnut ring that formed the reception. Kristen asked for Professor Harry Dean and was invited to wait on one of several armless reception sofas. She used the time to text Marcus and let him know she had arrived safely. Harry emerged twenty minutes later. He was wearing a white lab coat and was out of breath, a film of sweat covering his forehead.

'Sorry to keep you waiting,' he huffed. 'We've been dealing with a bit of a problem outside, as you might have noticed.'

'I noticed,' Kristen said. 'How long has that been going on?'

Harry sighed. 'It started a few days ago. Just a couple of demonstrators at first. Now it's an organised mob. It seems we've upset a number of religious groups.'

'They're objecting to your research?'

'It appears so,' Harry said. 'We've been running our trials for three years now, so I suppose it was only a matter of time before the word got out. We're lucky to have kept it under wraps for this long.'

Kristen followed Harry as he escorted her towards a set of lifts.

'It's not like this is anything new,' he said. 'Religious people have often been concerned about the advance of science. And sometimes with fair reason.'

Kristen cast her mind back to Marcus's birthday party, and how she, too, had become upset with Harry's work. She was embarrassed at the memory.

'It's an understandable reaction,' Harry said. 'I would feel the same if I thought someone was setting out to prove or disprove my faith. Of course, that's really not what we're trying to do here.'

The lift arrived and Harry waved her inside.

'Who would have leaked it?' she asked.

'It could have been anyone. We have two hundred employees at this facility alone. It was inevitable, really. I just worry we'll have news crews here soon.'

'But it's all safe and above board,' Kristen said. 'I mean, it's not like you're doing human cloning or something.'

Harry smiled weakly. 'True, and the subjects in our trial

are all volunteers who have been fully informed and have granted their consent.'

'As I have,' Kristen said.

'Yes, and now you're one of those whose anonymity and privacy might be threatened if this protest grows any larger.'

The doors pinged open on the third floor and Harry swept his hand, inviting her to exit. 'Let me show you the heart of the project,' he said. 'Or perhaps I should say the brain.'

Kristen stepped out of the lift and, for the very first time, into Harry's world.

3

Her first impression was of an ultra-modern hospital ward. On one side of the ring-shaped corridor were rows of glass-walled cubicles looking out onto the atrium. Most contained people lying supine on bed platforms, wearing their everyday clothes. Clinicians in lab coats with ID badges stood by the beds, each appearing to operate a machine shaped like a white cylinder at the head of the platform. Kristen stepped up to the glass as one bed slid a woman in her fifties into its tunnel opening.

'Are those … MRI machines?' she asked.

'Technically, fMRIs,' Harry said. 'Modified somewhat to be more compact.'

'We only had one MRI at St Anthony's,' she said. 'They cost a lot of money.'

'The foundation has very deep pockets,' Harry said, nodding. 'But I'm pleased to say we do give something back. When they're not in use, these machines and other equipment are loaned out to hospitals all over Switzerland. Sometimes even further afield.'

Kristen liked the idea of that. More staff bustled past them, some carrying tablets, others wheeling stainless-steel trolleys with monitor screens mounted on them. There was a tangible energy to the floor.

'Monday is our busiest day,' Harry explained. 'We usually scan our subjects at the start of the week. Then again on Friday to get a good before-and-after picture. The machines capture increased blood flow in the brain caused by new neural connections. What we in the field call neurovascular coupling.'

She nodded, like *neurovascular coupling* was a phrase she heard every day. 'And this whole floor is just for your research?' she asked.

'This and the level below,' Harry said. 'Most of the staff you see here are just trained on the scanner and the transcranial hardware, the God helmets themselves. The actual analysis is done by a smaller team of neuroscientists who are under my supervision.' He grinned. 'You know, as a boy, I always wanted to have super vision …'

Kristen indulged him with a smile that she felt he didn't deserve and returned to watch the woman being scanned.

'We perform more than four thousand scans here every week,' Harry said. 'We use AI to help us, but that's still a lot of data. Come on, let me show you the tech itself.'

They walked down the corridor, Kristen trying not to stare at all the different people as they went by, trial subjects just like herself. She estimated there were perhaps thirty scanning rooms in all. She didn't know how long it took to scan each person, but the logistics had to be challenging. No wonder they needed so many machines. At the end of the passageway, Harry stopped at a set of double glass doors. He lifted a lanyard and touched his ID card to a reader on the wall. The doors slid open with a loud *whoosh*. Kristen followed Harry through into an expansive space built into the central column. It resembled an indoor sports hall. Rows upon rows of black chairs stood on the white floor; at first sight the hall reminded her of a hairdresser's – behind each chair stood a hydraulic arm that bent and hovered over the seat. Attached to the end of each arm was a dome-shaped hood.

'These are our God helmets,' Harry said. 'It took the university who designed them five years to manufacture them all. I won't tell you what they cost to build.'

Kristen approached the first row, and the first chair. Hesitantly, she reached out and ran her fingers along the black hood. It was metallic and cold to the touch. She peeked under the dome. A canopy of hard steel wires formed a kind of inner helmet, with smaller metal cylinders connected at various points. She was no engineer, but she assumed these pins were probably magnets, and the small wheels attached to the hard wires allowed them to manoeuvre around the canopy as desired.

'It looks horrifying, I know,' Harry said. 'But it's all quite painless, I promise.'

Kristen stepped back from the machine and allowed herself to take in the whole room.

'There are sixty in total,' Harry said. 'We have to split the testing into two-hour slots to get everybody done. You, however, are going to be a special case.'

'I am?'

'You'll be doing your scans and sessions all on your own. As I explained to you, I can't just insert you into an existing trial midway through. But I convinced the board to consider a qualitative study, with you as the main subject.'

'Yes, you mentioned that.'

'What I probably didn't say was I had to use your personal story to convince them to sign off. I told them this test was focused on how the God helmet can affect someone who's grieving and who also has your religious background.'

He glanced at the floor, looking slightly ashamed. 'I had to make it ... worth funding, you see. I hope this doesn't upset you.'

Kristen's heart melted. She had bullied Harry into helping her. Of course he had to find a way to get things officially rubber-stamped. 'I understand, Harry,' she said. 'You have no idea how grateful I am for what you're doing for me.'

Harry looked up at her. 'Kristen, there are no guarantees this can help you.'

'I know,' she said. 'But I believe it will.'

She was sure of it too. Harry's machines could turn mystics into atheists. It might only be a few more weeks before the world started to make sense to her again. The way it surely did for Marcus.

'One more thing,' Harry said. 'We take safeguarding here seriously. So before I put you under one of these, I need you to have a talk with our resident psychiatrist. You'll need to have a fitness assessment with him before I can give you the go-ahead.'

Kristen thought back to the crowd of protestors. Harry had happily dismissed them as reactionaries. Yet he had a full-time psychiatrist to assess the subjects of his experiments. Had she truly considered the risks of what she was about to do? The rows of black God helmets stared back at her, as if daring her to back out. But she wasn't going to.

'Whatever you need,' she told Harry. 'I'm ready to get started.'

4

They rode the lift to the top floor and entered another circular corridor, this one lined with grey carpet. Harry knocked on an open office door halfway around. A man answered, around Kristen's age, dressed in a tailored suit and designer shoes.

'Adrian, this is Kristen,' Harry said and then, turning to Kristen, 'I'll see you in about an hour.'

The man introduced himself as Doctor Adrian Kemplar and beckoned Kristen inside. He invited her to sit on one of two sofas facing each other across a low coffee table. Aside from his desk, the only other furniture in the office was a wooden bookshelf, crammed full of books. A single window afforded views of the atrium below and the dome roof above. It was like peering out onto a mega shopping mall. As Kristen sat down, she noticed a large box of tissues that made her uneasy. The last thing she fancied right now was a therapy session.

'Welcome, welcome,' Doctor Kemplar said, taking a seat on the opposing sofa.

She detected a strong Australian accent. Folding her arms, she crossed her legs and rotated one foot nervously.

'Thanks for doing this, Mrs Hardy,' he said. 'Please relax. This is just an informal chat.'

Kemplar offered her a glass of water, which she politely declined. 'Professor Dean has told me about your particular … situation,' he said softly. 'I hope that's all right. He was probably more frank with me than the board, because of my specific role here.'

Kristen uncrossed her arms. She would have to trust this man if she wanted to get access to the God helmet. And she did. 'Harry probably told you I lost my daughter,' she said.

There, she thought. *How's that for an awkward opening?* But any hopes of turning the tables and making the psychiatrist feel uncomfortable backfired. He didn't even blink. Instead, his eyes searched hers out.

'Yes, I'm aware,' he said, gently. 'Do you want to talk about it?'

'Not particularly,' Kristen said truthfully.

'It's all right. We don't have to.'

He leaned back, smiling warmly. Though he had no notepad or laptop, Kristen couldn't help feeling he was taking mental notes to type up later. She just wanted to cut out the bullshit.

'Look, Doctor Kemplar, can you just tell me what it is you need me to say? I really want to get started. *Please.*'

Kemplar nodded. 'Mrs Hardy, my role here at the Bennett Foundation is to look after the psychological well-being of all the subjects on Harry's trials. I insist on regular sessions with everybody, to make sure their mental health stays okay. And that includes you. I don't know how you know Harry, or how you got yourself a space here. And frankly I don't care. But I do have a job to do. So if I think you're in any way negatively affected by your experience here I will eject you from the trial. Do I make myself clear?'

Kemplar delivered his warning in a friendly enough tone, but Kristen felt the veracity of his promise. She glanced around the room, noticing for the first time certificates and awards hanging above the psychiatrist's desk. All accrediting professional competence. Here was a man who took his role seriously. She had to respect that.

'I will cooperate fully, Doctor Kemplar,' she told him. 'I'll attend as many sessions as you deem necessary, and I'll be honest with you about my state of mind, to the best of my ability. I'm grateful you're here to make sure I'm okay.'

Kemplar seemed immensely pleased at this. 'I appreciate you saying that, Mrs Hardy.'

'Kristen, please.'

'Then you must call me Adrian,' he said.

'So why did you volunteer to be studied?' Adrian asked.

Kristen didn't hesitate to answer. 'Harry told me the helmet can stop me believing in God.'

The doctor stared into her eyes. 'And you're okay with that? Your file says you're a devout Catholic.'

'I'm more than okay,' she said. 'In fact, I'm hoping that's exactly what happens.'

He bit his lip thoughtfully. 'Kristen, are you sure about that?' he asked. 'Tell me, have you ever met or spoken to a de-convert?'

She frowned. 'De-convert?'

'Someone who has renounced their faith.'

She considered the question. There were people she had known from church who had stopped going over the years, but none had been close friends. 'Not as such,' she admitted.

'People de-convert from religions all the time,' Adrian said. 'But often they're not prepared for what the world looks like without faith. They don't appreciate how much it can provide meaning and purpose.'

'I understand,' Kristen said.

She wanted to tell him that she no longer had any

meaning and purpose anyway. What difference would it really make?

'There can also be a significant amount of disorientation and confusion,' Adrian continued. 'A loss of identity. It can cause people to feel hopeless, inducing depression. Perhaps even suicidal thoughts.'

She snapped her head up at this. This was a starker risk than she'd considered. 'Has that happened to some of the people in the trials?' she said.

'Thankfully, no,' he said. 'And my job is to make sure it never does. We believe in good quality aftercare here. But there's a reason you'll be given a lot of waivers to sign. There's a lot to watch out for if the experiment is successful. And even if you are happy with how your personality might change, there are likely to be more problems to face down the road that you may not have anticipated.'

'Like what?' Kristen asked.

'You may lose friends,' Adrian said. 'Faith communities often reject doubters, sometimes declaring them heretics, or cutting off ties. It can be very isolating. The Catholic church is quite a global community to be shunned by.'

'I don't know about the global community,' Kristen said. 'I do have friends from church, but I'm pretty sure they wouldn't abandon me if I told them I didn't believe anymore.'

'Don't be so certain,' Adrian said. 'I'm sure your friends are lovely, but people sometimes feel threatened by one of their own leaving the fold. It's just good to be aware of that. And then of course there's family.'

Kristen shook her head. 'My mother died quite a long time ago,' she said. 'My sister and I aren't close. As for my dad, I think he'd be delighted if I gave up on religion.'

'And what about your husband?' Adrian asked. 'How does he feel about you doing this? If you don't mind me asking?'

Kristen sighed. 'He's worried that it'll change me,' she said. 'That I won't be the same person he married.'

Adrian nodded. 'And he's an atheist, right? At least he declares so in his books.'

Kristen raised an eyebrow. 'You've read his books?'

The psychiatrist pointed at the bookshelf. Kristen turned and stared, eventually noticing that one of the shelves had all six of Marcus's *The Rites Stuff* series.

'I'm a big fan. Love the TV show. I've found he also has some fascinating insights into evolutionary psychology.' Adrian followed this with a serious look. 'I hope you don't find it weird that I have his books here.'

'Not at all,' Kristen said. 'My husband has a big following. I'm pretty used to it.'

Adrian nodded. 'Good. Something else you should be prepared for, Kristen. If this does what you hope it will, it won't just change you. It can have a permanent effect on Marcus as well. The question is, are you prepared for that?'

Kristen swallowed. The truth was she didn't know. This was a leap in the dark for her marriage. It would either be a good thing, or something she might come to regret. But she couldn't control what Marcus felt or wanted for her. Any more than he could control her. In the end, this wasn't only about him. This was her life too. And whatever happened, she needed to find a way to be at peace. 'I guess I'll have to be,' she said.

5

They talked a while longer before Adrian told her he was satisfied. From the landline on his desk, he called Harry and officially okayed Kristen for her first session. A woman arrived at the office shortly after and introduced herself as Amanda Tanner. She appeared to be in her late thirties, with straw-blonde hair pulled back into a tight ponytail. She was dressed in the same white lab coat Kristen had seen the other staff wearing and carried a tablet device in one hand.

'Has she signed all of the consents?' Tanner asked the psychiatrist curtly.

Adrian nodded.

'NDAs too?'

'She's one hundred per cent yours,' Adrian said.

Tanner looked Kristen up and down with a distinctly cool expression. 'Come with me.'

Kristen thanked Adrian Kemplar, then followed Tanner to the lifts and down again to the fourth floor, where she was led into one of the cubicle rooms with an fMRI machine.

'Bra?' Tanner said.

'Excuse me?'

'Are you wearing a bra?'

Kristen confirmed that she was. Tanner pressed a button on her tablet and the room's glass window went opaque. 'Please take it off,' she said.

Kristen unhooked her brassiere and placed it into a red plastic container that Tanner held out for her.

'Any jewellery?' Tanner asked. She tucked her thumb inside the T-shirt she was wearing under the lab coat and pulled out her necklace, as though Kristen might be too stupid to understand what she meant.

Kristen was struck mute for a moment, but only because she was staring at the small crucifix on Tanner's necklace, which reminded her of a similar one at home that she only just realised she had stopped wearing.

'Anything metal on your person?' Tanner pressed, apparently impatient with the lack of response.

'Uh ... just these.'

Kristen removed her wedding and engagement rings and added them to the container. She was led onto the white bed, where Tanner told her to be very still. She felt the bed platform move and then she was inside the bore of the cylinder. The thrum of what she guessed were its magnets resounded around her head. The scanning lasted twenty minutes before she was ejected again. Tanner looked at her tablet screen and nodded approvingly. Scan over, Kristen was led back to the main hall she'd been shown earlier. Harry Dean was already there, fussing over one of the God helmets at the end of a row. He looked up as the women approached.

'Ah, Kristen. I see you've met Amanda. She's going to be your Tech Manager. Everyone on the trials gets assigned one.'

He showed Tanner his tablet screen. 'I took the liberty of running the pre-diagnostics,' he said. 'We're good to go.'

Tanner didn't look at whatever data was on display, instead tapping her own tablet. 'I'll be the judge of that, Professor,' she said.

'Yes, of course you will,' Harry mumbled apologetically.

He extended a chubby hand towards Kristen. As she took it, he cupped his other hand over hers and gave her a kind stare. 'Good luck, Kristen,' he said. 'Let me know how it goes.'

Then she was alone with Tanner. Kristen had the sudden urge to go to the bathroom. She wasn't sure if it was just nerves, but the desire was strong. She asked meekly for permission, half afraid the surly Tech Manager would bite her head off. But having vented her annoyance at Harry, Tanner seemed to be marginally more relaxed. She told Kristen to go ahead but to be as quick as possible. Kristen thanked her and headed towards the sign at the far end of the room. On her way back, the oddity of where she was struck her again. As she weaved through lines of chairs, each with their integral God helmets, she had a sinking feeling she couldn't quite name. The sight of all this machinery no longer called to mind the inside of an enormous hair salon, but some awful dystopian future where human minds were uploaded into some cloud. She didn't know where the image came from. She wasn't especially interested in science fiction movies, but this was quite possibly the most other-worldly scene she'd ever witnessed. As she drew closer to her assigned chair and helmet, she caught Amanda Tanner watching her slowly, and the feeling of dread solidified. Kristen told herself she was overreacting. Harry knew what he was doing. And the institute had been using these machines on people safely for more than three years. Nevertheless, she couldn't shake the sense of foreboding. She recalled the protestors gathered outside the institute. NO FAITH IN SCIENCE, one of their signs had read. Yet she was about to put all of her faith – and her head – in that strange black dome. She hoped she wasn't making a terrible mistake.

'I'll need your phone,' Tanner said. 'And any other electronics you have on you. The magnetic fields can interfere with the equipment.'

Kristen fished her iPhone out of her handbag and handed it over. She removed her coat and folded it onto her lap. She settled hesitantly into her chair while Tanner typed something on her tablet. A noise started up, a light whirring that made Kristen jump. She twisted her head up and saw that a circle of red LED lights had lit around the base of the God helmet. It only added to the sense of menace. The Tech Manager leaned over, placing her hands on Kristen's shoulders to shift her position before guiding her head forward. Then she reached for the dome and slowly and carefully aligned it with the top of Kristen's skull. There she stayed, frozen as if she was a statue. Kristen blinked fast at her.

'Are you ready?'

Kristen nodded. But, in truth, she wasn't. Tanner pressed a button on her tablet and the hood lowered down. Instinctively, Kristen closed her eyes and the whirring sound became a low-level grinding. She felt the envelopment of the metallic cover and the touch of cold metal at the front and back of her head. Last chance to back out, she thought. She imagined Abigail as a ghost, standing next to Tanner with her arms crossed. *Oh, Mother, what on earth are you doing? You don't honestly think this quackery will work, do you?* Kristen blinked away the image. She dared to open her eyes and a black visor inside the helmet slid down over them.

'We're going to start with your prefrontal cortex,' Tanner said. 'Now, you might feel a slight knocking sensation, so don't be alarmed.'

Too late for that, Kristen thought. Her nerves felt shot. Even her lips had started trembling. No, not trembling. Moving. She was muttering. She recognised the words, barely even a whisper. *Hail Mary, full of grace, the Lord is with thee.* Ironic as it was, Kristen's base instincts had taken over. She was praying.

6

(crucifix) (star and crescent) (menorah) (the om symbol) (lotus) (yin-yang) (pentagram) (wheel of dharma) (crucifix) (star and crescent) (menorah) (the om symbol) (lotus) (yin-yang) (pentagram) (wheel of dharma)

The visuals flashed rapidly before her eyes, almost too fast for Kristen to register. She didn't feel a knocking, or indeed any sensation in her skull, but she did become mildly dizzy watching the fast *flick-flick-flick* as the images repeated over and over. Then came the music. Not a melody, but a drum beat. It sounded like the underlying rhythm to a song she thought she knew. She tried to concentrate on the track, but the visuals took over her attention again. Some of the icons were associated with other faiths, but others were unfamiliar to her. Harry had explained that much of the imagery she would see would be abstract, or be too fast to process. But he'd also told her not to underestimate what a person stored in their subconscious brain. In addition, her audiovisual stimulus had been carefully selected by his team of neuroscientists. It was, he assured her, based on years of research and tailored to her personal profile. This she noticed relatively soon after the first burst of images faded and were replaced by colourful illustrations that were distinctly Christian.

(bible) (fish symbol) (dove) (lamb) (chalice) (angels) (rosary) (bible) (fish symbol) (dove) (lamb) (chalice) (angels) (rosary)

And *now* she felt it. Not a knocking, but a light buzzing inside her skull. It didn't hurt; it was perhaps mildly uncomfortable at best. But a *psychological* discomfort. She visualised an invisible, electrified finger applying pressure, prodding different parts of her brain. And then it started to move faster as the drum beat increased and imagery changed again. A multitude of AI-generated pictures followed, of families smiling, of the earth, a single daffodil, the oceans, the moon, cityscapes and sunsets that all became a blur. Kristen reminded herself she didn't have to keep up with it all or try to analyse what she was seeing and hearing. It was enough to simply let it happen. The visor now showed her a cluster of amoebas, single-cell organisms dividing and splitting, dividing and splitting, and the tingling swept over to the right-hand side of her brain. *That's the part mostly responsible for creativity and storytelling,* she heard Harry say. She had told herself a powerful story many years ago. And, if this experiment was working, her brain was currently being rewired to tell her a new one.

It finally came to an end forty minutes later. All sensations ceased and the visor retreated back into its slot. The God helmet emitted a whirring sound as it moved up off Kristen's head. She blinked in the harsh clinical whiteness of the hall. Tanner stood in front of her, reviewing her tablet.

'Looking good,' she said. 'How do you feel?'

'I'm not sure,' Kristen said. 'A little dizzy.'

'Any nausea?'

'N-no,' she said.

At least she didn't think so.

'That'll change,' Tanner said coolly. 'Next week, we're going to increase the intensity. And start the CES.'

'The what …?'

'Cranial electrotherapy stimulation,' the other woman said. 'We're going to work on the amygdala. That's when you'll start feeling a change in your emotions.'

Kristen rubbed the sides and back of her head. It felt like there were cobwebs in her hair that needed brushing out. She didn't know what a change in emotions meant, but she had a feeling the effects of this experiment were only going to get stronger. 'What happens next?' she asked.

'Come back Friday for your after-scan and aftercare with Doctor Kemplar,' Tanner said. 'But for now, you are done. Congratulations.'

She said these last words with zero warmth. But Kristen didn't care. She didn't need this tech geek's approval or validation. She was proud enough of herself for taking this first step. And she was more curious than ever about where it was going to lead.

7

'So ... did Harry successfully scramble your brain?'

Kristen was back at Orchard House, reading a magazine on the sofa. Marcus had wandered downstairs for a coffee refill. He hadn't even started packing for his flight to the Philippines in the morning.

'I'm fine, darling,' Kristen assured him. 'It really didn't hurt at all.'

In truth, when she reflected on the experience, it reminded her of a documentary she had seen about an experiment in subliminal advertising conducted in cinemas in the late 1950s. The day after, it had all seemed quite innocuous.

'Do you feel any different?' Marcus pressed.

'No,' she said. 'Not at all.'

He looked at her as though she might be lying. 'And you're definitely going back?' he said.

'Every Monday and Friday,' she said gently. 'I told you, darling.'

'I still don't understand why,' he said.

He sounded like a sulking schoolboy and it pissed her off, more than a little.

'I mean, to erase the only thing that's ever brought you comfort in your life,' he said.

She put her magazine down and blew out a long plume of air. 'Let's talk about your trip, darling,' she said. 'Where are you guys going first?'

Marcus winced, clearly unhappy she was changing tack. But he answered her. 'Overnight in Manila, then straight on to Mindoro island,' he said, 'to interview some of the Hanunuo Mangyan tribe. Most of them are farmers. They mostly live in bamboo houses built on hillsides and have a very rich cultural tradition, including the Hanunuo script, recognised as a national treasure …'

She heard the beginnings of Lecture Mode coming on and was pleased. At least he'd moved on from judging her. She listened attentively as he continued, smiling at all the right intervals. The more he talked, the more he forgot all about his objections. It worked for a while, anyway.

'Kris, I'm just worried about you,' he said after dinner.

Kristen had made a curry. They had eaten together in the dining room for the first time since the funeral.

'And I'm worried about you too, darling,' she said.

She had heard so many stories about couples losing a child who become unable to live together. She didn't want this to be true for them. She reached across and squeezed Marcus's wrist. 'We have to be understanding about what we both need right now. I need Harry's help, and you need to work. So let's just be kind to each other, okay?'

He closed his eyes. Kristen wondered what he was imagining in that pained gaze. 'We're going to be so far from each other,' he said. 'It won't be easy.'

'FaceTime,' she countered. 'And lots of it. I'm sure the weeks will pass quickly. And we'll both be back here for our anniversary, won't we?'

Their fifteen-year milestone was coming up in November.

'I already sorted it out with Tim, darling,' Marcus said. 'I'll be back for the entire week, I promise.'

'Good,' she said, letting go of his hand. 'It's important we take time for each other. It's … sometimes couples can … in a situation like this. We just have to hope that we'll be strong enough.'

He squeezed her hand in reply, a sign to her that he understood what she was saying.

The next day, she drove him to Heathrow. They said little on the way, long silences where they both clearly didn't want to revisit their conversation of the previous evening. She followed the signs to the drop-off zone and gave him a kiss on the cheek.

He turned to her before exiting the Land Rover and smiled weakly. 'You know, there was a time when you would have said *prayed*,' he said.

'What?' she asked, confused.

'Last night. You said we just have to hope that we'll be strong enough. But normally, you'd have said *prayed* that we're strong enough.'

She looked at him, not knowing what to say. He was one hundred per cent right, of course. 'Marcus,' she said. 'Go. You'll miss your flight. I love you, darling.'

'I love you too,' he said.

He kissed her through the window, and then he was gone, through the sliding doors that took him into Departures. Kristen watched him disappear, then began the long drive home, to a house that felt even emptier than before.

8

She planned to FaceTime with Marcus three times a week, but his often hectic shooting schedule and the seven-hour time difference made it challenging. The first week, the reception at his hotel had been terrible, resulting in choppy conversations. He asked her how it was going at the Bennett Institute and she deflected by asking about him.

'You look tired, darling,' she said. 'Are you sleeping okay?'

She didn't mean jet lag. Marcus had had enough time to acclimatise now. He took her true meaning, however.

'Mostly I am,' he said. 'I, er, took the liberty of packing some of your sleeping pills from the house. Just in case, you know. And, on a couple of nights, well ...'

Kristen dismissed it with a wave. She couldn't judge him, not for that. Not after she herself had spent so long lost in the Fog. She could tell he was embarrassed to admit it so, out of sympathy, she changed the subject. 'And how's the shoot going?'

'Well,' Marcus said, looking relieved to change topic, 'today was ... educational. We found a small village where the villagers still practise *kutkot*.'

'*Kutkot*?' she repeated, not sure what he'd said.

'A ritual for the dead,' he said. 'I thought it had died out years ago. It was so strange watching it, Kris. I was struck by how, wherever you go in the world, people just can't seem to let go of their dead. Once I'd have called it primitive. But now … now I think I get it.'

A pang of sadness hit her just as his face pixelated and froze. 'Marcus?'

Kristen shook her iPad, but the connection was gone. The limits of technology, even in this modern age. She messaged Marcus to say she hoped they could try again later.

She received no response that night. At nine o'clock, and against her better judgement, she searched online for *kutkot* until she came across a video showing the ritual. Curious, she clicked play and, a moment later, her screen was filled with a small clearing in a jungle. Several people were standing around, presumably members of a tribe, though they were all wearing Western clothes. A young man, maybe eighteen or nineteen, stooped in the middle of the group, digging furiously into the dirt with a shovel. Kristen watched in fascination as the camera zoomed in on his handiwork. He'd created a small pit, from which the rags of some rotted material poked out from amongst a handful of tree roots. One object that she mistook for a root was a lighter colour than the rest. By the time Kristen worked out it was a human bone, the scene had changed. A bony corpse, complete with skull, now sat against the trunk of a tree. It was partially decomposed and the limbs had clearly been assembled like a nightmarish Guy Fawkes. The corpse was decked out in a beautiful dress and adorned with ornate jewellery. A multigenerational family surrounded it, all smiling and laughing. A child, perhaps nine or ten, was stroking one of the body's arms.

Subtitles at the bottom, the narrator's transcript, explained the *kutkot* was a tribal tradition of digging up loved ones from their graves and dressing and adorning them to honour their memories. The ghoulish scene transitioned to a cave, which showed members of the tribe moving the bones inside while the narrator explained how the dead person was to be venerated before being returned to the earth. *For you are dust and to dust you shall return,* she heard Father Nolan say in her head. She swallowed, hastily closing the video. One thing was for sure. She wasn't going to fall asleep any time soon.

9

As the weeks rolled by, Kristen's life followed a regular, predictable pattern. On Monday mornings, she drove to her local station and boarded a train to Gatwick in time to catch a lunchtime flight to Geneva. At the institute, protests consistently greeted her outside. The crowd of demonstrators seemed to grow a little with each visit, with a few more people holding signs and chanting angry slogans. Still there appeared to be no media interest, which she imagined Harry was probably relieved about. Once inside the institute, Kristen's routine never varied. She was met by a predictably frosty Amanda Tanner in one of the glass cubicle rooms for a fresh fMRI scan. Afterwards, Kristen would spend forty minutes to an hour under a God helmet, just her and Tanner alone in the great white hall. Sessions on Fridays were usually a little shorter. Once completed, Tanner took her for her end-of-week scan, for contrasting. Then came the follow-ups with Doctor Adrian Kemplar. Kristen would spend an hour with him in the so-called aftercare sessions. This was essentially therapy, where Kristen was encouraged to discuss her experiences over the week, and anything else going on in her life. As her trust in the doctor grew, she found herself opening up, often talking at length about her faith. Why she had first joined the church, what it was that she had valued about it. She also shared her vulnerabilities and confusion with him. How she couldn't square her belief in a God who was loving and kind with the unspeakable thing that had happened. Kemplar listened sensitively to it all and took notes, but seemed satisfied overall that the God helmet was not harming Kristen in any way.

She felt little change in herself as the sessions continued to accumulate. Her thought patterns seemed much the same, at least as far as she was able to tell. She still believed in God. And after three weeks had passed, she still regarded herself as a person of faith. She wondered if any of it was going to take. But she also knew the God helmet must be doing *something* to her. After each session, Amanda Tanner would list which areas of her brain they had targeted that day. *Primary visual cortex. Occipital lobe. Extrastriate cortex. Left temporal lobe, right temporal lobe.* And, of course, the regular small electroshocks to the amygdala. Things were happening. She would just have to be patient.

Marcus appeared relieved when Kristen told him about her progress during one of their video calls.

'Maybe this won't work, Kris,' he suggested. 'Maybe the technology won't have the same effect on you.'

She tried not to focus on the hopeful expression on his face. 'Darling, Harry tells me it most likely will.'

'It's just that you used to see the world as bigger and more wonderful than most other people,' Marcus said. 'It was a special gift.'

There he goes again, Kristen thought. He was talking as if her faith was the thing he'd most admired about her now. Like it had been someone else who had belittled it all these years.

'I just don't want you to be like me, Kris,' he said. 'Surely you'd be happier with the comfort of your beliefs?'

But Kristen wasn't sure she agreed. And if he really preferred her to stay as she was, she wanted him to be under no illusions.

'Darling. It's just going to be a matter of time. Harry said for some people it can take a little longer. But the technology works.'

Marcus was quiet for a while. 'Yes,' he said. 'I suppose you're right. Harry knows what he's doing. His machines can no doubt change anyone ...' He gave her a rueful-looking smile. 'Even someone with as strong a faith as you.'

'Darling—'

'But you could still walk away,' he suggested.

She shook her head. 'Marcus, I'm committed to finishing the trial. I promised Harry. He's gone out on a limb for me and it wouldn't be fair to him.'

Marcus sighed. 'It's all right, Kris. I do understand. You want to find peace. Believe me, I know what that's like.'

He reached out a hand towards her, positioning it so it appeared on her screen. Kristen copied him, wishing they really could feel the warmth of each other's fingertips.

'I love you,' he said.

'I love you too,' she said, reluctantly dropping her hand. 'Now come on, tell me more about *Homo Luzonensis* or whoever's bones you're all digging up this week.'

10

A week later, on the first Monday in November, Kristen's taxi pulled up at the institute as usual to find two police cars obstructing the gate, lights flashing. In the field across the road, the crowd of protestors that had become such a familiar fixture were being quizzed by several police officers. She couldn't hear what was being said, but it was clear there were some heated exchanges. Tobias, the German security guard who manned the gate, exited his hut and approached the cab, prompting Kristen to wind her window down.

'Good morning, Mrs Hardy,' he said.

They had become friendly over the last month, and Kristen looked forward to their brief, cordial interchanges.

'Sorry about the chaos,' Tobias said. 'We had an incident here last night.'

'Incident?' she asked, frowning.

'Those crazies broke into the facility,' Tobias said. 'Stole one of our vans and tried to drive it into the building.'

'Oh my God,' Kristen said.

It came out before she had chance to recognise that she had technically blasphemed, another first for her.

'They smashed through the glass,' Tobias explained. 'But

then they set off alarms inside the atrium and drove off in a panic. They torched the vehicle about a mile down the road.'

Kristen was speechless. 'Why on earth would they do something like that?' she said.

'You know what these religious types are like,' he said. 'Every day more turn up, getting more and more aggressive. It really was only a matter of time before someone tried something.'

The taxi driver, hearing this, looked relieved when Tobias offered to escort Kristen from there. The security guard led her around the back of the hut to the walk-through gate in the fence. He punched five digits on a keypad, buzzed her through and walked her across the car park before turning back. Kristen waved him goodbye and made her way to the institute's entrance where she saw that the glass doors were smashed. Harry Dean was standing in front of a line of yellow incident tape talking to a police officer.

'Ah, Kristen,' he said as he saw her approaching. 'Please excuse me for a moment, officer.'

'Harry—'

'I know, terrible, isn't it? Listen, I don't want you to worry,' Harry said. 'We're beefing up our security.'

'How did they get in?' Kristen said.

'Buggers cut the fence,' Harry said. 'At the far side of the site, where there's a CCTV blind spot. Clever, really.'

He shook his head vigorously, his puffy cheeks wibbling. 'God knows what they hoped to accomplish. It's not like we're going to shut our experiments down.'

'Tobias said they burned out the van?'

'Stupid, stupid,' Harry muttered. 'Who did they think they were hurting? That van was full of equipment to be donated to local hospitals, so it's sick people who are going to suffer now. But I'll be damned if I'm going to stop my important research.' He wagged a finger at her. 'Never give in to bullies, Kristen. Ever.'

Kristen nodded, told Harry she was sorry and asked if there was anything she could do to help.

'Just don't let them worry you,' he implored her. 'Please.'

'I won't,' she promised.

'Splendid,' Harry said. 'My apologies, I must get back to my statement. Have a fruitful session today.'

She did her usual fMRI scan, followed by forty minutes under the God helmet and the watchful eye of Amanda Tanner. By the time she was done, she had forgotten all about the break-in. Her only reminder was when her taxi arrived to collect her. As they pulled out through the main gate, the crowd was still there, watched by a now increased police presence. The jeering and chanting were angrier than ever. There seemed to be a lot more signs too. This time, she made a point of not reading them.

That evening, she had another video call scheduled with Marcus. It was just after seven in the morning over there. Her husband was still in bed, in his dressing gown, drinking a coffee with his laptop resting upon his lap.

'Darling,' Kristen said. 'Can you hear me okay?'

'Surprisingly clear,' he said.

She smiled. The film crew had apparently moved to a new hotel closer to their next location and had been rewarded with better Wi-Fi. Even Marcus's room looked like an upgrade; the headboard behind him doubled up as a bookcase full of coffee table books.

'How are *you* doing, Kris?' he asked.

She knew what he really wanted was another update on her psyche, but she skipped straight to telling him what had happened at the institute. Marcus listened carefully to the account, his expression becoming more grave as she talked.

'I don't like this, Kris,' he said when she was finished. 'I'm really worried about your safety.'

She was touched by his concern. 'Darling, it's all right. It's just a bit of protest vandalism.'

'I don't care,' Marcus said. 'It's bad enough thinking about what Harry might be doing to your brain. But on top of that, the idea he could be putting you in danger with these clearly crazy fanatics, it just—'

'I know, Marcus. These people obviously don't like what Harry's doing. But they didn't actually harm anyone.'

'They tried to break into the institute!' Marcus protested. 'What if they'd succeeded? You have no idea what they're capable of!'

She sighed internally. It wasn't like his concerns weren't legitimate.

'Kris,' he said, after a pause. 'If you don't feel safe there any more, I'm sure Harry would understand if you wanted to quit.'

Perhaps he had seen something in her expression, or maybe he was just trying his luck. But Kristen knew she had to make it clear, once again. 'Darling, please. I'm not going anywhere. And there's no need to overreact.'

He gave her a sceptical look.

'It's all right, honestly,' she said. 'The police are on the case. You don't need to worry about me.'

Marcus frowned. 'Are you quite sure about that, Kris?' he said. 'Because from here it looks like you're wading deeper into some dangerous waters.'

'There's no need to worry, darling,' she repeated.

It was the only thing she could think of to say. But she could see in his expression that her husband remained wholly unconvinced.

<h1 style="text-align:center">11</h1>

When Kristen returned to the institute on Friday, the glass doors had been fixed, and she was relieved to see things looked like they had returned to normal. She sat under the familiar God helmet as the cold Amanda Tanner monitored her brain activity from her tablet device. The images today were of spiral shapes and colours, the music, psychedelic pop. Both sensory inputs seemed far too abstract for Kristen to associate with any concepts or ideas, but she wasn't the neuroscientist. As the hydraulic arm of the God helmet lifted off her head, Kristen decided to risk conversation.

'I see the protestors still haven't gone away,' she said. 'My taxi driver this morning told me the break-in made the local news.'

She waited. Tanner sometimes responded to her social overtures while at other times, she fiddled with her tablet, pretending not to hear. By now, Kristen was used to her rudeness, and no longer took it personally. Today, however, she was graced with a response.

'It's almost as if they think we have no business messing with people's spirituality,' the Tech Manager said.

Her sombre tone caught Kristen off guard, and she prompted her for more. 'Do you really think so?'

'Do I really think what?' Tanner replied.

'Do you think the Bennett Foundation has no business … you know. Doing this.'

'I don't know. Maybe you could argue that we have more important things to research. Like actual brain diseases. Religion isn't on top of everybody's list of priorities.'

'But Harry said he thinks this will lead to greater discoveries that will help with other conditions,' Kristen said.

Tanner shrugged. 'We'll have to see, won't we? He's been running variants of this experiment for three years now and I'm not sure we've helped a single person.'

Kristen sensed there was more Tanner wanted to share. 'So you don't agree with this project? Why are you working here then?'

Tanner snapped her head up. 'I joined the foundation, not a single experiment.'

She sounded angry now, and Kristen would not have been surprised if she lost her temper.

'I … Listen, thanks. I appreciate everything you do here for me.'

'Sure,' Tanner said. 'Let's hope it cures some other disorder you didn't know you had, eh?'

She had a friendlier reception from Tobias as she waited for her taxi. 'They arrest anyone yet?' she asked.

The angry mob was still camped across the road. They seemed to have doubled in size, if that were possible, and the placards trebled.

'Not yet, Mrs Hardy,' the security guard said. 'The cops are pretty useless in my opinion.'

He kept his voice down in case the pair of police officers

standing on duty today might hear him. 'I'll be forced to do their job for them, I think,' he added quietly.

'Oh?'

'I have a copy of the security video,' he said. 'Those crazies better watch out.'

He made a V-shape with his index and middle finger and pointed at his eyes, and then at the crowd. Kristen nodded in what she hoped came across as solidarity. As her taxi pulled away, she caught her last glimpse of the demonstration in the rear-view mirror. She thought about all the hundreds of people who would be coming in and out of the institute over the week. People like her, who were willingly subjecting themselves to a machine that had the power to eradicate faith altogether. Were they as safe as they'd like to believe? Was she?

12

That night, instead of going home, Kristen stopped over at a hotel in London and caught the train out to Cambridge on the Saturday morning. She had not seen Bree since the funeral, and they had arranged a long overdue weekend to catch up. Bree picked her up from the station and they drove to the family home on the outskirts of Cambridge. The house was empty when they arrived because Darius had taken Poppy to the cinema, which made Kristen secretly glad. She loved the girl, but the sight of her just reminded her of her loss. If she was being honest, she wasn't looking forward to seeing Poppy over the next day or so. But somehow, she would have to find a way to cope. She sat on a bar stool in the kitchen as Bree fetched a bottle of wine from the fridge.

'So,' Bree said. 'I see you're not a dribbling vegetable at least. Yet.'

'I don't think you're allowed to say that anymore, Bee.'

Bree laughed. 'You know what I mean, Krissy.'

She popped the cork and poured out two glasses. 'Seriously though, has it made any difference?'

'It's hard to say,' Kristen said. 'Harry says neurological

changes might start to become apparent around now, but I just don't know.'

She accepted the drink and clinked glasses with Bree.

Bree took a sip from her own goblet and chewed her lip. 'You know what you should do? Come to Mass tomorrow.'

The suggestion made Kristen's heart turn to lead. 'Oh, Bee, I don't know if I can.'

'Course you can, silly!'

'I haven't even been to church since ...'

Bree planted her glass firmly on the counter. 'Come on, Krissy. This is what you said you wanted. To stop believing, right? What better way to see how that's going? You were part of that church for like, what, twenty years?'

'Fifteen,' Kristen said. 'But I take your point.'

She sighed, feeling a little apprehensive at the idea, though she wasn't sure why.

'Look,' Bree said. 'You don't like it, I'll leave with you. Bring you back here. But it's worth a try. Let's see how much of the bullshit you don't swallow any more.'

She reached a hand across and placed it over Kristen's. Kristen looked at it, then at her. 'Why do you go to church, Bee?' she asked. 'I mean, if you don't actually believe in it all? What's the point?'

'Who said I don't believe?' Bree said.

'Well, you don't seem to care whether any of it is real. You actually seem excited about the idea that I might lose my faith.'

Bree shrugged. 'I don't know,' she said. 'I've been a Catholic since I was little. I married a Catholic. Sundays, I go to church. That's just what I do. I've never really thought about it. Darius believes it more than I do. For me, I just think ... well, why give yourself a headache? You can overthink shit sometimes.'

Kristen smiled. 'Sometimes I envy you.'

Bree waved a dismissive hand. 'So you'll come to Mass?'

Kristen smiled. 'Yes, all right. Let's see how it feels.'

'Goody good,' Bree said, raising her glass.

They were heavily tipsy by the time Darius returned with Poppy a couple of hours later. It made things slightly easier for Kristen who, dulled by the wine, greeted her cheerily. She was even able to ask the girl questions about her life and school, which Poppy answered in her usual skittish way. As the afternoon wore on, however, Kristen's sobriety returned and, with it, the familiar dull ache. Fortunately, Poppy had a sleepover at a friend's house and it wasn't long before Darius whisked her off again. When the car pulled out of the drive, Bree put her arm around Kristen.

'What are you guys doing for Christmas?' she asked.

Kristen frowned. 'I … I don't know. We hadn't …'

'Then you're coming here,' Bree said. 'Get out of that house and come stay with us. We may not have the same square footage, but there's plenty of room.'

Kristen considered this. 'I … appreciate the offer, but I won't persuade Marcus. He'll want to be at home, writing. I know it.'

Bree bit her lip. 'Hm … okay, then we'll come to you.'

'What?'

'You can't be alone, Krissy. I mean, you have Marcus, but you know what I mean. You need noise. *Distraction*. We'll come early, stay all week. Unless …'

Kristen blinked. 'Unless what?'

'Unless you think having Poppy in the house—'

'No, no,' Kristen said, holding up a palm. 'That won't be a problem.'

She wasn't sure that was true, but something in her jumped at the prospect of having Bree right there for her, at the one time of year she'd been dreading since the funeral. It did make sense. Orchard House was spacious enough for all of them to not feel like they were on top of each other. She didn't know what Marcus would say, but she was sure she could persuade him. But was it too much to ask?

'But, Bree, it's your Christmas too,' Kristen said.

'Whatever,' Bree said. 'We'll do our relative visits early in December, then treat your place like a free Airbnb. It's perfect, really.'

Kristen found her eyes watering. 'Really? You really want to be there?'

Bree soft punched her on the shoulder. 'We'll be there with bells on,' she said. '*Christmas* fucking bells.'

A while later, headlights shone through the window as Darius returned. They ordered a takeaway curry and Bree proposed the idea of the visit. Her husband agreed, adding that it would be nice for all of them to be together, if Marcus had no objection. The trio watched movies in the living room. Bree and Kristen ate snacks and topped up each other's wine until Darius turned in at around ten. By the time Kristen went to bed, it was 2 a.m. and she had practically forgotten all about the experiment she'd agreed to.

13

As she shuffled in through the doors of Our Sacred Heart the next morning, Kristen experienced a strange blend of both nostalgia and dysphoria. Her many years attending the church seemed to contradict her sense of dislocation. It was like returning to a childhood home that another family had moved into and redecorated. Some familiar faces in the congregation smiled at her, and she was courteous enough to smile back. But she didn't feel at all connected to them. Father Connolly gave her a friendly wink and mouthed 'welcome'. After that, a kind of muscle memory took over, and she fell into old routines as natural to her as breathing. She found her spot next to Bree as she had done since they were girls. Darius was on the other side with Poppy, who was dressed in her Sunday best. So much of it was still familiar.

Yet, as the Mass got under way, Kristen discovered she was unengaged with the music, and unable to join in the singing. Instead, she felt as though she was watching a live performance of actors in a play. She glanced up at the old pillar and stared at the mural of Mary. It stirred no emotion in her. All she saw was dry paint. Curious, she tried other focal points in the church that she remembered. She cast her eyes to the altar. All she saw was a table with a white cloth on it. Just like any other tablecloth in anyone's kitchen. Connolly's robes too looked, *felt*, like fancy dress. As if he was on his way to a Halloween party. Connolly was still reciting the Mass, but as Kristen studied his lips, it was as though they were just uttering noises. Meaningless sounds for a meaningless ceremony. It was as if everything she had ever loved about church had been somehow stripped of its mystery.

She sensed movement. Bree was nudging her. A queue had formed in the aisle. It was time for communion. Kristen allowed herself to be guided from her pew and waited her turn to receive the wafer from Father Connolly. The priest smiled warmly at her. Instinctively, she held out her tongue as she had done a million times before. Connolly placed the wafer on it and she closed her mouth and eyes, trying to feel the peace this ritual once gave her. But it didn't come. It didn't feel like Christ's body, broken for her. Rather, it was like a cheap supermarket wafer that tasted dry and horrible. Without knowing she was about to do it, Kristen spat the remnants out onto her hand, drawing gasps from some of the congregation.

'I can't do this,' she said to Father Connolly. 'I'm really sorry.'

She wiped her hand with a tissue in her jeans pocket and turned away. She pushed past Bree, Darius and Poppy, then faces old and new in the queue, not stopping until she reached the back of the church. There, she pushed the doors open and stepped outside into the fresh Sunday morning air. It felt good to breathe it in. The doors slammed behind her with dramatic effect. Moments later, Bree emerged.

'Hey, girlie,' she said, placing a gentle hand on Kristen's shoulder. 'You good?'

Kristen nodded. 'It's not real anymore, Bee. I feel like God … isn't there.'

Bree nodded. 'I'll go get Darius and Pops. We'll go back to the house.'

'No, you guys stay,' she insisted.

'Don't be silly. We'll go back next week. We always do.'

As she was about to return inside, Kristen tapped her shoulder and Bree turned back. 'It's not just in there,' Kristen said, pointing at the church. 'I don't think God is anywhere. I don't think … I don't think He exists at all.'

Bree's eyebrows shot up as she considered what Kristen was saying. 'So you think the helmet thing fucking worked?'

Their eyes met as Kristen turned the question over in her mind, knowing that saying it out loud would cement what she was sure she already knew. She took a deep breath. 'I think it fucking worked,' she said.

14

By Sunday evening, Kristen was back in Orchard House again, curled up on her sofa with a cup of tea. The feeling was still with her, the epiphany that everything was different now. She was an *unbeliever*. As she explored this new mindset, she realised she was also experiencing some of the emotions Doctor Kemplar had warned her about. Like embarrassment. She felt foolish for ever having believed with such certainty that there was Someone Upstairs. It was strange to adjust to this new reality, and almost hard to believe that the helmet was doing what Harry said it could in such a relatively short time. She sipped her tea, trawling through her memories to times when she had felt close to God. Events in her life that she had once considered to be His work, she now reframed as being mere coincidences. It filled her with a kind of awful horror. Not the existential angst that she feared, which Adrian had also warned her about, but the realisation that she had wasted so many years believing in something that wasn't there. That she now believed had *never* been there. She even understood why Marcus had mocked her beliefs over the years. Oh God, Marcus. Thinking of him brought home just how much she was missing him. She decided to video-call him and was surprised to catch him awake given it was one in the morning in the Philippines. He was sitting up in bed, his face looking bleary and tired.

'You all right, darling?' she asked him.

'I'm fine, Kris,' he said. 'You?'

'I was just calling to say I miss you.'

And you were right by the way. The God stuff was all a sham. It was all bullshit and I'm sorry I didn't see that sooner. But she said none of this, instead asking after Tim and the rest of the crew.

'Everything's good here,' Marcus said curtly.

He didn't expand, and Kristen didn't press him. She suspected he had more on his mind. She had texted him yesterday to tell him about her experiment with attending Mass. As if to confirm her suspicions, Marcus dived straight in.

'So, what happened at church, Kris?'

She gave him a full account of her experience, going over it slowly so the words could come out right. 'I just felt so … disassociated from it all,' she said. 'It was strange.'

He was quiet for a moment. 'So, Harry's infernal device has finally succeeded in changing you.'

'Darling,' Kristen said. 'We've been over this.' She sighed. 'Look, in a couple of weeks you'll be home. Then you'll see. I'm the same woman you married.'

Marcus closed his eyes and pinched the bridge of his nose. 'Kris, it's late here. Can we talk about this again later? I really have to get some sleep.'

He ended the call, leaving her staring at the black screen and wondering if she might have lost more than just an internet connection.

She was too restless after her conversation to settle, her brain buzzing over Marcus's accusation. She felt uneasy at the thought she had fundamentally changed who she was. Yes, she was on a journey. And, yes, okay, she was changing how she perceived the world too. But so what? Didn't people do that anyway, as they grew and learned more about life? Surely people were more than just the sum of their beliefs? She was still fundamentally *her*, wasn't she? Still Kristen Hardy. Besides, there was no doubt this was already helping her make sense of Abi's death. After all, if no God existed, there was no one to blame. It seemed so much simpler. And she wasn't going to slow this journey down, not even for the man who she loved more than anyone else on earth. Kristen finished the last of her tea and stood up, knowing what she was going to do. She scoured the house, going from room to room, looking for anything that belonged to her previous life. And when she found something, she got rid of it.

Her rosary beads were first. Then her Bible. There were more items than she'd realised, from palm crosses to the old liturgical calendars she kept in the kitchen drawers. Even the silver crucifix was removed from its pride of place on the mantelpiece and put in her box of religious miscellany in the garage. It could all stay there ready to be taken to the dump. The whole exercise took a good couple of hours, but when she was finished, Orchard House was purged of her religious past. She was exhausted, but happy. This felt right, like the next step on the journey. This was her path now, whether Marcus liked it or not.

15

Over the next several days, Kristen felt like a new person. Walking among the various passengers and holidaymakers at the airport, she reflected on how much smaller the world had become compared to a hundred years ago. Advances in science and technology had changed the world so much that someone born in the nineteenth century would barely recognise it. It also occurred to her that all these advances owed nothing of their existence to religion. Flying back on Monday night, she had seen St Paul's Cathedral lit up in the London skyline and thought that, aside from being a testament to great architecture, it served no real purpose. Life seemed perfectly explainable in material terms now. Yes, there was still some mystery as to how the universe began, but Kristen now felt confident that scientists would one day find the answers. She wanted desperately to confide these new ways of thinking in Marcus, to let him know she understood him now better than she had ever had. She needed to win him over. But pinning down the time with her husband to discuss it all was tricky. The shooting schedule seemed to be ramping up. Their calls often had to be rearranged and when they did happen, they felt too short. On

Friday, Marcus called her to say he was still swamped but would be flying home on Sunday as agreed.

'I just need to wrap some things up here,' he said.

It was frustrating, but Kristen wondered whether it wasn't for the best. After all, some things were better discussed face to face.

'I totally understand, darling,' she said. 'I can't wait for you to come home.'

Sitting under the God helmet during her next session, her retinas bombarded with images from the visor and her ears fed classical music, she wondered why Marcus wouldn't want her to embrace these new ideas. After all, wasn't her new, rational self a better soulmate, a better fit?

'I want him to understand that I finally get him,' she told Adrian Kemplar during their aftercare session. 'That I understand how patient he must have been with me all these years.'

She had to hope Marcus would appreciate the positive changes in her once he got to see them first hand.

16

When Sunday arrived, Kristen was both excited and nervous. Marcus arrived back at Orchard House late at night, having insisted on making his own way from the airport and taking the train to their local station in the New Forest.

'It's going to be too late to fetch me,' he'd told her. 'And besides, you're flying back to Geneva in the morning. You need your sleep.'

He was right, of course. Kristen already felt heavy-lidded by the time she heard his taxi pull up outside Orchard House around midnight. Her husband grinned at the sight of her still awake to greet him.

'Happy anniversary, darling,' he said, kissing her cheek.

It wasn't strictly till Wednesday, but this was the start of a week together, one that Kristen hoped would heal some of the issues left unaddressed. Marcus wheeled his suitcase into the corridor.

'Did you get everything done that you needed to?' she asked.

'Yes, I'm all yours for the week,' he said, stepping into the lounge and breathing a deep sigh. 'Ah, home sweet home.'

'Tea, darling?'

'No thanks, Kris,' he said. 'Bed, if you don't mind. I'm feeling rather tired. The jet lag's a killer.'

Kristen nodded. That suited her. All she wanted was to curl up with his arm draped over her.

It was hard to get out of bed the following morning, but somehow she managed it. The day in Geneva felt long and arduous and she missed Marcus the entire time. When she pulled up at the house that evening, Kristen was relieved to be home. She was looking forward to their first proper evening together. She let herself in through the door and called out Marcus's name. Receiving no answer, she wandered upstairs. Her husband's voice was audible through the study door as she passed by. It sounded like he was on the phone. She flung her bag onto their bed in the master bedroom, then used the en suite to freshen up before heading back to the study. She was about to rap on the door when she heard Marcus still talking in a noticeably excitable manner.

'It was the serpent who deceived them,' he said. 'Yes, I see that now.'

Curious and puzzled, she pressed an ear to the wood.

'Yes, yes. Adam's original sin. And, as you say, exile from the garden. I follow.'

She frowned but kept listening.

'Yes, Father,' Marcus said. 'Yes, I see. I wonder that I couldn't before. Thank you.'

He sniffed. Was he crying?

'No, no,' Marcus said. 'No, she won't change her mind. She thinks this will bring her peace … yes, she told me about the communion. I'm sorry, Father. And in front of the very priest who married us. I … oh, I see. Yes. I suppose you are more forgiving than me, Father. I suppose that's your job. Thank you, yes. I will.'

Kristen heard the digital sound clip of a video call ending, and felt an icy finger run down her spine. Marcus, *her* Marcus, had been talking to Father Connolly. About *her*.

17

She could barely process what she'd heard. Instinctively, she moved away, headed downstairs, and plucked out whatever food she found in the cupboards to rustle up a late dinner, trying to make sense of things. Marcus appeared around twenty minutes later.

'Kris! When did you get home?'

She ignored him, continuing to stir her pasta in the saucepan.

'That smells wonderful, is there enough for both of us?'

She refused to look at him, instead asking him outright who he'd been speaking with earlier. He sighed. 'Yes, all right,' he said. 'It was Father Connolly. I've been seeking his … spiritual counsel.'

She stopped, spinning around like a whirling dervish. 'What the hell, Marcus? *You*?'

'I know,' he replied. 'But funny you should mention hell, though.'

'It is?'

'Father says our Abigail is definitely in heaven. Isn't that great news, Kris?'

'Marcus, what are you talking about?' Kristen said. 'You don't believe in heaven. Or hell.'

A potent mixture of anger and shock stirred inside her.

'Well, maybe I should have had more of an open mind,' he said.

'What?'

She felt like she was dreaming. Was this actually Marcus talking? 'I don't believe what I'm hearing,' she said. 'Since when did you start caring what *any* religions teach?'

He slammed a palm down on the kitchen counter, making Kristen jump. 'Since I lost my fucking daughter, Kris!'

The pot continued to boil, pesto sizzling, the spoon lying idle on the counter. Kristen swallowed. In all their years of marriage, she had never seen him lash out like this.

'If there's even the *remotest* chance,' Marcus said. 'That she lives on somewhere, her soul, her spirit ... I have to know.'

His voice became weak and tears formed in his eyes. Kristen almost choked on the words she spoke next. Yet she had to say them. 'Darling. She's gone. You know that, right? Gone forever.'

She took a step forward, placed a gentle hand on his chest. He pushed it off. 'How would you know?' he said. 'You've purposefully allowed them to amputate that part of you that felt the connection with the afterlife. You've been so fucking selfish.'

'Selfish?' she repeated, appalled at what he was saying.

'What if she's looking down on us now?' Marcus continued. 'Wondering why we aren't happy to know she's alive? Instead, you seem to want her to be dead. Maybe the thought of never seeing her again makes you happy.'

She slapped him. To her shame. Part of her knew this outburst came from his suffering; that, as cruel as he was being, he didn't know what he was saying. But it hurt just the same.

'Good!' Marcus said, rubbing his reddening cheek.

'Perhaps I've struck a nerve. Maybe this is some love for your daughter still there, after all.'

'Marcus!'

She screamed his name, flashes of rage rippling through her. Marcus paused, took a deep breath, and appeared to take stock of their situation. He had the good grace to look ashamed.

'I'm sorry, Kris,' he blurted. 'I didn't mean that.'

But Kristen wasn't ready to forgive him just yet. She turned away from him, stirring the sauce with all her might, waiting for him to leave her alone. Eventually, he must have realised she wasn't going to talk to him and he left the room. And her alone with a hundred confused thoughts.

18

She was so angry with him, she elected to sleep in the spare room. But in what passed as their first conversation an hour after the kitchen incident, Marcus insisted he would take it. Kristen raised no objection. He knew better than to apologise again or seek her forgiveness. In the morning, she was jolted awake by memories of what he'd said, and her anger returned. She dressed quickly without showering, wandered downstairs with her phone and found a private space in the garden, where the signal was strong. She video-called Father Connolly.

'Kristen?'

The priest was inside Our Sacred Heart, in the back room where the communion bread and wine were kept. Kristen didn't care about the intrusion; she'd wanted to see him on camera so she could challenge him to his face. 'I need to talk to you,' she said.

Connolly squinted at his screen, and his expression told her he saw she was deadly serious. 'I have morning Mass in fifteen minutes,' he said contritely. 'But we can chat for a short while now if you want.'

She came right out with it. 'Have you been giving spiritual counsel to Marcus?'

Connolly shot her a guilty look. 'Yes,' he admitted.

'How the fuck?' she said, flummoxed. 'When did this start?'

'It was about a week ago,' Connolly said. 'Marcus called me. He said he was studying the Bible. He asked if I could take him through what the church teaches about the afterlife.'

Kristen just stood there, gripping the phone stupidly. *Studying the Bible? Wanting to know about the afterlife?* How could this be the same man she married? But then she recalled Marcus's words the previous evening. *If there's even the remotest chance ... I have to know.*

'I did suggest he talk to Father Nolan,' Connolly continued. 'But I think your husband trusts me because I married the two of you. And, of course, I was the priest who christened Abi.'

Kristen's mind was doing cartwheels. There was a time when Marcus seeking out a priest would have made her happier than she could have imagined. But now it felt like a betrayal. 'You told him Abi was still alive?' she blurted. 'How could you do that to him?'

Connolly looked hurt. 'Because I believe that, Kristen. Don't you?'

She closed her eyes.

'Maybe I did ... once,' she said.

She felt a pang of grief as she continued. 'But I don't think anyone lives on, no. Only in our memories.'

The weight of the pause that followed was palpable.

'Kristen, what's happened to you?' Connolly asked gently. 'Marcus tells me you've enrolled yourself in some kind of scientific experiment – some machine that interferes with your brain?'

She ignored the question. The feeling of being betrayed

returned. 'What the hell were the two of you talking about last night?' she demanded.

'Last night? Marcus was asking me about the Garden of Eden.'

She blinked, confused. 'Eden? Why?'

'I don't know,' Connolly said. 'He seems fixated with the story of Adam and Eve, and the garden in particular. Kristen, I must be honest with you. Whatever's going on between you two, I am grateful that he is seeking answers. And I pray that God helps him find them.'

Kristen bit her tongue. She wanted to tell Connolly to stop speaking to her husband about religion and to mind his own business. But she was just being emotional. She knew deep down she had no right to control who Marcus spoke to, however much she'd like to. 'Look, Father,' she said. 'Whatever you do, please don't give him false hope. We lost a daughter. *He* lost a daughter. He needs to deal with that ... and, frankly, made-up fairy tales aren't going to help.'

19

She avoided Marcus for the rest of the day. When he came downstairs, she took her tea back up to the room. She knew she was being childish, but she wasn't ready to forgive him. In a previous life, she would have been compelled to, of course, but she felt no such obligation now. Marcus knew better than to stir the hornet's nest, so retreated into his space. She soon heard the familiar click of the study door followed by the soft tap-tapping of laptop keys. Her thoughts kept returning to her conversation with Father Connolly. It was clear that Marcus was in deep pain. She might not believe in the supernatural anymore, but it had only been yesterday when she had. What right had she to be angry at Marcus for seeking spiritual comfort? She was like an ex-smoker of faith, wasn't she? A hypocrite of the worst kind. But even though all of that might be true, it didn't absolve Marcus of the cruel words he'd said to her. For that, she needed more time.

They remained apart until the evening, when they passed each other briefly in the kitchen and Marcus risked another apology. Kristen, feeling a little calmer, acknowledged it with a non-committal nod. She cooked a chicken, left him half of it on the counter and took herself off to the bedroom once more. Later, she fell asleep watching her iPad, and woke up in the early hours to find a familiar arm draped around her. She hesitated for a moment, and then squeezed it gently back.

Marcus dropped her at the station early Friday morning. They were back on speaking terms, but she suspected it was a temporary truce, held together by Sellotape. How long before he brought up Abi's still being alive somewhere, and the friction would start all over again? They had tactfully avoided the subject for the last two days. But she was worried it would just be a matter of time. She was glad to be back in Geneva a few hours later, and relieved when the taxi dropped her by the institute's gate. Without her realising it, the place had become a sanctuary of sorts. Even the protests didn't bother her.

Sitting on Adrian Kemplar's sofa, Kristen delved into Marcus's recent odd behaviour.

'It's like we're trading places,' she said, recrossing her legs for the third time since the conversation started.

The psychiatrist nodded sympathetically. 'It's likely a coping mechanism,' he said. 'You told me yourself that Marcus expressed worry about losing you. Perhaps this is his way of trying to get that connection back.'

She shook her head. 'But this isn't like him, Adrian. He's never shown any interest in faith before. This is grief driving him. It must be.'

'Perhaps you mean this isn't like the old him,' Adrian suggested. 'Both you and Marcus are on a journey, and maybe your paths are diverging.'

'That's what I'm afraid of,' Kristen said. 'What if we're

moving so far apart we'll never find our way back to each other?'

Adrian was silent for a moment. 'Do you feel you can't join him on the new path he's on?'

She shook her head vigorously, rejecting the very thought. 'I've come too far,' she said. 'Invested too much.'

'Yes, you have. And has it been worth it?'

She closed her eyes, weighing the question. The world was a cruel and unkind place, she believed. The kind of place where babies were lost, and some children didn't live to see adulthood. But it made a hell of a lot more sense to her than it had ever done. 'Truth always matters,' she said. 'However hard it is to accept.'

Her flight was delayed coming back and it was after midnight when she pulled into the driveway. Marcus had insisted on waiting up for her. He asked her about her day, told her it had rained in the afternoon. The small talk signalled his desire to keep the peace and Kristen was grateful for it. After half an hour of niceties, however, she discovered that her silver crucifix had been replaced on the mantelpiece. Marcus must have found it in the garage and decided to put it back. Why on earth had he done that? Did he think she wouldn't notice? Part of her was tempted to have it out with him. But for the sake of harmony, she didn't say a word. The peace held. Kristen was relieved when she and Marcus enjoyed a wonderful Saturday together, sitting out in the garden, wrapping up warm and drinking tea in the weak November sunshine. Though they barely spoke, the natural rhythm they had always enjoyed as a couple returned. Kristen even allowed herself to think everything would work out and that maybe Marcus's behaviour was no more than a temporary blip. In the evening, he drove them to the Moroccan restaurant in Southampton where he had booked their anniversary dinner. During dessert, he produced a small black box and slid it across the table. Kristen blushed as she opened it. Inside were a pair of sparkling earrings that caught the electric candlelight.

'They're crystal,' he said. 'Fifteen years is crystal, I understand.'

She picked one of the earrings up and touched it to her earlobe.

'They're beautiful, darling. Thank you.'

She put the item of jewellery back carefully and reached into her own bag, producing a gold-coloured envelope. There was no card inside. Marcus detested greeting cards of any kind, which was why she hadn't even given him one on his birthday. He tore the envelope open and removed two printed PDF tickets inside. 'Cancun?'

'Mexico,' she confirmed. 'Just you and me. In January.' She paused, choosing her words carefully. 'We have Christmas to get through,' she said. 'Hopefully having Bree and Darius over will be a distraction.'

Of course, she had omitted mention of Poppy. Marcus had been surprisingly amenable to the idea of hosting, which she had not been expecting. But she knew it wouldn't be easy for either of them having an eleven-year-old in the house.

'The new year could be a new start for you and me,' she said. 'I thought maybe two weeks in the sunshine could help. New beginnings and all that.'

She was weeping, annoyed at herself, but also unable to stop.

Marcus dragged his chair around the table, put his long arms around her and squeezed. 'It's a lovely thought,' he said.

She sniffed and buried her face in his armpit. He was kind enough not to mention she had bought the tickets with their joint account, which she never replenished. He might have made a light joke about it, once, but this was not the time. He must have known what she was trying to do, what she was hoping to save. And by the way he held her, she could tell he loved her for it.

20

They went to bed early and made love for the first time in a long time. Kristen woke up on Sunday morning to an empty bed, with a hangover from the wine she had drunk the night before. She assumed Marcus was in his study and went back to sleep. Later, when she woke again, she was still alone. Her phone told her it was nearly one o'clock. She heard the sound of chatter and laughter. There was a visitor in the house. Puzzled, she dressed quickly and wandered downstairs. In the living room, she found Marcus chuckling at something a young man said. A man dressed in black and wearing a clerical white collar.

'Good morning, Mrs Hardy,' Father Nolan said.

'Darling, did you sleep well?' Marcus asked. 'I've just made some tea. Would you like some?'

Kristen stared dumbfounded at the pair as Nolan raised his cup.

'It's very good,' he said. 'Your husband is quite the brewer.'

Quite the brewer. What in the actual fuck? Kristen wanted to scream. Instead, she opted for something more congenial.

'This is a … surprise,' she said, looking over at Marcus.

'Oh well, I thought it was only polite to invite Father back,' Marcus said cheerily.

He rose from the sofa and sauntered to the kitchen where the teapot sat next to the Aga top.

'Back?' Kristen asked.

'Well, yes, darling,' Marcus said. 'I went to Mass this morning.'

'*You* went to Mass?'

When Marcus turned around he had a glow about his face that she had only seen once before, on a couple of Jehovah's Witnesses who had come to the door. At the time, she had found those other-worldly expressions cultish and unsettling. Now she suspected that she probably had that same glow about her for years and had not been aware of it. One person she had never thought it was possible to see it on was Marcus Tristan Hardy.

'It was wonderful, Kris,' Marcus said. 'I understand now why you always wanted me to go with you.'

'Marcus and I have been talking a lot about our faith this week,' Nolan said, earnestly.

It was as if he expected Kristen to leap for joy at the news. She wanted to grab his ears and shout into one of them that there was no longer any such thing as *our* faith. Marcus poured a cup of tea and wandered over to hand it to her. 'Yes indeed. What does the Bible say, Kris? I was blind but now I see!'

He chuckled again, leaving Kristen to look askance. When he saw she wouldn't take the tea, he looked disappointed. But then he shrugged it off with a smile. 'You know, Father Nolan agrees with everything that Father Connolly said about our Abi. That she's in heaven, Kris. Alive and well and happy.'

'She's with Christ for all eternity,' Nolan piped up. 'A reason to rejoice!'

The young priest's voice seemed to have lost some of its

croaky quality, Kristen thought. Perhaps the kid was excited about his new potential convert.

'You fucking rejoice, then,' she snapped. 'I'll continue to grieve for my daughter who, despite all the things this sincere but misguided idiot might have told you, is gone. She's not in heaven, Marcus. She's lying in the ground at St James's churchyard. You need to wake up to that.'

Unable to stand in the room any longer and be part of this ridiculous charade, she left through the front door, slamming it behind her. She walked out onto the road, glad they were at least a mile from the nearest neighbour and nobody could hear her shouting and think she was the crazy one.

21

Kristen's feet carried her in a direction she didn't quite understand at first. After about a quarter of a mile, it was clear she was heading towards the village. The further she walked, the more it dawned on her that this was not about getting away from the house and from Marcus and Father Nolan. At least, not only about that. She knew then where she was going. She had not visited Abi's grave since the funeral. A better mother might have attended the site fastidiously, of course, bringing fresh flowers every week and keeping the plot tended and neat. But then again, a better mother would have kept her child alive in the first place. She walked the remaining mile to St James's, along the narrow country lane that eventually became the village centre. A small collection of shops including a Post Office stood opposite a defunct red phone box that marked the entrance to the green. On the opposite end was the knee-high stone wall and arched entrance to St James's. Kristen passed through and continued around the back of the church to the graveyard. Many of the gravestones here were over a century old, some adorned with statues of angels. There was a time when she would have been comforted by the depiction of angelic beings standing watch over the departed, but this morning they felt more like gargoyles. She was repulsed by them. Nearest the corner of the graveyard, where the grass was newer and less trampled, stood the simple marble stone that bore her daughter's name. She lowered herself onto the damp turf.

'I'm so sorry, sweetheart,' she whispered to the headstone.

She ran her fingers across the inscription of Abi's name and the dates of her birth and death, then across the message she and Marcus had had carved underneath. *Until We Meet Again*. At the time, Marcus had insisted there be no religious verses so they had landed on this non-specific phrase, which was not from any holy book, making Marcus happy while giving Kristen the chance to express her belief that her daughter would live on. That they all would. Now, those words held no meaning for her. She yearned with everything inside her to be reunited with Abi. But with the numinous absent, the words were empty. Empty words over a plot of ground that would one day absorb the last remaining molecule of her daughter's body. Slowly, Kristen got to her knees and brushed off the muddy leaves from her jeans. *Until We Meet Again*. Once again, her anger turned to sorrow. It all boiled down to grief, didn't it? Marcus was consumed by his. Was it really any wonder that he would want those words to be true? That a person could be so desperate that they could move from being curious about faith to actually attending church? If anyone could understand that, surely it was her.

'I just want to know what this means,' she told him. 'Are you saying you are Catholic now?'

They were sitting in the garden again. When she had finally mustered the courage to return to the house, she found Nolan gone and Marcus at the table reading the Bible.

'As I said, Kris, my eyes have been slowly opened this

week,' he said. 'I can see how maybe there's more to life than just what we can see or hear or touch.'

She blinked hard at him. 'Didn't you once tell me that life was merely chance? Billions of years of evolution, and nothing more?'

Marcus swallowed a gulp of tea, frowning. 'I did,' he conceded. 'And I still know that is true, as a scientist. We are here because of survival of the fittest. Kill or be killed and all that jazz. But perhaps there are more answers to come, Kris. I'm digging deeper into the truth, darling, one hopes deep enough that our daughter can see.'

Except our daughter can't see anything any more, the cynical part of Kristen wanted to say. *The worms are eating her eyes.* But she couldn't bring herself to do it.

That evening, Marcus returned to the Philippines and Kristen spent the night alone in the house. They had agreed to video-call in the week, but she suspected whatever gains they had made may have been squandered. She felt more distant from him than ever.

FIVE

1

The following day, she flew back to Geneva. The God helmet did its usual thing, but Kristen was distracted as the visor delivered the rapid-fire images that flicked across her (*sunrise*) peripheral vision. Her mind was so focused on Marcus attending (*waterfall*) Mass, she only registered the occasional (*mountain*) image as the magnetic currents pushed and pulled on her brain. She wondered whether Marcus was talking to priests in the (*moon*) Philippines and seeking their counsel too (*island*). One thing she was sure of. There was nothing she could say that would put him off this new spiritual quest of his. She felt nothing but pity for him.

Afterwards, she met Harry for coffee in the facility's cafeteria, located on the seventh floor. He explained to her that the next stage would be all about cementing her neurological rewiring. 'We call it the binding phase,' he said.

It would begin the following week, on a Wednesday. Kristen would be required to attend the institute three times a week from then on, significantly increasing her sessions under the God helmet. Harry warned her that all the flying back and forth could also take its toll and she might consider occasionally staying in Geneva overnight. He also offered her a bumbling apology about not being able to provide accommodation at his apartment, which he explained was not especially female friendly. Kristen suspected he felt it might be inappropriate to host his best friend's wife while he was thousands of miles away. But she appreciated his earnestness and thanked him regardless. 'Listen, Harry,' she said. 'When it's all done, is that it? Will my brain stay changed?'

Harry shrugged. 'As I told you from the start, there are no guarantees. It's very possible the change will be permanent. But you may also find the effects wear off over time.'

Kristen nodded. She had gone into this knowing that, while the trials had mostly been successful, there were no long-term studies on those whose neurology had been significantly altered. She was worried, though. She happened to like her new, sceptical mind. 'How soon could the effects wear off?' she asked nervously.

Harry shook his head. 'I couldn't say,' he said. 'A year. Two. Unfortunately there's no way to know for sure.'

'But I'll be able to come back here for a top-up, right?' she asked, only half joking.

Harry smiled weakly. 'I'm afraid not. I do hope you don't feel I've misled you, Kristen. I know you've been in such pain.'

'You've been nothing but honest throughout,' Kristen said. 'I'm grateful, Harry. Truly.'

She reached out and clasped his hands. Harry looked forlornly at them. She let go, softly. 'I owe you,' she said. 'I always will. However this turns out.'

The rest of her week fell into its normal routine, but her video calls with Marcus concerned her. He appeared constantly tired. Kristen worried that returning to work was too much for him. On top of the demands of the shoot, he was obviously preoccupied with new questions about spirituality and the afterlife. She was too scared to ask whether he was still seeking counsel from priests. Instead, she gently suggested that perhaps he could ask Tim to send him back to the UK early. But Marcus insisted he was doing fine. 'Things are going really well, Kris,' he said. 'I need to stay here until my work is finished.'

He smiled at her in the dim light of his hotel room and told her not to worry. That he loved her. She said it back, of course, but all she could think about was having him home again. Christmas felt a very long way away.

2

On Wednesday, she made her first midweek visit to Geneva and officially started the next phase. The hydraulic arm hummed as it gently lowered the God helmet over her face.

'So, ready for the next step?' Amanda Tanner asked.

Kristen confirmed that she was. The visor extended out over her eyes, and the show began. She'd been told the new sessions would be ninety minutes and to prepare accordingly. But it didn't take long to notice that the audiovisual stimulus was far more condensed. The visor was feeding her hundreds of new images, all collaged together. The tempo of the music changed constantly, sometimes slow, sometimes fast. Sometimes it was a specific genre, like rock and roll or instrumental piano. Other times, that incessant drum beat. All while the magnets whirled around her skull. She told herself to relax, and for a while she did. But towards the end of the session, she started to feel sick. And then she *was* sick. All down her blouse. As the helmet was raised off her head, she saw Tanner holding out a damp flannel.

'Sorry,' the Tech Manager said. 'I didn't see you go till it was too late. You're being subjected to more currents now and the intensity can have an effect. Not everyone reacts to it, but it's also not uncommon.'

Kristen took the damp towel gratefully and dabbed at her clothes.

'Don't worry, the feeling will go after a while,' Tanner said gently. 'Do you have a change of clothes?'

'No,' Kristen said.

'I'll fetch you a white T-shirt. You'll need something to wear for the afternoon session.'

Kristen blinked dumbly at her. 'Afternoon?'

'Didn't Harry tell you? You'll be doing two additional hours after lunch. But you'll be done by three thirty.'

Kristen was confused. 'Harry told me I'd have to do three times a week. But he didn't say anything about double sessions.'

'It's part of the binding phase,' Tanner said.

Kristen pulled out her phone. 'I didn't know,' she said. 'I'll have to change my flight. How long will I be doing double sessions for?'

'The next three and a half weeks,' the Tech Manager said. She smiled, adding, 'But after that you'll be all done.'

After rescheduling her flight and adjusting her taxi pick-up time, Kristen sought out the institute's cafeteria. There she enjoyed a hot pasta lunch that replenished her emptied stomach. When she returned to the hall, Tanner was waiting. For the next two hours, she endured her second intensified session under the God helmet. She experienced more nausea and dizziness but the Tech Manager's lab-side manner was surprisingly empathetic. At one point, she even stopped the machine to allow Kristen to take a break and pop to the ladies' room. When she returned, Tanner handed her a box of nausea tablets.

'These should help,' she said gently.

She was so much nicer than her usual self that Kristen wondered if perhaps she had a secret twin sister.

That evening, she was supposed to have her regular chat with Marcus, but he didn't pick up when she called him. She didn't think anything of it, assuming he might have fallen asleep because of the time difference. It had happened before. But then he surprised her with a text shortly after midnight.

Kris, the Great Being exists.

She frowned and sent him a single question mark back.

Kristen heard nothing back from Marcus all through Thursday, though when she looked, she noticed he hadn't bothered to check his messages. On Friday, she returned to Geneva where, once again, the God helmet made her sick to her stomach. Tanner assured her it was all normal, reminding her that this was a programme meticulously engineered by Harry and his team of neuroscientists. Kristen would have loved to have had that reassurance from Harry himself. Rather disappointingly, she hadn't seen him since they'd last shared coffee together, despite this being her third visit this week. Still, Tanner was correct. She needed to trust the unique electromagnetic symphony that was playing inside her brain. And Kristen did. But that didn't mean she wasn't relieved when the helmet finally came off.

Somehow, she got through the afternoon session, which seemed to go for much longer than the promised two hours. She thought she spotted a recurring motif in the visuals, a series of geometric shapes that formed mandala patterns. Between them, she believed she saw other shapes too – a lotus flower, a dove. The music was back to classical, a violin concerto she didn't recognise but which had a screeching quality that unsettled her. Either that or it was just the onset of more nausea. The sensation of an invisible finger pressing on her brain was much stronger too, though she still didn't feel any physical pain. When the session finished, she felt proud of herself for not throwing up. The much softer face of Amanda Tanner even congratulated her for it.

Hours later, after landing at Gatwick, she switched her phone back on and discovered a flurry of texts waiting for her, all from Marcus. She spent the train journey from the airport studying them. But the more she looked, the more confused she became.

Kris, the Great Being is real

Another read:

The Great Being is truth

There were ten of these, mostly variants of each other. She scrolled up and down through the messages, puzzling over them. Was Marcus okay? Her phone sat heavy in her hand. She had no idea how to respond. As though Marcus could sense she was reading them, her phone pinged again, this time with a slightly more ominous message:

Be warned, Kris. The Great Being cannot be mocked.

A little perturbed, Kristen typed a message of her own back.

Marcus, we need to talk.

3

She pulled the Land Rover into the driveway and headed inside. Instead of making tea, however, she retrieved a bottle of red and poured herself a large tumbler. She figured she might need it. Marcus had texted her back, suggesting they have a call at eight thirty, UK time. Kristen gulped the wine down and filled herself up again, taking the bottle into the living room. She set her tablet up at the right angle on the armrest and waited a few more minutes until it was time. When Marcus appeared on her screen, he was in the hotel bed, the same head-board-bookshelf behind him. But tonight, he sat cross-legged, like a mystic yogi. He beamed when he saw Kristen. 'Darling!'

'Marcus, what's going on? Why did you send me all that stuff?'

Marcus looked perplexed for a moment, and then his face brightened again. 'Oh, of course. I should have told you, Kris. I've seen the Great Being!'

Kristen had to force herself to swallow her wine. 'You've seen what?'

He laughed. 'I know. Not words you thought I'd ever say.

I get it. But it happened one night, I was meditating on the garden—'

'Garden?'

'Of *Eden*,' Marcus said as though it was obvious. 'I was caught up in the story, the *mythos* if you will. The meaning of the serpent, original sin et al. Father Connolly helped me to understand what some of these symbols mean. But then I realised that it was all about the fruit.'

'What?'

'The Great Being walked through the garden in the cool of day, you see. Adam and Eve, *homo sapiens*, just wanted to eat. But it was up to the Great Being whether they ate or not. Whether they had *permission*. Do you see?'

Kristen didn't know what to say. It appeared from his expression that Marcus could tell that she didn't see.

'Am I going too fast, Kris? I apologise. I've had a number of epiphanies, darling.'

Kristen swallowed more wine. Watching Marcus continue to speak at such a rapid pace made her wonder if he'd taken something. 'Darling,' she said, slowly and very carefully. 'I don't think you're well.'

'Nonsense,' Marcus said. 'I've never been more in my right mind. The Great Being is real, Kristen. Don't you see what that means? It means there is One who has the power over death and life.'

'Darling, is Tim there?' she said. 'May I speak to him?'

Marcus laughed. 'I see you're scared, Kris. I was too. But you don't need to be afraid.'

Kristen shook her head fiercely. 'Darling, there's no such thing as a *Great Being*. Take it from me. I know better than anyone what it is to finally come to terms with that.'

He snorted. 'You haven't come to terms with anything,' he said. 'All you've learned is how to commit blasphemy!'

He leaned forward and ended the call. Kristen was stunned. Did he really just use the word *blasphemy*? She called him back, but he didn't answer, apparently too angry with her.

Marcus's strange behaviour left her head spinning. She scrolled through her contacts and found Tim Barnes's number. Unlike her, he was there on the other side of the world with her husband, in the same hotel. Maybe he could help. She wrote him a message:

Tim, it's Kristen. Sorry if I woke you up, I know it's super early there. Just wanted to ask if you would mind checking in on Marcus? I'm a little worried about his mental health.

As soon as she sent it, she wondered if she was betraying her husband. Whatever he was going through was his own private affair, and perhaps she shouldn't be involving others. But her concern for him was too strong for her to do nothing. She was relieved when she saw Tim was awake and already typing a response.

Sure, Kristen. Happy to.

She breathed a sigh of relief and then heard another ping.

Hope all is well with you.

That's debatable, she thought, but replied that everything was fine. She hoped it wouldn't be long before he talked to Marcus. Given his strange ramblings, the sooner the better in her opinion.

She slept fitfully, leaving her phone on in case Marcus called her back. She heard the ping of a text message, but when she rolled over to check, she saw it was from Tim.

Hi Kristen. I spoke to Marcus. I don't know exactly what's going on with him, but he says he just needs to be left alone for a while so he can process some things. It's not an ideal situation, of course, but I'm trying to be as supportive as possible considering what he (and you) have been through. I feel like I should leave him be while he works through whatever this is. I don't know if I've helped but I'm not sure what else I can do. Sorry.

So am I, Kristen thought. She was a little disappointed by Tim's lack of concern. But perhaps whatever conversation he'd had with Marcus had not involved any mention of Great Beings.

Eventually succumbing to the early dawn, Kristen rolled out of bed to make tea. She kept trying Marcus, but he continued to ignore her calls. She was still thinking about how to help him when it occurred to her that there was one other obvious person she could ask. Despite being just as far away from the Philippines as she was, maybe Harry could help. She doubted Marcus would listen to her, but perhaps his best friend could convince him that his new-found faith and the fantasies that accompanied it were clearly the result of a grieving father's despair. She decided she would discuss her concerns with Harry in person when she next saw him at the institute.

<h1 style="text-align:center">4</h1>

Marcus continued to snub her for the rest of the weekend. She went to bed Sunday night half concerned, but also half angry at him. On Monday morning, she still couldn't decide which feeling dominated as she flew back to Geneva. The first thing she did when she arrived at the institute was ask for Harry at reception.

'I'm afraid he's been off sick for a while,' the receptionist said. 'Is there anything I can help you with?'

Kristen sighed and politely shook her head. She would just have to wait, she supposed.

That night, back in the New Forest, her tired brain tried to figure out how to write a conciliatory message to Marcus. Her anger at his silence had turned once again to worry. She'd barely started composing her draft when Marcus messaged her instead, asking how her day had been. Such ordinary, everyday spousal concern might have comforted Kristen, offered some reassurance that things might be back to normal, were it not for the follow-up message.

Kris, the Great Being has the power over life and death

On Tuesday morning, she woke frustrated and confused. Marcus had not answered her when she had called him back, instead fobbing her off with a text that promised to call in the morning. Eventually, he did, but it was closer to two o'clock in the afternoon, around 10 p.m. his time. His face appeared on screen, looking paler than usual.

'Marcus?' she began.

'The Great Being will show you, Kris,' he said. 'So you'll know the truth.'

Even in the limited light of his hotel room, she could see a wild glint in his eyes.

'He'll give you two signs,' he said.

'Signs?' she asked. 'What are you talking about?'

'You'll see, darling.'

'See what?' She was feeling exasperated by him now.

'First, the heavenly chorus,' Marcus said. 'Then the angel in bright raiment.'

'What?' She heard a sound, perhaps a voice outside the door. Tim, maybe? Or one of the other members of the production crew. 'Marcus?'

'I have to go,' he said, and cut the call.

A few moments later, her phone lit up.

Heavenly chorus. Angel in bright raiment. You'll see

Overwhelmed, she called Bree and spilled her heart out about her husband's behaviour. Her best friend reacted with her usual sensitivity and tact.

'Woah, he sounds like he's going properly mental,' she said.

'Bree!'

'I'm just saying. Have you thought about calling his GP?'

'What's his doctor going to do from England?' Kristen asked. 'He's stuck in that hotel, losing the plot with no one to help him. He won't even talk to his producer.'

'You could fly out there,' Bree suggested. 'You've got the money.'

That much was true. But as concerned as she was, Kristen couldn't leave her obligations in Geneva. 'I'm on the last part of the trial,' she said. 'I can't do that to Harry.'

'Well, what about Harry?' Bree asked. 'Can he talk some sense into him?'

'I've tried to reach him,' Kristen said. 'He's been off sick, apparently. I really need him to be there tomorrow.'

She hoped he would be. It was starting to feel like she was running out of options.

5

After Wednesday morning's session, she made her way to Harry's office, hoping the walk from the hall to the lifts might dispel some of the residual nausea. But in the end it wasn't worth the trip. No one answered when she knocked on the door. She'd received no response to the gentle checking-in text she'd sent Harry yesterday either. Maybe the poor man was genuinely bedridden. He must have his reasons for not getting back to her.

She stood outside the institute's gates later that afternoon, waiting patiently for her cab. Tobias was off duty today, so she was alone with her thoughts, which were soon interrupted by yet another message from Marcus.

Kris, have you seen the signs yet?

She swallowed, not wanting to reply, and slipped the phone back inside her bag. Across the road, the demonstrators were gathered as normal. There was still a police presence monitoring them, and none still dared cross over. For a paranoid moment, Kristen imagined that Marcus had joined their ranks, that he was somehow involved in the campaign against the institute. She envisaged him among the crowd, angrily decrying the experiments the Bennett Foundation were conducting. Then she took a breath. Her husband might be going through something deeply strange and personal, but he was not some crazed religious fundamentalist. But even as she thought it, she was no longer sure she believed it to be true.

On Thursday, she woke up to another one.

Don't be afraid, Kris. The angel is just a messenger. They all have been, since the beginning.

'Goddammit, Marcus!' she shouted, throwing her phone across the room.

She went to the bathroom and used the time to calm down before returning to retrieve the device. She took a breath and called. Marcus did not pick up, playing whatever stupid game he was playing. She sent him a message:

Darling, I'd like you to see a doctor.

There must be one at the hotel.

Please will you call them, let them take a look at you?

She saw the ticks that meant he had read it. Then dancing dots as he wrote one back.

The heavenly chorus will be first.

She closed her eyes and sighed. He was becoming increasingly lost in this fantasy. What if he couldn't snap out of it? He needed to make peace with the fact that their little girl was gone forever. That was what she was doing. What she was still doing.

The graveyard at St James's was misty this morning, the night's fog not quite lifted. The extra chill in the air made her glad she'd worn her thick wool coat. Kristen laid the lilies she'd bought at the village florist against the headstone and knelt down on one knee. She wondered if taking Marcus here would bring him the closure he needed. She made herself a promise that when he came home, she would insist they visit the grave together. His desperate grief was crushing him, both in spirit and mind. She would do whatever it took to help him. Resolved, she stood up to leave but something unexpected caused her to shiver – and look around her. The graveyard was empty, but … she swore she heard singing. Far off, like a distant choir. Like a *heavenly chorus*. *No*! She needed to get a grip. She took a few steps, but as she neared the gate, the chorus started up again, causing her to spin around. Then it was gone. Nothing. Just gravestones and fog. Wait, there it was again! Faint. Lyrics muted and unintelligible. It was impossible to tell where the sound originated from. She clutched the front of her coat and hurried away, back towards the main road, and home.

That night, she slept uneasily again. She dreamed of a bright white cloud, descending from the sky over an ancient desert city that she recognised as Jerusalem.

6

In the morning, she made herself a strong coffee to counteract a night of half insomnia. She had been filled with trepidation about waking up to more of Marcus's messages, but there hadn't been any. The train journey to the airport was long and arduous, and she wondered how on earth she was going to get through the day. A familiar flight and taxi ride later, she was back at the institute. She made a beeline for Harry's office but once again found it empty. Harry had still not responded to her, and she'd given up leaving voicemails. He had to have his reasons, but this was getting ridiculous. As she returned to the lifts, she considered calling Marcus's parents in Spain. But she was reluctant to. It wasn't only that she didn't want to worry them, though she didn't. She simply didn't think they'd be able to help. Marcus had a familial but stand-offish relationship with them at best and her intuition told her he would dismiss their concerns just as he had done hers. She knew who her husband would listen to. But unfortunately he was nowhere to be seen.

• • •

She reported to the main hall, where she spent the morning dose of ninety minutes beneath the God helmet.

'Feeling okay?' Tanner asked when they were done.

Kristen gave her a thumbs-up, but it was a lie. The nausea was as bad as ever, even with the pills. 'By the way, any word on Harry?' she asked. 'Is he still sick?'

'As a dog, apparently,' Tanner said. 'He emailed the department yesterday. Some kind of virus. He said he hopes to be back in next week. But I guess we'll see.'

Yes, and we'll see if he ever replies to me, Kristen thought.

The afternoon session was hard on her again. The visor spun a medley of spirals that she was half sure kept forming the infinity symbol, accompanied once again by the rhythmic drumming. After the first hour, the anti-sickness tablets stopped working, and she reached for the emergency vomit bag Tanner had given her. She filled it with the remnants of the chicken salad she'd had for lunch. The God helmet whirred off her as Tanner rubbed her back soothingly.

'I'm so sorry,' the Tech Manager whispered. 'You're doing really well, Kristen.'

Who are you and what have you done with Amanda? she wondered.

Her aftercare session came next.

'How are you responding to the helmet?' Adrian Kemplar asked. 'I understand they've recently increased your exposure time?'

'Some nausea,' she said. 'But nothing I can't handle.'

'Good,' the psychiatrist said. 'Anything on your mind this week you'd like to talk about?'

Kristen sighed. She told him about Marcus's escalation of behaviour, and showed him some of the texts he'd sent her.

The doctor was taken aback. 'I … I didn't realise it was this serious.'

'I'm worried, Adrian,' she said. 'It's like he's having a breakdown or something.'

'It is concerning.'

'I just don't know what to do, short of flying out there myself.'

Adrian nodded. 'How long is he out in the Philippines for?'

'He's due home for Christmas,' she said.

The doctor was quiet for a while, thinking. 'What about Father Connolly?' he finally said. 'Didn't you say he was the first person Marcus reached out to when he started thinking about spiritual things?'

Kristen confirmed that he was.

'You said Marcus trusts him. Maybe he could ask the priest for help.'

She bit her lip, thinking it over. While she had hardly been keen on Connolly getting involved again in Marcus's strange religious awakening, she was also out of options. And Marcus did seem to trust him. It was probably worth a try.

She called Connolly on the way to Geneva airport and told him what had been happening.

'Visions of angels?' the priest said. 'Hearing the audible voice of God?'

Now that she confided in him, she wondered if his vocation meant he would automatically be inclined to believe Marcus's claims. But his response surprised her.

'Listen, Kristen,' he said gently. 'I've been doing this job a long time. I've seen parishioners claim to hear the voice of God, and some who see visions. Sometimes, I believe it's God behind it, but there are definitely other times when it's clear that the person needs medical help. I can hear the concern in your voice and I understand why you'd be worried.'

Kristen felt hugely relieved, and then guilty. 'Look, Father, I know I was angry with you last time we spoke, and I'm sorry. But I'm really worried about him.'

'I understand,' Connolly said. 'I'll call him, see if I can get him to talk to me. Leave it with me, okay?'

'Thank you, Father,' Kristen said. 'I really appreciate it.'

'Of course,' Connolly said.

She hung up and allowed herself, rightly or wrongly, to feel a modicum of relief.

7

Marcus broke his latest bout of silence and called her late Saturday morning. He was holding the phone so close to his face, his hazel eyes seemed to stare right through her.

'Darling?' she said, turning her own camera on. 'Are you okay?'

He frowned. 'Why wouldn't I be, Kris?'

She swallowed. 'You haven't been answering my calls.'

He snorted. 'And were any of them to tell me that you've witnessed the signs?'

Kristen was quiet. She didn't want to tell him about her recent experience in the churchyard. She didn't want to encourage him. 'No,' she said. 'I'm afraid not.'

'Then I haven't missed anything, have I?' he said, irritably. 'Anyway, we're speaking now, aren't we? So what is it you wanted to say?'

She inhaled. 'Darling, these messages you keep sending. The things you're saying. You're really worrying me. I think you need help.'

He laughed. 'Is that why you asked Father Connolly to check in on me?'

'I … yes.' There was no point in denying it, she thought. 'Are you angry?'

'Oh, no, Kris. Why would I be? Priest, imams, shamans … they're all emissaries. I had a long and fruitful conversation with the good priest. I told him what I'm telling you. The Great Being holds the power of life and death.'

Hearing him repeating this only upset Kristen further. 'Darling,' she said. 'What happened to your reason? Doesn't all this seem at odds with everything you always told me?'

There was a silence. After what felt like a long period of time, she spoke again. 'Darling, please listen—'

'No, you listen, Kris. Harry's machine has made you forget what your soul once knew was true. But the Great Being has told me you will come around. He'll send the angel tonight. I recommend you fall before him and beg for the Great Being's mercy.'

The screen blacked out as he abruptly ended the call.

'Marcus?'

But he was gone. This time, she didn't bother calling him back.

Father Connolly rang her next. 'Kristen,' he said. 'I thought you should know, I have spoken to him.'

'I know,' she said. 'He told me.'

'We talked for over an hour,' Connolly said. 'But honestly? He was mostly just rambling. He told me some kind of divine being has been communicating with him.'

'What do you think is happening to him?' she asked.

The priest hesitated. 'I wish I knew. All I can tell you for certain is that he believes it's very real.' His tone became more sombre. 'As to his claims of having visions and revelations from this so-called being … I've been doing this job for over forty years and I've never seen quite this kind of … hysteria.'

Hysteria. That was exactly the right word for it. She was

relieved that Father Connolly had confirmed it. 'What can we do?' she asked. 'There must be some kind of help for him?'

As soon as she said it, she wondered whether to tell the priest the whole truth. That Marcus was not the only one potentially seeing and hearing things. But she didn't want to muddy the waters.

'There's only so much I can do from thousands of miles away,' Father Connolly said. 'I did try and talk to him, but he was too incoherent. I might have better luck in person. When is he coming home?'

'They're all flying back just before Christmas,' Kristen said.

'Then perhaps I can visit him at the house,' Father Connolly said. 'If that would be okay with you?'

'Of course,' she said. 'I'd be grateful for anything you could do. And he does seem to trust you.'

'Yes, he kept referring to me as an emissary, as though I were some wise holy man or guru,' the priest said. 'But I think he's in a different place from when he first contacted me. Then, he was interested in Catholicism. But whatever he believes in now isn't any mainstream religion that I know. If I'm being honest, I'm worried about him.'

Kristen recalled Marcus's creepy warning before he'd hung up on her, and sighed. 'You and me both, Father,' she said.

8

She was convinced she wouldn't get to sleep that night, but she did. When she slipped into the bed at around ten, instead of her brain ticking over, she found her eyelids drooping. A sign of exhaustion. Not only was she flying to Geneva every other day and enduring the God helmet sessions, but the situation with Marcus had completely drained her. It wasn't long before the bliss of darkness took her.

The singing woke her up. She sat up slowly, rubbing her eyes and adjusting to the darkness of the bedroom. It sounded like it was coming from the forest outside. She shuffled out of bed and staggered to the bedroom window. The back garden was dark, and the silhouette of the treeline beyond the field somehow even more opaque, like the vacuum of a black hole. She pressed her face against the glass and shut her eyes, trying to listen. There. A distant choir. Was she going mad? She didn't think so. If this was an audible hallucination then it was a good one. A bright light appeared at the periphery of the garden, just out of view. The golden-yellow tint ruled out the pure white security spotlight that occasionally turned on whenever stray foxes or badgers wandered in front of its motion sensor. She couldn't see the light's origin point, however. Curious but cautious, she wandered slowly downstairs. Through the glass doors that led to the garden, she had a better view, but the mystery only deepened. The light was coming from one spot, an oval-shaped aura that … except it wasn't an oval, not exactly. It was a figure, a man in golden light, dressed in golden robes. *Bright raiments,* her mind said, before she had a chance to stop it. Majestic wings expanded out and up from the being's back, like a canopy unfurling in the gentle night breeze. Overtaken by fear (*awe,* her mind said), Kristen allowed her feet to somehow keep carrying her forward. Something was compelling her to get a closer look. She unlocked the patio door, turned the handle and stepped out into the night. And froze.

The figure was staring directly at her. Though its body was golden, its face looked as though it had been meticulously carved from marble, like a classical Greek statue. Pupil-less eyes fixed on Kristen and its mouth had upturned curves on the corner of its lips that made it impossible to tell snarl from smile. The hairs on her neck prickled and her atavistic instincts took over. She bolted back inside, slamming the door behind her, and sprinted for the kitchen. Though it was bathed in darkness, she could make out the set of knives on the island counter. She reached for the largest and sharpest, ready to whirl around if the being chose to follow her into the house. For a moment, she was convinced she heard heavy footsteps across the wooden floor, but it was just the pounding of her heart. She took a deep breath and exhaled, tried to slow her heart's rhythm so she could hear better. With as much stealth as she could muster, she crawled past the island and dared to peer around, into the living space. She hadn't switched on any lights on her journey downstairs, which meant only the dark shapes of furniture were visible. But it also meant she could tell straight away that there was no light emanating from inside. She sucked in air and summoned the courage to step back through the living room. The knife was clasped firmly in her hand, which she held defensively in front of her. It might have offered some reassurance if her arm wasn't trembling so much. A few more considered steps took her to the edge of a sofa, where the garden was fully visible.

There was nothing but inky black darkness. She ran to the door and double locked it, not daring to stare too long at the outside world. She was grateful all the other windows and doors were locked. She sprinted back upstairs and closed the bedroom door behind her. Her hand, still holding the knife, trembled, and her chest rose and fell in rapid succession. She glanced at the window and rushed over to shut the curtains. As if that would keep out the ... the what? Creature? Angel? But whatever the nature of that being was, there was one word that also described it truthfully. *Intruder*. She scooped up her phone on the dresser and called the police.

9

Several years earlier, a mobile police station had been set up in nearby Willowdale to cover the local rural catchment without needing to draw resources from Southampton. Tonight's responders, a woman and a man, arrived in less than twenty minutes. They introduced themselves by name, but in Kristen's anxious state, she forgot them immediately. She invited the officers into the kitchen and hastily recounted her story. Though initially sympathetic, they became visibly sceptical when Kristen described the appearance of her intruder.

'Angel wings, eh?' the female officer asked, scribbling in her pocket notebook. 'Like, as in fancy dress?'

'I know how it sounds,' Kristen said. 'I'm just telling you what I saw.'

The male officer, in his thirties with a ginger beard, folded his arms. 'And his clothes were glowing, you say?'

He challenged her with a stare. She started to regret her decision to call. Not that she could blame them for doubting her story.

'Can you show us where you saw this man?' the other officer asked.

Kristen ignored her accusatory blue eyes and escorted them through to the living room, pointing to the glass doors. 'He was standing out there,' she said.

The male officer opened the patio door and took a few steps out into the garden, which activated the automatic security spotlight. The patio slabs and surrounding glass were instantly flooded with bright, white light. But it was the pizza stove the policeman was most interested in.

'Would you say he was about here?' he asked, pointing directly at the stove.

Kristen's heart sank. In the spirit of wanting to be honest, she had to be straight with them about this too. 'Yes,' she admitted.

She squinted at the stove. The vertical pipe was around the same height as the angel had been. The female officer stepped out into the security light too, looking back at Kristen. 'And you said the intruder didn't move from this spot,' she said.

Kristen got the point. Now that she looked closer at the stove, she saw that it lined up with the rowan tree that grew by the hedge. Branches protruded from either side at the top. Seen from the right angle, they might well resemble wings. But that didn't fully explain it. For one thing, the security light had not been on. It had been the angel who was brightly lit, while the garden remained in inky blackness. She was certain of it. But she dared not say so. The last thing she wanted was for them to consider making a psychiatric referral.

'You know, maybe I did make a mistake,' she said.

'We'll take a look around anyway, if that's okay,' the man said. 'To be sure there's no one here.'

They returned several minutes later, having walked the borders of the garden, informing Kristen there had been no sign of forced entry.

'That outside light is pretty bright,' the male officer said.

'It might have dazzled you, caused you to see spots or things that weren't there.'

'Yes,' Kristen said. 'Now that I think about it, perhaps that's what happened.'

The officer nodded as his partner placed a hand on her shoulder. 'It's better to be safe than sorry,' she said. 'Please don't hesitate to call us if you see him again, okay?'

Yeah, so you can lock me up for sure, Kristen thought. She watched them get into their car, whose blue lights were still silently winking. The tyres bit into the gravel and they headed off towards their next call. Stove or no stove, Kristen *knew* what she had seen. It had been no trick of the light. Which only made her wonder if she was hallucinating things. Because if she was, she could think of at least one obvious explanation.

10

True to form, Harry did not pick up. She felt like screaming. He was the only one who might have an answer for her. After all, it was his God helmet that had been screwing with her neural pathways these last three months. She found it hard to believe tonight's episode wasn't connected. It was almost 3 a.m. now, which made it four o'clock in Switzerland. She hung up and went to bed determined to try again first thing. The adrenaline dump from her body was like a sedative in her veins.

Sunday morning arrived as dull and void of miracles as any other. Kristen was relieved to discover nothing but a plain old pizza stove standing in the garden. She kept trying Harry every hour or so, and kept failing. To distract her preoccupied mind, Kristen cleaned the house from top to bottom, listening to podcasts on her phone, working up a sweat. She took a much-needed nap around two but was woken by the sound of a text thirty minutes in. It was Marcus.

I know you saw the angel

She was afraid to talk to him, anxious it would send her over the edge – that by admitting to what she had seen, Marcus would somehow drag her into the dark vortex of his own delusions. She was also worried they might be sharing some kind of dissociative episode. She remembered how Marcus used to refer to religious services as mass hysteria, people effectively hypnotising each other into believing things they ordinarily would not. Had she and Marcus somehow formed such a bond? Her phone pinged again.

Repent, Kris. Before it's too late.

'Oh fuck off,' she said.

She put the phone down on the kitchen counter where it rang moments later, startling her. But then she saw whose name was on the screen.

'What's happening, Krissy? You haven't replied to my messages.'

Kristen closed her eyes and sighed. 'Oh God, Bee, I'm sorry,' she said. 'Lots more crazy stuff going on.'

'Any word about Marcus? Are you sending him to the looney bin or what? What's the latest?'

Kristen laughed darkly. 'He might not be the only one who needs a straitjacket.'

'Why's that, hon?'

Kristen brought her up to speed. It wasn't easy. She was worried her best friend would think she had lost the plot. And Kristen wouldn't blame her if she did.

'A fucking angel, are you kidding me?' Bree said. 'What the fuck did you do?'

'I called the police,' Kristen said. 'But that was a mistake. I think they're convinced I was making it up.'

She felt hot tears on her cheeks and realised she was crying. 'Bree, I'm scared. What if something's actually wrong with me? What if that God helmet did something to me?'

'Hey, hey, girlie. Don't freak out. You're still you, right? I mean, you know your own name and where you are and shit, right? You know who I am.'

Kristen wiped away a tear with the back of her sleeve. 'I mean, y-yes. B-but I'm seeing things. Things that aren't fucking there. And Marcus keeps texting me about it—'

'Fuck Marcus,' Bree said. 'Let him have his own crazy. You need to focus on you. Find out why the hell this is happening. When are you supposed to be back over in Geneva?'

'Tomorrow morning,' she said. 'But Harry hasn't been in for ages now. And he's still not answering my calls.'

'Fuck Harry. Talk to any one of the other friggin' boffins over there. Hell, talk to all of them. And don't stop till they give you some answers. Chances are they put the wrong setting on you or something. You're *not* nuts, okay?'

Kristen wanted to believe her. But it wasn't the only worry she had. 'What if there's permanent damage?'

'What if, what if. Stop with the *ifs*. Get your butt over there tomorrow and get some answers.'

Kristen nodded. It was wise counsel. 'Thank you, Bee,' she said.

'De nada. You want me to book a flight? Come with you, shout at them too, or whatever?'

'No, no. I'll be fine. Appreciate it though.' She sighed. 'I'll let you know what they have to say.'

'Good,' Bree said. 'And what about when you're back? We're still coming to stay, right?'

'If you still want to,' Kristen said.

'I'll be there with Christmas bells on,' Bree reminded her. 'Even if you and Marcus are a couple of whack jobs.'

Kristen hung up, feeling grateful she had a friend she could lean on. She wondered where Marcus was right now, who was there for him to lean on? She had another thought then. After her visit to the institute tomorrow, she was done with the God helmet. She didn't care about the study, or what she had promised Harry. When her business there was over, she was going to jump on the first plane to Manila and, one way or another, bring her husband home.

11

She had a knot in her stomach during her taxi ride to the institute. Even the sight of the placid lake waters did little to calm her nerves. At reception, she was told Harry had still not come to work. Disappointed but not surprised, Kristen made her way to the main hall and to her second order of business.

'All set?' Amanda Tanner asked.

'I can't do this any more,' Kristen said.

'Why?' Tanner asked, a concerned look on her face. 'What's wrong?'

'I think maybe … *me*,' she said.

They were in a small white consulting room. Bare, with only a desk and two chairs, Kristen in one of them.

'I have your scans right here,' Tanner said.

Kristen leaned forward to get a closer look at the tablet screen she was holding out. On it was a black-and-white contrast image of a brain. Tanner flicked the screen and Kristen saw the same picture, this time with more white spots in the left lobe.

'You can see the increased activity there in your temporal

lobe,' the Tech Manager said, 'compared to when you first started your sessions. Those are new neural networks.'

There were other contrasting shades of grey on the scan too, but Kristen had no hope of decoding any of it.

'Your rational brain is more closely connected than ever before,' Tanner said. 'The emotional storytelling part barely lights up anymore. There's been no mistake, Kristen. Your treatment path has been *away* from any faith or mysticism. There's no way you should be having these hallucinations from anything we're doing here at the institute.'

Kristen sank back in the chair. 'Then why, Amanda? I'm hearing voices. I'm fucking seeing angels. How do you explain that?'

Tanner looked away as if embarrassed. 'I'm sorry,' she said. 'All I know for sure is there must be another explanation.'

Kristen shook her head. 'Where's Harry? Where has he disappeared to? I really need to talk to him.'

'No one knows,' the other woman said. 'Apparently he phoned one of his team over the weekend to say he wouldn't be coming in for a while yet. He insisted we keep the police out of his office.'

'The police?' Kristen asked.

'Oh, you know. The break-in. They still haven't finished their investigation. Harry doesn't want them anywhere near his research.'

Kristen frowned. 'Did he say *why* he's not coming in? Is something going on?'

'He said it was for personal reasons,' Tanner said. 'No one has a clue what's happening. We've got a lot of paperwork backed up here. Things he would usually sign off on. If he doesn't turn up soon, he's going to be in a lot of shit with the board of directors.'

Kristen sighed and leaned back in her chair. What on earth was Harry up to?

12

Though it was a Monday, Kristen took the lift to Adrian Kemplar's office, hoping he might be free. He was just showing another patient out when she got there. 'Kristen, what a surprise,' he said, smiling.

'Do you have a minute?' she asked.

'Actually, I have forty-five if you need them,' he said.

She nodded. 'I think I just might.'

The psychiatrist listened patiently as she told him her story. When she was done, he was quiet for a while. Then he leaned back in his chair and took in a slow breath.

'Kristen,' he said. 'I'm going to ask you something and it's vital you are honest with me, okay?'

She nodded. She felt a tinge of nervous anticipation but her trust in the doctor remained firm.

'Have you been hearing voices that are asking you to harm yourself or others?'

It sounded so ridiculous when the question was said out loud that Kristen almost laughed.

'No,' she said. 'There are voices, but they're just singing. And the angel didn't say a word. It just kind of stared at me.'

Adrian asked her to describe each hallucination again, in much more detail. When she finished, he fidgeted with his hands as he appeared to chew over what she was saying. 'Have you spoken to Harry?' he asked. 'To see if it could be an adverse side effect of the tech?'

'I spoke to Amanda. She said she didn't see anything on the scans.'

'Well, that's good,' he said. 'But the techs have only really been trained to a certain level. You should definitely speak to Harry.'

'Harry's gone AWOL,' she said. 'Haven't you heard?'

The doctor frowned. 'I, er, heard he was sick?'

'No one knows what's happening,' Kristen said. 'Apparently he said he's not coming back any time soon. For personal reasons.'

'Strange,' he said. 'I didn't know that. I know he's not been in for a while.'

She buried her face in her palms. 'Adrian, I feel like I'm going insane.'

'I'm sorry.'

He leaned forward and gave her a serious look. 'I'm afraid I need to ask you something else, Kristen.'

She swallowed but nodded.

'When we had our very first conversation, when I first assessed you, did you keep from me any previous history of psychiatric treatment or related medication that you didn't want to share with me?'

She shook her head. Emphatically no.

'Next question. And this is another delicate one. How do you feel about the possibility that these experiences may indeed have a psychological or medical explanation? Are you open to exploring this?'

He was essentially asking if she could accept she might

actually be losing her mind. She considered her response carefully.

'I'm not thrilled about the possibility,' she admitted. 'But yes, I'm open to it.'

The doctor tapped his pen, looking down at his notepad. 'What do *you* think might be going on?'

She was annoyed at his inability to offer a tangible explanation. 'Well I don't have a fucking clue,' she said. 'But Marcus seems to think it's the Almighty himself, trying to get me to believe in His existence again.'

'Do you believe that?'

'I ... I don't know,' she said.

It was hard to admit it. But the truth was she was beginning to doubt herself. To doubt what she knew about the world. She was crying now. 'I need to know what's happening to me,' she said, blowing her nose on a tissue. 'Please, Adrian. Help me.'

He reached across the low coffee table and touched her wrist. 'I will,' he said, 'I promise. I might need to refer you to someone in the UK. Someone who might be able to prescribe you the right antipsychotic medication ...' He paused, seemingly conscious of his language. '*If* it's needed. But what I can tell you is I don't think these are *your* hallucinations.'

She sniffed. 'You don't?'

'Think about it,' he said. 'Who mentioned the choir and the angel to you in the first place?'

She considered. 'Marcus.'

'That's right. Then suddenly you hear singing at your daughter's grave. And then ... lo! An angel appears in your garden! But it was Marcus who planted both those ideas in your head, wasn't it?'

She thought it over and realised he was right. 'Okay,' she said. 'But what about the dream I had? About Jerusalem?'

'Maybe just associative,' Adrian said. 'Images, thoughts you connect with your previous faith.'

'But I still saw that angel,' she said. 'What does that fucking mean?'

'I don't know,' he said. 'Perhaps some kind of hypnosis or suggestion. Hopefully we can find out. In the meantime, I'm assuming you're not doing any more sessions on the God helmet?'

She chuckled darkly. 'I don't think that would be wise, do you?'

'Most definitely not,' Adrian said. 'And I wouldn't sign it off anyway.'

13

She left Adrian Kemplar's office with one question still burning in her mind. Where the fuck was Harry? Without realising she was going to do it, she pressed the first-floor button instead of the one for the lobby. She emerged into the busy white corridor and hurried past the glass-walled cubicles full of subjects getting their early scans. She tried not to think of them as lab rats risking their sanity on Harry's experimental machines. As she rounded the bend, she saw Amanda Tanner exiting a cubicle up ahead. The Tech Manager glanced her way, then hurried quickly across to the stairwell as if suddenly remembering an urgent appointment. Perhaps she still felt awkward about her subject's unexplained psychosis. As Kristen passed the main hall on her right, she did not look at the rows of God helmets, which she was now convinced were evil and dangerous. At last, she reached Harry Dean's office. This time, she didn't bother knocking. Instead, she glanced quickly behind her to make sure no one was watching, and slipped quickly inside.

Kristen shut the door firmly behind her. A walnut desk dominated the room, with a single desktop computer and a large leather chair. Apart from a mousepad and mouse, the only other items on the desk were two old-fashioned stationery trays, which were stacked full of folders and papers. She sat in the chair and checked the door again. She didn't think she was doing anything illegal. But if she was asked by a member of staff what she was doing, she wouldn't have an answer. All Kristen knew for certain was that something was scratching at her, a niggle that wasn't going away. It bothered her that Harry had not told anyone at the institute why he was taking a leave of absence. But it worried her more that he had not responded to her many texts and calls. She felt as though she was more than just another test subject. She was the wife of his best friend. It just didn't make any sense. She exhaled and pressed the computer's *on* button. The start-up jingle was followed by a password prompt. A dead end.

She turned the machine off again and tried the top desk drawer. Inside was a large portable hard drive with a single lead and USB jack. She had no idea what was on it, and without being able to access the computer, had no way of telling either. She tried the middle drawer, and was rewarded with a beautifully bound faux-leather book. She opened it and discovered it was a calendar diary, a page per day. Various appointments were scribbled in pen. Kristen's heart quickened as she flicked through the last couple of weeks trying to make sense of them. Some looked like consultations with other doctors at the institute. There was a regular team leaders' meeting on Wednesdays. Fridays, Harry attended a cross-departmental meeting, the purposes of which eluded Kristen. There was nothing written in for the evenings or weekends. This was strictly a work-related diary that told her nothing except Harry had obviously missed a bunch of important engagements. She pulled the final drawer out and found a den of bad snacks. Crisps, chocolates, sweets, biscuits. *Oh Harry,* she thought. *You must start taking care of yourself.* She sighed and closed the drawer again. She rocked back in the chair, looking around the desk.

The trays were the only thing she had left to go through, and they looked full of dull paperwork. Still, she had come this far. She pulled out the first tray, flicking through the folders inside. The top one contained several invoices from companies she supposed were suppliers to the institute. Some were from a catering company that delivered fruit, another set from a private car hire firm which Kristen assumed ferried the institute's employees around. Several more recent invoices were from manufacturers supplying parts with names and serial numbers she had no hope of decoding. There were also personal receipts mixed in, travel expenses, restaurant bills and the like. Kristen supposed they were all costs that Harry was responsible for signing off. She set the folder aside and cast her eye on a letter sitting loose on the tray underneath. It was from a doctor at a hospital based in Geneva.

Dear Professor Dean,

We were very sorry to hear about the incident at your facility. We trust that the foundation is suitably insured. Our neurology department here was particularly disappointed as we were looking forward to the loan of a Magna-Stim XK machine, as promised.

As discussed when Doctor Scherrer and I visited you back in February, we have many patients suffering from major depressive and anxiety disorders who might benefit from its therapy.

May I enquire as to whether the institute would be able to spare another machine? As ever, we are grateful for the foundation's consideration and generosity.

I look forward to hearing from you in due course.

Yours sincerely,

Doctor Schmid

(on behalf of the Neurology Department at Mont Blanc Medical Centre)

Kristen had a pretty good idea what the Magna-Stim XK

was. A *God helmet*. She remembered how Harry had told her the institute sometimes loaned its equipment to surrounding hospitals. This medical centre must have been promised one of the machines. She frowned, considering the implications of the letter. It suggested that the machine had been damaged here at the institute. The use of the word *incident* presumably referred to the activists who had broken in many weeks ago. But they'd failed to get into the main building, hadn't they? Hadn't the smashing of the entrance doors set off the alarm, causing the intruders to flee? She placed the letter back and flicked through the rest of the paperwork. It consisted of more invoices but nothing more of value. She should probably leave before someone caught her. She opened the office door a sliver and peered out. The coast was clear. She slipped out into the corridor and towards the exit, no closer to understanding what had happened to Harry. Or what the hell was happening to her.

14

As she crossed the institute's car park, she wondered if Harry was in some kind of danger. She wasn't sure where the thought had come from. It was only a suspicion, based on zero evidence, but the idea grew stronger the more she entertained it. As usual, the demonstrators were on the far side of the road, waving their placards and signs decrying the work of the institute. She felt their hostility, as strong as ever. Tobias waved and stepped out of his booth to open the gate.

'Still no arrests then, I take it?' she asked.

It was a rhetorical question. Several weeks on, the police still had nothing. The security guard responded with a half smirk as he punched in the code to allow her through. A thought struck her as he held the gate open for her. 'Hey, Tobias, I'm curious about something. Did the police ever provide a crime report?'

'Yes, of course,' Tobias said. 'Why do you ask?'

'Did it mention anything about whether the thieves, vandals, whatever, also damaged a Magna-Stim XK? One of the so-called God helmet machines?'

Tobias raised an eyebrow and gave her a suspicious look. 'Yes,' he said, 'it did. The machine was listed as part of the van cargo. It was supposed to be on its way to a medical facility in Geneva. How did you know that?'

'Doesn't matter,' she said. 'But the God helmet ... it was damaged in the fire, right? When the thief torched the van?'

'We can safely assume so,' the security guard said. 'The vehicle was entirely burned. Anything not made of metal probably melted, but ... what's the English ...? Nothing was *salvageable* as far as I know. Any reason to ask?'

'I'm just trying to make sense of something,' she said.

'Look at you, Mrs Hardy. A sleuth in the making. Are you going to help me catch the bastard? He worked alone you know.'

'Alone?' she said, puzzled.

'Yes, I studied the *überwachungsaufnahmen*,' Tobias said.

Seeing her confusion, he clarified. 'The security footage. I thought there were two or three in the van because the cabin was very dark. But then I put the film through an AI tool which can lighten. Then I see only one driver, very clearly. I already share with the useless police but still they cannot find him!' He shrugged his shoulders as if to emphasise his frustration.

'I see,' Kristen said. 'He's not here today then, I take it?' She pointed at the protestors.

'Not that I can see,' Tobias admitted glumly.

'I'm honestly surprised the police haven't ID'd him by now,' Kristen said. 'Especially if they have his face.'

Tobias reached inside his security jacket and took out his phone. 'He was clever, wore a ... what do you call this one?' He pulled his fingers across his face.

'A balaclava?'

'Yes, *balaclava*. But that doesn't mean we won't know it's him.'

He showed her a photo on his screen. The image was black and white and had the grainy tone of CCTV footage. It looked like a screengrab taken from a video. Kristen squinted, leaned in closer and saw the Bennetts van. It was pulling away from the building's entrance. Tobias helpfully flicked his finger and thumb and expanded the shot so she could see the windscreen clearly. The sole occupant of the van sat behind the wheel and was indeed wearing a balaclava. For a moment she was puzzled by what Tobias was getting at. And then she saw it.

'His head almost touches the roof of the van,' Tobias said. 'He has to be close to two metres tall.' He popped the phone back in his pocket and jerked his thumb towards the crowd across the road. 'I'm sure it's just a matter of time before I notice him.'

Kristen smiled nervously as her taxi pulled up to the gate. As it drove her away, she tried to tell herself she wasn't thinking what she was thinking. That at six foot three, her husband was about two metres tall. Except she was thinking *exactly* that.

15

Her driver tutted when she told him she no longer wanted to go to the airport. But he grudgingly accepted the new destination she gave him just south of Geneva. Kristen had found Harry's address in her inbox, among Marcus's fortieth birthday invitees. Half an hour later, the taxi cruised through Champel, an upscale neighbourhood favoured by expats. They passed several art-nouveau-style apartment blocks before arriving at the number Kristen had. She gave the grumpy driver a compensating tip and hurried to the main entrance. A concierge behind a desk greeted her warmly. 'Can I help you, madam?'

'I hope so,' she said. 'I'm a friend of Professor Dean's. I believe he's a resident.'

'Are you a friend or relative?' he asked cordially.

'Friend,' she said.

The concierge picked up a phone and, after a minute or so, shook his head. 'I'm afraid he's not answering,' he said.

'Is he at home?'

'I'm afraid I don't know, madam. My shift started this afternoon, but I haven't seen him come or go.'

'Please,' she said. 'He's a really close friend of mine.'

She showed him pictures on her phone of herself and Harry, taken at Marcus's birthday party. She explained that Harry had not been seen for many days, and was not answering calls. Seeing her worried expression, the concierge nodded sympathetically. 'Sure, let's check in on the professor,' he said.

His calm voice reassured Kristen and he escorted her towards the only lift, recessed further back into the foyer. The lift was bigger inside than she expected, resembling a freight elevator. Harry lived on the third floor. The concierge, who introduced himself as Johannes, led her to apartment number fourteen and pressed the buzzer. When there was no answer, he removed a bunch of keys from his black jacket and selected the one he wanted. He turned the key in the lock and pushed the door open hesitantly.

'Professor Dean? Are you home? Is everything okay?'

Kristen was grateful that Johannes was willing to risk invading Harry's privacy, but at the same time part of her worried about what lay beyond the door. Johannes pushed it all the way open anyway, and Kristen followed him inside. The sight that greeted her was familiar from her previous video calls with Harry. She recognised the Scandinavian decor and white walls. In the centre of the living room, empty takeaway containers and plastic water bottles were scattered everywhere, leaving a lingering smell. The detritus surrounded a pile of floor cushions positioned at the centre of the room. But that wasn't the focus of Kristen's attention. That honour belonged to a machine resting above the cushions. More accurately, a Magna-Stim XK. It had no integral chair, but the hydraulic arm and dome were unmistakeable. Kristen caught her breath as she approached the machine, running her hands over the dome as if to confirm that it was really there. Johannes, meanwhile, moved through the rest of the apartment, calling out Harry's name over and over with no response. Kristen circled the God helmet, trying to put together the pieces of the puzzle.

'What is this?' Johannes asked as he rejoined her in the living room.

'Some sort of experiment,' she said. 'I think.'

'Aha,' Johannes said. 'I wondered why they brought it here.'

'They?' she asked, confused.

'The professor and the other man. From the photographs you showed me?'

'Other man?'

'Yes, the tall one in the photos.'

It was already winter outside, but Kristen could have sworn the temperature in the room dropped a degree or two. 'You saw Marcus here?'

'I don't know his name,' Johannes admitted. 'He and the professor carried this machine through the lobby. It was covered in a sheet, but I recognised the, how would you say?'

He made a dome-shaped gesture with his hands. 'I offered to help them, but they said no. I think the professor was angry that I wasn't minding my own business. They got into the lift and that was that.'

Kristen felt like time had slowed. Marcus and Harry attempting to sneak a God helmet into Harry's apartment?

'And when was this, Johannes?' she asked, her voice croaking.

'I would say perhaps two months ago.'

Kristen nodded. Around the same time of the break-in. A van was taken, supposedly with the God helmet inside. And then the whole thing set on fire, nothing but non-combustible metal parts remaining. The same parts that could have easily been on those invoices she'd sifted through in Harry's office. Delivered straight to the institute, smuggled out and then deliberately left in the van to make it look like the torched remains of a Magna-Stim XK. She circled the room as though she was a detective at a crime scene, trying to avoid stepping on yellow polystyrene takeaway boxes. A curly white strip caught her eye, one of several scattered across the floor. She knelt down and scooped it up. It was a zip tie which appeared to have been severed as if cut with scissors or pliers. Frowning, she quick-walked past Johannes and headed into the hallway. She heard him protest and follow her. By the time he caught up with her, she had already found the room. It was the second of the two bedrooms. The bed featured a bedstead that also doubled up as a bookshelf. Having only ever seen it cropped on screen, she had mistakenly believed it to be a hotel room. On the desk was a laptop. She sat down, flipped the lid open and typed in a single password.

Abigirl1.

'Please,' Johannes beseeched her. 'The professor's privacy!'

'This is my husband's computer,' she said calmly.

The desktop appeared and she scrutinised the folders, looking for more clues. She found a folder labelled 'Great Being'. In it was a series of videos that had been saved onto the hard drive. The thumbnail of each one showed the face of her husband, Marcus Hardy, who, it seemed, had not been living in the Philippines as she had supposed, but here in Harry's apartment.

16

Johannes was asking her more questions but she ignored him, hitting play on the first video. She saw Marcus staring into the camera.

'First session, November second,' he said. 'I feel confident I understand the basic principles of how the technology works. With a little help from Harry—'

'What's that?' Harry cut in.

Kristen could hear his voice, but he was off camera.

'I said, I feel confident with your help I can master this thing,' Marcus said.

He waved a tablet in one hand, similar to the kind Amanda Tanner used for Kristen's sessions.

'Aury,' Harry said in a cautionary tone. 'There are no guarantees this will work.'

'Yes, you said.'

'And you shouldn't be filming! If anyone were to find this …'

'Relax, old boy,' Marcus said, 'it's just for personal use. Besides, you're in the clear. If the police suspected anything, they would have arrested you by now.'

Harry's face appeared behind Marcus. He was shaking his

head furiously. 'I shouldn't have helped you,' he said. 'If it wasn't for the fact that I owe you my life, I would not have. For the record.'

Marcus tutted. '*Et tu*, Harry? What about Kristen? You didn't hesitate to help her.'

'Yes, well, I owed her too,' Harry said. 'But at least with her I could make a legitimate case to the board. This is … well, unorthodox. I could go to prison, Aury. So please. Delete the damn video.'

'I promise,' Marcus said. 'As soon as I am finished.'

Except he hadn't, Kristen thought. She skipped to another thumbnail below. Marcus reappeared, talking to camera. His face looked pallid, a thick sheen of sweat on his forehead.

'… initial symptoms are mild nausea,' he said. 'Nothing to report so far but Harry confirmed it does take time.'

Kristen anxiously clicked on the next video.

'November fifteenth,' Marcus's face said. 'Ten a.m. I think it's starting to work … I feel the pain lessening, the grief fading. For which I can only say thank you, Harry. It could all be autosuggestion, of course, but I do feel different …' He smiled. 'Like it's possible that Abi *is* still alive, somewhere. It's … such a comfort … I can't tell you …'

He buried his face in his palms and sobbed. Kristen couldn't bear to watch. She sped up the video. When she resumed play, the lighting behind Marcus's face had changed, suggesting it was evening. His eyes looked red and puffy.

'… going to speak to Father Connolly,' he said with a sniff. 'I think he can help answer some of my questions—'

She stopped and scrolled down. It was hard to say how many videos Marcus had made. Part of her did not want to continue, but she clicked on another file anyway.

'November twenty-third,' Marcus said. 'I'm back and ready to start it up again. I couldn't tell Kris anything. Not until I'm one hundred per cent sure where this leads. I think I may have ruined our anniversary though by going to Mass ...'

Fast forward.

'I'm increasing the intensity,' Marcus said. 'Harry says it's dangerous but if there's any chance this will show me where Abigail is now, maybe even help me see her, it'll be worth it.'

It felt for Kristen like the room was tilting, like someone else was moving the slider along.

'... making sure to drink plenty of fluids. Just finished another ninety minutes, repeating the same session twice—'

Fast forward.

'December second. I had the dream again,' Marcus said. 'This could be a glimpse of the true reality that lies beyond this one ...'

She closed the file down and took a breath. In the next video, Marcus was holding a plastic bag under his chin. At first Kristen thought he might be hyperventilating but then he opened it up and vomited into it. When his retching ended, he addressed the camera again.

'Two thirty,' he said, looking at his watch. Beads of sweat rolled down his forehead. His eyes appeared larger as if fuelled by the use of amphetamines. His speech had sped up too. 'I believe the priests and prophets are likely emissaries on the long journey to revelation. If I'm right, it all fits with our evolutionary purpose. It is within the great chain that we all find our place ...'

Kristen shut her eyes. When she dared to open them again, Marcus was shouting at someone off camera. 'Fuck you. Of *course* I understand the risks!'

'Aury!' she heard Harry shout back. 'You've gone seventy-two hours non-stop with only a half-hour break between sessions. The human brain is not meant to be subjected to that much current. You need to follow my programme—'

'*No*. Harry. I need to go deeper. Much, *much* deeper. The things I'm starting to see now, they're just the surface.'

'No, you need to stop this, now—'

Kristen heard the two men argue vigorously, then the video finished. There was one file left in the folder, undated, but it looked like the last one Marcus had recorded. She clicked on it and saw her husband's face again. His eyes displayed an ethereal, milky quality as if he were lucid dreaming.

'I had to do it,' Marcus said. 'Harry was resisting far too much!' He burst into tears. 'I saw him suffer,' he blurted. 'I heard his screams. But I had no choice. He was going to try and stop me.' He looked around the room nervously. 'I need to take him away from here before someone comes looking. A neighbour, or the damn concierge downstairs.'

He leaned forward into the camera and his face filled the screen. Kristen felt his piercing stare. 'I have no idea who any of this is for, any more. I started off thinking maybe Kris would find it, maybe she would understand what I had to do. But now perhaps the police will see it. If so, I say good. By the time they do, its will will be done. I am its servant. We *all* are. As it was before, ever shall it be.'

Then the screen went black.

Kristen slammed the lid back down hard. 'Shit.'

'What is wrong?' Johannes asked when he saw her face. 'Is Professor Dean all right?'

She turned to him, tried to speak, but couldn't. She was unable to say aloud that she believed that Harry Dean might be dead. Murdered by her deranged husband.

17

Tim Barnes answered after the second ring. 'Kristen, how are you? Nice to hear from you.'

'Marcus,' she said. 'He's not been out there with you?'

'With us?' Tim said. 'No. He left us barely a month into the shoot. I assumed he told you.'

'No,' she said, 'he didn't.'

Tim told her what had happened. Out of the blue, Marcus had announced that he was going to leave the production and he had no idea when he'd be ready to return to the show. 'It was so sudden,' he said. 'I tried to warn him he was leaving us in the lurch. We barely had a third of the footage we needed and none of his narration. But he didn't care. He just packed his bags and walked out.'

'So when I asked you to check up on him … he wasn't at your hotel?'

'No,' Tim said. 'I wasn't even at the hotel. The whole crew had to come home early. We've missed all our deadlines. It's likely the BBC will postpone the next season. I thought you knew all this.'

Kristen shook her head. 'You must have wondered why I reached out to you.'

'It did cross my mind,' Tim admitted. 'But I thought you just wanted my help. I did call him, as you asked. And he told me he was doing something important and personal. But I assumed he was home, with you. What's wrong, Kristen? Is Marcus okay?'

'No, not really,' she heard herself say.

Tim pressed her for more, but she didn't have the bandwidth to explain. But at least now she understood why Tim had not seemed overly concerned with Marcus's odd behaviour. The reality was, he hadn't seen it.

'Is there anything I can do?' Tim asked.

'Thanks, Tim, but no,' she said, and ended the call.

Darkly, she wondered if there was anything anyone could do for Marcus now.

'Wait, slow down,' Adrian Kemplar said. 'You're going too fast. You're *where*?'

Kristen pressed the phone to her ear as she told him again. She was sitting on the living room sofa with Marcus's laptop resting on one of its arms. Johannes paced nervously around her. He'd wanted to call the police, but Kristen had asked him to hold off for now. 'Marcus has totally lost his mind,' she told the psychiatrist. 'And now I'm worried he might have harmed Harry.'

'This doesn't make any sense,' Adrian said. 'I thought he was in the Philippines?'

'So did I.'

Kristen described in detail what had been going on in the apartment and shared her suspicions about the break-in.

'Wait, so Marcus stole a God helmet?'

'And Harry helped him,' she said.

'But why?' the doctor said. 'Harry wouldn't jeopardise his job at the institute, surely?'

'I think Marcus bullied him into it,' Kristen said. 'He

saved his life once, many years ago, and Harry has always felt indebted. My guess is the break-in was Marcus's idea.'

Adrian said nothing, seemingly at a loss for words.

'He wanted the same thing I did,' Kristen said. 'Help to get over Abi. But he did the opposite to me. He asked Harry to design a programme that would *open* his mind to spirituality. Only he overdid it. He went way beyond the limits of what was safe.' She gripped the phone harder, barely believing what she was saying. 'I think the protestors were the perfect cover,' she said. 'Marcus probably thought the police would suspect one of them was behind it, especially if the whole thing was staged to look like protest vandalism. He must have persuaded Harry they'd get away with it.'

'Please, madam, we can call the police now?' Johannes said.

Kristen held up a finger. She was about to continue when she realised there was a sinking feeling inside her that was growing stronger by the minute.

'Oh God,' she said. 'Adrian, it's all my fault.'

Guilt stabbed at her as she uttered the words and her eyes welled up. 'If I hadn't asked Harry to use the machine,' she said. 'If I hadn't gone down this path—'

'Kristen,' the psychiatrist said. 'Please listen to me. Marcus is responsible for his own decisions. You have no way of knowing that he wouldn't have done this anyway.'

'Except I do,' she said, rubbing tears from the corners of her eyes with the palm of her hand. 'Marcus saw me, saw my determination.'

She shook her head vigorously and began compressing the files into a zip folder and attaching them to an email. 'The question remains as to what damage he's done to himself. I'm sending you the videos now, I want you to take a look. He keeps referring to some *It* that he believes he's doing the will of, as a servant or something. It could be this Great Being he's been talking to me about, I don't know. Maybe you can make more sense of it.'

She asked for Adrian's email address, then cc'd herself. A second later, she heard the whoosh of the email as it sent.

'Is this from Marcus?' Adrian said, confused.

'Yeah, sorry, I'm using his email account,' she explained.

Adrian acknowledged the receipt of the videos and told Kristen he was downloading them. When it was done, she asked him one more favour. 'I have a young man here keen to talk to the police,' she said. 'I think we need to get them involved. Harry could be lying injured somewhere or ...'

She tried to finish the sentence but still couldn't. 'I've tried calling Marcus several times but it keeps going straight to voicemail,' she said. 'I think he's deliberately turned off his phone. My flight leaves in less than an hour. I know it's a lot to ask, but I wondered if you could deal with the police here?'

Adrian paused. 'Shouldn't you stick around? They'll likely want to question you.'

'I'm not going to be of any use to them,' she said. 'I don't know where Marcus is, and I had no idea about any of this.'

She had already thought this through before calling him. 'The police need to find Harry,' she said. 'As a priority. But it's also possible that if Marcus ...' She forced herself to continue. 'If Marcus has ... *done* something to him, he might have fled the country. He could be on his way home right now. I need to get back there.'

An awful quiet hung in the air.

'I get it,' Adrian said at last. 'I'm happy to talk to the police, no problem.'

'Thank you,' she said.

She handed the phone to Johannes. 'This gentleman is going to assist the police with their enquiries. Can you introduce yourself?'

The concierge nodded and took the phone. Kristen gathered her things for the airport. She stared at the laptop.

Should she take it? No, this was likely to be evidence the police would want. She looked at her watch. In an ideal world, she would stay. But if Marcus had fled back to England, she needed to find him, and fast. After all, if he really had killed his best friend, what else could he be capable of?

18

She barely made her flight. Kristen spent the entire journey replaying the scene she had found at Harry's apartment. So much of Marcus's behaviour made sense now, yet the implications were frightening. The state of her own psyche still remained a mystery, but for now she needed to concentrate on what was happening to her husband. She had started this. So now she needed to do everything she could to try and stop it. If she could stop it. Kristen felt guilt weighing her down again, following her all the way through Arrivals, until it was suddenly replaced by anxiety. Out of nowhere, she heard the sound of angelic singing. Worried her hallucinations had returned, she was relieved to discover it was only a children's choir on the concourse, singing Christmas carols to raise money for some charity. At Gatwick train station, she tried Marcus's mobile again. Her call went straight to voicemail, like all the others. There was now little doubt in her mind that he had turned his phone off. The air was bitterly cold when she stepped out of her local station. She had to scrape ice off the Land Rover's windscreen before daring to drive back to Ashworth. Orchard House was dark when she arrived, with no sign of anyone home. She opened the front door wide and called out Marcus's name. No response. She stepped inside, closing the door behind her, and went straight to the kitchen where she turned the boiler on. In the living room, she stopped to stare briefly at the pizza stove, her strange would-be angel. In the moonlight, it looked nothing like her heavenly visitor. Her phone vibrated. Thinking it might be Marcus, her heart quickened as she pulled it out of her bag. But it was Adrian Kemplar.

Hope you got home safe. Have spoken to the police. Will update you fully tomorrow.

She rang him back immediately. 'What? What did they say?'

The doctor sighed. 'They're not convinced a crime has been committed,' he said.

'What? You showed them the recordings, right?'

'Yes. And they do agree that Marcus is likely having some kind of psychological breakdown.' Adrian's voice was soft and kind as if the very sentence might upset her.

But she was beyond that now. All that mattered to her was locating Marcus and finding Harry. She realised she'd lost the thread of what Adrian was saying.

'... and because Harry had actually told the institute he'd be absent, they think it's possible he might just be away on some urgent business and he could well return in his own time. Long and short of it, they don't regard him as a missing person. At least, not yet.'

She shook her head. 'What about Marcus practically admitting he'd hurt Harry?'

'I know, they watched the clip,' Adrian said. 'They say he only claimed to have harmed him. There's no evidence of any physical violence in the apartment and the concierge confirmed that no neighbours reported any screaming.'

'So what? Maybe they just didn't hear it.'

Kristen could barely believe what she was being told.

'They *do* want to interview Marcus, however,' Adrian said.

'In fact, they said to tell you if he gets in touch, to please ask him to come voluntarily to the station here in Geneva.'

She let out an incredulous laugh.

'Look, I know,' Adrian said, picking up on her frustration. 'They weren't unwilling to help, they just said there was not enough evidence. They're also coming here to the institute tomorrow once they've had a chance to look at all the footage. Maybe they'll be more convinced then.'

She shook her head. This wasn't what she was hoping for. Surely they needed to prioritise finding Harry? 'So what do we do now? Harry could … well, what if he …?'

'He might be fine,' Adrian said. 'The cops are right in that we only have Marcus's word that he harmed him. And Johannes spoke to the other concierge who works in the building. Neither of them remembers seeing Marcus dragging a body out of here in the middle of the night or anything.'

But Kristen wasn't convinced. 'So what now? We just wait?'

'I suppose so,' the psychiatrist said. 'Marcus will resurface sooner or later. And Harry might well show up unharmed too. Until then, I don't know what else we can do.'

She sighed.

'I assume there's no sign of Marcus there?' Adrian asked.

'None,' she said. 'Wherever he is, he hasn't been home.'

Except she was wrong about that. Later that evening, she went to fetch a jumper from the bedroom wardrobe and her gaze chanced upon strange black markings on her favourite pair of leather boots. She picked one up and held it under the bedroom light. A single word had been scrawled on the shaft in black marker pen.

SHAME.

It was Marcus's handwriting. Kristen put the boot down and noticed that the word had also been written across her knee-length beige leather coat. The same was true of Marcus's leather jacket, the one he rarely wore. She spun around, convinced her husband was standing behind her. But she was alone. Instinctively, she crept over to the study. The door was unlocked. She pushed it open with force as if the act would dispel any ghosts or malevolent beings (*angels in bright raiment*, she thought while trying not to). Nervously, she fumbled for the light switch, bathing the room in sixty-watt brightness. Her husband's sacred workspace was untouched apart from an object she recognised sitting on the desk. It was Marcus's leather-bound journal. He always took one on his work trips abroad. It shouldn't be here. A single word was written across the cover.

SHAME.

She opened the journal and discovered pages of hand-written script inside, untidy and spider-like. She tried to read Marcus's handwriting, but it was too erratic, as if he'd written everything when drunk or asleep. Occasionally, phrases were underlined or written in capital letters she *could* make out. In the middle of the journal, however, she found a paragraph that was legible:

There have always been predators. We used to know this, deep in our psyche. When we came from deep water and the deep forests. From Eden we emerged, we evolved, and we built campfires. But, in time, we forgot the dangers that lurked in that old darkness. As we grew crops, formed communities, the stories we used to tell changed. They morphed into religions, metaphors for the real truth.

Then, two pages later, she found another:

From the beginning, every creature that clawed its way out of the mud and shit has been hunted. Including us. We were born to run, to flee nature's deadly tooth and claw. But we forgot that Something must have started the chain.

She also found a number of references to something called the *Apex* and the *Great Chain of Being*. She stepped back from it all, needing a moment to draw in a deep, stabilising breath.

Marcus had been here. In the house. And in the last twelve hours. But what the hell was this graffiti about? She reached for her phone. Like some kind of amateur detective, she took pictures of the journal's pages and the items Marcus had written the word *shame* on. But it wasn't her who was going to study them for clues. She typed a long message to Adrian Kemplar, then attached all the shots from her phone's photo library. If anyone could untangle this, it would be a trained psychiatrist. She waited while the message sent and a couple of minutes later, Adrian sent her back a supportive message, promising to take a closer look. These, plus the many hours of video Marcus had also left behind, were going to be a lot to wade through. Kristen didn't envy him the task. Especially since it was all clearly the ramblings of a person who had lost their mind.

19

She called Willowdale police station and pressed upon them as best she could that her husband needed to be found as a matter of urgency. An hour later, she was paid another visit. Unfortunately for her, it was by the same pair who had come out to her before.

'No angels this time, eh?' said the male officer, grinning.

His name badge reminded her that he was PC Grant. This time, they all sat in the living room and Kristen offered them tea. The officers nodded politely and indulged her. The teapot was empty and it was getting late by the time she had finished her story. The other PC, whose name was Lyndsey Stock, had a lot of questions about the institute in Geneva. She looked increasingly puzzled as Kristen described the God helmets, often glancing across at her colleague. Kristen wasn't sure whether they believed such technology existed or if it was another fancy of Kristen's overactive imagination.

'And you believe one of these machines has made your husband delusional?' Stock asked.

Yes, and it's all my fault, Kristen wanted to say. But she only nodded. 'I can put you in touch with someone at the institute tomorrow who can corroborate everything I'm saying.'

'And Marcus was here at the house today?' Grant asked.

'Yes,' Kristen said. 'When I was in Geneva. But he's gone now.'

'So it's possible he might return home still?'

'I don't know where he is,' she said. 'But I do know he's not in his right mind. Please, you have to find him.'

She opened the email on her phone, and the video files she had sent to Adrian Kemplar. She clicked the last attachment, the one that would make the best argument. She went full screen and jacked up the sound to maximum. The pair watched in fascination as Marcus ranted about having to 'stop' Harry, the expression in their eyes changing the longer the video played. She saw she finally had them convinced.

After she closed the clip, PC Grant swallowed. 'Okay, I … I can see why you want to find him. Tell you what. I'll put the word out tonight and alert the other stations in the area. Perhaps in the meantime, you might put together a list of friends and contacts, anyone at all your husband might be staying with. I mean, those you haven't checked with already.'

'He doesn't have anyone he's that close to,' she said. 'Trust me.'

'We'll make this a priority,' PC Stock said, clearly sensing her distress.

Kristen teared up. 'I'm just so worried,' she said. 'What if he's wandering out there somewhere? Lost and confused?'

Stock reached across and touched her arm. 'We'll find him, Mrs Hardy, don't worry.'

'How? He's turned his phone off! He could be anywhere!'

'Well, we can call on the NPAS.'

She sniffed, blew her nose. 'The what?'

'The National Police Air Service. We can put in a request for a helicopter,' Stock said, 'to comb the local area. If he's lost in the forest, he'll be picked up by the infra-red camera.'

Kristen's eyes widened. 'You can do that?'

'We can,' Stock said. 'We'll need to get it authorised. But I believe with your husband's clearly unwell state, we could justify the expense.'

They told her they ought to get going, to put the request in action as quickly as possible.

'Don't expect to hear from us till tomorrow morning, Mrs Hardy,' Stock said. 'Unless we find your husband before then.'

She led them to the door, thinking it was over. But PC Grant had one more thing to say. 'What about you, Mrs Hardy? Have these machines affected your own mental health? Do you need support? We can refer you to a—'

'I'm under the care of Doctor Adrian Kemplar,' she said quickly.

It had dawned on her that her honest confession might raise concerns for her mental state too. Especially after her previous call about the angel. The last thing she wanted was to be sectioned.

'He's fully qualified,' she said. 'I can give you his details. You, er, can talk to him tomorrow.'

'Yes, perhaps we will,' Grant replied.

She tried not to read too much into that.

'In the meantime,' Stock said, 'if Marcus does come home, call us straight away.'

Kristen promised them she would. The cruiser drove off into the night, leaving her feeling vulnerable and alone.

20

She went from room to room, making sure all the windows and doors were locked. Marcus only had a key to the front door, so she made sure to put the chain on just in case he did show up. She didn't think he would hurt her, but she intended to wait for the police before letting him in, just to be safe. As she returned upstairs to change into her pyjamas, she remembered someone Marcus *could* be with. Young Father Nolan. Marcus had attended Mass with him, after all. She wondered whether he had gone to St James's. *Shit*. She called the presbytery straight away. No one picked up, but it was close to midnight now. She left a brief message, asking Father Nolan to call her back. If Marcus was at the presbytery, at least he might be getting some spiritual counsel. As much of an atheist as she felt she was now, she figured that any help he received could only be good. She closed her eyes just as her mobile rang, startling her. For a second, she thought Marcus had turned his phone back on. But it wasn't him.

'Bree!' Kristen said.

'Sorry, hun, I know it's super late. But Darius said I should make sure we're still on.'

'Still on?' she said, confused.

'For tomorrow. Christmas bells on, remember?'

'*Right*,' Kristen mumbled. She had completely forgotten their visit was due.

'So what happened in Geneva?' Bree asked. 'You figure out what the hell they've been doing to that lovely brain of yours?'

Instead of answering, Kristen laughed darkly. 'You have no idea what kind of day I've had, Bree. I don't even know where to begin.'

'*What*? Spill!'

So Kristen spilled, starting with how Marcus had been lying to her and what she'd found in Harry's apartment. When she'd finished, she waited for what she imagined was going to be a tirade of more questions. But Bree's response was briefer than that. 'Oh. My. God. *Hun*!'

'I know,' Kristen said.

'And you have no idea where Marcus is now?'

'The police are out looking for him,' she said. 'I'm so worried, Bree. I'm going out of my mind.'

'Of course you are, girlie. Of course you are.'

'And I'm worried he might have hurt Harry,' Kristen said. 'Maybe worse. The video I watched, it … was like he was someone else.'

'God,' Bree said.

She gripped the phone tighter and felt a flush of anger directed at herself.

'It's my fault, Bee. If I hadn't gone to the institute in the first place …'

'Don't even,' Bree said. 'At least you told Marcus what you were doing. He's been lying to you this whole time. This isn't on you, Krissy.'

Her words echoed Adrian Kemplar's view. But Kristen still couldn't help feeling she had helped start Marcus down a path.

'Maybe forget coming,' she suggested. 'Stay where you

are. Things are super crazy down here.'

'Bullshit,' Bree said. 'You fucking need us, girlie.'

'But what happens if Marcus turns up?'

'We call the police,' Bree said. 'Besides, we'll have Darius with us. And I for one would feel better with you having a man in the house right now.'

'And what about Poppy?'

'What about her? We'll make up some story about where Uncle Marcus is. And if he does turn up, the three of us will be there to deal with him. It's got to be better than you being stuck out there on your own, Krissy.'

Kristen considered her situation. Alone, in an empty house. A missing husband, out there somewhere, maybe lost. Of course she needed her best friend. Now more than ever.

'You sure, Bee?' she said.

'See you tomorrow, you daft mare.'

<h1 style="text-align:center">21</h1>

That night, she had another religious dream, but there was no Jerusalem this time. Instead, she saw a celestial being with four wings, two covering its body and two outstretched behind it. She recognised the creature from the Old Testament Book of Ezekiel. A cherubim with four faces, one of a man, another a lion, another an ox and finally an eagle. The being glowed with a golden sheen that shone as brightly as the angel in the garden had done. As she stared at its brilliance, she heard Marcus say: *It's just nature, darling. Kill or be killed and all that. We're just fighting for our place in the food chain.* She sat bolt upright in bed, her hair and skin wet through with sweat, her breathing laboured. She reached for the lamp and turned the switch. Light flooded the room. She stared at her phone. It was just after 4 a.m.

Resigned to the fact that she wouldn't be able to get back to sleep, she swapped her usual tea for a mug of coffee and sipped it in the living room, trying to shake the strange dream from her mind. The sky gradually turned purple, revealing a hard winter frost on the lawn outside. Kristen continued to gaze numbly out of the window until PC Stock called her at a quarter past seven.

'Just to let you know, we got approval on the helicopter. It did a search for your husband overnight, but there was no sign of him.'

'There wasn't?'

'That's good news, Mrs Hardy. It means he wasn't out in the forest alone, so he's likely taken shelter somewhere. Hopefully that means he's safe.'

That's a relief, she thought. *Of a sort anyway.*

'Will you keep looking for him?' she asked.

'Not with the helicopter. We have to justify every NPAS request and it's already covered the whole forest. But rest assured, we've put the word out with all our patrols across the county. If anyone spots him, they'll call it in.'

Kristen sighed internally. She'd hoped they would have found Marcus already, but she appreciated they were doing all they could.

'Thank you, officer,' she said.

As soon as she hung up, she remembered the presbytery and called again. This time, she was happy to hear Father Nolan pick up. 'It's Kristen Hardy,' she said. 'Sorry to call so early, but I wondered if you've seen Marcus recently?'

'Mrs Hardy,' replied the reedy voice. 'I got your message. I was going to call you. As it happens, your husband *was* here, a couple of days ago.'

Kristen's heart beat faster. 'He was?

'Yes, he was visiting Abi's grave,' Nolan said. 'I did ask after you, but he said you were in Geneva.'

Kristen shut her eyes. This was the first time he had gone to the grave that she knew of. She pressed Nolan for more details.

'Well, he told me that he'd been having a lot of spiritual revelations,' Nolan said. 'In particular, about something he referred to as the great ring ... or ...'

'The great chain of being?' she suggested.

'Yes, that's it. I don't know what he was referring to

exactly. But he kept calling me an *emissary*. To be honest, he didn't quite seem himself. I hope everything is all right?'

No, she thought. *Everything is very much not all right.* Anger stirred inside her. By her reckoning, Marcus had already been using the God helmet a couple of weeks before Nolan had shared Mass with him. If the young priest hadn't encouraged him, perhaps he would have stopped altogether. But that wasn't true, was it? It was clear from the video diaries that Marcus had fully intended to keep going. And besides, it wasn't the kid's fault. He was only being true to the things he believed, many of which Kristen herself had believed only yesterday.

'Mrs Hardy? You still there?'

'Listen, Father,' she said. 'Do me a favour. If Marcus shows up again, you call me. Straight away, okay? Can you do that?'

'Of course, Mrs Hardy,' he said.

She cut the call before he could ask any more questions.

22

When the front door bell rang at eleven thirty, she felt a deep sense of relief. At last, here were her reinforcements. Never had there been a more welcome couple standing on her doorstep. Bree lurched forward, throwing her arms around her, as Darius shepherded Poppy around the two women and into the hallway.

'I'm so glad you're here,' Kristen whispered in her ear. 'It's all so crazy.'

'Don't you worry about a thing, girlie,' Bree said. 'You're not alone now. The friggin' cavalry has arrived.'

'Bree!' Darius said, covering Poppy's ears.

'What? I said *friggin'*.'

Kristen let go of her friend and escorted her out of the cold. In the entranceway, she crouched down and placed her hands on Poppy's shoulders. 'Hey, sweetheart, would you like some ice cream? There's a tub in the freezer. If it's okay with Mum?'

The girl looked at her mother.

'Go ahead, Pops,' Bree said.

Poppy nodded shyly back at Kristen, who offered her hand and led her into the kitchen. Kristen was pleased to discover that it was less painful interacting with her this time. More than that, she actually took pleasure in watching Poppy devour the strawberry scoops she handed to her in a bowl. At Kristen's invitation, Bree and Darius made themselves at home. Darius took the luggage upstairs to the guest bedroom while Bree freshened up in the downstairs bathroom.

Later, the four of them sat in the living room, spread out between the two long L-shaped sofas. Poppy lay between Bree and Darius, earphones in, shuffling her legs around as she watched a show on her tablet. She was oblivious to the conversation the adults were having, and Kristen preferred it that way. Darius was asking her about Marcus's visit and the graffiti he'd left behind.

'Can I see the items?' Darius said. 'I mean, if you don't mind?'

'Sure.'

Kristen took them upstairs to the bedroom and showed them the jacket and boots, laying them out on the bed. Darius examined a boot and the word written on it.

'These are all made of leather,' he said.

'Yes,' Kristen said. 'The journal in the study is too.'

'It reminds me of something …' Darius frowned as he tried to remember. 'Yes, from Genesis!' he finally said. 'The story of the Garden of Eden. Adam and Eve felt the shame of their nakedness and tried to cover themselves in fig leaves.'

Kristen recalled the account. *The Lord God made garments of skin for Adam and his wife and clothed them,* she quoted.

'Some have interpreted this as God giving them a more permanent way to cover their shame,' Darius said.

'I always thought the fig leaves were about Adam's shame,' Bree said. 'Like the Garden of Eden was super cold or something.'

Darius ignored her. 'It was the realisation that they were

naked,' he said. 'Which they only knew because they ate from the Tree of Knowledge. I think all this leather reminded Marcus of the animal skin that covered Adam and Eve before God expelled them from the garden.'

'But why? It makes no sense,' Bree said.

'There likely isn't a why,' Kristen said. 'Any more than there's a *why* I'm seeing supernatural beings in my own garden.'

'It's those stupid machines,' Bree said. 'Clearly they've been fucking with both your brains.'

Kristen shook her head. 'Marcus's, maybe. He purposely put himself on a path to crazy. But all my religious instincts, my faith, went away. The sessions were working, remember? I couldn't even attend church with you guys. How could I now be hallucinating things as well?'

Darius put the boot back down and regarded Kristen carefully. 'Have you considered the possibility that maybe what you saw was real?' he asked.

She raised an eyebrow at him. 'Real?'

'I understand why you went to Geneva,' Darius said. 'But Kristen, what if you're wrong? What if that *was* an angel? Surely it can't be that long ago that you've forgotten what it's like to have your mind opened to the things of God?'

She responded with another head shake. 'I'm sorry, Darius, but that doesn't make sense. Marcus is seeing and hearing things too, and he's gone off the rails. I think he might even have ...'

She closed her eyes tightly and made herself say it. 'I think he might have murdered Harry,' she said.

'I hate to suggest this, Kristen, but what if Marcus's experiences are also real ... what if he's being influenced by something evil?'

Bree looked at her husband. 'Like, *devil* evil? You're talking about some kind of full-blown exorcist shit?'

Darius didn't reply, but stared at Kristen earnestly. 'What

if you, on the other hand, have been called back to God? What if these dreams and visions are a sign? Not of whatever Marcus is being drawn to, but the opposite. What if God is overriding what the helmet was supposed to do in order to call you back to Himself?'

Kristen was dumbstruck by the idea. 'But for what reason?' she asked. 'And even if there was such a thing as God, which I no longer believe, why would He need me? Couldn't He accomplish whatever He wanted to without me?' She exhaled before continuing. 'Bree's right. The best explanation is something went wrong with the helmets, somewhere. It has to be.'

'Maybe,' Darius said. 'But I still believe in God. And I just wonder if maybe it's possible that God is calling you for some higher purpose. Maybe something way beyond your limited understanding. Maybe beyond any of ours.'

The women both stared at him sceptically.

'Hey, I'm just trying to keep an open mind,' he said.

23

Though she was not in the mood, Kristen allowed Bree to talk her into opening a bottle of wine. They were alone, sitting on stools on opposite sides of the kitchen island.

'Just ignore him,' Bree said. 'He's just getting overexcited. He never was comfortable with you deciding to have your noodle messed with. He thought it was, I don't know, blasphemy or something.'

'Oh really?' Kristen said. 'He never said anything.'

'He's too polite,' Bree said. 'And kind. Try not to judge him, Krissy. He means well. But he believes in angels and demons and all that shit. He's a proper Catholic, so I guess he can't help it.'

'It's okay.'

Kristen had not sensed any malice from Darius. Although he'd been animated at the idea of some kind of supernatural showdown, he'd struck her as well-meaning and sincere. As for the theory he advocated, it disturbed her more than she'd let on. Yes, she'd protested the notion, intellectually at least. She couldn't accept an other-worldly explanation. But her strange experiences had all the hallmarks of perceived reality. Put another way, it had all *felt* real, whether it had been or not. She sipped her Chardonnay, trying not to let crazy thoughts into her head. The only thing that mattered was finding Marcus. Maybe then the knot in her stomach would finally loosen.

'Hey,' Bree said. 'How about we watch a movie? Take our minds off this shit for a while. There's nothing you can do right now except let the police do their job, right?'

Kristen nodded keenly. Bree was completely right. What they all needed was a distraction.

They watched a mindless all-ages comedy about a big dog that gets adopted into a large family. Kristen barely paid attention to the film, her mind becoming increasingly numb as the afternoon wore on and Bree kept topping up her wine. Kristen had dragged a beanbag out for Poppy from the downstairs storage cupboard. The girl took to it like a fish to water, nestling deep into it to watch the movie. Kristen also made her a big bowl of popcorn and tried to ignore the awful pang of grief as memories of rainy-day movie afternoons resurfaced. Darius seemed embarrassed at his earlier outburst and kept quiet throughout the film. After the credits rolled, Kristen felt chilly and offered to fetch blankets or turn the heating up. Darius shrugged, but Bree and Poppy were keen on both options, so she rose from her seat. She was about to head to the laundry room, where she kept spare blankets, when a snippet from the television caught her attention. Darius had flicked over to the news, where a reporter's voice had just uttered the words *'producer of* The Rites Stuff*'*. When Kristen saw the monitor, she was confused. There was a photo of Tim Barnes, smiling, his arm around his husband Steve.

'... police are not saying whether the murders are hate-related, an official this afternoon stating that no lines of enquiry have been ruled out ...'

Kristen blinked hard at the TV and felt as if she was having another one of her recent bizarre dreams.

'Hey,' said Bree. 'Isn't that—?'

'Oh my God,' Kristen said, cupping her hands over her mouth.

Her knees buckled, and she went down on them, her legs losing their strength as she tried to absorb what she was watching.

'... *the double murder is believed to have taken place last night. The couple were discovered by a visiting neighbour, who described wandering into a scene not unlike something from a horror movie ...*'

The segment cut to said neighbour, a stout man in his sixties who looked genuinely like he'd seen a ghost.

'*It were 'orrible,*' the man said, in a strong cockney accent. '*I thought it were like some kind of Satanic ritual. I don't even wanna describe what I found —*'

'Bree, take Poppy out of the room, will you, please?' Kristen said.

She was surprised at how calm her voice was. Somehow, she knew where this was all leading. Bree didn't hesitate, marching Poppy into the dining room as quickly as she could.

'*... I mean, whoever it was, they was savage,*' the witness continued. '*To do what they did to two of the nicest blokes you ever met ... some people are sick in the world, I tell ya.*'

On screen, the scene cut to a police officer taking questions from the press, outside Tim Barnes's house in Kingston. Kristen's mouth was as dry as sandpaper.

'*Can you confirm this was a homophobic hate crime?*' one of the journalists asked, shouting to get his voice heard above his peers.

'*We have no comment at this time,*' the officer said.

'*We heard the word "shame" was written in blood on the sofa. Wouldn't this indicate —?*'

'*We can't comment on the specifics of the case,*' the officer insisted.

'*Shame?*' Darius murmured. 'You don't think ...?'

Kristen did not reply. But unfortunately, yes. She really did think. It was surely too much of a coincidence to be anything but.

'I mean, if it was a leather sofa, therefore animal skin. Maybe ...'

Kristen could barely hear him. Her husband's voice was whispering in her head.

It's just nature, darling. Kill or be killed and all that.

She remembered Marcus's manic speech to camera, back at Harry Dean's apartment.

I saw him suffer. I heard his screams. But I had no choice.

It was as if something tilted in the world. Outside, the light faded. Icy mists had formed on the windows. Kristen touched her forearm with one hand and discovered it was trembling.

24

She called the station in Willowdale and asked to speak to Stock or Grant. The man who answered told her neither had begun their shifts and asked her what her call was about. When she told him, she was put straight through to the station's Duty Officer, who introduced herself as Sergeant Christina Harris. Harris listened quietly as Kristen outlined her suspicions.

'But you have no evidence your husband was involved?' she asked neutrally.

'No,' Kristen admitted. 'But I'm sure of it. He's not well, and he's, er, he's been missing for a couple of days.'

She heard keys tapping on the other end of the line. 'Ah yes,' the sergeant said. 'We've been searching for your husband in the locale, I see. But now you think he's in Surrey?'

'I think he might have been last night,' Kristen said. 'I'm worried he might have ... hurt Tim and his husband.'

Yet again, she couldn't bring herself to say the word *murder*, despite what she believed in her heart.

'I see,' Harris said. 'Have you by any chance heard from your husband?'

Kristen confirmed she hadn't. She heard more light tapping of keys. 'I'm just looking at the national report,' Harris said. 'Victims were … Tim and Steve Barnes. What exactly was your husband's relationship with them?'

'Tim was Marcus's boss,' Kristen said.

'Did your husb … did Marcus harbour any animosity towards him that you knew of?'

'No, none,' Kristen said. 'But he's not himself. I don't know if you have a record of this, but there are these machines that … well …'

She told Harris what she had told Stock and Grant. When she had finished, she wondered if the connection had been cut. But eventually the sergeant responded.

'Mind-control machines? I have to be honest, Mrs Hardy, it sounds a little like science fiction.'

'I get that,' Kristen said. 'But I promise it's true.'

'And you think this machine could have made Marcus murder those men?'

She shut her eyes, felt a stab of pain in her heart. 'I don't want to,' she said. 'But, yes.'

'Hmm.' Harris was silent for a while. 'Okay,' she said finally. 'I'll pass this on to the Met police. If there's anything behind what you say, I'm sure they'll be in touch in due course.'

'Thank you.'

'In the meantime, it says here you yourself have reported seeing visions of things that weren't there? Is that right?'

'Yes,' Kristen confirmed.

'And how are you doing now? Any hallucinations? Hearing any voices?'

'No,' Kristen lied. 'I'm absolutely fine.'

'I see,' Harris said.

There was something about her tone Kristen didn't like. A subtle but present suggestion that she was being judged. She half suspected they had a folder on her named 'Crazy Lady'.

Even so, when Harris eventually hung up on her, Kristen knew she had done the right thing by calling.

Bree rustled up an early dinner for Poppy, while Darius retired to his room to answer work emails. Kristen kept her friend and her daughter company as pasta boiled on the stove. Bree moved with confidence from cupboard to fridge to oven. She knew the kitchen inside out after spending all those weeks looking after her. And now here she was, doing it again. It made Kristen feel both guilty and grateful. The women refrained from discussing the murders in front of Poppy, but there was a lot of unspoken tension. They were both equally quiet as Poppy wolfed down her pasta at the small kitchen table, looking into each other's eyes to read the subtle unspoken dialogue between them. Kristen's phone rang, making her jump.

'How are you doing?' Adrian Kemplar asked when she picked up.

Kristen stepped away from the table, distancing herself from Poppy. 'Not good,' she said. 'Something terrible has happened.'

Checking she was out of earshot, Kristen told him about the murders of Tim Barnes and his husband and the graffiti their killer allegedly left at the scene.

'My God, that's awful,' Adrian said. 'I'm so sorry. Were you close?'

'Tim was a friend,' Kristen said. 'They both were.'

'I'm sorry,' he repeated.

Neither of them spoke for a moment, and then the psychiatrist got to the reason for his call. 'Kristen, I've been watching all the videos and studying all the pictures you sent me.' He let out a slow breath. 'And I think I may have a hypothesis. About the specific nature of Marcus's ... psychosis.'

Psychosis. Murders. What was even happening? she wondered.

'I think Marcus has been trying to construct a meta-narrative.'

'Meta what?' she asked.

'It's just a fancy word for a belief system. A story that would make sense of whatever religious or spiritual epiphanies he's been experiencing from using the God helmet.'

'Okay ...' Kristen said hesitantly.

'In the video diaries, he starts off following Harry's programme, taking it slow and easy. After a few sessions, he becomes more open to the notion of God and religion.'

'Yes, that's right,' Kristen said, remembering Marcus's interactions with Father Connolly and Father Nolan.

'We can see him fixate on some aspects of that faith that now make sense to him in a way they hadn't before. Like the notion of an afterlife, an all-powerful divine being etcetera. He develops an interest in the Garden of Eden.'

'He kept talking about Adam and Eve being allowed to eat the fruit,' she said.

'Yes, that makes a lot of sense,' Adrian said. 'I think the anthropologist in him saw Eden as a metaphor for our evolutionary past, the jungles and forests we first emerged from.'

Kristen recalled the snippets she'd read from the legible parts of Marcus's journal.

Doctor Kemplar continued. 'As Marcus starts to spend an increasingly unhealthy amount of time with the helmet, his beliefs get more bizarre. But he's still trying to make sense of his revelations in a way that fits with his knowledge of evolutionary development. I believe he eventually found that ... in an idea called the *Great Chain of Being.*'

'Yes! He kept talking about a Great Being,' Kristen said.

'Something about it sounded familiar,' Adrian said. 'Then

I remembered. There was a chapter dedicated to it in his third book. So I looked it up. Page sixty-six. There's an illustration there that I think explains everything.'

'Wait,' Kristen said. 'Can you hold on?'

She ran upstairs to Marcus's study and pulled out the paperback from the shelf. 'Sixty-six? Okay, got it.'

She was looking at an image that she half recalled. An old black-and-white illustration of a stack of creatures in a kind of pyramid. She knew it was famous and that maybe she'd even seen it at a museum or something once.

'During the Middle Ages, it was widely believed that everything in the universe had a specific place in it,' the doctor explained. 'This idea was called the Great Chain of Being. It's been used to justify social and political hierarchies throughout history, and Marcus was more than familiar with it, as you can see.'

She traced her finger down the illustration from top to bottom.

'What you're looking at is a depiction of the divine order of creation,' Adrian said. 'God is at the top and all life forms are arranged underneath, in descending order of importance.'

'Yes, I see it.'

'The chain attempts to organise and categorise all life into one system. God is at the highest pinnacle, then angels, man, and after that, all the animals down to inanimate objects like plants and rocks at the very bottom. Every creature has a specific place and function, a place on the ladder.'

'Yes,' she said, trying to follow.

'There are a number of themes in Marcus's ramblings,' Adrian continued. 'Things he keeps coming back to. But the core of these is this idea of hierarchy. Specifically, that the most powerful being of all is at the top of the ladder. But it seems Marcus has moved beyond the Judeo-Christian concept of God. Or the God of any religion known today. Instead, he calls this great being the Apex.'

She sat down in the study chair, trying to wrap her head around it.

'I think Marcus believes the Apex ultimately has the divine right to take the life of any creature down the ladder. As they do the creatures below them.'

Kristen closed her eyes.

Kill or be killed and all that. We're just fighting for our place in the food chain.

'But it gets worse,' Adrian said. 'From what I can glean, he believes he thinks he's doing the will of this Apex. It's possible he might have committed these murders for this reason.'

'But why?' she asked, perplexed.

'I don't know for sure. But given his conviction that this being has the power to grant life and death for every creature that ever lived, I have a suspicion. And you're not going to like it.'

'Tell me,' she said.

'I think Marcus believes this Apex is going to bring your daughter back from the dead,' he said.

25

The adults shared a silent dinner around the table, a stir-fry Kristen whipped up at the last minute. Poppy sat with them playing cards by herself so no one dared say anything. After the meal was over, however, Poppy retreated to the sofa with her tablet and Kristen told Bree and Darius everything Doctor Kemplar had told her.

'So he thinks God is some kind of ... predator?' Darius said.

'I think so,' Kristen said. 'Like an apex predator. With the ultimate power over all other lives.'

Darius looked pensive. 'And Marcus believes this being will bring your Abi back?'

'That's what Adrian thinks,' Kristen said.

No one said anything for a moment.

'Kristen,' he said, 'have you thought any more about what I said? That what's happening to Marcus could be the work of the devil?'

Kristen rolled her eyes. 'Oh, come on.'

'I'm serious,' he said. 'What if God wants to use you to stop Marcus from killing any more people, somehow?'

She shot him an angry look. 'You think Satan made my

husband go on a crazy murdering spree just so God could make me his divine cosmic agent?'

Darius looked away. 'I don't know. But *something* isn't adding up. I still think maybe those dreams and visions you've been having might mean something.'

'Hey, you're freakin' her out!' Bree said. 'Leave her alone with that crap. Can't you see she's scared enough already?'

'I'm just trying to make sense of it all,' Darius said. 'I still believe in God, and in good and evil. And there's evil going on here. Maybe three murders so far. And Kristen could have been given signs from God.'

'Now you sound like Marcus,' Kristen said.

She wanted to add *by which I mean bat-shit crazy*, but didn't. Darius was an old friend and she knew he did not mean any harm. Bree glanced over at Poppy as if to make sure she was still immersed in her film. The girl was, but Bree dropped her voice to a whisper anyway.

'Who friggin' cares whether there's supernatural shit involved, Darius?' she said. 'If Marcus is out there murdering people, the police need to find him. And quickly.'

'What if he doesn't want to be found?' Darius asked.

Before either of them could answer, Kristen's phone rang on the table, and Marcus's name flashed up.

26

Seeing the word 'Marcus' fill the screen snapped them all back to reality. Kristen glanced nervously at her friends. Bree nodded. Darius did too, and then suggested she put it on speakerphone so they could all hear.

'M-Marcus?' Kristen said, her voice trembling.

'Darling!'

'Where are you, Marcus? The police are out looking for you.'

'Naturally,' he said, and laughed. 'Still, they won't be able to stop it now.'

Kristen felt her heart go icy. 'Stop what?'

'The will of the Great Being,' Marcus said.

'You mean the Apex?'

Marcus laughed again. 'I see you've been reading my journal. Fine, let us finally speak Its holy name.'

'And what *is* this Apex's will, darling?' she asked.

'To give us our Abi back, Kris. Surely you've worked that much out by now.'

The cold feeling crept across her chest now, spreading all around her. 'Marcus, darling,' she said. 'Abi is dead. You *know* this.'

This time he laughed so hard his voice made the phone's speaker crackle. 'Well, lucky for us the Apex can grant life back to whoever It pleases.'

'Marcus, listen—'

'No, Kris. *You* listen. We don't have much time. It's all coming together now, but you need to stop these doubts. It's getting ridiculous.'

'Marcus,' Kristen said. 'Did you hurt Tim? Did you … did you …?'

'Kill him? Is that what you want to know? Yes. Happy now?'

Kristen let out an involuntary sob. She had suspected, of course, but hearing the awful confession from Marcus's own lips was another story. 'You murdered them both?' she said. 'In cold blood!'

'Nature is cold, Kris. But if it makes a difference I had no choice. They refused to give me the knife.'

'What knife?' she asked, confused.

'From Luzon island,' he said. 'The one the *Homo Luzonensis* used for hunting. You remember, don't you? How it had been so well preserved in that cave. It was a sign, you see. The Apex was moving everything into place. Making Tim bring the knife all the way across the world, just for me.'

'Why?'

'So that I can cover my shame,' he said. He tutted, as though this should be obvious.

'Shame?' she asked, just echoing his words now.

'For not having believed,' Marcus said. 'Not respecting the Great Chain. I was ignorant, Kris. Even with all my studies and so-called knowledge.'

He surprised her by suddenly crying. 'I was so confused and upset by what happened,' he sobbed. 'I just didn't … couldn't understand how it could ever make sense.'

Once she might have felt pity, but now there was only

anger. *How dare he?* He didn't deserve any sympathy after what he'd done.

'Then the helmet started working,' Marcus continued. 'I began to see …' He sniffed hard, like he was determined to get through his speech. 'The Apex took our daughter, Kris,' Marcus said. 'That is Its right. The lion hunts the gazelle. The Apex hunts us. It's just the order of things. But thankfully It can be merciful too. It told me how we can get her back.'

The emotional dam finally broke inside Kristen. 'Marcus, you are not sane!' she snapped. 'Don't you see? The helmet screwed your brain up. None of this is real. There is no Apex!'

'Harry tried to tell me the same thing,' Marcus said. 'But he was wrong.'

Darius looked up, exchanging a concerned glance with Kristen. She leaned forward, grabbed the edges of the coffee table and steeled herself for the question. 'Where is Harry?' Kristen asked. 'Did you kill him too?'

'You need to understand, I had no choice,' Marcus said.

Kristen closed her eyes in despair.

'Harry didn't believe the Apex was real.' Marcus grunted, a frustrated sound. 'There isn't much time,' he said. 'The Apex Itself is coming. You need to stop your unbelief, right now and get on fucking board.'

'On board with what?' she asked.

'I've made a deal, Kris,' Marcus said. 'It's going to bring our princess back. But only if we do what It wants.'

'Darling,' Kristen pleaded. 'You are not well. You need to hand yourself in to the authorities.'

'It'll make its presence known to you this very night,' Marcus said. 'So be ready.'

'Marcus, wait—'

But the call had already ended.

27

She dialled Willowdale station immediately.

'He actually confessed to the murders?' Sergeant Christina Harris said, sounding shocked.

'Please,' Kristen said, 'you *have* to find him.'

'We've been doing our best,' Harris said. 'I don't suppose he gave you a clue as to his whereabouts?'

Kristen cast her mind back. 'I don't think so,' she said. 'He called me from his mobile so he could be any—'

She stopped short as an idea struck her.

'Mrs Hardy?'

'Hang on,' she said.

She pulled her phone away from her ear and tapped the app named 'FamilyFinder'. Her breath caught in her throat as she waited for it to load. But when it did, only her device was showing. Marcus's was greyed out. 'He must have removed his device from the app. He could be *anywhere*.' She groaned. 'Oh my God, what if he's on his way here to the house?'

'For what it's worth, I don't think it's likely,' Harris said. 'You told me yourself he knows the police are out looking for him, right?'

'You don't understand,' Kristen said. 'He's not in his right mind.'

'Be that as it may, Mrs Hardy, he clearly knew he needed to escape the scene of the crime at the Barnes home. Which means whatever his mental distress, he obviously knows the consequences of being caught. I sincerely doubt he'll risk being arrested.'

'But you can't guarantee it,' Kristen said. It was more of a statement than a question. 'Can you send someone round at least?'

Harris paused. 'I can put in a request to Southampton. But they may not have the resources. Plus, they'll need to be convinced your life is in danger. Did Marcus threaten you?'

'Well, no, not exactly …'

'Has he indicated to you that he intends to come to the house?'

She remembered Marcus's words. *The Apex Itself is coming.*

'Not personally,' she admitted.

'Look,' Harris said, 'given what you've told me, I think there's another way we can escalate this. Marcus is clearly using his phone again, which means we should be able to locate him.'

'But the app—'

'The app doesn't matter,' Harris said. 'We can triangulate his position using phone towers.'

Kristen was relieved to hear it. 'You can? Well, that's great!'

'But we need to get permission from his network provider. It's a whole legal thing and it can take a while. Do you know who he's with?'

Kristen gave her the name of Marcus's mobile network company.

'Okay,' Harris said. 'Let me contact them now, see if I can push this through. It's the end of the working day though, so I doubt we'll even get the process started tonight. In the meantime, are you alone in the house? Is there anyone with you?'

'My friends are here with me,' Kristen said.

'Good. Like I say, I doubt he'll risk coming there. But if he shows up, you call us immediately. Understood?'

Kristen promised.

28

Darius took Poppy upstairs to bed. Kristen thought maybe she would have picked up on the strange tension going on in the house, but all the girl seemed interested in was the Christmas tree her father had promised they would go out and buy tomorrow.

'What if he *does* come here, Bee?' Kristen said, when she was sure they would not be overheard. 'What if he tries to hurt us?'

'Don't worry, hun,' Bree said. 'Darius is going to be downstairs.'

She was repeating the offer her husband had made an hour earlier to sleep on the living room sofa, with everyone else upstairs, which Kristen had gratefully taken up. She had locked all the windows and doors using bolts and chained the front door. Marcus still had his front door key, but he wouldn't be able to gain access easily. But while she was concerned about Marcus visiting, she was also starting to wonder whether that was all they needed to worry about. She didn't say anything, but the questions about her own psyche were resurfacing in her mind. Somewhere deep inside her, a primal fear threatened to take over. The fear that Marcus's delusions were real. Kristen recalled what Adrian Kemplar had said about her suggestibility. But if she really was being gaslit by Marcus's fantasies, why had she become so susceptible? Hadn't she spent the last three months rewiring her brain to be more sceptical about such things? Amanda Tanner had shown her her scans, hadn't she? Not that Kristen could make sense of them, of course. But what reason would Tanner have to lie? She heard footsteps and saw Darius had returned. She looked at the two of them imploringly.

'What if it's not Marcus you guys need to worry about?'

'What do you mean?' Darius said.

'What if it's me?'

Bree laughed. 'Daft mare!'

'I'm serious. What if I'm the next one to go full psycho on you guys?'

Bree put her glass down and squeezed Kristen's arm. 'Krissy, I don't know what the hell is going on with you. But I do know you. And you would never hurt a fly.'

Kristen shook her head. 'Wouldn't I?' she said. 'Are you sure? Three months ago, I would have said the same thing about my husband. And now look where we are.'

Bree said nothing, but Kristen clocked her giving Darius a concerned look and him returning one. It was obvious neither of them could think of anything to say that would comfort her.

<h1 style="text-align:center">29</h1>

It was dark when Kristen opened her eyes. Dark, and freezing cold. The clouds obscured the moonlight, but it was enough to see she was standing in her back garden. She was in her gown and barefoot. But how had she got here? She spun around, trying to remember. She touched the skin of her cheek and the film of sweat she discovered brought back memories of a dream. Of her, running through the foliage. Running from a predator. No, not a predator. *The* predator. She spun around. The patio doors had been flung open. She had no watch but it felt to her like the witching hour. Perhaps 3 or 4 a.m. There was a crunch, the loud snapping of branches, and her breath caught in her throat. From here, she had a clear view of the gate and beyond. Something moved in the adjacent field, some kind of creature, onyx-dark. It was hard to discern its shape, but it had an unnatural gravity and presence that she could sense even from here. Her stomach flipped. The *Apex* was here. Marcus had been right all along.

The dark shape paused and she felt every cell in her body freeze up with fear. It was hard to comprehend. It was like understanding something fundamental for the first time, something primal. This being was the first and the last, the Alpha and the Omega. She knew that It was looking at her right now, in the same way she knew the ocean was made of water, or that the sun would rise in the sky tomorrow. The only problem was, she was no longer sure the sun would rise for her. She remained cemented to the spot, spikes of fear shooting through her body whenever she considered inching back towards the house. Her heart raced. Part of her might have been inclined to pray, even after everything. But she understood now that there was no God apart from the Apex, harrowing be Thy name. Her existence hung in the balance, as fragile as a spider's web. The Apex need only decide to pounce and her life would be snuffed like a candle wick, just as poor Abigail's had been. There was nothing to do now except wait for the end to come.

SIX

1

It felt as though eons passed. Kristen did not know how she managed to stay standing, shaking with terror.

Eventually, for whatever reason known only to Itself, the Apex moved away, deeper into the forest. Preying on other creatures down the food chain, perhaps. But mercifully, sparing her. A hand touched her shoulder and she screamed.

2

'Kristen,' Darius said. 'What are you doing out here?'

She gasped, flinging her arms around him in terror. 'It's here,' she whispered in his ear.

Bree made a hot toddy, something Kristen hadn't had since she was a child. She sipped it slowly at the island and Darius and Bree sat on stools either side of her. Bree rubbed her back.

'It was just a dream, girlie,' she said. 'You're okay, honestly.'

'No,' Kristen said. 'No, it's real. It's here. Marcus was right.'

'No, he isn't, hun. You just took an express train to Crazy Town, that's all.'

'Bree!' Darius said.

'I'm just saying it's in her head. There's nothing out there, hun. Nothing that will hurt you.'

'What will hurt her?' asked a young voice.

Poppy, dressed in her pyjamas, had wandered downstairs. 'I heard screaming, Mum. Is ev-everything okay?'

Kristen glanced at the poor scared girl, unable to answer.

The whisky's warm effect trickled down her throat and across her chest.

'Everything's fine, doll,' Bree said. 'Aunty Krissy just had a bad dream, that's all. Isn't that right, Krissy?'

Kristen saw the whites of Poppy's eyes and wanted nothing more than to protect her from the horrible truth. 'Th-that's right, darling,' she lied.

Poppy instantly relaxed and switched into excited mode. 'What time is it, Dad?' she asked. 'When are we getting the tree?'

'It's only just gone four, sweetie,' Darius said. 'Why don't you go back to bed?'

Poppy shook her head. 'I feel like I'm too awake now.'

'Me too,' Bree said. 'Why don't we all have some early breakfast? Think you could manage something, hun?'

It took a moment to realise that Bree was addressing *her*. Kristen smiled weakly, still pretending for the sake of the girl.

3

Dawn light streamed through the windows. Bree made everyone pancakes and sat Poppy in front of the TV to watch cartoons. Kristen remained at the island, trying to make sense of what she'd experienced. The logical part of her wanted to believe it was all in her mind. But she couldn't deny what had happened, even if she couldn't explain it. Fear was its own truth. Just because a rabbit fleeing for its life cannot grasp how a hunter's rifle works doesn't mean the threat isn't real. Kristen did not fully understand the Apex. But that didn't change reality. It was here. Somewhere in the forest, still watching and waiting near the house. The question was why? What did It want? And did it have anything to do with whatever Faustian deal Marcus had managed to negotiate? Anxiety gripped her as she studied her house guests – Bree scrolling through her phone, Darius reclining in the single armchair, snoring softly, the only one of them to manage going back to sleep. They'd both had their theories about Kristen's mental state, Bree's grounded in scientific reality, Darius in his Catholic beliefs. But neither was prepared to believe two truths that Kristen now accepted, deep in her gut. One, that Marcus was right about the Apex and the reality of

Its existence. And two, it was no coincidence It had decided to seek out their location. Given Its fundamental predatory nature, It was clearly here to hunt.

Kristen spent the next few hours watching the garden nervously, wondering what to do next. But by lunchtime, she had made a decision.

'Maybe you should try to get some sleep, girlie,' Bree suggested as she cleared more plates away.

Kristen shook her head. 'I'm okay, Bee. I feel … okay. I appreciate it. I tell you what, though. I'll have a cigarette.'

She nodded at Bree's handbag.

'Really?'

'Really.'

Bree fished out the packet and offered it across. 'I'll join you,' she said.

'No, you stay here,' Kristen said. 'I'd rather be alone for a while. No offence.'

'Sure, whatever you need, Krissy.'

Kristen took the cigarette and the lighter Bree gave her and pulled on a coat before venturing into the garden. She lit the tip, dragged on the butt a few times, and glanced back towards the house. Bree, Darius and Poppy were all in the living room, focused on the TV. She needed to do this for them, and for the girl in particular. Kristen flicked the rest of her cigarette onto the wet grass, where it dampened out immediately. She headed towards the gate. A moment later, she was across the field. And then on to the woods, under the overcast sky, where she knew the Apex waited. Where she planned to negotiate with It as Marcus had done. To beg and plead for It to at least spare her friends.

4

She entered through a copse, trees surrounding her like grey-silhouetted sentries. Everything was coated in fog. Fear gripped her, seizing the muscles in her legs and arms. She stopped to place a hand against the trunk of a nearby tree. What was she thinking? This had clearly been a mistake. She felt a quickening inside her, the feeling of being stalked.

'Krissy?'

Bree appeared, standing behind her. 'The fuck, Krissy. What are you doing out here?'

'It's not s-safe,' Kristen said. 'Get back in the house, Bree. Quick!'

'What's not safe?' Bree asked her.

'It's here,' Kristen said.

'What's here? Come on, Krissy, I'm freezing my tits off here. Let's go inside.'

'I'm going to ask It to spare you.'

'Fuck's sake, Krissy.' Bree reached for her arm just as a booming crunching noise came from within the fog, less than twenty feet away. Bree startled, and snapped her head towards its point of origin.

'What is that? A horse or—'

'Bree, *run!*' Kristen yelled.

The stomping became louder. The here-and-now of her friend in danger redirected her fear-adrenaline. She grabbed Bree's hand and tried to yank her back towards the house. But she was met with resistance. Her best friend was rooted to the spot, presumably mesmerised by the sight of the ancient predator that was charging at them. Kristen dared to look too and saw the Apex in Its full grotesqueness. In another place and time, removed from the danger, an outside observer might have marvelled at the Being's chimera-like qualities. It resembled the creature from the Book of Ezekiel that she had seen in her dream. Except that creature was only a representation of the real truth. For the Apex sported a lion's head, then a serpent's. But then a wolf's, a vulture's, a bear's, a hyena's. All these heads vibrated, moving at super speed, each rapidly transposing the one before. They swapped out so fast they all blurred into each other. For a moment, both women stood transfixed as the predator's faces changed, including once into a fang-toothed fish, a deep-sea creature Kristen had once seen in a nature documentary. And then stranger faces, ones she assumed belonged to ancient orders, to species now long extinct. The Apex stopped, then lunged forward. A powerful ape-like arm struck Kristen and sent her flying into a tree. She dropped to the wet, peaty floor like a stone, the wind knocked out of her.

'Get the fuck off me!' she heard Bree yell.

Kristen rolled over, to be greeted by the upside-down view of the hulk of a beast carrying her best friend off like a prize. *Boom-crunch, boom-crunch* went the Apex's legs as It vanished into the mist again. Kristen closed her eyes, a stab of deep grief jabbing her. She had lost her best friend to the One that had power over life and death. Just as she had lost Abi.

'Kristen! *Kristen!*'

She felt the world shake before realising it was just her body. Opening her eyes, she blinked in confusion as a man kept shouting her name. Then she knew who he was.

'Darius!'

'What happened?' he asked, anxiously. 'Where's Bree?'

She let out a sob. 'The Apex,' she said. 'The Apex took her.'

Darius shook his head. 'No, that's not possible. What really happened? Tell me!'

The fear in his voice had crept up a level. 'Was Marcus here?' Darius said.

'It took her,' Kristen said miserably.

'Oh, for goodness' sake,' Darius said.

A scream came from the forest, far off in the fog. A voice Darius would recognise all too well. It died as quickly as it had begun.

'Dear Lord, no. *Bree!*' He let go of Kristen, letting her slump back onto the mud, and ran into the veil of white fog, disappearing as quickly as Bree had done.

'Darius, don't!' Kristen yelled after him.

Darius had no idea what he was running towards and she failed to warn him in time. She reached out a feeble hand, then let it fall uselessly onto the ground. It was a small mercy that Darius's own cry of pain was as short-lived as Bree's had been, followed swiftly by a dull thud. *The power to take life*, she thought. Like a lion sinking its fangs into a gazelle, or a hawk snatching fish from a lake.

It's just nature, darling.

As it ever was, so ever shall it be.

5

She could have stayed that way, lying in the mulch, just waiting out her own inevitable fate. Were it not for the image of Poppy, who she suddenly remembered was still very much alive in the house. It was what galvanised her to push herself up from the ground. Somehow, she made it onto her knees and then her feet, though her legs were still shaky. There was no more sound from the white fog. The entire woods had become whisper-quiet. She sensed the Apex might be retreating again, deeper into the forest. It never crossed her mind that It might have spared Bree's and Darius's lives. Those cries of agony were all she needed to know about their fate. One goal propelled her forward. She had to try and get Poppy to safety. Each step she took back towards Orchard House felt like she was stuck in treacle. Eventually, however, she made it across the field and through the gate, into the back garden. Poppy stood behind the glass doors staring out wide-eyed at the sight of Kristen in her dirty clothes covered in mud. She stepped back as Kristen opened the door and collapsed onto the carpet by her feet.

'Wh-where's Mum and D-dad?' Poppy asked her.

Kristen did not dare to open her eyes and meet the girl's

imploring look. There would be no redemption in her answer. Instead, she rolled onto her back and let out a low, deep sob. This, in turn, triggered Poppy, who burst into tears. They stayed that way for a few moments, not a word passing between them. Eventually, Kristen managed to get a hold of herself enough to sit up, clutch her arms around her knees and rock back and forth. She looked at Poppy, a confused, frightened little girl, and her protective instincts kicked in again. She had to take her far away from here.

'Darling, you need to change out of your pyjamas,' she said. 'Go fetch the bag Mum packed for you.'

'What h-happened to her, Aunty Krissy?' the girl asked, her voice a few octaves higher than before.

Kristen opened her mouth, her scrambled brain searching for a way to frame the answer. But none came.

'Just pack,' she said.

She pushed against her knees, got to her feet. 'I'll help you,' she said.

It was less packing and more throwing as much as possible into a holdall. Once Poppy's bag was full, Kristen did the same. The girl followed her into the bedroom, tears running down her cheeks, repeating the question about her parents over and over. Kristen still could not reply. Her mind was now occupied with where they should flee to. She knew that the Apex was all-powerful, that in truth, It could stop time, bend the laws of physics if It wanted to. Which meant there wasn't anywhere It could not find them. But she sensed that the forest was its natural home, as was the darkness that fell upon the earth each night. It lived, as It had always lived, in the deep blackness that men and women used to keep at bay with campfires. Where the known world met the unknown. So where to, then? London, perhaps? Urban, built-up areas, saturated with Wi-Fi, electricity and people? That seemed like the best bet. It only made half-formed sense, but it was better than no plan at all. Bags finally ready, she threw them hastily in the Land Rover and returned for the girl. She grabbed Poppy's hand and led her out and across the driveway. She felt some resistance as Poppy protested that they couldn't leave her mum and dad behind. Kristen pulled her hard across the gravel. It was too late for Bree and Darius, but maybe there was still a chance for her. This thought was the last she remembered before she sensed a powerful presence, Ancient and Evil, approach from behind. Poppy screamed and the next thing Kristen knew a blunt force pushed her against the car, and her head hit the side of the door handle. Then everything went black.

6

She wasn't sure how much time had passed when she finally came to. Her cheek was wet and when she touched it, her fingers came away painted with blood. A panicked thought followed. *Where is Poppy?* Kristen scrambled to her feet, ignoring the chafing of the gravel against her palms. She looked around, but it was futile. The Apex was long gone now. But where had It taken Poppy? Had It killed her already? Maybe she was lying dead somewhere nearby. Kristen couldn't bear to look. Instead, she staggered back into the house as she debated her options. She could call the police. But she believed Marcus was right. They would not be able to thwart Its will. What possible good could they do? First things first. She needed to get the blood out of her eyes. In the kitchen, she washed her face and applied a plaster to her cut. Her phone rang. A video call request, Marcus's name on the screen. Sick to her stomach, she pressed answer.

'Praise the Apex!' Marcus cried when he saw her face. 'You're alive!'

'Marcus,' she said. 'Something's happened—'

'The Apex visited Its wrath upon you,' Marcus said. 'Hunted your friends. I know.'

A hot tear rolled down one cheek. 'Poppy ...'

'Yes, I know. But don't you worry, darling. The Apex has brought her to me.'

'Wh-what?'

Marcus flipped his phone around and she went from seeing a crop of his face to the outside world. It looked like he was somewhere in the forest. The connection broke up, but then sharpened just in time for her to see Poppy lying on the grass. Kristen could just about make out her chest rising and falling. The girl was unconscious but still alive. In the screen, she saw Marcus's free hand, waving the flint dagger he'd stolen from the Barnes house.

'Everything is almost in place, Kris,' he said. 'The girl is almost ready to be offered.'

'Marcus! What the fuck do you mean *offered*?'

'The Apex will need a sacrifice,' he said petulantly. 'A *life for a life.*'

He flipped the camera back to a close-up of his face. There was something on his head. But before she could discern what it was, he moved the camera closer until she saw nothing except his flaring nostrils. 'You will need to join me, though,' he said. 'To make sure we've both covered our shame.'

'I don't understand,' Kristen said. 'Please, don't hurt her!'

Her head was reeling. She had no chance against the all-powerful Apex. But at the same time she couldn't just sit there and do nothing. Futile or not, she had to try and save Poppy.

'I see you, Kris, I know what you're thinking. You're fond of the girl. I understand. But she's not our Abi. And, just so you know, if you contact the police, I *will* kill her. And then there's no chance of Abi coming back to us.'

'Oh, Marcus.'

She didn't know what to tell him. But she needed to play

along, at least for now. He was too volatile. 'Where?' she said. 'And when?'

'Tonight,' Marcus said. 'Half past five. Come to the spot where the Apex took Abi. Where she fell.'

'Marcus, I'll never find that,' she said.

'It's all right, Kris,' he said. 'Just open the FamilyFinder app.'

'Your phone's not on it,' she said.

He smiled. 'Been trying to find me, have you?' he said. 'It's all right, I've added it for you. It'll take you straight to me. But the Apex said you must wait until it's dark. Not before.'

He started to sing a song, one Kristen half recognised. But before she could place it, he spoke again.

'Just make sure you come alone,' Marcus said. 'Or she'll die a pointless death.'

He hung up. Kristen put her phone down and threw up.

7

She wiped the vomit from her mouth and tried to stop shaking. She felt powerless, like an ant trying to work out how to fight back against the shoe that wants to stomp on it. There was no way that she could see to rescue Poppy. The Apex had dominated the heavens and the earth since the start of time. What chance did she have? She sank her face into her palms as she considered her options. One thing she knew for sure. As much as she yearned to see Abi again, she could never, *ever* live with paying such a price. Her heart sank as she wiped the snot from her nose and allowed a feeling of hopelessness to wash over her. A siren sounded, warbled and far off. Her phone again. She scooped it up from the counter. It was Adrian Kemplar.

'Kristen, it's me. Something's happened here. I need you to listen carefully, okay?'

He spoke to her in calm, measured tones but the words didn't sink in and she had to ask him to repeat himself. 'Amanda Tanner has been arrested,' the psychiatrist said. 'She's in police custody now.'

'What?'

She wasn't sure she was hearing him right. Tanner? Why? What had she done?

'The police have been here at the institute,' Adrian said. 'They've been interviewing the staff involved with the God helmet trials. Amanda must have been spooked by them because when it was her turn she broke down and confessed to manipulating your sessions.'

The next question blurted out of her. 'Manipulating them how?' she asked.

'For the last three weeks, she's put you on a different programme designed to reverse everything it had done before. Your instincts were right. The helmet's been changing your neurological pathways in the opposite direction. She's been *trebling* the recommended exposure time too. It explains the visions you've been having. It's good news, Kristen. It means you're not going insane, after all.'

She barely took in what he was saying. 'It's ... definitely not real?' she said, desperate to believe what he was telling her.

'Nothing you've been seeing is real,' Adrian assured her. 'Your brain has been tricking you. I know it all *seems* real. But I can promise you it isn't.'

She felt a strange kind of ebbing, the tension in her muscles and limbs letting go. *It's all an illusion.* She couldn't fully process this, but she trusted him.

'Why?' she asked. 'Why would Amanda do this?'

'She's been very vocal in her opinions about the time and resources dedicated to the God helmet trials,' he said. 'She believes passionately the money ought to be spent elsewhere.'

Kristen remembered something Tanner had said about the trials.

He's been running this particular experiment for three years now and I'm not sure we've helped a single person.

'The police told me what little they know,' Adrian continued. 'Apparently she has a father with late-stage

Alzheimer's. It seems Harry promised to pull some strings and get her dad on an experimental new drug trial the Bennetts were sponsoring in the UK. But only if she switched the helmet programme without telling you.'

Kristen felt ill. '*Harry* was part of this? Why?'

'I'm afraid I don't have an answer,' Adrian said. 'The police have had no luck finding any trace of him. I think they're coming around to the idea that he may have been murdered after all.'

'Marcus pretty much confessed to it,' Kristen said.

'You've heard from Marcus?'

'Over the phone. I've already told the local police here.'

'Dear Lord. Okay, I'll pass that on. Any idea where he is?'

Kristen didn't answer, her thoughts still caught up elsewhere. 'It doesn't add up, Adrian,' she said. 'Why would Harry ask Tanner to alter my programme?'

'I don't know,' Adrian admitted. 'I just wanted you to know there's a rational, scientific explanation behind the things you've seen. So you can put your mind at rest.'

She thanked him and hung up without telling him what was happening closer to home. Her mind was too busy spinning with the implications of this news.

She found the energy to stand. In fact, strength was slowly returning to every part of her body. She carefully sidestepped the pool of sick left on the carpet and made her way through the doors and out into the garden. There, she sucked in a lungful of icy air. Less than twenty minutes ago, she believed that an ancient all-powerful predator ran the world and everything in it. And that it was about to sacrifice the life of an innocent girl. Now, the mist had been lifted from her eyes. It was *all* the God helmet after all. It had been since the beginning. The angel in the garden, the choir ... all just subliminal suggestion, illusions in her mind. Just like the

Apex itself. Despite all she had seen and heard, everything she believed she had intuited, it did not exist. There was no longer any reason to be afraid of the dark beyond the campfire.

Relief flooded her chest, but also confusion as she rewound the recent past and replayed her experiences in her head. Whatever she had seen was a figment of her imagination, a result of her suggestibility. But that didn't mean there wasn't anything to fear. She hadn't just imagined what happened to Bree and Darius. She might have been tempted to wonder, except she felt the plaster on her cheek and bruises from whoever had slammed into her. *Someone* had killed her friends. *Someone* had taken poor Poppy to be sacrificed. But now she could be sure that it was no Being from the beginning of time. No, that something was a some*one*. The same person it had been all along. There was and always had been only one Apex. And Marcus Hardy was his name.

8

She had so little time. Sunset was barely three and a half hours away. She ran through the possibilities in her head. She could call Sergeant Harris. After all, she knew exactly where Marcus was going to be, and when. But she also believed him when he said he would kill the girl if she brought the police. If he thought his chance of making the sacrifice the way the Apex intended was gone, he would have nothing to lose. No, her only hope was to try and talk him into letting Poppy go. Difficult, seeing how caught up he was in his delusions. She needed a way to build trust somehow. Who would Marcus trust? A priest. *Emissaries*, he called them. Could a priest persuade him to surrender Poppy? He might be too far gone to listen. But right now, it seemed like her best shot. She called the presbytery at St James's first, but no one picked up. So Kristen rang the one priest who already knew her husband was in a dark place.

Father Connolly listened patiently to her story. He expressed horror and sorrow as she described how her friends had been killed. And disbelief when she told him that Marcus had abducted Poppy Clarke. Then she told him her plan. Connolly was quiet. 'Kristen, you should get the authorities involved,' he said. 'This is the wrong way.'

'No, this is the only way,' she said. 'He'll kill her if he spots anyone in uniform.'

'And if you bring me? What if that makes him kill her too?'

'I'm counting on him giving you a pass,' she said. 'You need to convince him not to harm Poppy.'

'I don't like it,' Connolly said. 'Playing into his delusion is high risk. This really should be left to the authorities.'

'Then Poppy's dead,' Kristen insisted.

She could tell he still wasn't convinced. 'Look, it's like a hostage negotiation,' she said. 'They send in someone skilled and professional, you know. I'm sorry, Father, but in this situation, that's you. You can reach him.'

'Kristen, what if he can't be reached?'

'Then that poor girl is dead anyway. Please, Father. I'm begging you. Help me.'

'Why me? Couldn't you contact Father Nolan? He's closer.'

'I tried him already,' she said. 'He's not answering his phone. But you're by far the better option anyway. Marcus *trusts* you. You married us. And you were the one who baptised Abigail. You said it yourself.'

Connolly reluctantly conceded her points. With a deep sigh, he agreed to help. 'I'll drive down now,' he said. 'If the traffic's light, I can be there in three hours.'

'Thank you,' Kristen said. 'For being brave. There's a child who's counting on us.'

'That's what worries me,' he said.

She showered quickly, changed into a sweater and jeans, and put on a pair of outdoor shoes. While she waited for

Connolly, she went out back again, pacing the woods behind the field, looking for signs of either Bree's or Darius's body, but found no trace of them. It felt strange to be back out here. Different even from just a few hours ago. Her mind was still coming to terms with what Doctor Kemplar had told her. But there was another worry now. Just because she knew she had been hallucinating all this time, it didn't mean the hallucinations would stop. And if her past experience were anything to go by, when they returned, she would not be able to distinguish reality from fantasy. She would have to try her best to hold on to her sanity. Poppy's life hung in the balance.

She heard the car pull up a little after quarter past three. When she opened the front door, Connolly was dressed not only in his usual black cassock and white collar, but full priestly apparel: surplice, stole, chasuble and a rope around his waist made of braided wool, which Kristen remembered from her church days was called a *cincture*. The priest pointed to his head, which sported a zucchetto skull cap, and shrugged. 'I thought if I am going to be an emissary, I'd better look the part,' he said.

She gave him a weak smile and let him in, offering him something to eat or drink. But Connolly only wanted to use the bathroom and get going.

'I suggest we go and see him early,' he said.

'You think so?' she said.

'I'm not saying we ambush him,' Connolly said. 'We approach directly, waving the white flag. If he's not at the appointed meeting point yet, maybe he'll be feeling less … *sacrificial*.'

Kristen understood his macabre meaning. She opened up the FamilyFinder app and selected Marcus's phone. A moment later, a blip showed his location. 'He's … here,' she said. 'In the village.'

She flipped the screen around to show Connolly the flashing spot just off the village green.

'Do you know where that is?'

She swallowed, nodding. 'That's St James's church,' she said.

They took the Land Rover, a vehicle familiar to Marcus should he spot them approach. Connolly agreed to drive as Kristen kept an eye on the app. Her mind was racing as fast as the speedometer. Why was Marcus at the church? Had he been visiting Father Nolan? And was that why Nolan didn't pick up the phone earlier? The app vanished, replaced by an incoming call. She recognised the name she'd saved in her contacts.

Willowdale Police Station

Probably Sergeant Harris checking in. She shook her head and cut off the call.

'Who is it?' Connolly asked.

'No one we have time for now,' she said. 'Just drive.'

Connolly obliged. Outside, daylight was fading fast. Tall hedgerows on either side of the lane dimmed the already crepuscular light. It was within this reduced visibility that the priest hit the brakes sharply as an animal appeared unannounced in the lane. The tyres screeched and Kristen's hands went instinctively to the dash to protect herself.

'What—' Kristen drew in a sharp breath. 'It's okay, Father,' she said. 'It's just a deer.'

It was indeed a deer. But not just any deer. Kristen recognised it as a roe, the kind she had spotted in the forest once in what felt like a lifetime ago.

'It's not in the least bit afraid,' Connolly observed.

The deer stopped in the road as if unaware it could have just been run over. It stared at them with neutral dark eyes, not even fazed by the vehicle's harsh headlights. Kristen leaned over and tapped the horn, but the creature stood resolute. She recalled what she'd told Abi once, about how lucky it was that hunting had ceased. 'They can finally live without fearing death,' she'd said. She remembered again the assurances Adrian Kemplar had given her that nothing she'd experienced had been real. Whether she saw angels, demons, or the Apex Itself when they finally encountered Marcus, it would only be in her head. Just like this deer, she had nothing to be afraid of. The only danger she faced was from the man she had married. And right now, she'd never felt more determined to stop him. The deer wandered off into a gap in the hedge, and Kristen urged Father Connolly to hurry.

9

The priest parked in the gravel car park next to the church. There was no answer when they knocked on the presbytery door. She instructed Connolly to wait in the small porch, while she went around the side of the Edwardian house. The kitchen window had no curtain or blind obscuring it. Kristen cupped her hands over her eyes and pressed against the glass. Through the misty pane, she saw an empty kitchen table with place mats set out.

'Hello!' she called. 'Marcus? It's me!'

No answer. She frowned, pulled away from the window. 'Father Nolan? It's Kristen Hardy. Is Marcus there with you? I'm with Father Connolly. We only want to talk.'

Silence greeted her from inside. She continued on and discovered a blue door. She knocked once and tried it, this time with success. The door opened and she found herself in a utility room. She called out for Father Nolan and Marcus, loudly announcing her presence. No response. It was a short walk to the lounge, which was cloaked in darkness with the curtains drawn. Hesitantly, she stepped onto the carpet, trying to avoid bumping into the larger, darker shapes which she took to be sofas and chairs. She fumbled her way to the hallway and let Father Connolly in.

'I don't think anyone's here,' she said.

'What does the app say?'

Kristen frowned. She'd checked it just moments before they pulled up. She pulled her phone from her jeans pocket. 'He's … moving away!' she cried.

Connolly peered over her shoulder. 'South,' he confirmed. 'That blip's going pretty fast too. Looks like he's running.'

Kristen squinted at the dot as it blinked further and further away from the house. 'He must have left just as we arrived,' she said. 'But where's he going? Did he even notice us?'

Connolly shrugged. 'I think I saw movement in the upstairs window,' he said. 'Why don't you stay down here?'

'Be careful,' she said, without being sure why. Connolly nodded and started up the stairs. Kristen, meanwhile, fumbled along the wall, eventually finding a light switch. The living room sprang into brightness. She checked the phone. Marcus was almost a quarter of a mile away now. If he had passed through the back garden, he would be deep in the forest by now. Her thoughts were interrupted by a disturbing groan coming through the floorboards above. It sounded like someone in pain. Father Connolly's voice echoed down shortly after. 'Oh, you poor, poor man. Oh no.'

'Father?'

Her heart beat faster as she found her feet carrying her with increasing urgency towards the staircase and up the bare wooden stairs. On the landing, she deduced the groans were coming from a room two doors away. There, sitting on the bed near the window, was Father Nolan. Connolly was next to him, a bear-like arm around his shoulders. As Kristen neared them, she might have got the impression from Nolan's position that he was looking out of the window, but she could now see the priest was cradling his face. Two bandages had been strapped across his eyes. She approached gently, dropping to her knees beside him.

'Father?' she said, placing a gentle hand on his shoulder. 'You all right?'

The young priest sobbed so quietly she barely heard him. Or the words he whispered. 'He … he took my eyes,' Nolan said, choking.

'Wh-what?'

Nolan seemed to stare at her through what Kristen now understood were two gauzes covering empty sockets. There was a small wrapped hand towel on the floor, the starched white blotted with red. Kristen had a sinking feeling about what lay inside that towel.

Nolan sobbed louder. 'H-he had this old d-dagger, made of stone or something. I thought he was going to k-kill me. But … he … t-took my eyes.'

Kristen and Connolly exchanged appalled looks. With some difficulty, Nolan told them what happened, his voice slurring in places. The previous day, Marcus had turned up at the presbytery unannounced, asking for help. The young priest could not bring himself to tell them the nature of Marcus's request, only that he was thoroughly disgusted by it and refused. With his advantage of height and physical strength, Marcus had overpowered Nolan, repeatedly punching him in the head until he passed out. When he awoke, he found himself tied to the bed and gagged. He described how he could hear Marcus moving around downstairs for hours before leaving. Nolan had stayed bound and helpless for the next twenty-four hours, until a couple of hours ago, when Marcus had eventually returned. The older priest and Kristen listened patiently as Nolan described how Marcus had told him that if he was going to be blind to truth, he might as well *make* him blind. Kristen shivered as she heard how he had forced Nolan to swallow a load of sleeping pills before he performed the operation.

'He was researching how to do it,' he said. 'On h-his phone. As I sat there, waiting. He-he ... *argh* ...'

Nolan struggled to continue. Kristen could see the sedative effects of the cocktail Marcus had given him had not entirely worn off, but at least they were sparing him what was going to be excruciating pain when they did.

'He s-said he wouldn't kill me,' Nolan said. 'B-but only because I was an emissary. He was wearing ... he was wearing ... I can't ... he was naked apart from the ...'

Nolan descended into dark sobs of despair, unbearable to watch. Father Connolly wrapped both large arms around the kid's shoulders and rocked him gently as Kristen examined the gauze on his head. There was no blood haemorrhaging that she could detect. This procedure had been performed with impressive precision for an amateur. But then Marcus had always been a quick study.

'You're not going to die,' she told Nolan. 'But you do need medical attention. We need to call an ambulance.'

'And the police?' Connolly said.

'No, not yet. The responding paramedics will call them anyway. You and I still have to track Marcus down.'

Connolly gently untangled himself from the wailing Nolan and moved over to the dresser to pick up the landline. A second later, he dialled 999. Kristen, meanwhile, turned to Nolan and rubbed one of his arms gently.

'They're on their way,' Connolly said. 'They said thirty minutes.'

'Father,' Kristen said, addressing the young priest, 'I'm so sorry about what happened. But I need to ask you ... what did Marcus want you to help him with?'

Nolan bawled, and Kristen waited patiently for her answer. It didn't come. But then it didn't need to. For as she looked over the bed, she noticed something leaning against the wall that she hadn't seen until now. A shovel, freshly caked in dirt.

10

Kristen had to see for herself. Connolly initially protested, reluctant to abandon the younger priest. But he trusted Kristen's insistence that Nolan's life was not in any immediate danger. He followed her out of the house to the graveyard, falling silent when he saw the mound of dirt beside the lopsided headstone. In the hole, barely visible in the moonlight, were pieces of a broken coffin lid.

'He took her,' Kristen croaked.

'Lord have mercy,' Connolly said.

The grave had to be six feet deep, at least. It must have taken several hours to dig it, perhaps more considering Nolan had refused to help. From the young priest's account, it sounded like Marcus had begun the exhumation last night and finished it off in the last couple of hours. Kristen stared at the desecrated resting place, unwilling to believe her own eyes. Had no one been by the graveyard today and seen what had happened here? Perhaps someone had and thought it was being dug with relevant permissions. But the only permission Marcus had sought was that of his imaginary predator-god. She was trembling, biting hard on her knuckles, stifling the scream she wanted to release. She had to put this out of her mind right now. Poppy was still their number one priority. But it wasn't easy to shake the feeling of revulsion as she checked her phone to track Marcus's position. 'Shit,' she said. 'He's a long way off now.'

She had to force herself not to visualise how Marcus was managing to run at such speeds carrying his macabre cargo.

'Are you *certain* we don't wait for the police?' Connolly said.

Kristen shook her head. *No*. Darkness had already fallen. They needed to get moving.

And so into the woods. Kristen wished she had brought a proper torch as she tried to follow the blip while using the phone's weak light. She would have to trust the two of them would get their night vision soon. Sweat cooled down her back, the animal adrenaline keeping her eyes and ears alert. It was an effort to keep pushing the visuals of Abi away. She had an awful picture of a youthful, decomposing body, wearing the same dress she had worn at Marcus's party, looking like the kutkot corpse she had seen online.

Oh, Mother, what a palaver this all is. Why didn't you just agree to go with Father on his walks?

No, she shouted inside her head. *Just stop it*. She told herself to concentrate on that blinking white dot, seeing it get ever nearer with every step they took. It was approaching five fifteen. Instead of being early, they would likely arrive exactly when Marcus had instructed. *As the Apex wills it*, she thought. She wondered what she would say when they eventually caught up with him. They should have rehearsed something, she and Connolly. *Fools*.

'Kristen?'

'I'm all right, Father. Let's hurry!'

The dot was still too far away.

• • •

Deeper and deeper, further away from the light of any campfire and into the heart of Marcus's Eden. The trees became sentries blocking the way. They were waist high in brambles. Thorns scratched at Kristen's arms and legs. Then she checked her phone one final time and guided them out. The pair found themselves in a natural glade. At the same time, the clouds parted way above and bathed everything in lunar light. It served not only to illuminate their position, but heralded a dark silhouette. The figure of a man stood near a large rock that Kristen was pretty sure was the same rock Abi had hit her head on. The man appeared to have an animal head on top of his own. *A wolf's head*, was her first thought. Was she imagining things? Could this be more hallucinations from the God helmet? She heard Connolly gasp, and as the two of them took a step forward, Kristen got the clarity she wished she hadn't. It was Marcus. A skull was strapped over on top of his head, secured with string or perhaps torn, bloodied rags. It was not a wolf. But it was canine. She knew, too, who it belonged to. Marcus's naked body was dressed entirely in an animal skin, with dark brown fur that would have once belonged to Zane, Tim Barnes's Labrador. Her husband moved aside, and she saw he was clutching Poppy by the hair in one hand, while holding the flint dagger in the other.

'Kris! You're here!'

Behind him, two lifeless bodies were lying on top of one another. There was just enough moonlight to see that one was Bree and the other Darius.

11

Kristen was grateful that the clouds moved again, darkening the view of her dead friends. She could still just about make out Poppy struggling under Marcus's arm. Though she could not see the girl's face, she could imagine her terror.

'Who's that with you?' Marcus demanded.

'Marcus, it's me, Father Connolly,' the priest said.

'Father?' Marcus replied, sounding confused. 'Have you come to bear witness? The younger one did not understand what I have to do.'

'I'm here to help,' Connolly said cautiously. 'Perhaps we can talk?'

Kristen called out to the girl. 'Hey, Poppy. Don't you worry,' she said, projecting as much confidence into her voice as she could. 'Aunty Krissy is here. I won't let anything happen to you, sweetheart.'

Marcus sneered at this and pulled the girl closer to his body. Father Connolly took a cautious step forward. Kristen sensed him flinch and figured he must have registered Bree's and Darius's corpses. 'Marcus, what is this? What have you done?'

'What?' Marcus shot back. 'Oh, you mean *them*? That

wasn't my choice, Father. Kristen's friends would have tried to oppose the will of the Apex. And I'm afraid they paid the price for that.'

'Tell me, Marcus … how do you claim to know the will of this Apex?' Connolly asked. 'Does It speak to you?'

Marcus tittered. 'It speaks to all of us, Father. You should know this. You're an emissary for fuck's sake. Are you as blind as that cunt Nolan?'

'Marcus, please,' Father Connolly said. 'Remember our conversations? How you came to me? Remember how we talked about how Abi would live again in heaven? This isn't God's will, Marcus. Please let the girl go. You need to trust me as you once did.'

'I was seeking the truth from you,' Marcus said. 'But your religion was just a shadow. I know what lies behind it, Father. Harry's machine has shown me.'

Kristen, meanwhile, was calculating her chances of reaching Poppy before her husband could bring that awful old blade down. She didn't like the odds. Maybe she could try talking to him, perhaps distract him long enough to create an opening.

'Hey, darling,' she said. 'What are you wearing?'

'This?' Marcus tapped the skull fastened over his head with the dagger. 'I should have bought her a dog, but I didn't. So now I wear my shame.' He laughed bitterly.

'Darling,' Kristen said. 'Don't you see what's happening? The most rational explanation for what you're experiencing is that the God helmet messed with your head. All this stuff about the Apex. Believing that our darling Abi can come back from the dead. It's just the programming in your brain. Think about it, darling. *Please.*'

She took a step forward too, opening her palms towards him to show she was not a threat. Now she had a better view of Poppy. The poor girl was shaking from head to foot.

'Oh, Kris,' Marcus said. 'Don't you see yet? The Apex is here.'

'Darling, I don't think that's right. I think there never was an Apex. I think it was you who killed Harry. You killed Tim and his husband and poor Zane.'

Kristen sensed movement and saw Father Connolly was by her side, also attempting to move in an unthreatening manner.

'Marcus, let's talk about the shame you mentioned,' Father Connolly said. 'In Genesis, God covered Adam and Eve's shame because they sinned. But we're all sinners, Marcus. What you've done to these poor people … what you're doing right now … it's also sin. But God can forgive you if you turn away from your sins. Why don't you put the knife down?'

'Oh, Father,' Marcus said, sighing. 'This is not sin. It's a life for a life. Isn't that what your Bible says? That was why she was born, don't you see? She's the same age. It was *meant* to be!'

Poppy whimpered. Kristen inched closer.

'Marcus,' Father Connolly said, gently. 'It is wrong to take an innocent life. Give the girl to Kristen. You can take me instead. You can have *my* skin for this Apex of yours.'

'No!' Marcus screamed.

The reaction made Kristen and Connolly jump. Marcus lifted Poppy clear off the ground by her hair. She cried in pain and clutched his hand, her feet kicking the air.

Marcus looked at Kristen. 'If we give the Apex this sacrifice, we can both wear the girl's skin and cover our shame. Then It will be satisfied, and *she* will live.'

He put Poppy down again. The moon peeked out from the cumulous again, allowing Kristen to follow Marcus's gaze. A dark shape, about Poppy's size, lay next to the rock. Kristen snapped her head back, unable to acknowledge what it was.

'Marcus,' she said, forcefully. 'You always taught me truth was important, no matter how difficult to accept. And the truth, my darling, is *there is no Apex*. It's been you. You all along. *You!*"

'Really? Then who is that?' Marcus asked, pointing with the knife.

She heard a loud crunch as something large and powerful burst out from a cluster of trees. Kristen spun around and her heart turned to ice. Something ancient, with vibrating heads, stared at her, into her very soul. 'Are you seeing this, Father?' she asked.

'Yes,' Connolly said.

After that, it all happened very fast.

12

Her only thought was to run, her natural survival instincts kicking in. She sprinted away, heart pounding. Only when she reached the edge of the glade did she dare to look back. In a snapshot, she saw her husband had slung Poppy to the ground as Father Connolly rushed forwards. Marcus buried the dagger into Connolly's ribs. The burly priest cried out in agony.

Kristen wanted to go back, but she had no more say than a fox being chased by a pack of hounds, or a fish swimming away from the jaws of a great white. So she turned and ran, weaving through trees as, behind her, the loud snapping of branches signalled the Apex in pursuit, ready to devour and kill, as It had always done since the dawn of time. She forced her legs to go faster, her feet to push harder off the ground. Some part of her brain cried out in Adrian Kemplar's voice. Urged her to think about this, just for a second. She *knew* her brain had been messed with. The Apex had never been real. But then, how had Father Connolly seen It too? She needed to get away from the thing's clutches. A fallen tree blocked her path in the patchy nocturnal light, but she saw it just in time and managed to vault over the top. She heard a loud thud behind her as the Apex collided with the tree, followed by a loud scrabble as It attempted to climb over. Hearing Its angry, frustrated cries, all she could think was how It would show her no mercy when It caught her, and that only made her even more afraid. She wanted to run but her legs were like stone. Cold terror shocked her up and down like a Taser gun as the dark ancient fear returned. And made her its prisoner.

13

The last thing Poppy Clarke remembered was passing out at the driveway at Orchard House when someone, or some*thing*, had attacked her and Aunty Krissy. When she had come around, she had been somewhere in the forest, tied to a tree with an old shirt. Abigail's dad, Mr Hardy, had been standing over her, waving that horrible old knife. It was clear from the start he had become a crazy person. He was wearing some weird animal skin and a skull on his head and he was angry and shouting. He threatened to hurt her if she called for help or tried to run. Poppy believed him. Mr Hardy had told her to wait, saying he was going to fetch Abigail, which didn't make any sense since Abigail was dead. When he was gone, Poppy was too scared to cry out for help in case he had lied and was still nearby. She hoped someone would come by, but the forest was large, and no one did. She closed her eyes and sobbed quietly, afraid of what Mr Hardy was going to do. She knew he must have hurt her mum and dad, perhaps badly. She shivered in the increasing cold and prayed to Jesus that Aunty Krissy would find her.

· · ·

Finally, it got dark and Mr Hardy returned, covered in mud and dirt. He cut Poppy free, grabbed her arm and took her away. They walked for maybe ten minutes, his fingers pinching her wrists painfully, but she knew she wasn't strong enough to break free. Eventually he stopped in a clearing at a spot Poppy recognised. This was where Abigail had hit her head and died. Something covered in dirt and rags lay next to the rock. It had a horrible smell that turned her stomach. Not far away, she was greeted by a sight that made her heart feel so heavy it hurt. Her mum and dad, lying on top of each other, their skin cut a hundred times and soaked in blood. She understood that they were dead and had to force herself to look away. Then she had heard footsteps approaching. Mr Hardy snatched her up and pressed the tip of the knife to her neck. Aunty Krissy had come. She was not alone! Poppy recognised old Father Connolly from church too. The adults talked to each other and then everything went crazy. Aunty Krissy saw something in the bushes and asked Father Connolly if he could see it too. Poppy couldn't, because the next thing she knew Mr Hardy had thrown her aside and she hit the ground hard. She winced in pain, and when she opened her eyes Mr Hardy was stabbing poor Father Connolly with his knife. She opened her mouth to scream but all that came out was dry air. Mr Hardy roared and circled Father Connolly as he collapsed, the animal skin flapping around his body as he moved. He kicked the big priest on his side, rolling him over. His eyes were open, just like people on TV looked when they died. Then Mr Hardy ran over to her and grabbed her hair again. He dragged her across the ground and flung her on top of the same rock that Abigail had hit her head on.

'Hear, O Apex, Giver and Taker of life! Accept this life as a sacrifice, as a life you are owed!'

Poppy did not understand what the words Mr Hardy was saying meant but she did understand that he intended to kill her. She tried to get up, but Mr Hardy kicked her down with his bare foot, pinning her against the hard stone. She felt despair again as she realised that no one was coming to help her. Mr Hardy slowly raised the knife above his head and started spouting strange words again. But then she saw something – behind him, over by the tree. Groaning, but moving. Impossible … and yet. It took her a while to understand that, somehow, it was her mother. *Her mother was still alive.*

14

The Apex closed in on Kristen. She remained terrified, helpless as it slowly stumbled towards her. This was it. The end of her life, at last. As it was, ever shall it be. But as she closed her eyes, waited, she recalled Adrian Kemplar's warning again, about however real things seemed, they weren't. *Think,* she told herself. *Remember the God helmet. Remember all the sessions. This is just your brain hallucinating. The Apex isn't real.* She summoned what courage she could. It wasn't easy. All her senses were telling her she was about to die. But somehow she moved her body, even as she sensed the dark shape reach her position. She ran forward and stumbled onto a bank with a steep incline. Though it was dark, she could see a bank on the opposite side and a narrow stretch of ground below her, perhaps twenty feet down. She knew what this was, from the few times she had been out walking in the forest. This was called a *hollow way*, where an old trail had slowly become overgrown, flanked by banks on either side. She took a leap of faith, literally, springing off the end and landing hard on the other bank. She grabbed a tuft of long grass, which served as a solid handhold.

The sound of wheezing and heavy breathing echoed from

the bank opposite. She dared to turn her head back and saw the dark shape scramble down the other slope but fail to see the drop. The creature fell, tumbling head first and landing on the ground below, with an agonising whelp of pain. The cry sounded too weak to belong to the Ultimate Predator at the very top of the universe's food chain. Kristen lowered herself far enough to see where her pursuer had fallen. As she did so, the clouds above drifted apart again, and extra moonlight illuminated the gully. The chimera of faces she had seen before had morphed into a series of rotund, pink, more human faces, sheened with sweat. Then many faces became one. Rather than the fearful Apex, Kristen instead saw the lumbering, hulking mass of Harry Dean. Harry was on his back, wheezing and puffing. His head rolled side to side. 'My *leg*!' he wailed. 'It's broken!'

'*Harry*?'

She had assumed Harry had been murdered in Geneva, and was both relieved to see him and confused in equal measure. She let go, carefully slid down the bank and dropped to the ground. Moving quickly to his side, she knelt beside him. It was as if he was caught in a fever, his brow sweating, his state delirious. 'I *can't* let you escape,' he bawled. 'It will kill me!'

But his anguished cry told Kristen that the heavyset man was no immediate threat to her.

'Who will kill you, darling?' she asked, examining his left leg, which he was clutching desperately.

'The Apex!'

Harry's initial assessment was correct. He had broken his femur by the looks of it. No easy feat, in Kristen's experience. But then he had landed with over one hundred and sixty kilos of gravity behind him, so maybe it wasn't that surprising. She prodded the already swollen skin and Harry yipped with pain. He looked at Kristen with imploring eyes that glowed under the moonlight.

'Please, Kristen, It holds my life in Its hands. It spared me once, but It won't show mercy again.'

He started to cry like a little boy. Kristen was puzzled but there was no time to get answers. It had been stupid of her to run. Her lizard brain had moved her body involuntarily and she had abandoned the very person she had come to save. 'You won't die from a broken leg,' she said. 'And I don't know if you can even make sense of my words, Harry, but there *is* no Apex.'

She turned, leapt up onto the bank on the left, frantically crawling her way to high ground. When she reached it, she sprinted back in the direction of the glade, hoping beyond hope that her mistake had not already cost Poppy her life.

15

Poppy had never seen her mother move with such speed or determination. Mr Hardy was still babbling while her mum scrambled on her hands and knees, forwards, forwards, until she was close enough to launch herself at Mr Hardy. This she did, screeching like a wild animal. Her momentum caught Mr Hardy off guard, the impact of her body slamming into his back, sending him head first into some bushes. Wheezing and struggling, her mum slithered towards her, her clothes soaked in red. She reached out to Poppy and pulled the girl gently to her. 'Run,' she whispered in her ear.

'Where, Mummy?' Poppy gasped.

'Anywhere. *H-hide.*' Spittles of blood flew from her mouth as she spoke.

Poppy nodded, wide-eyed.

'*Goood girl,*' her mum said, and smiled with reddened teeth. '*Go!*'

Not needing to be told twice, Poppy sprinted into the woods. She heard Mr Hardy roar and quickly glanced back, just in time to see he had returned to the spot where the rock was, still clutching his knife. The last thing she heard her mother say was 'Come on then, you crazy fuck.'

16

Kristen returned in time to witness two miracles. The first was the sight of Poppy fleeing the scene and escaping into the woods. The second was Bree, who was somehow still alive. She was on the ground, snarling at Marcus, who hovered over her, waving the flint dagger. Kristen grabbed a large, heavy stick from the ground and charged at her husband, full of righteous anger. She let out a warrior's cry. Marcus turned, the dog skin flapping with his movements. The Labrador's skull had fallen off his head, but he didn't look any less deranged. She had to shut out the memories of the man she married as she swung the stick like a baseball bat. It connected to his head with a loud crunching sound and Marcus fell backwards and rolled away from them. She dropped to Bree's side, and hurriedly examined her wounds. Marcus had cut her extensively. She was bleeding from so many points, there was just no way Kristen, even with all her years of training, could help. How she was still breathing was anyone's guess. Maybe it was sheer force of will, or the power of a mother's protective love. Bree tried to speak, but could only gurgle blood. Kristen wiped back her friend's sticky, crimson-stained hair and cradled her head gently. 'It's okay, Bee,' Kristen said. 'You're going to be okay.'

But she knew she was lying. A sound erupted nearby and Kristen's heart quickened. Marcus was already on his feet. Groaning, he rummaged around for the knife. Kristen wanted to get up, but she was rooted to the spot by thirty years of friendship. Marcus cried out in joy, having found his prize. He held the dagger up to his eyes. 'Thank you, O Apex,' he cried.

He glanced over at Kristen and Bree. But instead of rushing them, he vanished into the forest. Kristen realised he still needed Poppy to complete his insane plan. A weak, bloodied hand touched her face.

'Save h-her,' Bree said. 'Promise me.'

Kristen stared into her eyes. 'I will,' she said. 'I *promise.*'

Then she stood up, breaking the bond that fought against her to stay where she was. It was the hardest thing she'd ever had to do, but she had no choice. Leaving her best friend in the world to die alone, she picked up her stick and chased after Marcus.

17

Poppy did not know how long she had been running. Many times she thought she heard Mr Hardy catch up to her, or felt his breath hot against the back of her neck. But each time she was mistaken. She found the river and used it to guide her way in the dark. The muddy bank caused her to slip and fall more than once, and she had to right herself each time. She finally risked stopping to catch her breath, and squinted at something she saw hovering over the river. It was the tyre swing. Shivering, with sweat rapidly cooling on her body, she approached the willow trunk, saying a silent prayer of thanks to Jesus. She thought about swimming across but the water was deep and freezing. Instead, she shuffled along the trunk, then climbed down the rope using the handholds and tucked herself into the tyre. She arched her back and swung on the tyre until it was as high as it could go. *Momentum*, she remembered as she let go. She landed on her heels, which hurt so much that she had to bite her hand to stop from crying out and giving away her position. The tyre swayed back and forth like an out-of-control pendulum, and now she worried that Mr Hardy might see it. But maybe he was still too far away and the swinging would stop in time.

She stumbled towards the fallen tree and quickly crawled inside until she had to crouch. Her fingers touched the candle wick the girls had used when Abigail had first taken her here. There wasn't enough wax left to light, but she wouldn't have dared anyway in case she gave herself away. She slunk down cross-legged and tried to get her breath back as quietly as possible. Eventually, her chest rose and fell in a steady, slow rhythm. Outside, she heard the ambient noises of the night. These included unknown scurrying of smaller creatures and a distant owl hooting. She was freezing, her nerves shredded. Exhaustion racked through her body while her mind wanted nothing more than to stop thinking about all the horrors it had witnessed.

She heard a snap, the sound of branches crackling and something moving outside. Then Mr Hardy's voice, singing in a low-pitched timbre. 'All things bright and beautiful … all creatures great and small … all things wise and wonderful … the Apex eats them all!'

A mixture of howling and laughter followed. 'Apex, who art in Eden, hallowed be Thy prey, Thy hunting done, the hunt must be done …'

A loud snap, this time of a branch directly outside the hollow. She jumped, startled. Footsteps grew louder, approaching the mouth of the trunk, and Poppy bit her bottom lip so hard it bled. She heard a loud sniff.

'Mmm,' said a gruff voice. 'I think you might be … I … I … oh, Apex is that you? My Lord and my God is that you walking through the garden in the cool of the night? It is you, isn't it? What? Yes, the girl is here!'

And with that, the footfall went quiet. Poppy listened carefully, hoping to hear the sound of Mr Hardy's diminishing footsteps as he walked off into the distance. But there was only silence. Then two arms reached into the trunk and yanked her out of her hiding place.

18

Kristen listened to the light wind and the sounds of the woodlands. Where, oh where, was Marcus? She stumbled upon the river, then ran alongside it. Her chest burned, her muscles ached. The moon kept dipping in and out of cover, giving her only brief flashes of her immediate surroundings. But there was no sign of him anywhere. She tried not to think about Bree, cold and alone as the remaining life ebbed out of her. She had to find Poppy. Up ahead, she saw something that made her stop. A round, hoop-like object that appeared to be suspended above the river. She remembered something Poppy had said that fateful day back in the summer. Something about a secret hiding place.

'It's inside a tree,' Poppy had said. 'Near where the tyre swing is.'

Yes, Kristen could see it now. It was on a rope, dangling off a willow that arched over the water. This must have been what Poppy was referring to. Maybe the girl had come here herself to hide. Then Kristen heard the singing. Not a hallucination of a heavenly choir this time, but Marcus's own voice.

19

Poppy screamed as Mr Hardy dragged her by her hair and towards the river before wading into it. The water was ice cold. She kicked and waved her arms, swallowed horrible mouthfuls of it, thinking she was going to drown. Mr Hardy kept pulling her along regardless. Whenever Poppy's head burst above the water's surface, she heard snippets of his shrill singing.

'Each deadly jaw that opens ... each scorpion that stings ...'

When they were about halfway across, Poppy came up once more to gasp for air and twisted her head around, just in time to see a figure traversing the river from the other side. It was coming towards them. Some exhausted and frightened part of her wondered if it might be her mum, come to save her again. Poppy barely registered that it was Aunty Krissy before she saw her leap forward and swing a big stick that landed squarely on Mr Hardy's chest. Mr Hardy was either caught off guard or lost in his own crazy singing. Either way, he staggered backwards like a drunk man, letting go of the knife. At the same moment, Poppy surprised herself by biting down hard on Mr Hardy's wrist, enough that he let go of her too. She sank to the riverbed, landing on her feet. The surface was an inch or so above her head, forcing her to swim upwards. As her head burst through, she watched Aunty Krissy launch herself onto Mr Hardy, pulling both of them under the water. For a few terrible moments, there were only bubbles. But then Mr Hardy flung his upper body up, panting for air. Aunty Krissy's head popped up too, but his strong hands grabbed her and pushed her down again.

Meanwhile, Poppy kicked and splashed as she spat out rancid water. She wanted to help Aunty Krissy, but she was no match for crazy Mr Hardy. Worse, her body was starting to cave. She felt her legs go weak and rubbery as the remaining strength drained out of her as if through a colander. She could barely stay afloat, spluttering and coughing as her head slipped under again, panic rising in her throat. Alarmed, she glanced frantically towards the bank. She could reach that, maybe. If she tried. She *had* to try.

20

Marcus shoved Kristen back into the unbearably icy water. Even as she struggled, she came to terms with the awful truth that the arms that held her down were the same arms that once held her during their first dance. But this was no longer her husband. The man who was forcing her face down towards the riverbed had become just another animal in the circle of life. Her own personal Apex, struggling for dominance as much as any goblin shark from any deep-sea nightmare. His arms were too powerful; she tried in vain to swim up, but she was pinned down too deep. Because of his height, his whole upper body was still above the surface, while Kristen was already feeling the pressure of intrusion of water into her nose and ears. The increasing *thud-thudding* of her chest told her her oxygen was running low. She scraped uselessly at the riverbed, trying to find a pebble or a stone she could wield as a weapon before the rest of her strength drained. She heard vibrations in the water, which at first she put down to her heartbeat, but soon worked out it was Marcus, still singing, still praising his predator-god, mangling a hymn he must have originally learned in school. She could no longer tell if her own eyes were open. Either everything had turned literally black or she was starting to lose her sight before she passed out completely. Still, life struggled on. As it had struggled on since the beginning of time. And, as every fish flapped desperately when it was out of water, and every fallen gazelle still kicked and bucked as the lions devoured its flesh, so Kristen Hardy ran her hand desperately along the mud of the bed. Her survival instinct finally paid off as her finger found something sharp and pointed that felt like it was made of old stone.

She was not a doctor, but she had enough understanding of basic anatomy to know where to strike first. She slashed at his ankles, at the Achilles tendons, and knew it delivered crippling pain by the change of vibrations in the water. She worked quickly, cutting under the knee, and when one hand released her, she brought the blade across his other wrist. Then, using his buckled knee as a lever, she pushed her body out of the water, her head emerging first as she spat out the river and coughed. The moon was out once more, and she saw Marcus's wide-eyed face stare at her in disbelief. He looked intently into her eyes with savage anger and hate. Nothing in that face belonged to the man she had loved. She could tell by his expression that he could not believe she had cut him. It was even worse when he realised she had also buried the knife deep into his stomach. He opened his mouth, and a dark crimson liquid spilled out. Then Marcus Hardy's body went limp.

<h1 style="text-align:center">21</h1>

She didn't know how she managed to drag him onto the bank. Some kind of adrenaline boost, something in her system that kicked in when she realised she was going to live after all. She laid him gently on his back, and he spat and gurgled, his hands clawing at his stomach, which sported a wound that didn't require her years of nursing to tell her was fatal. He tried to speak, with increasing difficulty. Kristen might have walked away then, or staggered away, but the wife in her just couldn't. The sky above the trees cleared, and she noticed a change in Marcus's eyes. A new kind of epiphany, marked with sadness. Maybe the realisation that he was about to lose his own place in the Great Chain. And despite all he had done, Kristen was filled with compassion as Marcus's breathing became increasingly laboured. She leaned forward, pressing her ear to his lips so she could grant him the mercy of listening to his last words.

'Praise the Apex,' he whispered. 'It works in mysterious ways.'

'Shush, darling, save your strength,' Kristen said, smoothing his hair back as tears ran freely down her face.

'N-no, Kris,' he managed. 'I was wrong, don't you see? *I*

was the sacrifice. And now the Apex has restored to you a daughter.'

He looked over her shoulder and smiled, a smile that faded as life left him. Kristen closed her husband's eyes and turned slowly as she heard someone approach. A shivering, frightened girl walked slowly towards her across the bank.

'Aunt-ty Krissy?' Poppy said.

Kristen shut her own eyes and felt her heart flood with pain and loss, mixed with unexpected gratitude. Was Poppy really here? Was she really going to live? She opened her eyes again. The girl was still standing there.

ONE YEAR LATER...

1

'Aunty Krissy, can I go in the water, please?'

Kristen looked up from her book across to the sunlounger next to her. Poppy was pointing excitedly at the beach, which from here looked as inviting as the Pacific Ocean behind it. Okay, honey,' Kristen said. 'But stay where I can see you, okay?'

'I will!'

The girl bolted across the powder-white sand towards the waves that lapped against it. Kristen smiled as she watched her go. She wasn't worried. There were plenty of other kids at the Cancun resort, and at least two lifeguards on duty that she could see. Besides, she wanted to encourage Poppy to have fun whenever she could. Especially after all she had been through.

It had been quite the year, for both of them. Kristen still remembered that night. How they had both lain there in the mud, freezing and shivering, desperately holding each other for warmth. Fortunately, the police had found them quickly, having been alerted by the paramedics who had attended to Father Nolan. Kristen and Poppy were rushed to hospital and treated for hypothermia. The bodies of Father Connolly, Bree and Darius and, of course, Marcus, were taken to the coroner. An extensive area of the forest had been cordoned off as a crime scene, as the authorities attempted to work out what had happened, eventually liaising with the police in Geneva to put the complete picture together.

Funerals were held. There was a small, quiet service for Marcus, in a crematorium, attended by close friends and family. Henry and Rosalind were there, the devastated looks on their faces throughout utterly heartbreaking for Kristen to watch. Bree and Darius had a joint ceremony. It was especially hard on Poppy, who spent two hours sobbing uncontrollably into Kristen's chest. Kristen cried with her, continually stroking the girl's head. She was surprised when Bree's mother came up to her afterwards and asked her if she would be willing to become Poppy's legal guardian.

'It was in Bree's will,' Rachel Honeywell said.

Years ago, Kristen and Bree had agreed to be godparents to each other's children. But Kristen never imagined either of them would actually have to do anything about it.

'Don't *you* want to take her?' Kristen had asked.

'Of course,' Rachel said. 'But with Frederick's dementia, I need to focus on taking care of him while there's still time. Besides, it's what Bree wanted.'

There was no objection from Darius's parents either, as long as Kristen promised to keep Poppy fully involved in their lives, which she was more than happy to do. The paperwork was all signed a week later.

2

Kristen's phone rang from inside her beach bag.

'Adrian?'

'Hey. Sorry to call you on your holiday,' the psychiatrist said. 'How is Mexico, by the way?'

She watched Poppy as she laughed and splashed about with the other kids as the surf crashed around them. 'Better than I'd hoped,' Kristen said.

'Glad to hear that. Listen, I have the results of your latest scan. You said you wanted to know?'

Kristen had agreed to return to the institute every week for an fMRI scan. The team of neuroscientists who had all worked under Harry had offered to analyse the state of her brain since Tanner's damage. They had reported a steady decrease in frontal cortex activity, which they told her was a strong indicator that the hallucinations were slowly, but surely, receding. But this was the call she had been waiting for.

'Kristen? You there?'

3

His voice faded as Kristen closed her eyes. She was suddenly back in the courtroom at Harry Dean's trial. The memories were still vivid. Adrian on the stand, testifying that the neuroscientist was not himself. Then Harry's own testimony, in which the awful truth had come out. Kristen still recalled the coffee they'd shared at the institute when he'd warned her the sessions were about to increase. What she didn't know then was that that would be the last time she would see Harry Dean in his right mind again. Later on that week, Harry returned to his apartment as usual to find Marcus had offered to cook one of his favourite dishes, supposedly as a thank you for risking his career to help him.

'I was just relieved to see him acting normally,' Harry said. 'He'd been abusing the God helmet and was starting to say some pretty weird things.'

Harry had accepted the meal, not knowing it was drugged with the sleeping pills Marcus had taken from Orchard House. The next thing he knew, he was awake on the floor, gagged, his hands zip-tied behind his back. Drawing on everything Harry had taught him about how the tech worked,

Marcus used the God helmet to completely rewire Harry's brain, using the same programme originally created to help him, to awful excess. Harry wept as he described how Marcus subjected him to non-stop violations of his mind for over a hundred hours. Kept prisoner in his own home, Harry was only given basic food and water, and a bucket to relieve himself in. During this time, Marcus taught Harry all about a Great Being he had started to call the Apex, force-feeding his ideas into Harry's newly susceptible mind.

'Marcus told me It had hunted me in the woods once many years ago,' Harry said. 'It had made me ingest deadly nightshade, but in Its mercy also decided to spare my life. He said I owed It my life now, but It would not demand it back if I joined him in doing Its will.'

Harry believed everything Marcus told him without question. In fact, he was so terrified of the Apex and Its power, he even thanked Marcus for forcing him to see the truth. From that point on, he was as malleable as putty.

After releasing him, Marcus persuaded Harry that Kristen needed to have her mind opened too, just as theirs had been. As a zealous convert to her husband's strange religion, Harry had readily agreed. But both men knew Kristen would not do so voluntarily.

'I said "Aury, we would need to be clever about this."'

Sitting at the back of the courtroom, Kristen's skin crawled listening to how the men had conspired against her. Harry told the jury that his first suggestion was to return to the institute and take over Kristen's sessions personally. But Marcus had been adamant that they stayed away from the public gaze.

'He said "We're not our old selves any more, old boy."'

There was a certain mania about them now, Marcus

explained. The intense eyes, the fast-paced speech, the agitated mannerisms. These changes in behaviour would be obvious to anyone who knew them. They must *not* be discovered in case someone called the authorities. Because then, Marcus had stressed, Kristen would never be able to have her eyes opened. Determined to please Marcus, Harry resolved to find another way. He accessed Amanda Tanner's personnel file on his home computer, not knowing he was looking for leverage until he found some. The notes in the file contained Tanner's primary reason for applying to the institute. A father back in the UK with advanced Alzheimer's. An idea struck Harry. He called Tanner and offered to give her father a place on a new and very promising drug trial, *if* she switched Kristen's programme during the binding phase. Tanner did not take much persuading. She loved her father dearly and his current prognosis allowed her to set aside any ethical objections. She promised to implement the new programme Harry sent her. Kristen remembered how much happier Tanner had become in those last few weeks. Now she understood why.

'What happened next?' the Crown prosecutor had asked Harry.

'The Apex came to Marcus in a dream,' Harry said. 'It told him both our destinies lay back in England. That It was going to bring his daughter back.'

So Harry had called the institute to say he would be going away for a while. Later that same night, he and Marcus snuck out of the apartment building through the fire escape. They caught a taxi to a car rental place near the airport, where Harry acted as normal as possible in front of the desk clerk and managed to secure a rental. He drove them across the border to France, and then onto the Le Shuttle bound for the UK. They headed straight to the New Forest where Marcus had spent a lot of time as a boy and where, coincidentally, the Apex was currently patrolling. While they waited for Its next instructions, the men lived off the land, hunting lower animals like squirrels, as was only right in the Great Chain. It was during this time that Marcus first visited Abi's grave and the house, where he'd left his strange graffiti and diary. In due course, the Apex appeared to Marcus again, to tell him It was ready to grant life back to Abigail Hardy, though, of course, It had certain conditions.

Harry recounted how he and Marcus retrieved the hidden rental car from the forest and drove to Kingston, arriving around midnight. Harry waited in the car outside the Barnes's home while Marcus rang the bell, and a puzzled Tim Barnes eventually buzzed him in. Kristen felt chills down her spine as Harry told the court how, half an hour later, Marcus came running out of the house carrying a dead Labrador in his arms. All the way back to the New Forest, Harry kept looking over his shoulder at the dead dog in the back seat, and then back at Marcus who was holding an old knife in his hands. It was covered in blood, just like Marcus's clothes.

Of course, Harry believed all of this was somehow serving the will of the Apex. He had not meant to harm anyone, his barrister insisted. He simply could no longer tell fantasy from reality. It was also almost impossible to know exactly what he was hallucinating at any given moment. Harry described how he and Marcus would occasionally see the same things, but often experienced their own distinct delusions. At times, they even mistook each other for the Apex, just as Kristen had done with Harry. What remained clear to him, however, was that Marcus knew the will of the predator-god best. Harry believed he was being a good servant when, at Marcus's request, he went to Orchard House to spy on Kristen and her new house guests. He believed he was doing Its will even when he knocked out Bree, Darius and Poppy and delivered them to Marcus.

It had taken many days to get through the neuroscientist's testimony. Harry would often stop speaking and vanish into a kind of trance. Twice, he descended into wild screaming as he saw something in the courtroom that wasn't there. Only Kristen had a pretty good idea what It was.

4

'Kristen? You there?'

'Sorry, Adrian,' she said. 'I was just thinking about the trial.'

The psychiatrist was quiet for a moment. 'It's all over now,' he said gently.

That much was true, about the trial part at least. Harry Dean had been sentenced to a minimum of three years in-patient treatment at the most prestigious mental health hospital in the UK, ironically originally opened by the Bennetts. Amanda Tanner was also prosecuted and sentenced to five years in prison. With the story all over the news, and the press asking awkward questions, the Bennett Foundation officially denied all knowledge of the God helmets' potentially adverse effects. The board of directors at the Geneva institute promised to shut down all such experiments and stop all the current trials with immediate effect. The protests outside the facility stopped shortly after that.

Except it wasn't all over for Kristen. Not yet. 'Tell me,' she said. 'I'm ready.'

'I'll email you the full report,' Adrian said. 'But the long and short of it is you're going to be okay. The doctors here are confident that your brain will heal itself completely and return to its factory settings, so to speak.'

'I see. Thank you, Adrian. For everything.'

Kristen hung up, sighed deeply, and closed her eyes, letting the sunlight paint red patterns on her lids. For the last twelve months, she had continued to see and hear things. Heavenly creatures, angelic singing. And yes, sometimes, the Apex. The incidents were becoming less frequent, but it was good to know that one day she would be able to go to bed and know for sure no dark nightmares awaited.

When she opened her eyes, Poppy was still playing in the sea. It was heartening to see her laugh again. It had taken a long time. After Bree and Darius's funeral, Kristen had sold Orchard House. Partly because there were too many awful memories, but equally because she hadn't wanted to drag Poppy out of school and halfway across the country. She bought a house in Cambridge for the two of them to begin a new chapter. She returned to nursing and started work at St Anthony's hospital again. At home, things were stilted and strange for the first few months. Poppy was constantly quiet and Kristen tried her best to connect with the girl.

'I lost my mum when I was young too,' she said once, over dinner. 'It's hard, I know.'

Poppy had burst into tears and ran upstairs to the sanctuary of her bedroom. But things were slowly improving. When Kristen first proposed the Cancun trip, she expected Poppy to baulk at the idea. But the girl seemed keen. Kristen was glad, especially as the tickets she had originally bought as an anniversary gift would otherwise have gone to waste. As it happened, the trip had done much to bring Poppy out of her shell. And maybe, just maybe, they might finally start to become their own family. Poppy was not Abi, of course. She never would be. But Kristen would look after her and love her, honouring the memory of the dear friend she missed every day. The idea of them forging a new bond brought back memories of that night, and Marcus's haunting last words. She hated that technically speaking, he had been proved right.

5

That night after a full dinner at the buffet restaurant, they walked along the beach. The moonlight lit their footsteps in the talcum-soft sand.

'Aunty Krissy, look at all the stars,' Poppy gasped, pointing up. 'They're so bright!'

'Yes, they are,' Kristen agreed.

They stopped and sat down for a moment, feeling the humid air and listening to the rhythm of crashing waves. Kristen spotted a crab by her foot, feeding off the corpse of a fellow crab, and suggested they shuffle along a bit. Poppy had no interest in the crab, still mesmerised by the unencumbered view of the constellation of Orion. Kristen took it in with her. The dazzling night sky reminded her of the night she had camped with Bree all those years ago when they were girls. How awestruck she had been then, convinced that beauty such as this meant that there must be meaning behind this strange universe.

'Do you think Mum and Dad are up there, Aunty Krissy?' Poppy asked, interrupting her thoughts.

Kristen met her gaze, then reached over to gently squeeze the girl's hand.

'You know what, honey? I don't know.'

And she didn't. Yet once she had believed. Would she do so again, she wondered? When her brain finally returned to its *factory settings*, as Adrian had put it. And if she did, how would she feel about that? She had set out trying to make sense of Abi's death, which still remained an enigma. Marcus would once have said that was because life was nothing but blind chance. That all of us were here because our ancestors successfully killed or ate their rivals, just as the crab beside her was doing right now. Yet despite all that happened, and all that the God helmet had done to her, she couldn't help but think that perhaps it wouldn't be such a bad thing to believe again. To think there had to be something transcendent that lay behind those brilliant stars. Something beautiful and redemptive. Otherwise, it would only beg the question. All those millions of years of blood and struggle. All those hundreds of billions of deaths. What had any of it ever been for?

ENJOYED THIS BOOK?

If you liked *The Apex*, I'd be very grateful if you'd consider leaving a review on Amazon (it can be as short as you like). It makes a huge difference for an author like me and helps readers find my books more easily.

FANCY A FREE EBOOK?

Get a thrilling ebook for free when you sign up to receive my occasional newsletter. I promise I'll never spam you. And you can opt out any time.

To get your free copy, just go to **dmsearle.com/ebook**

ACKNOWLEDGEMENTS

My thanks to all my beta readers who gave their time and feedback on earlier drafts. Thank you to Lesley Jones and Manda Waller for their fabulous editing and proofing skills — and to Stuart Bache who did such a phenomenal job on the cover. I also want to thank you, the reader, for joining me on this journey.